GOODBYE DEMONS

a novel

JJ Harrigan

Copyright © 2026 John J Harrigan

Published by Salty Books Publishing, LLC
(1870 Foothill Trl, Shakopee, MN)

All rights reserved.

ISBN: 978-1964354095
Library of Congress Catalog Card Number:
2026903246

Book design, Salty Books Publishing
Cover design, Brad Knefelkamp

1

*"Who was the second woman to fly across the
Atlantic?"*

Autumn 1977

Manhattan Skating Club

This was the chance of a lifetime, and Angie swore she wouldn't blow it. To concentrate on her preparations, she dropped down to one class at NYU. She did elaborate stretching exercises and weight training. She followed a dietician's meal plan and skated five days a week under the guidance of her coach. Angie concocted a brilliant plan to capture the Gold at Nationals and guarantee her a slot on the Olympic team.

Her coach objected. "No woman has ever done a triple axel, and you're not ready."

"I did it in practice. You saw me."

"You fell. A perfect double axel that you're capable of doing trumps a triple axel that you screw up."

Angie was determined to do the triple without falling. To build up her quads so she could jump high enough, she put a barbell on her shoulders and did repeated sets of knee squats every other day. She followed those with deadweight lifts to develop her hamstrings and glutes. To keep this weight training from hampering her flexibility, she combined each lifting session with an elaborate stretching routine. She sandwiched all of this between once-a-week ballet lessons to help her move with grace. Hours were spent experimenting with background music in order to find the piece that would mesh best with her movements.

Not only did she need the strength and agility to do the jump, she also needed to spin fast enough to complete the three-and-a-half turns during the short time she would be in the air. Less than a second. She used a harness to suspend herself above the ice while she practiced spinning as fast as she could. When she finished the spinning exercises, she raced up and down the rink several times to enable her to reach the speed that would be required.

Bruising falls came each day. It wasn't until a week before the competitions that she completed a triple. She grinned triumphantly at her surprised coach. Then on the next try she took a nasty fall that left her limping when she rose from the ice. Her coach sped over to her. After making sure Angie had broken no bones, she again warned her to stop trying the triple axel.

"You're not ready. It's a riverboat gamble."

"I have to take the gamble when I've got the chance."

"You'll have a chance next year. You'll be stronger and more experienced. That'll be the time to do it."

"In the meantime, some other girl might do it first, and nobody will ever hear about me. Even if I do one the next day. Can you tell me who was the second woman to fly across the Atlantic? Or the second guy to climb Mount Everest?"

The Boston Garden

Her stomach churned so badly Angie thought she'd barf. She sat on a bench awaiting her turn while she picked at one of the sequins on her costume. A part of her wanted to storm out of the stadium and chuck the whole thing. But quitting now would be to throw out all those years of preparation. She would let down a lot of people: her coach, the Skating Club that sponsored her, and especially her father Charlie, who had supported her quest since she'd started at age four. To calm her jitters, she focused on her routine. She pictured the sequence of moves her choreographer had worked out to fit the music that would be playing over the loudspeaker, the popular Beatles song, "Let It Be."

If she could reach enough speed when she hit the part in the song that called for her to leap into the air, she would go with the triple axel. If not, she'd do consecutive doubles.

As soon as she glided onto the ice, the jitters disappeared. She blotted out the fourteen thousand spectators and began with a graceful figure eight to the rhythm of the music, skating frontwards on the way out, then backwards as she coasted back to her starting point. Her left hand pointed forward, and her right hand held her right foot which was raised behind her.

With the boost to her confidence from the successful opening, she roared back to center rink. The music came to the point to launch her triple axel. With all the strength she could muster, she jumped from her left skate. She folded her arms across her chest and crossed her legs at the ankles as she rose. Spinning to the left, she made a complete rotation. Then a second. Then a third. She needed only one more half-rotation to land backwards on her right skate.

But she hadn't launched her jump with enough force to reach her maximum height. As a result, her right skate blade touched down on the ice before the half rotation was complete. Rather than being in line with her motion as she landed, the blade was almost perpendicular. It jammed in the ice causing her knee to buckle. She went sprawling, her kneecap crashing on the ice.

A fall would not be fatal to her performance if she could recover and complete her routine. Ignoring the pain in her knee, she tried to rise onto her left skate. The moment she put weight on her twisted right leg, it gave way, sending her tumbling back onto the ice again. For the first time, she heard the crowd. A huge collective gasp. And the mocking sound of the Beatles' Paul McCartney chanting the refrain.

2

"Bless his horny little heart."

May 1978

Tunis

Angie Parnell pressed her forehead against the window as the jetliner came down over the Mediterranean. She searched beyond Tunis for the brown expanse of the great Sahara. Instead, she saw coastland with brilliant beaches and green vegetation. A good omen, she hoped. Her light brown fingers drummed on the armrest as the plane touched down and began its taxi to the terminal. Before the engines cut off, she stood up, gathered her carry-ons, and prodded her seatmate, Sarah, to move into the aisle. She couldn't wait to start this reboot of her life.

She followed Sarah and their ten companions down the steps of the plane. A tall woman with a frown marched across the tarmac toward them. A thick, billowing skirt hung over her ample hips, and she stepped forward with long authoritative strides.

"Welcome to Tunis!" she boomed, as her frown morphed to a smile. "My name is Blaire Jones, and I'm the local Peace Corps director." She moved through the dozen volunteers, giving each one a hearty handshake. After ushering them through customs, she put them up for the night in a small hotel a block from the Peace Corps office in Tunis.

Peace Corps Office, Tunis

The next morning, the volunteers began an orientation program at Blaire's office. A sideboard held a coffee urn for the volunteers and an array of pastries. Angie picked a small cookie and brought it to her seat next to Sarah at the long conference table.

Blaire brought in a Tunisian teacher to review acceptable and unacceptable behaviors in Tunisia. The rules seemed clear enough. "Remove your shoes before entering a home," said the teacher. "Always bring a gift when visiting someone. Don't use drugs. And, for the female volunteers, keep your skirt hem below the knee."

Angie glanced at the long, blue denim skirts she and the other women wore. No chance of those offending anyone. Or the shapeless white blouses, either.

"Any questions?" asked the teacher.

Angie asked in Arabic, "Should we wear a hijab like you're wearing?" Angie held a cookie she had picked off a tray of refreshments, and she pointed with it at the silky green and yellow covering on the woman's hair.

The teacher fingered the attractive headdress. "It's optional," she said. "No one expects you to dress according to Muslim traditions." Then a sly smile crept onto her lips. "However, there is one thing you must correct immediately."

Puzzled, Angie paused as she was about to take a bite from her cookie. The woman's smile broke into a laugh. She pointed at the cookie in Angie's left hand.

"You must never eat with your left hand. Or shake hands with your left hand. That hand is reserved for unclean purposes."

Angie shifted the cookie to her right hand and blushed in embarrassment as the other volunteers burst out laughing. The instructor laughed as well, then said.

"However. I must compliment you on your Arabic. It is very good."

The compliment felt gratifying. Angie had been the standout student in the volunteers' three-month Arabic class. The distinction she got helped make up for the put-downs she sometimes received from the other volunteers for being youngest in their group and the only one not to have completed college.

She wondered if the taunts were aimed less at her age and more at her Cuban background. Although none of the volunteers made racial slurs, Angie had the darkest complexion among them, and she recalled the first day in the cafeteria when she sat alone at a table, and only Sarah joined her.

When Angie pointed out that no other volunteers had joined them at their table, Sarah had responded in her smooth Kentucky drawl, "They're just putting on airs, and it doesn't make a lick of sense. When we get out on our assignments, they'll learn that we're all in the same boat, and what you were before doesn't matter."

Angie reflected on the irony that the closest friendship among the group was hers with Sarah. Angie came from a mixed-race background but had grown up in affluence in New York. Sarah was the only southerner in the group, having grown up poor in the hardscrabble coal mining town of Harlan, Kentucky. And Sarah was right. Where they came from didn't matter now. Angie had spent a lifetime navigating racial and cultural crosscurrents at home, and she'd become an expert at getting along where she didn't quite fit in. Maybe in Tunis, she would fit in as well as get along.

Belvedere Park

Blaire topped off the weeklong orientation program by hosting a party to introduce some embassy personnel who had resources the volunteers could tap into once they reached their assignments. She hired taxis to bring everyone to the party at her second-floor apartment in the tony neighborhood of Belvedere Park.

After her week in the drab hotel, Angie reveled in Blaire's middle-class apartment. A colorful Persian carpet graced the living room floor, and Blaire had hung black and white photos of the nearby ruins of ancient Carthage on the walls. Next to a window overlooking the street below sat a coffee table stacked with American novels translated into Arabic. A placard invited the volunteers to take two or three books and give them as gifts to the Community Association leaders in their assigned communities and to contact the embassy's cultural affairs office if they wanted more. Angie grabbed two copies of *To Kill a Mockingbird*, which had been one of her favorite books in school. She and Sarah could present one to their association director when they found out who he was, and Angie could read the other one to strengthen her command of Arabic.

As she fingered through the other books, a deep male voice behind her said, "Hello."

She turned to face a tall young man wearing a light blue blazer.

"I'm Stevie Parker," he said.

Stevie had a head of crew cut blond hair. Not only was he tall, but he had the broad shoulders of a weightlifter. He was much too big to be called by the diminutive, Stevie. Steve the Giant would be more like it.

She extended her hand. "Angie Fernández Parnell, and this is my friend, Sarah."

Stevie held onto her hand a fraction of a second longer than she wanted. She motioned to a set of empty chairs. "Could we sit for a moment? I've been standing all day, and my knee's a little sore." As she sank into the chair, she said, "Sarah and I are being assigned to Ettadhamen on Monday."

Stevie grimaced.

"What does that mean?" Angie asked.

"What does what mean?"

"That face you just made when I said Ettadhamen."

"I've only been there once, and it's not the worst neighborhood in Tunis. But it's not like this." He gestured toward the plaza outside the window of Blaire's apartment.

"I wouldn't expect it to be like this," said Angie, trying to appear nonchalant. "What do you do here in Tunis, Stevie?"

Before answering, he moved his chair closer to Angie's. Uncomfortable with the closeness, she edged her chair back and glanced up at Sarah, motioning with her eyes for Sarah to sit across from Stevie.

"I'm the assistant director of TACC," he said.

"TACC?"

"The Tunisian American Cultural Center." He handed business cards to them. "We offer all sorts of events, from English classes to art shows. You must come down to visit us so I can show you around."

Just then, Blaire called for everyone's attention, and Angie turned away from Stevie.

"We have several people I want you to meet," said Blaire. "First is a Foreign Service Officer from the embassy who's promised to give us some background on developments in Tunisia." She swept her hand toward a tall, slender man in a charcoal gray suit. "Mr. James Bryan Whitcomb, the third."

"The third." Sarah giggled.

Angie nudged her in the ribs. "Hush. I want to hear this."

She leaned forward to get a better view of the speaker, who looked distinguished. His thick, dark brown hair had no trace of gray, not even at the sideburns. He couldn't be more than thirty.

He spoke with confidence. "What you're most likely to hear people talk about will be last year's general strike. The government jailed many of the leaders and broke up the unions."

"What do we say if people ask us about it?" said Sarah, loudly, and in her slow Kentucky drawl. Sarah had strong feelings about unions, Angie recalled. The only way she'd been able to afford college was a scholarship from the miner's union for children of men killed in a mining accident. Sarah would resent the idea of unions being broken up. She planned to enter law school after the Peace Corps and become a labor lawyer.

Whitcomb smiled. "Since you're not here as spokespersons for the U.S. government, you're free to say whatever you want."

"What do *you* say?" Sarah followed up.

Whitcomb smiled again. "Well, my job, unlike yours, *does* require me to be a spokesperson for our policy, which is to support the Tunisian government. I always need to walk a tight line between supporting the status quo and pressing for democratic change."

"Sounds like upper class mush," Sarah whispered to Angie.

"It makes sense to me," Angie replied. "He's conflicted, like we all are."

Another volunteer raised his hand. "In the Islamic world overall, what is the biggest problem we face?"

Whitcomb paused and looked to the ceiling for a second before replying, "I think the fundamental problem is the widespread poverty in the region that feeds so much political instability. We need to improve peoples' lives, the way you Peace Corps volunteers will do."

Angie felt pleased that the Foreign Service Officer believed she and the other volunteers would improve peoples' lives, but she overflowed with anxiety about what she and Sarah would encounter when they showed up at Ettadhamen in two days. And Stevie's cryptic comment about the neighborhood had upped her anxiety. She raised her hand to ask Whitcomb to elaborate on the role he had mentioned for the volunteers. Before she could speak, Blaire intervened.

"Mr. Whitcomb will hang around later to carry on this fascinating discussion privately. But right now, there are some other people who have resources that might be useful to you."

Blaire introduced a multitude of people who all blended together in Angie's mind: an embassy nurse, a librarian, a consular officer, and a cultural affairs officer who reminded them to take some of the books on the coffee table and give them out. They came from the State Department's book translation program, and they wouldn't do anybody any good if they just sat in a Tunis storage room.

The party began to break up, and Angie still wanted to talk with the tall Foreign Service Officer who was now standing by the door. Just as she moved toward him, Stevie Parker tapped her shoulder.

"It was a pleasure to meet you," he said, extending his hand to her. "I look forward to showing you around TACC, when you're free."

"That would be nice," said Angie offhandedly. She'd already forgotten what TACC was. "At the moment, I have a question for Mr. Whitcomb before he leaves." And she turned away.

She hurried to the door and stepped in front of him before he could leave the room. Smiling up at him, she said, "That was a very nice thing you said about the volunteers."

He responded with a smile that gave her a warm feeling. "I believe it," he said. "Stability in the region might depend less on the people I see in the diplomatic world and more on the lives of the people you will work with every day." He paused before asking, "Where will you be assigned?"

"Ettadhamen," said Angie.

He didn't grimace, as Stevie had at the mention of Ettadhamen, but he did raise an eyebrow. Before Angie could ask what the raised eyebrow meant, he handed her his business card and gave a friendly smile. "I admire your courage in taking on your assignment. If I can be of any help, don't hesitate to call."

Once Angie and Sarah were back in their taxi for the ride home to their dreary hotel, Sarah asked, "Why were you so abrupt with Stevie? He's a hunk, bless his horny little heart."

Angie laughed. "Bless his heart?"

"Just something we say in Harlan County. But you didn't answer my question. A good-looking guy shows interest, and you give him the brush-off. Why?"

"He makes me uneasy. He sits too close."

Angie slumped back in the seat of the taxi, her lips turned down, and her hands squeezing the copies of *To Kill a Mockingbird*. Blaire's party had done nothing to ease her anxieties about taking up residence in Ettadhamen.

Maybe joining the Peace Corps had been a big mistake. She'd much rather be on an ice rink for one of her figure skating competitions, wearing one of her sequined outfits as the spotlight traced her gliding along the ice.

3

"A shapeless skirt like that."

June 1978

Ettadhamen

Angie gritted her teeth as she and Sarah sat in a van enroute to Ettadhamen. They rode in awkward silence until they turned into a street marked with a sign in Arabic and French, Cité Ettadhamen.

"I'm a little anxious, Sarah," said Angie, as the van edged past the sign and up a narrow, dusty street. "What if this association director we're going to work for is difficult?"

Sarah grinned. "Just don't extend your left hand to him and we'll be okay."

"You're never going to let me forget that. Are you?"

"Nope."

The van stopped at a free-standing single-story adobe building with an Arabic sign that said, *Ettadhamen Community Association.* Coming out to meet them was a thin, fortyish man, with a front tooth missing. Omar, Angie knew, from the photo Blaire had shown them. He helped them place their bags inside the office. The stale smell of cigarette smoke swamped Angie as she stepped inside.

"The first thing we must do is get you into your housing, and I've found you a nice, well-lit place with plumbing."

He led them a block down the street, then turned onto a dirt lane that was lined with one- and two-story houses made of sundried earth and straw. Several of the two-story houses had laundry laid out over old wrought iron balconies. Each house abutted its neighbors, and none had front lawns. Omar beamed with pride as he ushered them into a small, single-story house midway down the lane.

"It even has running water," he said as he strode to a small kitchen table by a sink at the rear. He pulled open a curtain behind the sink to reveal a flush toilet covered with grime.

Angie and Sarah stared in shock at their new residence.

"Fortunately, I wasn't expecting the Waldorf Astoria," said Angie.

"And your expectations were met," quipped Sarah, as she swept her hand toward two small rooms plus the kitchen area. A layer of dust covering all the surfaces. Each room had a single bulb dangling from the ceiling, and the kitchen bulb was burned out.

"Could you find us some cleaning supplies?" Angie asked Omar.

It was nearly five o'clock before they got the place scrubbed clean enough to be comfortable. They rinsed off their sweaty bodies at the cold water tap in the kitchen, their only water source for cooking, bathing, and laundry.

Exhausted, they sat on two kitchen chairs. A neighbor knocked on the door to introduce herself. She was small, no taller than Angie, and looked to be in her early twenties.

"I want to welcome you to the neighborhood."

Sarah jumped up and extended her hand. "I'm Sarah and this is Angie. We are so pleased to meet you. What is your name?"

"Rania," she said. "Markets will be closed now, so I brought some food to hold you until tomorrow morning when you can get something."

Rania uncovered the plate to reveal a bed of couscous, pieces of lamb, dates, and some of Tunisia's round, flat tabouna bread. "Let me show you where the market is, so you'll know where to go in the morning. Just give me a moment to tell my husband, and I'll be right with you." She stepped toward the door.

Humbled by the woman's generosity, Angie turned to Sarah. "Rania's house is as small as ours, and she probably doesn't have a lot of food to spare. I don't feel right taking it."

"You can't snub her by refusing it. The only thing we can do is accept her kindness and do something in return when we get the chance."

Tunisian American Cultural Center

Stevie Parker leaned back in his chair, his feet propped up on his desk. His mind wandered to the Peace Corps volunteer he had seen at the party over the weekend. He'd been charmed by that long, curly black hair, that golden complexion, and that perfectly trim figure. She seemed a little icy. She hadn't paid nearly as much attention to Stevie as she had to that Foreign Service Officer blabbing about politics.

Stevie thought he should do something nice for her before that foreign service guy started taking an interest. Something simple and considerate would do. And he knew just the thing.

When the office closed at 4:30 p.m., Stevie hopped onto the Vespa he kept chained to a post behind the TACC offices. Ettadhamen was only fifteen miles away.

The trip took forty-five minutes in rush hour traffic. He circled the neighborhood, looking for the address given to him by his friend Blaire. He stopped at a store and bought three ice-cold bottles of Coca Cola. Who wouldn't want a nice cold Coke at the end of a hot summer day? He imagined Angie's gratitude as she tilted her head back and brought the cool bottle to her lips.

Stevie parked his scooter in a big asphalt parking lot that had emptied out for the day. He chained the bike to a post, picked up the three Coke bottles by the necks, and walked up the street, looking for Angie's address. He stopped. There she was, barely fifty feet ahead, standing in front of a small house with her Peace Corps partner. Stevie couldn't remember the partner's name. With a rush of adrenalin at finding her so quickly, he headed in her direction.

Precisely at that moment, another woman joined the two Peace Corps volunteers, and the three of them began to walk up the lane, then turned left, obviously headed somewhere. If Stevie ran after them now and tried to give them the Cokes, it would be awkward. Instead of looking like someone making a friendly gesture, he'd look like he was interfering. Angie might brush him off again as she had done at the party.

With a deep sigh, he headed back to his motor scooter. He'd try again some other day.

Ettadhamen Community Association

The next morning, before checking in with Omar at the Community Association Office, Angie did her daily stretching exercises. She finished by balancing on her left foot while she raised her right leg behind her. Next, she reached her hand over her shoulder and came within inches of being able to grab the foot extended out behind her. A month earlier, she'd been unable to do this. Her bad knee was healing up nicely. If she could just continue making progress, maybe she could return to ice skating competition after all.

"Why do you go through these strange exercises every morning," said Sarah.

"To stay agile."

"You just want to impress that FSO you were ogling at Blaire's party."

Angie grinned. "I wouldn't mind seeing him again."

"Forget it, partner. He lives in a different world than we do."

Finally, eight-thirty rolled around and they skipped into Omar's office to present him the copy of *To Kill a Mockingbird* Angie had picked up at Blaire's party. She was certain he would enjoy it.

Omar was sitting at his desk smoking a cigarette when they arrived. He stubbed the cigarette in an ashtray, but the smell of smoke continued to hang in the air. He turned the book back and forth, admiring its covers. Smiling, he opened it to the title page and asked both women to sign it for him. Angie had to force herself not to stare at the gap in his teeth when he smiled.

Having put him in a good mood, she broached the idea of a lending library.

"We can get dozens of books in Arabic from the embassy. Everyone in the neighborhood can borrow them."

"It will take too much administrative time to keep track of the books and make sure they are not stolen."

"In that case, we could just have a reading room."

"I don't have enough space in here for that."

Angie scowled, and Sarah jumped in with another idea. "One other thing we could do, Omar, would be to offer some English conversation classes. That would help a lot of people here find jobs with the international agencies here in Tunis."

"You are most certainly correct," he said, beaming a bright smile. "It still leaves me with a space problem, but I have an idea. Let's go for a little walk."

He led the women down the dirt lane where their house was. They ambled past the brown stucco buildings and stopped at an asphalt parking lot. He pointed to a small house next to the lot. "The Community Association was given this house as a gift, but the board of directors hasn't decided yet how we should use it."

He pushed open the door to reveal a large room that contained several tables and chairs. In the back was a small office. Everything was covered with dust, and the front window had a big crack. A dim sixty-watt bulb cast a weak glow when he flipped a switch.

"If you cleaned this place up, we could probably let you use it for the reading room and the English conversation classes you want to set up."

"Probably?" asked Angie.

Omar shrugged. "I can't say for certain. But if you got it cleaned up and we called it the Outreach Center for the Community Association it would be hard for the board to turn you down."

"We'll do it," said Angie. She looked at Sarah for confirmation. Sarah nodded her approval.

"You'll need to do a good job. When I present my idea to the board, I want this place to sparkle."

Sarah and Angie accompanied Omar back to the association office to pick up his cleaning supplies again. Then they spent the rest of the day sweeping out dust, washing surfaces, and rearranging the furniture.

"I wish we had some Windex," said Sarah as she wiped at a smudge on the cracked window.

Midway through their efforts, Angie commented, "I have to hand it to you, Sarah. When he started putting us off, I was ready to scream at him for dragging his feet. If it hadn't been for you sweet-talking him, we never would have gotten this space."

"Do you know what?" said Sarah. Leaning on the mop clutched in her left hand, she extended her right hand to Angie.

"What?"

"We make a pretty good team."

Covered with dust, the two women grinned as they stood shaking hands.

———

Omar returned two days later to inspect their work, and he brought the community association's vice president, Mrs. Trabelsi, a forty-something woman wearing a long blue dress and a colorful embroidered vest. Angie and Sarah toured them through the space they had cleaned up and organized.

"We plan to use this table for practicing English conversation," said Angie, indicating a table with four chairs. "If the Peace Corps can get us some instructional materials, we'll also use this area for English classes. We're going down to their office tomorrow to see what they've got."

Sarah pointed to the table in the corners. "And over there, we're going to display books in Arabic so people can use this as a reading room."

"What kind of books?" Omar asked, suspicious.

"Our director Blaire got us a list from the embassy," said Angie. "Maybe Mrs. Trabelsi would help us pick the best ones."

Mrs. Trabelsi nodded her willingness and added, "You need a sign out front so people will know you are here."

Omar shrugged. "I don't have enough funds in the budget to buy a sign."

"Omar, your janitor's son Mahmoud is artistic. Get him to paint a sign for you. That won't cost much."

"I don't know if he could do that. He's not very strong."

"He's as strong as any other teenager. He just walks with a limp. That's all," said Mrs. Trabelsi.

"What happened to him that he has a limp?" asked Angie.

"He had polio when he was little," said Omar. Angie cupped her hand to her cheek. Her stepfather Charlie walked around with a permanent limp he had acquired from a bout of polio as a child, and she felt that this gave her a bond to Mahmoud, even though she hadn't yet met him.

Mahmoud painted a sign for them on a flat sheet of wood that was almost two meters wide. Their neighbor Rania came over to help him fasten the sign to the front exterior between the door and the window. The four of them stood in the street admiring Mahmoud's artistry. He had cleverly inserted the colors of the Tunisian flag by giving the sign a bright red background that highlighted the Arabic words in white.

Community Association Outreach Center
English Conversation Sessions
Free English Classes
Reading Room
Tutoring

"Looks classy, Mahmoud," said Angie in Arabic, smiling at the wiry boy.

"You call it a reading room, but you don't have anything here to read."

"When the books arrive, we'll give you the first one," said Sarah.

A week later, a van from the embassy's cultural section pulled up with three boxes of American books, all translated into Arabic. Angie and Sarah arranged them alphabetically on the table in the corner. Louisa May Alcott, Pearl Buck, Emily Dickinson, Ernest Hemingway, Henry James, Harper Lee, John Steinbeck, among others.

Doctors without Borders

The following morning, Sarah woke up with a toothache. "I can't go downtown with you, Angie. But while you're at the Peace Corps office, see if you can get the name of a dentist."

Angie's shoulders tensed as she got onto the crowded bus to head downtown. She'd never ridden a public bus in Tunis, and she recoiled at the odors of the sweaty bodies crushed around her. This was as packed as the New York subway at rush hour. When a young man got up from his window seat to exit the bus, Angie sat down before anyone could squeeze past her. She welcomed the breeze of fresh air through the window.

At the Peace Corps office, it took only a few moments to get a list of dentists and to order the language materials she and Sarah needed for their English classes. This gave her the rest of the morning free to explore the narrow streets of the neighborhood. She spotted a shop window with a placard in French, "Médecins Sans Frontières.

She stepped inside to find a woman sitting at a battered wooden desk, smoking a cigarette. A sign on the desk gave her name, Antoinette.

"Good morning," said Angie in Arabic.

"I don't speak Arabic," said the woman in English.

"How did you know I speak English?"

"You don't look Tunisian, and no self-respecting French woman would wear a shapeless skirt like that."

Looking down at her long, blue denim skirt, Angie frowned, but the woman continued without paying notice. "I'm guessing you're American."

"Yes. I'm Angie, and I'm with the Peace Corps. The reason I stopped in was because of your sign. Do you have any dentists? My friend developed a bad toothache and needs to see a dentist."

"Our medical staff hasn't arrived yet, but I can give you a list of dentists we've approved."

She pulled a sheet of paper from a file cabinet. Angie compared the list to the one she'd gotten from the Peace Corps office and circled two names that appeared on both lists. Then she looked up at Antoinette.

"What exactly does Doctors Without Borders do?"

Antoinette ran a hand through her long brown hair. "We send medical personnel to poor areas of the world where people lack basic treatment. As the local administrator, I organize backup support for our medical people when they arrive."

"Is this a new thing?"

"We were formally organized in 1971. But the seed was planted three years earlier in Paris in The Revolution of 1968."

This triggered a memory in Angie, but Antoinette seemed a little acerbic, and she might think Angie was showing off if she mentioned it. Her pause led Antoinette to say,

"You look thoughtful about something."

"I remember that," said Angie, tentatively.

"You remember it?" Antoinette guffawed. "You would have been a child."

Angie jutted her jaw forward. "I was nine. I was visiting Paris with my dad."

Antoinette furrowed her brows. "You just happened to be visiting Paris with your dad during a revolution?"

"He was there on business. While he was out one day, I wandered from our hotel to the Sorbonne where it looked like a war was going on."

"It *was* a war. He never should have left you alone."

Angie chuckled at the memory. "When he found out I'd left the hotel, he was furious."

She rattled on as the French woman stared at her. "I remember college students getting teargassed as they threw stones at the police. I couldn't avoid the teargas, and this young doctor by an aid station rinsed it out of my eyes for me. Then he sat down on the curb next to me to take a break. I remember him lighting up a cigarette. Can you imagine that? A doctor smoking?"

Antoinette cast a glance at the cigarette between her thumb and forefinger, and Angie realized that she had just criticized the woman. Served her right for the comment she'd made about Angie's skirt.

"Do you remember his name?" While she waited for Angie to answer, Antoinette leaned back in her chair.

Envious of how relaxed Antoinette looked sitting back and blowing smoke out her nostrils, Angie asked, "Could I try one of those?"

"You smoke? After what you just said?"

"You just look so restful with it. Let me see what they're like."

Antoinette lit a cigarette for her and repeated her question. "Do you remember this doctor's name?"

Angie coughed from the cigarette.

"You have to inhale the smoke into your lungs," said Antoinette. She took a deep breath to demonstrate.

Angie tried again but coughed even harder as she tried to swallow the smoke. As she pulled the cigarette from her mouth, she gazed at it slack-jawed; it was disgusting. She crushed it in the ashtray.

"His name, Angie. What was the doctor's name?"

"Bayard? Bartram? Bernard? Something like that."

Antoinette's eyes widened. "Bernard Kouchner?"

"I can't remember if he even told me his last name. But he looked important, and he was helping people."

Antoniette flashed a big grin. "He's one of the founders of Doctors Without Borders. It didn't get off the ground until a few years later when he came back from Biafra, but you met him right when the idea started."

That's a stretch, thought Angie. But why burst her bubble? She nodded, and Antoinette grinned, as though she had found a kindred spirit.

"What an incredible thing," said Antoinette. Then she looked at her watch. "Angie, I have to go somewhere just now, but I'd like to talk more. Come back again, and I'll show you a nice affordable place where we can have lunch."

Angie took Antoinette's phone number, then hurried to the bus stop. She couldn't wait to get back to Ettadhamen and tell Sarah about the fascinating Antoinette, who bounced from grouchy to peppy.

4

"You're asking for trouble."

July 1978

Peace Corps Office

On a bright sunny morning, Angie answered a knock on the door and found a smiling Mahmoud standing at the stoop.

"Omar sent me to tell you that you got a call from the Peace Corps Office."

Since Angie and Sarah did not have a phone of their own, they relied on the phone in the Community Association office to contact the world outside of Ettadhamen. "What did they say?" asked Angie.

"They have some packages for you, and they want you to pick them up at 2:00 o'clock."

When they arrived at the office, they found two big cartons sitting on Blaire's gray steel desk. Also sitting at the desk, to Angie's dismay, was Stevie Parker. He stood up to shake hands with the two volunteers. As before, he held onto Angie's hand a moment longer than she liked. She pulled her hand loose and backed away half a step.

Stevie pulled a long knife from a sheath on his belt, tested it for sharpness with his thumb, and sliced open the boxes. He then wiped the blade on his pantleg and smiled with satisfaction before inserting it back into its sheath. Angie stood transfixed as she watched the ritual.

The first box held textbooks, worksheets, language cassettes, and a cassette recorder. Sarah lifted the box an inch off the desk, frowned, and let it drop. "Lord Almighty, this thing weighs a ton. How are we ever going to get this out to Ettadhamen on the bus?"

"No problem," said Stevie. "Blaire asked me to drive them out there for you in the Peace Corps pickup truck. You two can ride along."

He taped the boxes shut, then loaded them into the bed of the Ford F-150 pickup. Its gleaming two-tone red and white exterior stood out next to the single-colored vehicles parked in the street by the office. Angie hung back until Sarah climbed in to take the seat next to Stevie.

On the way to Ettadhamen, Stevie carried on a steady stream of talk. He had played football for the University of Oklahoma but failed to get picked up in the draft for the pros.

"What happened?" asked Sarah. "If you played well enough to be on a powerhouse team like Oklahoma, I'd think the pros would have snatched you up."

"My coaches had me blackballed."

"Why?" asked Angie.

"They didn't like me."

Angie glanced at Sarah. How could college coaches exercise a blackball in a draft run by the pros?

He tapped his fingers on the steering wheel. "Hell, I was our best linebacker. In the final game, I blitzed the quarterback three times and sacked him twice." Stevie grinned at the memory and stopped tapping the steering wheel.

"Impressive," said Sarah. "Why did you go to work for the State Department?"

"Since I couldn't break into the pros, I was at loose ends. Then I saw this recruitment notice for people to staff cultural centers the State Department has set up around the world. They gave me a great course in Arabic, and I've been at the center for six months now."

"That sounds similar to my story," said Angie.

"You were a football player?" joked Sarah.

"Of course not," said Angie, poking Sarah in the shoulder. "I injured my leg figure skating and was sidelined for a year, so I joined the Peace Corps."

Stevie took his eyes off the road and grinned at Angie. "I knew we'd have something in common. You little ladies should come down and visit us at TACC."

"Little ladies?" Angie said, bristling at the term. "I guess we women would seem like that to a boy like you."

Stevie turned his eyes back to the road, apparently oblivious to Angie's insult.

"Have you made some good friends at TACC?" asked Sarah.

"I'm the only American, and the Tunisians resent me. They'd like to get rid of me."

Sarah and Angie exchanged glances again. Most Tunisians they'd met had been pleasant. They rode the rest of the way in silence.

Stevie toted the boxes into their library-classroom and slit the boxes open with his knife. Angie watched, wide-eyed, as he slipped the knife back into its sheath.

"Why do you carry that big knife?" she asked.

"It's useful, as you can see." He pointed to the two boxes he'd just opened. "And it's a deterrent."

"A deterrent?"

"This isn't the safest place in the world. You might want to think about carrying some protection as well."

After making his farewell, Stevie drove off to return the truck to the Peace Corps office. Sarah asked Angie, "Why did you hang back when we got into the truck?"

"I didn't want to sit next to Stevie."

"He's a super stud. Why wouldn't you want to sit next to him?"

"He's creepy. Not creepy enough that I'd call the cops. But that knife of his spooks me out."

"Everybody carries a knife in Harlan County. Besides, he might be right about us needing something for safety."

"Not a single person in Ettadhamen has threatened us since we got here. I wish I'd felt this safe in New York."

Then Sarah changed the subject and grinned. "You really zapped him with that, 'a boy like you' line."

Angie pursed her lips into a frown. "I hate doing that kind of stuff, especially since he was helping us out. But you can't let people put you down."

Ettadhamen Community Association Office

Angie and Sarah drafted a flyer in English promoting the English offerings at their outreach center. Then they got Mahmoud to translate their draft into French.

"We need a copier to duplicate this thing so we can distribute it," said Angie.

"Omar has one," said Mahmoud.

Angie looked at her watch. Noon. "He'll be out to lunch right now, so we're kind of stuck until he comes back in a couple of hours."

"My father's the janitor," said Mahmoud. "He gave me a key so I can get into the office when I need to do something for him."

They followed the gangly teenager up the dirt lane toward the Community Association Office. He limped up the steps to the office and pulled a key from his pocket to unlock the door. The smell of the cigarette smoke struck Angie like the fumes from an outhouse. Even after two weeks in Ettadhamen, she still wasn't used to it.

Mahmoud walked past Omar's desk to the back room and pointed.

Sarah did a doubletake. "I thought you meant a real copying machine."

"This is a real machine. It makes copies," replied Mahmoud, his lips turned down at Sarah's complaint.

"I'm sorry," she said, setting her hand on his arm. "I didn't mean to insult you, Mahmoud. This is what we would call a mimeograph machine."

"I haven't seen one of these in years," said Angie. "My dad used to have one." She turned the handle on the rotator drum to see if it worked. "We can make do. All we need is a stencil."

Mahmoud pulled a box of stencils from a cabinet, inserted one into a typewriter, and removed the ribbon. Angie sat down and began hitting the typewriter keys, copying information from the flyer they'd drafted. She made three mistakes in the first two lines. She ripped out the stencil and replaced it.

"You do it," she said to Sarah. "You couldn't be any worse at this than I am."

It took them two hours to cut a satisfactory stencil, put ink into the machine, and roll off three hundred flyers. Their hands were purple with the ink when they finished. At that point, Omar came through the front door and scowled at them.

"Where'd you get the paper for this?" Omar snapped as he examined one of the flyers.

"Right over there," said Angie, pointing to several reams of paper sitting on a shelf.

"Those stencils and that paper are expensive. You're going to have to get the Peace Corps to reimburse me for this."

Angie, Sarah, and Mahmoud went out the door and left Omar to stew about the unauthorized use of his paper supply. They walked up the dusty streets passing out flyers to teens and preteens they met along the way. "For free?" asked one boy in passable English.

"Yes," Angie replied in Arabic, smiling. "You could practice your English, and you'd help us with our Arabic."

Outreach Center

Just as they passed out the last of their flyers, Stevie Parker stopped his Vespa in the parking lot next to their makeshift classroom.

"Oh, no," said Angie. "Here comes the football hero."

"Don't be so negative," said Sarah.

"How are you girls doing?" said Stevie, a big smile on his face."

"We women are doing well," said Angie. "What brings you out here?"

"I thought I'd share these bottles of cold Coke with you." He lifted his left hand with three bottles dangling by their necks between his fingers.

"Bring them up to our house," said Sarah. "It will be more comfortable there."

She led them toward their house, where she pulled three kitchen chairs out by the front door. Stevie placed his chair so close to Angie that their shoulders nearly touched.

Angie edged her chair away. "Give me a little room, Stevie. It's too hot to sit this close."

The three of them leaned back in their chairs, savoring the drinks. Sarah pressed the cool glass bottle against her face as though it were an icepack. "God, Stevie, this feels so good. Thank you."

They watched a group of children playing hide-and-seek across the street.

"Those kids all look so happy," said Angie, smiling, looking back and forth from Sarah to Stevie.

"But they're all dirty, and the girls will be pregnant by the time they're eighteen," he said.

Angie watched Sarah's back stiffen at Stevie's prejudgment, even though she suspected he was right. "They just get married sooner than we do," Sarah said.

"Stevie's got a point," said Angie. "Even Omar complained about the health habits of people here. I wonder if he would let us bring in the embassy nurse to give a talk on health and hygiene."

Sarah and Stevie nodded, and the conversation drifted off to other topics. Finally, Sarah stood up.

"Thank you for the Cokes, Stevie, but Angie and I have to desert you now and go to a Community Association meeting. There'll be a mob of people there, and we want to make sure they all see these flyers we've made up."

As Stevie rose to leave, he looked at Angie and said, "Is there anything you need that I can pick up for you in town?"

Angie clasped her hands and looked down at her lap as she thought about it.

"There is one thing, although I doubt that it exists in Tunis."

"What?"

"As I told you the other day, I was a figure skater before I joined the Peace Corps. Of course, there are no ice rinks in Tunis, but if Sarah and I had roller skates, we could use that parking lot after it empties out at the end of the day. It has decent pavement." She waved her hand at the empty lot at the end of the lane.

"What are your sizes?" asked Stevie.

"I'm a six, and I'd guess Sarah's a seven. Don't waste any time looking for them, Stevie. But if you ever run across a couple of pairs, I'll pay whatever the person wants for them."

Community Association Meeting

At the association meeting, Omar dismissed the idea of having the embassy nurse come out to Ettadhamen to give a lecture on health and hygiene. "She'll probably want to talk about birth control, and that would upset a lot of people."

"We can warn her away from that topic," said Angie.

"Let me think about it."

"I know what 'let me think about it' means," said Angie as they headed home after the meeting. "It means 'no way.'"

Sarah changed the subject. "You said you wanted to get rid of Stevie, and then you asked him to find you roller skates. You're sending him a mixed message. Why?"

Angie grinned. "If he finds them, I'll teach you to skate, which you're going to love. If he doesn't, which is more likely, he'll be too embarrassed to keep pestering me for a date."

"Horny guys are never too embarrassed to pester you."

"What would you do?"

"Well, I wouldn't lead him on by getting him to do me favors. You're asking for trouble."

5

"The closest friend I ever had."

July 1979

Community Association Office

Mahmoud popped his head through the door of the outreach center at mid-morning.

"Omar wants to see you."

"About what?" asked Sarah.

"I don't know, but he spent an hour this morning arguing with Mrs. Trabelsi about a nurse. Maybe it has something to do with that."

Omar extended his arm with his hand pointed down, gesturing for Angie and Sarah to approach him. They sat on the two chairs by his old wooden desk, and he leaned forward.

"I persuaded some of our women that a presentation on health by your embassy nurse might be beneficial. But only if the nurse doesn't mention birth control."

They set a tentative date for the lecture, and the two women left. Once they were out of Omar's hearing range, Angie asked, "Why is Omar grabbing credit for this? According to Mahmoud, it was Mrs. Trabelsi who pushed him into it."

"Who cares where the credit goes, as long as we can get the nurse out here to do it," replied Sarah.

They grabbed the noon bus into town and were pleased when Nurse Loretta Weldon readily agreed to give the lecture. Another request sat in the back of Angie's mind, but she hesitated before asking it.

"Do you remember that Foreign Service Officer who spoke at the party Blaire gave for us?"

"James Whitcomb?"

"He seemed to have an appreciation for initiatives like this that help ordinary people. Do you think he'd want to come?"

"I can ask," said Loretta.

"Don't tell him I suggested it."

Sarah laughed at Angie. "As we say in Kentucky, partner, you're barking up the wrong tree."

The nurse looked to be stifling a grin as she witnessed the exchange.

Outreach Center

It took an effort for Angie to curb her enthusiasm when James Bryan Whitcomb showed up with Nurse Weldon. He smiled at the two volunteers as he shook their hands. He wore the same charcoal gray suit he had worn at the party. Why anybody would wear a dark business suit to Ettadhamen on such a hot summer day mystified Angie. No matter. She was delighted to see him.

Her delight swiftly turned to embarrassment when only three girls showed up. Nurse Loretta spoke almost no Arabic and the audience had limited English, so Angie served as interpreter. She had prepared herself by asking Loretta for a list of medical terms she would mention. Angie looked up each one in her English-Arabic dictionary. Then she double-checked the words with Mrs. Trabelsi to make sure she pronounced them correctly.

Everything worked well until the nurse mentioned the danger that high blood pressure posed to the heart. Angie forgot the word for heart, and every circumlocution she could think of left blank faces. She gestured with both hands toward her chest.

"This organ here," she said, embarrassed. "The one that goes *thump-thump, thump-thump, thump-thump.*"

The girls in the room giggled, and Angie insecurely looked out to see the FSO grinning at her discomfort. Finally, one of the girls blurted out, "Qalb."

On a chair in front of Angie sat the oldest girl in the room, Omar's niece Yasmine. She held a baby boy on her lap, the younger of her two children. Yasmine was only eighteen, and Angie shuddered to think of how many more children she was likely to have. Although Omar had prohibited Loretta from introducing the topic of birth control, he couldn't object if one of the girls asked about it and the nurse responded. When no one raised a question about birth control, Angie waited for an appropriate moment. She saw her chance when the nurse mentioned the importance of hygiene for small children. Angie smiled warmly at Yasmine, who had just lifted her baby to her chest.

"Yasmine, you have such a beautiful little boy, and you do such a great job of keeping him healthy." She reached down, caressed the baby's head, and smiled at him. "Do you think he'll have any younger brothers or sisters?"

"If Allah wills it," said Yasmine, with no expression on her face.

"You have some choice in that," Angie replied, fishing for the girl to ask what kind of choice she had. When the fished-for question never came, Angie let the issue drop.

At the end of the talk, Angie and Sarah apologized for the meager attendance. Loretta rationalized it, "Their husbands and fathers probably objected."

James Whitcomb smiled sympathetically. "You did your best, and that's what matters. At the very least there are three girls who learned something that will make their lives better."

Angie thanked him for his kind comments, but she felt chagrined at the low turnout and her flubbing the translation of the term "heart." He was probably so unimpressed that she would never see him again. She vowed to herself that she would never invite any more speakers to Ettadhamen. If Sarah invited one, she would have to handle the translation herself.

Ettadhamen Parking Lot

A week after the hygiene lecture, Stevie marched up the lane, beaming as he held up two pairs of white roller skate boots. Angie eyed the boots with nervous pleasure. As nice as it was to have the skates, this would complicate her relations with him.

"Where did you ever find these?"

"I can't tell you how many people I had to talk to."

"I'll have to get a money order from my bank at home before I can pay you. Is that okay?"

"That's no problem," he said. "What I would like to do is show you around TACC."

"We'll do it, Stevie, but the next two weeks are really busy here. Maybe after that."

When Stevie left, Sarah made fun of Angie. "Any more bright ideas, Wonder Woman?"

"If you were the one he was hitting on, you'd brush him off, too."

"You wanted to get rid of him, and now you're indebted to him."

"Oh, shut up," said Angie, lifting the skates. "Let's try these out in the parking lot."

Sarah skated with her for five minutes, then went to sit on a stack of old automobile tires on the edge of the parking lot. Angie experimented with various movements she could manage on roller skates while wearing a full skirt. She finished by gliding back to Sarah on her left foot and raising her right leg as high as she could, given the long skirt she was wearing. The roller skate boot was a little heavy for this maneuver, however, that might work to her advantage. When she got back to an ice rink, the figure skates would seem light by comparison.

Two teenage girls watched with mouths hanging open, Yasmine's younger sister, Fatma, and one of her friends. Angie pumped her way toward Sarah, sat down next to her on the stack of old tires, and toweled the sweat off her face.

"God, I've missed this, Sarah. Bumpier than an ice rink, but it'll do."

She smiled as the two girls approached her.

"Can we try that?" asked Fatma.

"Of course," said Angie.

Fatma wore a hijab and a long robe that trailed behind her. When the two girls collided and fell, Angie jumped down from her seat on the tires. They just giggled and got back on their feet. After fifteen minutes, Angie motioned for them to stop.

"I have to get my dinner now. If you come back tomorrow, I'll give you lessons."

The next day, a third girl joined the skaters, raising Angie's expectations that the group would grow. She drafted a telegram to her father, Charlie, in New York City. She'd take it to the post office in the morning to send it. "Need six pairs of roller skates sizes 5, 6, and 7 STOP Pay from my savings account and take out an extra fifty dollars you can send me STOP Love Angie STOP."

Ettadhamen

That evening, Angie found it hard to concentrate as she sat on a chair in front of their house reading *To Kill a Mockingbird*. When Sarah sat down next to her, Angie said, "I don't know what to do about Stevie. Maybe I should just accept one of his date requests and then be so obnoxious he never asks me again."

Sarah gave a teasing grin. "You must admit, Angie, he is attractive. At least with him you'd get to hang around an accomplished athlete."

Angie looked up, scowling. "I'm a more accomplished athlete than he is."

"He played Division I football."

Angie felt her back stiffen. "He butted heads with a bunch of pituitary aberrations. Why does that make him accomplished?"

"All you do is roller skate."

Angie threw her book on the ground. "All I do? I already told you I was a competitive figure skater. A year ago, I won a bronze in the Figure Skating Sectional championships, and last fall, I was a contender for the Olympic Team."

Sarah frowned skeptically. "You never told me that. What happened?"

Angie paused and cast her eyes down to the ground before lifting them to look at her partner.

"What happened? It's a video tape that plays over and over in my mind, like a bad dream."

She glanced down at the ground again, and Sarah stayed silent, waiting for her to continue.

"We were at the sectionals at the Boston Garden arena last year, and I was determined to become the first woman to do a triple axel in competition."

"The triple axel?"

Angie gave a short laugh. "I keep forgetting that you don't speak figure-skate language. You jump in the air and spin three times."

"Sounds impossible."

"It's possible, all right. But your timing has to be perfect. To jump high enough to do the three spins, you need to be moving forward at breakneck speed. And you have to do all this in sync with the music that's playing over the loud speakers."

"What was your music?"

"The Beatles' 'Let It Be.' To me, that's their greatest song. After my mother died, I played it all the time, because it made me feel like I wasn't alone. I played it so much I drove Charlie crazy."

"Who's Charlie?"

"My stepdad."

She picked a stone off the ground and listlessly threw it into the street before turning back toward Sarah. "Then I made one little mistake and blew it all in a fraction of a second. I fell when I came down from the jump and injured my right knee."

"Badly?"

"I fractured the kneecap and tore the ACL."

"What's the ACL?"

"It's the ligament at the front of your leg that holds the knee steady."

"And if it hadn't been for that, you'd have made the Olympic team."

"Without doubt, if I'd succeeded at that triple axel. That's why I had to take the chance."

"How come you never told any of us about this?"

Angie shrugged. "You're always complaining about some of the volunteers putting on airs. If I bragged about it, I'd be putting on airs, and you guys would resent me."

Sarah set her hand on Angie's arm. "Pay them no mind, as we say in Harlan County. I never meant you when I said 'putting on airs.' You're as down to earth as they come. But I'm so sorry you had that accident."

"Don't be. The knee is healing nicely, although it took a couple of surgeries. The morning exercises and roller skating help me maintain body strength and agility. I may have another shot at that triple axel after all. The only question is when."

Sarah's jaw gaped, and her eyes widened. "When? You'd desert me?"

Angie placed her hand on Sarah's wrist and smiled. "No way. You're the closest friend I ever had. We've got a job to do here in Ettadhamen, and we'll do it together."

"Plus," Sarah pointed her finger at the sky, "That FSO James Whitcomb is still on your radar."

Angie buried her face in her hands. "After that fiasco of the nurse's lecture, he must think I'm the most incompetent person in Tunis."

6

"Why hadn't she thought of that?"

July 1978

Ettadhamen

When the parking lot emptied out at the end of each work day, Angie offered skating instruction to anyone who showed up. Afterwards, she experimented with moves she felt it was safe to do on the pavement of the parking lot. It had enough bumps and pockmarks that she was afraid to skate full speed or try any jumps.

She came home one night to find Sarah looking worried. "What's wrong?"

"We haven't seen Yasmine all week, and she used to come to the English conversation session every day."

"Let's go see if she's okay."

They hoped to get Yasmine's address from Omar, since she was his niece, but the association office was locked when they stopped by. They asked for people's help as they walked along the narrow, dusty streets. Many people didn't know Yasmine by name, so Angie had to give a description. The sun had set by the time they found her house, almost a kilometer from the parking lot. A ring of women and girls surrounded the dwelling.

Angie saw Mrs. Trabelsi at the front door and asked, "What happened?"

"Yasmine's little boy is ill."

"What does he have?"

"Measles," said Mrs. Trabelsi. "It's contagious, so no one can go in, but Yasmine should know that you cared enough to come and give her support."

Angie and Sarah peered through the doorway into a stifling, small, dark room that had only a single overhead bulb for light. Yasmine cradled her baby while sitting on a mat on the floor. He was covered with spots and his breathing was raspy. Next to them sat the father, looking down at the floor and saying nothing.

Mrs. Trabelsi got Yasmine's attention and pointed to the two Peace Corps volunteers. Yasmine looked anguished, and she barely nodded.

Angie didn't know how to make a gesture the Tunisians would see as one of sympathy, so she tried to mimic the look on Mrs. Trabelsi's face. She squinted and tightened her lips.

One of the women at the door headed out, squeezing past the two Peace Corps volunteers. Sarah asked her, "How long has the baby been like this?"

"Too long."

"Why doesn't she go to the doctor?" Angie asked.

The woman gave Angie a piercing glare. Her eyes swept down Angie's white cotton blouse. As wrinkled as it was, Angie knew, it looked luxurious compared to the faded robe the woman wore.

"Why doesn't she just fly the child to Paris?" retorted the woman sarcastically. She clicked her thumbnail against her upper teeth and pushed her way through the crowd into the street.

Embarrassed by the exchange, Angie turned her attention back to Yasmine. The baby's breathing became more labored. He began to gasp. As he tried to breathe, he hacked, his body shook, and his chest heaved. Gradually the coughs weakened and finally stopped. The baby lay dead in Yasmine's arms. She fell forward, sobbing.

Angie began to feel as though she were intruding on Yasmine's very private, painful moment. She nodded sadly to Mrs. Trabelsi. Then she and Sarah squeezed through the people who stared sullenly at the two healthy Americans.

When they got back to their house, they dropped onto their cots and stared silently at the ceiling. Angie couldn't blot out the image of the baby struggling to breathe. She remembered the time after her mother had died. How empty their home had felt. Now Yasmine's house would be like that.

Poor Yasmine.

If Yasmine's baby had been vaccinated as the embassy nurse advised, he would still be alive. Had Mahmoud gotten the polio vaccine, he would not have a shriveled leg. Most likely, none of the children had been vaccinated against measles. Or the other childhood diseases. Somebody ought to do something.

Tunisian American Cultural Center

Stevie Parker sat in his TACC office sharpening his knife. He drew the blade back and forth across the whetstone fifty times, and the blade made a pleasing *swish* as it moved across the stone. He relished the calming effect of the routine and thought of Angie. He wondered if she was using those roller skates he had gone out of his way to find for her. He needed an excuse to visit her again.

A mouse wandered across the floor interrupting Stevie's thoughts. He threw his knife at it. It missed and stuck in the leg of a wooden chair. Startled by the noise, the mouse scurried back to a small hole.

As Stevie got up to retrieve his knife, one of the TACC secretaries appeared in the doorway, looking startled at the knife stuck in the chair leg.

"What do you want?" barked Stevie. "You should knock before you intrude on someone."

The secretary's eyes widened, and she paused in the doorway.

"Well, come in as long as you're here. What do you want?"

She stepped tentatively toward him and handed him a sheet of paper. "I wanted to show you this flyer for a chess tournament we're going to sponsor. You might want your English language teachers to announce it in their classes."

Stevie grabbed the flyer and dismissed her, then smiled. Just what he needed. Given the popularity of chess among teenagers, Angie could use the contest to reach kids in Ettadhamen. This, added to the roller skates he'd already gotten for her, was bound to win some points with her. He'd bring this out to her the first chance he got.

He pulled out his knife that was still stuck in the chair leg. He wiped it off and put it back in its sheath.

Doctors Without Borders

Angie returned to Doctors Without Borders, arriving mid-afternoon. She took a seat on the chair in front of the desk and looked down at her hands on her lap. "Yesterday, I watched a baby die from the measles."

"I'm so sorry to hear that," said Antoinette with a grimace.

"Is there any way Doctors Without Borders could give these kids their shots so this doesn't happen again?"

Antoinette shook her head and lifted her hands, palms up. "I wish I could, Angie. But we can't inoculate children just because they need it. We'd have to have permission from the city. And we'd have to know that they hadn't already gotten their shots."

"If they'd already gotten their shots, Yasmine's baby wouldn't have died," Angie snapped.

Antoinette scowled, and Angie feared that she had just insulted her new friend. "I'm sorry for snapping at you," she said, "but even if some kids did get their shots, a lot of them haven't. Mahmoud, who painted our sign, didn't have a polio shot. You're the only one who can get these shots for them, Antoinette."

"If I commit our resources to what you want, I won't have enough left for the things we were sent here to do." Antoinette pulled a cigarette from the pack on her desk and lit it.

"Sarah and I can help with the resources," said Angie. "We can provide space for you. We'll get the embassy nurse to help give the shots, and we'll use the teenagers to help set up and organize things for you. If you need a truck to transport your stuff, I can borrow one from the Peace Corps office."

The more Angie talked, the more her excitement built and she started believing that it might be possible to do something. Even the skeptical look on Antoinette's face failed to deter her.

"The only added cost to you will be the vaccines. How much are they?" Angie asked.

"How many kids?"

"A few hundred in my neighborhood. Probably triple that when people in surrounding neighborhoods hear about it and sneak in."

Antoinette rose out of her chair and opened a drawer in her file cabinet. She pulled out a sheet of equipment costs and ran her finger down it. Then she jotted numbers down on a pad of paper.

"We could do the MMR and DPT for $10,000."

"What are those?"

"MMR is the vaccine for measles, mumps, and rubella. DPT prevents diphtheria tetanus, and whooping cough." She added, "We'd also need a couple of thousand for supplies to administer the vaccines and keep them safe."

"That's a lot," said Angie, her excitement waning as she realized the complexity of the task.

"And if you plan on a thousand children, that's more than your embassy nurse can handle. I'll need to hire a dozen trained people to give the shots. And I'll want a doctor on site in case there are any adverse reactions."

The complications of doing all this started to overwhelm Angie.

Holding the cigarette between the thumb and forefinger of her left hand, Antoinette used her right hand to scribble more figures on her note pad. "For fifteen total we could do all that and add the polio vaccine."

Polio! Why hadn't she thought of this? Her stepfather Charlie walked with a permanent limp he had gotten after a childhood bout of polio. And he had a soft spot for causes that helped kids. She pointed at the heavy, black, Bakelite telephone on Antoinette's desk. "Can you make long distance calls from that phone?"

"If I couldn't, I'd be out of business," said Antoinette, looking down at her fingers where her cigarette had burned down to a stub. She pulled out a new one.

Angie wrote a phone number on Antoinette's note pad. "Call this number. Tell whoever answers that Angelita needs to talk to her father."

"I thought your name was Angie."

"My dad calls me Angelita."

Antoinette looked at the number. "Where is this?"

"New York."

"That'll cost a fortune."

"Reverse the charges," said Angie. "My dad will be delighted to pay for the call. And let me try one of your cigarettes again."

Antoinette lit up two new cigarettes, handed one to Angie, and picked up the phone.

"Keep your expectations in check," she said. "This won't happen as quickly as simply calling cross town."

Once again, Angie began choking on the cigarette. She stubbed it out in the ashtray. Antoinette frowned. "These things are expensive. If you keep ruining them, I'm going to stop giving them to you."

Angie stood up to pace the floor as they waited for the call to go through, and Antoinette twirled her finger through her hair. Finally, an hour later, she got a connection. She handed the phone to Angie.

"Charlie, it's me, Angelita."

"What happened?"

She laughed. "Nothing happened. I just need your help."

"Are you okay?" He shouted so loud his voice carried across the desk. Antoinette smiled.

"Oh, it's so good to hear your voice. I've been missing you. And Evie, too. Tell her that I miss her. Charlie, I have an opportunity for you to vaccinate all the kids in my neighborhood."

"That isn't something I should do. Their government should do it."

"They do. But they can't afford to do it for everybody."

"How much?"

"Fifteen thousand dollars."

"Fifteen K?" he shouted into the phone.

Charlie was generous, but fifteen thousand dollars would be a stretch. She made it sound easy.

"Charlie, I'll bet you already give that much to charity." In fact, she knew he did, because she had once peeked at an income tax return he'd left sitting on his desk.

He responded, "When I had you working in my accounting department, didn't anyone ever mention opportunity costs? If I divert something to one cause, I lose the opportunity to give it elsewhere."

"I understand that Charlie, but this is a onetime thing. With fifteen K in hand, we can leverage it and get a lot of local help." Leverage was a popular term with her businessman father. She lifted her free hand in a pleading gesture, even though he couldn't see it. Across the table, Antoinette grinned at the sight.

"What about liability? If you give one of those kids an overdose, who knows what could happen?"

"It's all going to be administered by Doctors Without Borders, and they'll have a physician on site. All they need is the fifteen K to buy the vaccine."

Angie paused. What felt like minutes went by without a response from Charlie. She took a deep breath. "One of the kids I work with has a shriveled leg from polio. We can stop other kids from getting it if we vaccinate them."

If this argument didn't bring him on board, nothing would, she calculated. She felt a tinge of guilt at playing on his emotions this way, but she was desperate, and she held her breath as she waited for his response. Several seconds passed before he came back in a muted voice.

"I'll cover it. Just don't do this to me too often."

Angie exhaled a long sigh. "I can't thank you enough, Charlie. I'm going to give the phone to Antoinette who can explain where to transfer the money. Then I must go. If I miss my bus and have to walk home, it'll be dark by the time I get there. Love you."

Flashing a wide grin, she held out the phone to Antoinette. "Whatever you do," Angie said before releasing the phone, "don't tell anyone how you got the funds for this. It would totally screw up my relations with the other Peace Corps volunteers if they found out where the money came from."

Antoinette squinted at Angie in her plain clothes, who had just raised enough money to inoculate a thousand children. She cupped her hand over the mouthpiece.

"Your secret is safe," she said, seeming to understand Angie's need for confidentiality. "Don't leave yet. I'll drive you home. You're much too valuable to risk alone on the streets after dark."

Ettadhamen

Anxious to share the good news with Sarah, Angie pushed the car door open even before Antoinette came to a complete stop.

"One second, before you get out Angie," said Antoinette.

With one hand resting on the door handle, Angie turned toward her friend. "What?"

"I'll come by in the morning so you and your partner can introduce me to your association director. Don't mention this to him in the meantime. We need his support on this."

"Antoinette, he'll jump at the chance for this. It was his niece who lost her baby."

"Maybe," said Antoinette, "but he also doesn't want his people to think he's handing control of the neighborhood over to the Americans."

"Control of the neighborhood?" said Angie, her voice rising. "All we're trying to do is help people improve their lives."

"True, from your perspective and mine. Look at it this way. From what you've told me about your job, you've got people reading American books that will bring in ideas alien to the culture, maybe even be subversive to it. You want young girls to learn about birth control, which is taboo. You're trying to get teenage boys and girls to mingle, even though that's a very nuanced relationship here. You also want them to learn English from you, which will leave them somewhat influenced by you. And now you're taking over a task that would have been done by the local public health officials if they'd only had the resources. To some people this will look like cultural imperialism."

Angie was stunned to think she might be seen this way. She continued sitting in the car, even though she'd pushed the door open.

"That's a gross distortion. We're just trying to make sure that no more babies die from measles. How is that any different from what Doctors Without Borders already does?"

"There is a big difference. Médecins Sans Frontières is a respected, international, non-political entity that nobody sees as a puppet for the CIA."

"Puppet for the CIA? I've never even seen anyone from the CIA."

"The puppet never sees the puppeteer."

Angie shook her fists. "If I don't use resources available to me, babies will die. But if I do use them, you're telling me I'm a puppet for the cultural imperialists."

"Trust me, Angie," said Antoinette. "I'm not calling you a puppet. I'm telling you that there will be some people in Ettadhamen who think this way, and we have to do this in a manner that won't feed into their resentment."

She paused, and when Angie didn't respond, she continued. "For us to be able to do this, the support of your association director is crucial. We have to sell the idea to him in a way that makes him look like a benefactor to the neighborhood and not a tool of outside influence. So, introduce me to him tomorrow, and then let me do the talking."

Angie spent half the night tossing back and forth on her cot. In less than an hour she'd gone from euphoria over raising the necessary resources for the vaccinations to utter dismay that the whole project might fall apart if Omar thought he would be seen as a puppet of the CIA.

She recalled the Foreign Service Officer, James Whitcomb, who'd stressed how important the Peace Corps volunteers were in making peoples' lives better. How excited she'd been at that idea! And what could put it into practice better than vaccinating several hundred kids? How would he react to this idea that they were all just a bunch of cultural imperialists? She didn't want to control anything. She just wanted to ensure that no more kids in Ettadhamen got polio or measles, as had Mahmoud and Yasmine's baby.

7

"I'm not asking you to marry the guy."

July 1978

Ettadhamen

The next morning, Angie and Sarah brought Antoinette to the Community Association Office. They quickly discovered that Omar had a limited command of French and considerable difficulty following Antoinette's accent when she spoke English. Since Antoinette did not speak Arabic, Angie served as their interpreter. Antoinette pulled a small book from her big purse.

"After Angie told me what an avid reader you are, I wanted to give you this book by one of France's great writers, Jean-Paul Sartre."

Angie frowned. She had not told Antoinette that Omar was an avid reader. His copy of *To Kill a Mockingbird* still sat on a shelf behind his desk, its spine unbent. Why was Antoinette making this up?

"As you know," Antoinette continued, "Sartre was a strong advocate for independence throughout North Africa."

Omar thanked her for the book and leafed through it. Antoinette let their conversation drift to her positive feelings about Tunisia, the ruins at Carthage, the Bardo museum, and the Medina old town with its mosques, palaces, and narrow streets. When Omar lit up a cigarette, Antoinette reached into her big purse and lifted out her own pack. Angie's eyes bulged. She had never seen a woman smoke in public in Tunis. For all of Antoinette's sophistication, she might jinx this project if she smoked in front of Omar. Angie sighed in relief when Antoinette let the cigarette pack drop back into her purse.

Finally, Antoinette got around to the business at hand. "Médecins sans Frontières is a highly respected, politically neutral entity that has saved countless lives around the world. I felt horrible when Angie told me about the terrible tragedy of your niece's little boy dying of measles. If you used some of our resources, you could prevent your niece's tragedy from ever happening again to her or to any other parent here in Ettadhamen."

Antoinette was the best salesperson Angie had ever seen. She made it sound as though Omar would be the mastermind behind the whole project. He would earn the undying gratitude of hundreds of parents in Ettadhamen, and his reputation would grow among the public health authorities in Tunis. Angie got so engrossed with Antoinette's approach that at one point she forgot to translate. The conversation came to a pause until Antoinette nudged her to put something she had said into Arabic.

Omar agreed to accompany Antoinette to the public health office the next morning to get official approval for the inoculations. Additionally, he offered to provide enough additional space to carry out the vaccinations. He pledged to spread the word among the school principal, the imam, the association board members, and the other leaders of the neighborhood. And he put Mahmoud in charge of a signup sheet in his office. The first one thousand children to be signed up would get vaccinated.

Angie shook her head in admiration as they left Omar's office. When Antoinette dropped behind to admire some flowers outside the building, Sarah nudged Angie.

"Do you realize that this idea you came up with for the vaccinations is going to be sold as Omar's farsighted plan and Antoinette's brilliant execution?"

"Just so I don't have to watch any more babies die of measles, I don't care who gets the credit."

Antoinette caught up with them as they continued walking to the outreach center building. The moment they got inside, she pulled a cigarette from her packet. "Oh God," she said. "I've been dying for one of these. When he lit up in front of me, I thought I was going to suffocate."

She inhaled deeply and blew a burst of smoke into the room. Angie cringed at the realization that the smell would linger for the rest of the day. However, this was no time to be fastidious.

The tactful diplomat that Antoinette had been with Omar disappeared, and the no-nonsense administrator returned. She needed things done properly. She ordered Angie and Sarah to monitor Mahmoud's list of children to make sure that every name was legible and there were no more than a thousand names. If anybody came in after that, they would be put on a waiting list and only get the vaccine if someone failed to show up. Sarah and Angie should draft an attractive flyer about the event that could be distributed through the neighborhood.

As she inspected their space, she swiped her hand across a tabletop and held up a finger for them to see the dust she'd picked up.

"It's too dirty in here. If I see anything that will compromise the sterility of our equipment or put the children at risk, I will take back all the vaccines and give them to the Clinique St. Augustin." Then she pointed a finger at them. "And if that happens, it won't be me who will face the wrath of the disappointed parents here. It will be you two."

Before she left, Antoinette ordered them to organize the shot stations the way she wanted them. A place for a portable refrigerator to hold the serums. Five stations where the shots would be given by qualified personnel. And five more stations in Omar's office. A table and chair at each station. Space for the children to line up. Space for them to sit and wait for ten minutes after the shots to look for any adverse reactions. A table for holding cookies and fruit juice that would be given to each child after the shots.

"Pretty bossy," said Angie, after Antoinette went out the door.

"Bossy or not, she's the one who knows how to set up things for the shots. You hear?"

Angie smiled. "That's a new one."

"A new what?"

"Your Kentuckyisms. *You hear?*"

"Well, make sure you do hear. We need her."

Outreach Center

Vaccination day dawned sunny and hot, but with a welcome drop in humidity. Antoinette used the Peace Corps pickup truck to bring in her equipment. Sarah arranged for the teenage girls in the English class to be the first to get their shots. That would leave them free afterwards to assist the mothers when they brought in their babies. The girls eased the fears of the small children as they waited to be stuck by a needle. They offered cookies and juice to each family after their shots were completed. At the end of the line, each child's name was checked off the master list Mahmoud had compiled, and each parent given a card showing which shots the child had received.

At midday, Blaire Jones showed up with a Tunisian photographer, who lined Blaire up for a photo with Sarah and Angie. "We're very pleased to see you here Blaire, but Sarah and I are too busy keeping all of this organized to show you around."

"We won't interfere," said Blaire. "I need to get a few shots of the good work you two are doing. While we're doing that, we'll just wander around and observe things." The photographer snapped several photos, including some of Sarah and Angie overseeing the assembly line of children moving through the shot process.

After the final inoculation was given, Stevie spent two hours helping with the cleanup. He put the last box into the bed of the Peace Corps F-150 pickup truck and lashed a tarp tightly over the load. He would leave the truck sitting on the dirt lane in front of Angie's and Sarah's house until morning when they would drive it into the city to return all the borrowed equipment.

With some anxiety, he pulled Angie aside. "There's a nice French restaurant near TACC. Now that we're finished here, would you like to grab a bite?"

His heart rate went up as he asked the question. It was such a reasonable suggestion for two people who had worked side-by-side all day that she couldn't possibly turn him down. If he could just get her alone for a pleasant dinner, he was positive he could get her to enjoy herself.

"Oh, that would be nice, Stevie," she said with that smile he found so enchanting. "But Mrs. Trabelsi has prepared a thank you supper for Sarah, Antoinette, myself, and the nurses. I can't abandon them."

She cast her eyes down to her shoes as though she had a twinge of guilt. With all the help he'd given, she should have invited him to the supper. He certainly wasn't going to beg. Cautiously, she looked back up at him.

"I could ask Mrs. Trabelsi to invite you as well. But since it will be all women, you might feel out of place."

The obvious implication that he would be unwelcome among the other workers felt like a slap in the face.

"Maybe some other time," he responded with a half-smile. Then he left to retrieve his motor scooter from the pole where he had chained it.

It couldn't possibly be true that the supper would be all women. Were they not going to invite Omar, the association director? Or that runt Mahmoud? Or the doctor who had stayed all day to monitor the process? After all that Stevie had done for them, it was galling that they couldn't even invite him to the thank you dinner.

His anger grew as he revved the engine of his little Vespa. He engaged the clutch and sped onto the street so fast a pedestrian had to jump out of his way.

Ettadhamen, Home

They were finishing off their supper dishes a week later, when Sarah folded her dishtowel over a rack and turned to Angie. "After all that work Stevie did for us on shot day, we should accept his invitation to visit the Tunisian American Cultural Center," said Sarah.

Angie drew her head back and looked up at the ceiling. "Doesn't it spook you out that he always carries that knife on his belt?"

"I already told you. Half the guys in Harlan County carry knives."

"Stevie has a fetish about it. You should see the weird look on his face when he tests the blade for sharpness."

"I'm not asking you to marry the guy, Angie. Just go with me to check out TACC. It's the decent thing to do after all the work he did for us, and we can see if they have any resources we can use."

Tunisian-American Cultural Center

Elated, Stevie skipped to TACC's front entrance to greet Angie and Sarah. Angie's willingness to visit must be a subtle apology for the way she'd snubbed him on the vaccination day.

"Come in," he boomed. Their white blouses were darkened with sweat from the hot humid air. "You need to get out of that sun."

He toured them through the first floor gallery that was also used for lectures by visiting American scholars, receptions, and occasional concerts. Bright paintings from the most recent art show hung on the walls. "Next month we're going to use it for a youth chess tournament. We have room here for 150 kids, and a hundred have already signed up." He handed a flyer to Angie and said, "Do you think anybody in Ettadhamen would want to enter the contest?

"Let me post it and find out," said Angie. "We bought a chess set right after we opened the center, and it has become one of our most popular attractions."

At the end of their visit, he maneuvered Angie away from Sarah. To set her at ease, he rested his hand on her shoulder. Inexplicably, she pulled back.

"Would you join me Saturday at a reception we are holding for a French novelist? Afterward, there's a nice French café where we could get a bite to eat."

"I'm not dating right now, Stevie. Our director has discouraged us from doing that."

"Dating Tunisians, yes. That's understandable. You guys are stuck out in that slum all day long. I'd just like to help you get out a little."

She scowled. "It's not a slum. It's my neighborhood."

"Whatever." Why was she so defensive about her slum? "Everybody needs some break time now and then," he added.

"I'll have to pass for now," she said. "I don't want to upset Blaire."

Stevie frowned. "Check it out with her. I'm sure she wouldn't mind if you guys socialized a little."

After they left, Stevie went back to his office and mused about the visit. He was pleased to have learned that Angie was using the roller skates he had gotten for her and was giving lessons. Why did she include that teenage boy Mahmoud in the lessons? And, from what Sarah said, she put her hands on him while he skated. She shouldn't do that.

To soothe himself, he pulled his knife from its sheath and began running the blade across the whetstone.

8

A siren in the distance.

August 1978

Ettadhamen Parking Lot

Angie decided that she needed to be more blunt with Stevie. They could remain acquaintances on a friendly basis, but she had to make it clear that she was not going to date him.

Her chance came a week later when Stevie arrived just as she was helping Mahmoud learn to skate backwards. She had to grab his arm to help him balance. From the corner of her eye, she saw Stevie glaring at the sight of her touching the boy.

At the end of the session, Mahmoud took off his skates and began to wander away, leaving Angie alone in the parking lot with Stevie. She glided over to the stack of old tires to sit down while she unlaced her skate boots. He teetered as he walked toward her, and as he came closer, she smelled alcohol on his breath.

"I wanted to double check with you what happened. Nobody from Ettadhamen signed up for the chess contest." Chess slurred out as *chesh*.

Angie stiffened as Stevie stopped in front of her.

"We posted your flyer and promised bus fare for anyone who went," she said. "If no one has responded, it must mean that nobody is interested."

"Would you be one of the referees? Afterwards we could grab a bite at that French restaurant."

The mild turndowns she'd given him earlier hadn't worked. She decided that she had to be emphatic.

"Stevie, I don't want to date you."

"Why not?" he demanded. "A guy from Oklahoma's not good enough for you?"

The hair on her neck started to rise. She needed to calm him down.

"You're a very nice person, Stevie, and I appreciate your asking me out, but I just don't want to date."

"You won't date me!" he snapped, his voice rising. "But you've got your hands all over that little Arab kid prancing around in those sissy white skates."

Her smile froze, then disappeared. "Technically, they're not Arabs. They're Berbers." She couldn't resist the temptation to correct him. "And who I choose to associate with is none of your business."

"You're so smug! Like you're so much better than everyone else!"

Towering over her, he bent forward so his face was only inches from her own, vapors from the alcohol and his lunch wafting toward her. Involuntarily, she placed her hand on his chest to keep him away. At the touch of her hand on his chest, his hand jerked and pulled a large knife from the sheath on his belt. Angie's eyes widened and her mouth dropped open.

"Let's see how smug you are now."

He raised the knife above his head as if to attack her. She tried to push herself away, but she'd been sitting precariously on the unsteady stack of tires. The mere act of leaning backwards pushed her off. She landed on her tailbone, and a jolt of pain flashed up her spine. Because she fell backwards so fast, Stevie's knife missed her upper body. Instead, it came down into her right leg, slashing it from the upper thigh, almost to the knee. Another flash of excruciating pain hit her.

Stevie lunged at her again. Her right leg was immobilized by the pain, but she was able to lift her left leg and kick in his direction. The hard toe of the skate caught him in the eye. He dropped the knife and grabbed for his bleeding eye. Angie screamed, and Stevie sped away.

Angie grasped her thigh in a vain attempt to stanch the flow of blood. She called for help, but her voice was weak. Her mind was growing woozy. She heard shouts and saw Mahmoud come running.

Sarah suddenly appeared and pulled off her own denim skirt to wrap tightly around the wound. Women poured out of their shacks to help. Rania came running with a towel to cover Sarah's bare legs and protect her from prying male eyes. Before she passed out, Angie thought she heard a siren in the distance.

9

"Look at this rationally, Ms. Parnell."

August 1978

U.S. Embassy, Tunis

James was taking a coffee break when he first heard the rumors of a violent confrontation between two American government employees. It sounded like the issue might end up in the Tunisian courts. If that were to happen, he feared for the treatment of the Peace Corps volunteer, as a woman and a foreigner. He left his coffee cup on the table and headed for the office of embassy consul, Walter Bedell. One of the consul's jobs was ensuring fair treatment of American citizens by foreign governments.

"I've heard that a Peace Corps volunteer is about to be charged with assaulting our contract employee at TACC," he told Bedell.

"Mr. Parker plans to hire a Tunisian lawyer to press charges. What's the political section's interest in this case?" asked the consul.

"None," said James.

"What is your personal interest?"

"Also, none. I just have trouble believing that a violent attack on Mr. Parker would have been made by a person compassionate enough to have organized several hundred vaccinations of children. Especially considering that she barely comes up to my chin, and he's the size of an NFL linebacker."

"I appreciate your concern," said the consul, "but I'm limited in how much I can tell you."

"Send Parker home before he can stir up trouble. If one of our employees ends up in the Tunisian courts, who knows what damage that will do to our overall relations with the Tunisian government?"

"I'll tell you what, James. I'll let you worry about things in the political section, and you let me take care of consular matters."

Clinique St. Augustin

Angie woke up in a hospital bed with her leg and tailbone throbbing. The fog of sleep receded, and the room slowly came into focus. The smell of antiseptics. A photo of sand dunes hanging on the white wall across from her. Bouquets of flowers on a table just beneath the picture. And the memory of Stevie's knife slashing into her leg.

At her side, a middle-aged Tunisian nurse in a white uniform adjusted an IV bag dripping fluid into Angie's wrist.

"What time is it?" Angie asked.

The nurse said something in French that Angie couldn't understand. She looked at the logo on the nurse's cap: Clinique St. Augustin.

"I don't speak French," she said in Arabic.

"I said to lie still," responded the nurse in Arabic.

"What time is it?" Angie repeated.

"Nine o'clock. Now lie still and let those pain killers do their job."

Nine o'clock? How could it be nine o'clock with sunlight streaming through the window. My God, she had been unconscious since the previous afternoon. The throbbing in her leg and tailbone diminished as the morphine took effect. She began to feel pleasant, and her mind drifted until she fell back asleep.

At noon, the nurse brought in a tray of food. Just a croissant, coffee, and fruit juice. "How does your leg feel?" she asked.

"Better than this morning, but still throbbing," said Angie.

"I'll be back shortly with your next dose of pain medication. In the meantime, try to eat something."

Angie took a sip of fruit juice and set the cup back on the tray as a silver-haired gentleman came into her room.

"I am Walter Bedell," he said. "I'm the embassy consul."

She felt pleased that such a high official had come to see how she was.

"I needed to see you," he said, "because of the situation that has developed."

"Situation?" The word put her on edge. "This was an assault, not a situation."

"I was trying to be tactful. Mr. Parker claims that you kicked him in the eye with the toe of your roller skate boot. He lost sight in that eye, and he's asked a lawyer to press charges against you in the Tunisian courts."

She sat up and tore the bed sheet off her injured leg, showing a long white bandage from knee to groin. Spots of blood oozed through. The effort of moving sent a surge of pain along the leg.

"Does this look as though I could have attacked him? If he'd been sober and in control of himself, he'd have killed me." She glared at Bedell.

The consul ignored the bandage. "I'm sorry for your injury. However, it's important for you to understand that you don't have diplomatic immunity. So, if he succeeds in getting charges filed, you could be tried in Tunisian courts."

Angie could no longer hold herself up. She collapsed back onto the bed and groaned. A nurse returned to the room and glowered at the consul. She motioned for him to leave as she checked the pain medications dripping into Angie's wrist.

Clinique St. Augustin, Sarah

Late on the second morning, Sarah pushed the door open to Angie's room. She put her hand on Angie's forehead and felt pleased not to find a fever.

"I've been so worried about you," she said as she sat down next to the bed. "I wanted to see you yesterday, but they said you couldn't have visitors. Will you be okay?"

"My doctor predicts a full recovery."

Sarah sighed. "I'm so relieved."

"I have other problems. The embassy consul came to see me, and he thinks I'm the one who's at fault. Stevie's trying to press charges against me."

"What?" Sarah shouted. A nurse looked into the room and made a shush sound. Sarah lowered her voice.

"Don't worry, Mahmoud saw the whole thing. When they hear him, they'll forget all this nonsense of charging you."

"They'll never believe a kid from Ettadhamen over somebody who works for the State Department," said Angie.

"In this case they will. We all saw Stevie carrying that knife on his belt all the time. Besides, when the women of Ettadhamen moved in to take care of you, I picked up the knife carefully so I wouldn't smudge Stevie's fingerprints. I was afraid it might get lost if I gave it to the police, so I waited till this morning and brought it to your friend, Mr. Whitcomb, at the embassy."

Angie grinned for the first time. "Clever, Sarah. I think you're going to make a great lawyer."

Sarah beamed at the compliment, but she didn't want to wear out Angie, who kept nodding off. When she fell asleep, Sarah left.

Clinique St. Augustin, Bancroft

Angie woke up when a new nurse holding two containers of pills came into the room.

"I can give you more morphine. Or, if your pain is down to a tolerable level, you can take these Tylenol."

"Let me try the Tylenol," said Angie.

After lunch, a mid-forties gentleman came into her room. "My name is Edward Bancroft, and I'm a legal officer with the State Department," he said. "How do you feel?"

"I'm trying to get off the morphine and use these instead." She lifted the Tylenol container for him to see. "Thank you for coming to see me. The consul told me I might be prosecuted and handed over to the Tunisian courts. I can't tell you how scary that is. We need to get it stopped."

Bancroft smiled and patted the back of her hand as it rested on the bedspread.

"That's all been taken care of. Mr. Whitcomb gave me the knife he'd gotten from your partner, Sarah, and we found Parker's fingerprints all over it. She also gave a very credible account of the incident that contradicts Parker's story."

Angie let a smile creep onto her lips. "So, the charges have been dropped?"

"We evacuated Mr. Parker to New York for emergency eye surgery. And without him here to pay the bill, his lawyer will drop the case."

"You helped him get away? He won't face assault charges?"

"It's in nobody's interest to have a trial in Tunis. The publicity of a trial here would undermine the goodwill that was created by your vaccination project. And it's up to the Department of State to decide whether to press charges in the U.S."

"Whether?" She slumped deeper into the bed, and the movement shot another stab of pain into her bruised tailbone. "You've got to get him off the streets. He could come after me again the moment I got home. Or somebody else."

"I appreciate your fears, Miss Parnell."

"Ms. Parnell," she said, her mood growing more sour.

"Ms. Parnell," repeated the lawyer. "There are complications. The hospital in New York made a preliminary diagnosis that he suffers from paranoid personality disorder. If he claimed an insanity defense, conviction would be very difficult."

"You should prosecute him anyway."

Bancroft pursed his lips and bowed his head. "The problem with a trial is that you lose control over events. Any competent defense attorney will go to extraordinary lengths to discredit you."

"How can I be discredited for telling somebody I didn't want to date him?"

"Please try to look at this rationally, Ms. Parnell."

She rose to a sitting position so she wouldn't have to look up at him. As she shifted, one of the stitches on her leg pulled against the tissue. She winced, but Bancroft continued talking as though he didn't notice.

"You will be accused of provoking the attack. You accepted rides from Mr. Parker. You cajoled him to buy roller skates for you. You went out of your way to visit him at his place of work. You got him to do heavy work on the day of the vaccinations. Despite being in a culture with very strict rules on male-female relations, you put hands on an underaged Tunisian boy. You'll be accused of promiscuity, maybe even pedophilia."

"That picture is a complete distortion of the truth," she snarled.

He raised his hands, palms out. "I agree with you. But your reputation will suffer damage because of it."

"Even so, how could anyone justify his attack?"

"His attorney will deny that he attacked you. He was offering the knife as a present when you kicked him in the eye, which caused the knife to fall into your leg. So, the injury is your own fault, not his."

"There isn't a jury in America that will be convinced by that absurd story."

"It doesn't have to convince them. All it has to do is give one juror a reasonable doubt about Parker's guilt."

He raised a finger and pointed it at her. "If that happens, Parker will walk away a free man. You, on the other hand will spend years agonizing about the distorted picture his lawyer painted of you."

He paused again, and she refused to comment.

"The best thing for you is to let it go away so you can proceed with your life."

Angie continued sitting upright, glaring at him. "What do you want from me, Mr. Bancroft?"

"I have a release agreement for you to look at. Your medical insurance through the Peace Corps will cover your immediate medical expenses. However, you will have ancillary expenses such as travel and medical supplies and counseling that might not be covered. If you sign this agreement, the State Department will pay for them."

He held out the document, but she didn't take it.

"We'll also pay college tuition for you to finish your degree and advance you an immediate ten thousand dollars to help you get back to normal."

He set the document on her lap. She looked down her nose at it, horrified by a sudden realization. The term normal, in the lawyer's mind, no doubt meant the ability to walk around with no more than a slight limp. It probably didn't mean the ability to jump and twist and spin and hold her leg suspended in the air as she'd have to do as a competitive figure skater. And do it better than anyone else who challenged her on the rink.

Tears welled in her eyes at the fear that she might never again skim across the ice in a choreographed ballet of exotic movements. She looked down at the papers so the lawyer couldn't see her eyes, and she forced them shut until the tears stopped. Then she looked over at Bancroft.

"This is premature. I plan to return to competitive figure skating after the Peace Corps, but I don't even know how my injuries have impacted that. I need to see a sports medicine specialist. Will you send me to Paris to see one?"

"That seems a little extravagant when your doctor here predicts a full recovery and we're already making you a generous offer."

Angie snarled. "I want to talk with my father, who will want to check with his New York lawyers."

Angie swore that Bancroft blinked at the term New York lawyers. He responded without delay.

"Of course," he said. "We'll do whatever we can to help you get your life back on track as rapidly as possible. Fortunately, there are some American attorneys here in Tunis who could make a quick assessment of this document for you."

"I want to speak with my father," she repeated.

"We'll take you down to the hospital director's office later this afternoon and place the call to him from there."

Clinique St. Augustin, Charlie

The embassy lawyer walked by her side as an attendant wheeled her to the hospital director's office. The attorney backed out of the room and closed the door to wait outside.

She had to be careful what she told Charlie. He would indeed demand that his New York lawyers put in their two cents, and they could drag out a case like this for years. She'd be lucky if he didn't fly immediately to Tunis to escort her back to the States personally. He would take charge of everything and pressure her not to return to Ettadhamen.

These thoughts got interrupted as Charlie's voice burst through the phone. "Angelita, I've been worried sick about you."

Tears came into her eyes at the sound of his voice.

"I didn't mean to worry you. I just had an accident while I was teaching one of the kids at Ettadhamen how to roller skate."

"If you're okay, why are you in the hospital?"

"I bruised my tailbone badly and injured my leg. The doctors just wanted to be thorough."

"You should come home and get checked out by a sports medicine specialist."

"No, Charlie. I'm not coming home now."

There was a long pause on the line before Charlie spoke again. "Querida, you've got a figure skating career at stake. If you won't come home, at least have the Peace Corps send you to the best sports medicine specialist they can find in Europe. You suffered this injury while you were on duty, so they owe you that."

She promised to follow up on his suggestion to see a specialist in Europe. She wanted to get the conversation away from her injury before he raised too many questions. She asked how her half-brother Michael was doing and her friend Evie who worked in Charlie's office.

They chatted for twenty minutes, and tears flowed down her cheeks as she hung up the phone. She dried them and waited a moment to regain her composure before opening the door for the embassy lawyer, Bancroft. She was damned if she'd let him see her crying as he escorted her back to her room.

"My father insists that I get a second opinion from a qualified sports medicine doctor in Europe before I do anything else."

"We'll use the best one we can find," said Bancroft, gritting his teeth.

"How do I get there?" She gestured toward the wheelchair where she sat. "I can't even walk yet."

"We'll medivac you there as soon as your doctor here says you can travel."

10

"A PR shill?"

August 1978

Clinique St. Augustin, Blaire

On the third morning, a nurse propped a pair of wooden crutches against Angie's bed. "You need to start moving around," she said. She placed the crutches under Angie's shoulders and instructed her to put her weight on the hand grips rather than the armpit rests.

"Wow," said Angie, as she swung her bad leg forward through each step. "It feels great to get out of that bed."

She went out the door to explore the hallway. Making it to the end of the corridor, she did a one-eighty and lowered herself onto a bench. It felt good to escape the aroma of antiseptic that lingered in her room.

No sooner had she sat down than Blaire Jones stepped out of the elevator into the hallway.

"It's great to see you out of bed," said Blaire as she made her way toward Angie. "How do you feel?"

Angie edged to the end of the bench to make room for Blaire to sit. "Quite good," she said. "The hospital will release me in a couple of days, and the embassy agreed to send me to a sports medicine specialist in Paris. They can evaluate the surgery I got here and set me up with a program of physical therapy exercises I'll need if I'm ever to return to competitive figure skating."

Blaire grinned and handed Angie a copy of the *New York Daily News*.

"What's this for?"

"Turn to page seventeen."

A quarter-page photo showed Angie calming a small Tunisian girl as she stared tearfully at a vaccination needle stuck in her arm. The headline said, "Local Peace Corps Volunteer brings health and wellness to Tunis slum."

"Blaire, we weren't supposed to be seen as the ones doing this. It was Doctors Without Borders. And it's insulting to call Ettadhamen a slum. It's just a poor neighborhood."

Blaire put her hand on Angie's wrist. "You're missing the point. Publicity like this, combined with your figure skating achievement, puts you in an extraordinary position."

"Position for what?"

"To be the public face of the Peace Corps. You could do wonders to boost recruitment and public support. You can be to the Peace Corps what Joe DiMaggio is to Mr. Coffee and what Dorothy Hamill is to shampoo."

"You want me to become a PR shill?"

"Not me. The central office in D.C.."

"Forget it. Those people in Ettadhamen saved my life. I'm going back there to finish out my assignment with Sarah."

"Every day you are there will be a reminder of what happened to you."

Angie stiffened. "The first time I skated, when I was four, I fell down on that hard ice, and it hurt like hell. The teacher refused to lift me up. She put out her hand and said if I really wanted to become a figure skater, I'd take her hand and pull myself up. That's what going back to Ettadhamen means. It's pulling myself up."

"Just give it some thought, Angie. You don't need to decide right now. We can talk when you get back from those sports medicine people in Paris."

Ettadhamen

After the trip to Paris, Angie returned to a surprise party at Ettadhamen. Above the door to her house was a banner Mahmoud had designed, WELCOM HOM ANGIE.

A steady stream of people stopped by to wish her well. The girls from her skating group handed her a package and explained that it was a gift from several mothers of the children who had been vaccinated. Angie unwrapped it and pulled out three long Tunisian skirts, in a colorful array of green, blue, red, yellow, and orange. She stood up to hold one of them against her legs. It was long enough to cover her bandage and elegant enough to wear at formal events.

Mahmoud handed her another packet. The boys from the center had chipped in their savings and bought a chess set designed in Arabic motifs. She put the board on a table and set the king and queen in place. They stood looking majestically out over the room.

"You guys shouldn't be giving me presents. I should be giving presents to you. You saved my life, I didn't save yours."

Rania replied, "In the next neighborhood, three children have died of diseases in the past year. Thanks to those vaccinations you arranged, my baby is healthy."

After everybody left, Sarah buttonholed Angie about her trip to the sports medicine specialists in Paris. "What's the verdict?"

"I have a good shot at returning to competition, and they set me up with a physical therapist here in Tunis to guide me through a rigorous set of exercises I can follow. So, it's do the exercises and hope for the best. What went on here while I was gone?"

"I talked with Mr. Bancroft."

"That creep. He should be disbarred."

Sarah laughed. "The reason the embassy was able to evacuate Stevie so quickly was because they cut a deal with the Tunisians."

"He told you that?"

"Not in so many words. Two facts were clear." She raised a finger and said, "First, the Tunisians gave up jurisdiction of the case, even though they originally did not want to do that."

"You sound more like a lawyer every day. What was the second fact?"

"The U.S. might be willing to fund some specific programs for the Justice Ministry. However, there is no causal connection between that and Tunisia's willingness to let Stevie be evacuated."

Angie rolled her eyes.

"The good news, though, is that they're seeking a permanent commitment of Stevie to a psychiatric ward. If he's committed, you can stop worrying about him attacking you again someday. And in a commitment hearing, his lawyer won't attack your reputation, which he would do in a criminal trial."

Angie waited several minutes to respond. "I'll think about that, Sarah. The settlement offer Bancroft made to me still doesn't sound right."

"That's another thing that didn't make a lick of sense to me. So, while you were gone, I found an American lawyer here in Tunis who's willing to look at the agreement for you. We've got no way to know if he's any good, but at least he's a lawyer."

"Was he referred to you by Bancroft?"

"No."
"Let's call him in the morning."

11

"On strike against men."

September 1978

Peace Corps Office

Four Peace Corps Volunteers took seats around a long conference table. Angie grabbed the back of her chair for balance as she lowered herself into the seat and tucked her injured leg under the table. Blaire Jones came into the room along with a Tunisian man and woman.

"Next week," said Blaire, "the American ambassador will host an important reception for two members of Congress who are visiting. They have asked to meet some Peace Corps Volunteers, and we thought you four would be the ideal ones to do that."

Three of the four volunteers at the table had played roles in the vaccination project at Ettadhamen, Sarah, Angie, and Ben, who was still trying to score points with Sarah. His Peace Corps partner, Keith, had not participated in the project, but he was invited to the reception, Angie suspected, just so Blaire could show off an equal number of male and female volunteers.

As Angie pondered this, Ben asked, "Why us? I'd feel out of place at a reception like this."

His partner, Keith, nodded his agreement. Blaire frowned, then put on a reassuring smile.

"Oh no, you won't be out of place at all. You four are all pleasant and articulate. The perfect people to help build solid support for the Peace Corps."

Sarah spoke up. "For me, it would be exciting to go. But what would we do there? We won't know anybody."

"Just mingle. When someone comes up to you, be pleasant. Talk frankly about your projects, and if you see someone standing alone, introduce yourself."

"What do we wear?" asked Sarah.

"As Peace Corps Volunteers, no one expects you to dress up. Just wear what you're wearing now."

"In that case, I can't go," said Angie.

Blaire's smile morphed into a scowl. She lounged against the back of her chair in what Angie saw as a gesture of exasperation. First Ben and now Angie had thrown a monkey wrench into Blaire's grab for glory.

"Why not," asked Blaire.

"This skirt doesn't always cover my bandage." She lifted the hem three inches, and sure enough, the bandage showed. "Everybody from the embassy probably knows about it, so that doesn't bother me. But I don't want to advertise it to everyone else."

"Wear one of those long skirts you told me the girls from Ettadhamen gave you."

"If I wear one of those skirts while Sarah wears what she has on now, I'll stick out like a sore thumb, and everyone will ask me why. I shouldn't have to deal with that."

"Nobody's going to ask about your skirts," Blaire blurted.

"If Angie won't go, I won't go," said Sarah.

"Neither will I," said Ben. "I agree with Sarah. None of us has the right to make Angie uncomfortable."

"This is absurd," snapped Blaire. "We need you people there to show off the Peace Corps."

"You should all feel free to go," said Angie, trying not to show her sense of glee at giving Blaire some discomfort. It served her right for trying to turn Angie into a PR shill. "For my part, I refuse to put myself in a position where I might be embarrassed."

"Suppose Sarah wore one of your long skirts as well. Is that acceptable to you?"

Angie nodded.

"Good," said Blaire. "Now let's get back to business. One reason we want you at the reception is to serve as interpreters, especially for the Congressmen. It will be a plus for them to see that our volunteers are fairly good at Arabic."

The volunteers laughed again. Sarah spoke up.

"Fairly good? Blaire, we speak Arabic better than any other American I've ever met here."

"And we're proud of that," said Blaire. "However, there is an issue we have to deal with." She brought her hand to her chin and looked a little sheepish.

"The Arabic speakers at this reception will be educated people who hold important positions. They use vocabulary and gestures subtly different from what is common in the neighborhoods where you live."

She gestured to the two Tunisians who flanked her at the table. "We want you to spend some time with these two language teachers to go over some of the differences in phraseology and gesticulation."

The four volunteers burst out in laughter. They understood exactly what Blaire meant. She didn't want anybody to unwittingly use some street phrase they'd picked up that was the Arabic equivalent of *fuck*.

———————

After the meeting broke up, Blaire pulled Angie into her office for a private conversation. Sarah waited in the lobby while Angie set her crutches on the floor and lowered herself into a molded plastic chair facing Blaire's gray, metal desk. The official portrait of President Jimmy Carter hung on the wall above Blaire's head.

"The embassy lawyer, Mr. Bancroft, would like to close the books on the settlement he offered you, and he asked me to sound you out on it."

"Why doesn't he just talk to me directly?"

"Maybe he thinks you got off to a bad start with him. Let's face it, you were a little snarky."

"He talked about ten thousand dollars for damages. That's too low."

"If ten thousand was too low, your demand of half a million was preposterous."

"That's what my lawyer recommended. What did Bancroft come up to?"

"Mister Bancroft," corrected Blaire. "Not Bancroft."

"What did Mister Bancroft come up with? She stressed the word Mister.

"Fifty."

"Tell him to bring a copy out to Ettadhamen so I can give it a final read."

Blaire reached into her desk drawer to pull out a folder.

Angie lifted her crutches and rose to her feet. She pointed one at the closed door. "Let me consult with Sarah first."

She and Sarah went over the agreement line by line. "I don't like haggling over this," said Angie, shaking the papers in her hand. "It makes me feel grubby."

"Get that idea out of your head," said Sarah. "Suppose the injury from Stevie's attack turns out to be so bad you can't even go back to skating for pleasure."

Angie jammed her crutch onto the floor, making a thump noise.

"I *will* skate again, Sarah. I'll do it if it kills me. If I can't skate competitively, maybe I'll set up a free skating school for kids in Spanish Harlem."

"You'll need a lot more than fifty-thousand dollars for that."

Angie gave a wry smile as she scratched out fifty thousand and wrote in one hundred thousand. She signed the document and crutched her way back into Blaire's office where she dropped the agreement on her desk.

Residence of the American Ambassador

James Bryan Whitcomb III strode toward the ambassador's residence. Like all junior officers at the embassy, one of his duties at diplomatic events was to make guests feel comfortable. This might lead to picking up a new piece of information he could pass on to the State Department. More likely, it meant a dull evening of chitchat.

He was surprised to see Peace Corps volunteers in the reception room and pleased to spot Angie Parnell among them. Although he had met her, he knew very little about her. Her white blouse contrasted beautifully with her dark complexion, and she looked elegant in her long, colorful skirt. She had intrigued him at their earlier meetings, but he'd never seen her look so stunning.

She was chatting with the Minister of Culture who seemed to enjoy her presence. When he was pulled away to meet someone else, she scanned the room, and her eyes paused on James. He took a step toward her, but precisely at that moment the Peace Corps director, Blaire, touched her arm and pulled her away.

James plucked a gin and tonic from the tray of a passing waiter, a good drink for a warm evening. The air conditioner was losing its battle with the heat generated by the crush of bodies in the room. He spotted a friend from the Spanish

Embassy, and they began to talk about a mutual acquaintance they both disliked.

The Spaniard commented, "He is such a—how do you say it in English— Hijo de puta."

James shrugged. He had no idea what the phrase meant. Then a woman's voice popped up from beside him.

"Son of a bitch."

Peace Corps Volunteer Angie Parnell had edged within hearing distance of the two men.

"I beg your pardon," said James, frowning. Should he rebuke her for her language?

She picked up on his displeasure. "I just wanted to help your friend who was searching for an English term. What I said in English was actually less coarse than what he said in Spanish, which was, 'son of a whore.'"

Her flippant response annoyed James, but his Spanish friend smiled and asked, "Where did you pick up this colorful Spanish vocabulary, señorita?"

"I grew up with it."

Before either man could respond, the Spaniard was called away by an older man, and James found himself alone with the woman. He was curious to know how she had grown up speaking Spanish, but he was still irked by her attitude and said nothing. Fortunately, Angie broke the ice.

"I didn't mean to cause any embarrassment, Mr. Whitcomb. If I offended your friend, I apologize." She extended her right hand, which he took and held for a second.

"He looked more amused than offended," said James. "But we do have to mind our language in settings like this." Oh my God, that sounded stuffy, he thought the moment he said it. She didn't seem to notice.

"I'm glad I ran into you," she said. "I want to thank you for the flowers you sent me when I was in the hospital."

She smiled brightly, and James smiled in return. "I felt bad about what happened to you. Especially after you got all those kids vaccinated."

"You heard about that?"

"All Tunis has heard about it. And half of D.C.. Blaire has no doubt sent that photo of you with the little girl to the two congressmen who just came in."

He pointed to the entrance, where the ambassador ushered in two smiling men in their fifties.

"I know, that's why we're here. It's really important to Blaire that we talk with them."

"You don't want to?"

"I don't want to end up saying anything that could reflect badly on her."

"Just tell them about your vaccination project. That was a hell of a coup."

She smiled, tilted her head down and looked up coquettishly from the corners of her eyes. "Just a moment ago, you frowned on words like that."

When he didn't respond, she added, "It never seemed like a coup. I just asked the local administrator of Doctors Without Borders if she would help us."

"And they committed thousands of dollars of resources?"

"Isn't that why they exist?"

"With limited resources, it just seems a little extravagant to spend them in Ettadhamen."

Her lips turned down. "Where in the hell should they spend them? Belvedere Park where you probably live?"

Her eyes flashed, and James stood silent for a moment. How could such a captivating woman be so annoying?

Before he could say anything, she added, "I must move on, Mr. Whitcomb. My director will be angry if I don't mingle."

Two hours later, the reception began winding down. One of the congressmen had kept Angie on her feet interminably while he explained the misguided mission of the Peace

Corps. Even providing vaccinations for hundreds of children in Ettadhamen didn't impress him.

"It was a one-shot affair. Today you saved a few. Tomorrow you'll be gone, and everything will go back to the way it was. These people need to take responsibility for themselves."

Standing still in front of the congressman was causing her injured leg to ache, but she couldn't tell him she needed to sit down. He'd ask what was wrong. If he found out about her having been slashed, he'd no doubt find something in that to hold against the Peace Corps as well.

Eventually, the ambassador called him away to meet someone else. Angie found a couch and eased herself into a sitting position.

"Miss Parnell?"

She looked up to see James Whitcomb with his hands clasped. What a disappointment he'd turned out to be! First, criticizing her language, and then looking down his nose on Ettadhamen.

"I just wanted to apologize for the comment I made earlier. It was uncalled for. I also want you to know how sorry I am for that attack on you last month. The embassy took much too long to get your side of the story."

"I appreciate the sentiment, Mr. Whitcomb. But I'm too exhausted at the moment to talk about it."

"I understand. However, if you want a friendly ear over coffee some afternoon, I'll be very glad to meet with you."

"At the moment, I'm on strike against men."

He looked stunned at her brusque response. He turned to walk away, looking stylish and trim in his charcoal gray suit. Maybe she was overreacting. Of all the embassy people, he was the only one who admitted she never should have been left twisting in the wind, fearing that she'd be turned over to the Tunisian courts. He disappeared out the door before she could say anything.

12

"An inside joke."

September 1978

Ettadhamen Community Association

Angie sat in Omar's chair as she spun the dial on his telephone. She hated making personal calls in front of him and sighed with relief when he went into the backroom to give her some privacy. Even without him eavesdropping, she gulped a deep breath as she waited for a connection to James' office. When he finally came on the line, she pretended as though her last words to him had not been, "I'm on strike against men."

"What a pleasant surprise to get your call," he said.

"I want to invite you to Ettadhamen for that coffee you suggested," she said in a rush. Her fingers twisting the telephone cord as she talked.

Afterwards, she grinned as she told Sarah about James' impending visit.

"Lord Almighty! What happened to your strike against men?"

"I'm just trying to make peace with the Embassy."

"I can see why. He's a hunk."

"The last time you called someone a hunk, he tried to kill me."

"Let's hope that James will be more civilized than Stevie was."

Angie began the visit by introducing James to Omar, who stressed how much he appreciated Angie's help in the vaccination project he had organized. The project was part of his elaborate development plan to improve the neighborhood, if he could just get adequate resources. Angie dragged James away before Omar embarrassed her by asking for money from the Embassy.

Back in the house she shared with Sarah, Angie brewed two cups of Cuban café con leche. She awkwardly made chitchat with James, until it came time to take him to the Outreach Center for the English conversation group. But most of the girls stayed mute in the presence of the tall American in a business suit. Desperately, she fished for a way to break the ice.

"In case you meet Americans," she told the girls. "One thing you want to learn is how to greet them. I will demonstrate."

She made James stand in front of the group, while she approached him. She smiled, looked him in the eye, and extended her right hand. "I am pleased to meet you, Mr. Whitcomb. I am Angie Parnell."

She turned back to the girls. "Then, if you want him to stick around, you do this."

She dipped her head to the side, smiled, and looked up at James coyly from the corner of her eyes. The girls laughed. Finally, she'd gotten a reaction.

"What if you want him to go away?" said one.

James smiled. "Easy. Just tell him you're on strike against men."

The girls looked blank, but Angie laughed. My God, she thought, an inside joke, and I barely know this guy.

"This was very enjoyable," James said to Angie at the end of the visit. "May I reciprocate by taking you to lunch this weekend?"

Lake Tunis

James showed up the following Saturday in a Buick sedan much too big for the crowded streets of Ettadhamen. He wore a white polo shirt. It was the first time she'd seen him out of a business suit, and she liked the fit of the shirt over his tapered build. Angie wore a colorful blouse she'd brought from home and a faux silver bracelet she'd bought in the market.

They rode in an uncomfortable silence to a French café on the nearby Lake Tunis. As they sat looking out at the water, James said.

"Tell me about yourself. Why did you join the Peace Corps?"

"I took a bad fall in a figure skating competition last fall, and the injury put my career on hold for at least a year. The Peace Corps seemed like a great way to do some good while I recovered."

He gave a sympathetic frown. "It sounds like there was something else at work besides just the fall."

She looked out at the water lapping at the shore of the lake as she weighed how much to tell him.

"I've always had a problem fitting in. Being a competitive skater didn't help, because the training is so intense you don't have much time to socialize with other kids. Added to that, because I'm American, Cuban, and part-Black raised in a White family, I never had that solid sense of a single identity that most kids had. Most of them knew where they fit in. When I started college, all of this got worse."

"College should have helped," said James. "Most people have an identity crisis when we start college, so lots of the other students would have been in the same boat."

Angie sat up straight and tapped her finger on the tabletop. "Here's how it worked out. I'm at NYU and the sororities invite a girl named Parnell to their rush parties. Then I show up, part Cuban, part American, part White, and part Black. Everybody's nice, but nobody follows up with an invitation to pledge the sorority."

"That sucks," said James.

"Then I go up to Harlem to check out the City College of New York where there's more minorities."

"And?"

"I'm much too pale. 'High yellow' is what this one girl sneered when I flirted with a guy she had her eye on."

James fidgeted. He used his napkin to wipe his lips that didn't need wiping. "I had moments at Duke when I didn't fit in, but nothing like that. I don't know what to say, Angie."

She put her hand on his, then withdrew it. "Maybe nobody knows what to say."

They were quiet for a moment before James asked, "Did things improve when you got here with the Peace Corps?"

"Nobody makes an issue of my background, and that's refreshing. Until recently, I can't say I fit in any better here than I did at home."

"Until recently?" he asked.

"What changed everything was watching that baby die of measles. I felt so bad for him gasping for breath." She dipped her head and swallowed as she recalled the moment. "And I felt even more so for his mother, Yasmine, who could do nothing to help him. It changed the way I saw the world."

She took her hand off his. "Sarah and I worked our butts off getting the vaccination project organized. That galvanized our friendship and brought us a lot of acceptance in the community. Today we walk around Ettadhamen like we belong there."

He responded with a warm smile. "So, you do fit in now?"

"I don't know how to describe what it feels like, James. Imagine your great sense of pride in knowing that the project never would have happened if you hadn't been there. Everyone who participated can say the same thing. Sarah, Antoinette, Mahmoud, everyone. It's humbling when you learn your picture is the one that gets sent out to newspapers around the country, while these other people get very little credit for what they did."

He was leaning toward her as she told him this, staring into her eyes.

"There's another aspect of it, too," she added. "I think before I got here, I saw people as abstractions. North Africans, maybe, or Tunisians. Now when I think of North African, I think of Yasmine, whose baby died, and Mahmoud, who walks with a limp, Omar who's well-meaning but clueless. They have hopes and dreams and feelings just like you and I have, regardless of the fact that their lives are much harder than ours. And their lives will still be hard after I've left and gone back to New York. That's humbling too."

She leaned back in her chair and shook her head, sending her long, curly hair swaying in the breeze.

"To answer your question, I feel like I belong here, but I know I will leave. I'm proud of what I did. I'm rambling, because it's all jumbled up in my mind."

She stopped talking to take a sip from her wine.

"I don't think it's rambling. It's captivating," said James.

"Enough about me." Angie leaned toward the table. "Tell me about you. Why'd you join the Foreign Service?"

"My story's not nearly as dramatic as yours. Remember that old novel, *The Ugly American*?"

She shook her head.

"It was about Americans overseas leaving a bad impression. It had a big impact on me. And the Vietnam war was going on. When Bobby Kennedy called for ending the war, I became a true believer in him."

Angie's eyes widened. "You worked on his campaign?"

James shook his head. "I was only fifteen, and he didn't have any campaigns in North Carolina where I lived, so no, I didn't work for him. But I raved about him and collected so many of his posters that I drove my parents nuts. They're Republicans and thought that Bobby Kennedy was just one step removed from Lenin."

She laughed.

"It probably sounds goofy. When he got shot, I became even more convinced that we needed to stop our senseless wars and stop sending ugly Americans abroad. Joining the Foreign Service seemed like the right thing to do."

Angie peered at him over the rim of her wine glass. She'd never met a man whose passion to make the world a better place was so similar to her own. She'd arrived at that passion in a much more visceral way than he had. A traumatic injury that interrupted her skating ambitions and then a traumatic moment of watching a baby die of measles. His journey had been much more cerebral, a book he'd read and a presidential campaign he'd followed from afar. As long as they shared the same passion, what difference did it make how they'd gotten to that point?

"I don't think that's goofy at all," she finally said, grasping his hand. "When I was nine, I actually met Bobby Kennedy, and I felt the same way you felt when he got killed."

Carthage

The next Saturday, James drove her to Carthage where they visited the Carthage National Museum. They wandered past old pillars and stood before a trellis made of stone. Because of her leg injury, Angie struggled on their climb to the top of Byrsa Hill where the ancient Phoenicians had built their fortress. By the time they reached the top, her leg began throbbing, and she had to sit down to relieve pressure on it. When she was ready to move on, James held her arm to steady her as they walked down the hill back to his car.

On succeeding weekends, they toured the magnificent Bardo Museum, shopped in the Medina of Tunis, and took a day trip to the resort town Hammamet where they strolled along the beach and ate lunch at a seaside restaurant. They even rode a camel. Their guide snapped pictures of them bouncing along on the backs of the giant animals on the edge of the desert.

Angie sent a photo of them on their camels to Charlie. She relished speculating about how he would react.

Belvedere Park

At the end of August, James invited her to a party to meet some Foreign Service couples. She winced. "Other than you, my experience with the diplomats hasn't been very encouraging," she said.

"We're just like you, only stuffier."

"I'm stuffy?"

"Sorry, that didn't come out right."

"Could Sarah come as well? It'd be easier if I had another friendly face there, and I've been neglecting her lately."

"No problem," said James. "There's a guy in the consular section who's single. I can pair them up."

The party took place in James' second floor apartment in the upscale Belvedere Park neighborhood. A colorful Persian carpet hung from a side wall, and the apartment overlooked a narrow street lined with palm trees. She and Sarah each wore the long skirts Angie had been given by the Ettadhamen girls. Angie also wore a yellow silk blouse she'd found at the street market.

People had barely arrived when they began arguing about Iran. If she had once felt uncomfortable with the older Peace Corps Volunteers who all had college degrees, she felt intimidated by the knowledge that James' friends showed in their intense debates.

"What the hell are we going to do?" asked one. "Iran's almost paralyzed by those unending strikes and demonstrations."

"We've got to get the Shah to take a tougher stand," said George, a pudgy young man. "Or all the good things he's done will go down the drain."

"What good things?" asked James.

George scowled. "Well, he gave women the right to vote. And he's modernizing the country."

James objected. "He's created a police state that we keep propping up with more arms than anyone needs. We should shift our support to the reformers and help them build a bridge to the future."

"¡Excelente!" exclaimed Angie, raising her wine glass toward the ceiling. Everyone looked at her, and she grinned sheepishly.

Sarah finally contributed to the conversation. "This seems very personal to all of you. Why is that?"

"Any one of us could be assigned there," said George, who had wanted the shah to get tougher.

"And right now, it's very dangerous," added another. "I can't stop thinking about that Western movie house the rebels torched last August and burned 400 people to death."

Angie cringed.

"If my next assignment is Iran, I won't go," said a third. "I refused to expose my family to a place like that."

"What about you, James?" asked George. "Your assignment here in Tunis is almost up. What'll you do if your next one is Iran?"

James leaned against the Persian carpet on the wall and twisted the glass of Burgundy in his hand. "You have to take the bad with the good. Tunis has been very good. If it hadn't been for Tunis, I wouldn't have met Angie."

She felt warm and pleasant as he put his hand on her shoulder. A few people oohed. George pressed James.

"So, what'll you do if Iran is next?"

James shrugged. "If that's where they need me, that's where I'll go. Maybe I can help build that bridge to the future."

Angie beamed at James' courage, and a warm romantic glow washed over her. Later, as the guests began to leave, she realized she would have liked some time alone with James. With moonlight streaming through the windows, this would be the perfect moment to let him lure her into his bedroom. However, she could hardly do that and leave Sarah twiddling her thumbs on the living room couch.

On the ride home, she gave Sarah the seat by the passenger door, while she wedged herself against James. She spent most of the trip with her hand resting on his thigh.

13

"Mixed couples won't work in the Foreign Service."

November 1978

Hippodrome Restaurant, Tunis

A week before Thanksgiving, Mahmoud knocked on Angie's door.

"You have a telephone call at Omar's office. It's from a Mrs. Bentley at the American Embassy."

She didn't know anybody by that name, but she stepped quickly to Omar's office. "Mrs. Bentley?" she asked when the phone picked up on the other end of the line.

"One moment, please," came a voice in English with a Tunisian accent. After a long pause, another voice came on the phone.

"This is Mrs. Bentley."

"This is Angie Parnell. Did you call for me?"

"Yes. I'm the wife of the First Secretary in the Political Section of the Embassy."

The First Secretary was James' boss, Angie realized. Why would she call?

"A friend and I want to treat you to lunch at the Hippodrome Restaurant next Monday. Could you meet us there at noon?"

"Of course. But what is the occasion?"

"No occasion, my dear. We just want to get acquainted."

She wore the same outfit to the Hippodrome that had captivated James at the embassy reception the previous summer. Her only jewelry was the bracelet she'd bought at the market and a crescent shaped pair of earrings she'd brought from home. These paled in comparison to Mrs. Bentley's pearl ear studs and matching necklace. She and her companion, Mrs. Smith, had thin, gaunt faces that reminded Angie of the famous American Gothic painting Charlie had once dragged her out to see. Angie had to bite her tongue to keep from smiling at the comparison.

"Would you like something to drink?" asked Mrs. Bentley.

"An iced tea, please," replied Angie.

"You must try this Chardonnay. It is magnifique, as the French say. The French had a big influence on Tunisia, you know."

Angie furrowed her eyebrows. Influence is a strange thing to call it, she thought. France invaded the country in the 1880s and held it as a colony for the next seventy-five years.

All three women ordered the same dish with thin tomato slices, olives and a deviled egg. A waiter poured the Chardonnay. It wasn't until they finished their salads that Mrs. Bentley got down to business.

"My husband Arthur and I like your friend James very much, and we think he is destined for a distinguished career."

Angie nodded.

"I understand that James is quite infatuated with you."

"We get along," said Angie. "We met at the ambassador's reception in August."

"And things are getting serious between the two of you?"

Angie stiffened. This was none of the woman's business. "It's a little early to think along those lines," she said.

"Saying it is a little early, implies that there is a distinct possibility."

"A distinct possibility of what?"

"Of you two getting serious."

"Getting serious meaning what?"

"Maybe thinking of marriage?"

Angie squirmed in her chair as she replied. "This is not something James and I ever discussed, and I'm uncomfortable talking about it behind his back."

The woman smiled and set her hand on Angie's wrist.

"I certainly don't want to make you uncomfortable. Do you think it really is a good idea for the two of you to push this relationship?"

"We enjoy seeing each other. Why should we stop?"

"Because of what it might lead to."

"Meaning?"

"James comes from a distinguished family, and he would be a marvelous catch for someone like you."

Angie's pulse skyrocketed. Her hands jerked on the tabletop, and she put them on her lap to hide her clenched fists. She forced herself to remember that she was talking to a person capable of harming James' career prospects.

"He shouldn't date a Peace Corps volunteer?"

"No, my dear. There's nothing wrong with being a Peace Corps volunteer. However, relationships are much more enduring if the partners come from similar backgrounds."

"Mrs. Bentley, do you know anything about my background?"

"You may tell me if you like."

Trying not to expose her anger at this reaction, Angie wrapped her feet tightly around the legs of her chair. A tremor of pain shot through her right leg, as the sudden motion pulled one of the muscles still weakened from the slashing. She had no intention of demeaning herself by justifying the position of her family. Her father had built a hedge fund which by now had enough assets to buy this entire restaurant if he wanted to. She refused to mention that. If she did, she would be pleading for acceptance. Her eyes drifted out to the oval racecourse, where a trainer was leading a horse by the bridle. Mrs. Bentley spoke again.

"Do I need to spell it out for you?"

Angie's eyes came back from gazing at the racehorse and looked unblinking at Mrs. Bentley.

"Please do."

"You will cause great harm to James' career if you lead him on to the point of wanting to marry you."

"I'm hardly leading him on. And I don't see how my friendship hurts his career."

Mrs. Bentley took a deep breath.

"You come from different backgrounds that will cause problems for both of you."

Angie clenched her fists again. Just as she'd thought, the whole business of different backgrounds was a euphemism.

"Is it the Cuban part of my background you object to? Or the African part?"

"My dear, we don't object to anything. Do we Mrs. Smith?" Mrs. Smith shook her head. "But mixed couples won't work in the Foreign Service."

Angie unhooked her legs from the rungs of her chair and jumped to her feet. Another stab of pain shot through her wound.

"With all due respect, this is the most insulting thing anyone has said to me in a long time."

"I do not mean to insult you. Please sit down."

She motioned at the chair. Remembering that this was the wife of James' boss, Angie resisted the urge to storm out of the restaurant. She lowered herself onto the chair.

"I am not criticizing who you are, Miss Parnell."

"Ms. Parnell."

Mrs. Bentley rolled her eyes, but said, "Ms. Parnell. I'm just trying to help you and James understand what you will face. There are some people who will hesitate to invite mixed couples to their social gatherings. You yourself will feel shunned, and James will be passed over for sensitive posts. In time, his career will languish."

She reached out to touch Angie's shoulder, but Angie shrunk back.

"I do not believe that," she said, struggling to keep her voice calm. "Every time I visit the embassy, I see Black and Hispanic Foreign Service officers. They seem to get along quite well with everyone else."

"But you don't see mixed couples."

"That will come. You can't hold back the future."

"It isn't just the Americans who have trouble with mixed marriages. So do the local people. You and James would be ostracized right here by the Tunisians."

"The mothers in Ettadhamen didn't care about my color when I got vaccination shots for their children."

"My dear, they are colored, too."

"The people at Doctors Without Borders didn't care about my color when I organized the process for them."

"Well, they're French. The French are a little odd, themselves."

Mrs. Bentley stood up to leave.

"I did not want to be the one to bring this up, but somebody had to. Please understand that my only motive is to teach you and James about the gravity of your situation before it's too late."

Angie refused to stand up when the two women left. She clenched her fists and tried to stifle the rage that coursed through her body as she watched Mrs. Bentley walk through the door.

She slapped her cloth napkin on the tabletop. Of all the Foreign Service people she'd met, none had shown the disdain of Mrs. Bentley. Not even that scuzzball lawyer, Bancroft, or the consul. They had all been accepting. Mrs. Bentley was clearly the outlier, the leftover from an ancient past.

That knowledge didn't make the experience any less gut wrenching. What if Mrs. Bentley was right in the last analysis? What if Angie's acceptance by James' Foreign Service friends was like the welcome she'd gotten at the sorority rush parties? Everyone was nice, but the invitation to join never came.

She'd never enjoyed talking with a man as much as she did with James, and she wanted to continue seeing him. She was certain that he also wanted to continue seeing her. However, it was his career, not hers, that might be at risk. The more she saw him the more she exposed him to the risk. Did she have the right to continue doing that?

Belvedere Park

The Saturday after Thanksgiving, Angie stood by the parking lot waiting for James. It felt good to be out of the plain denim Peace Corps skirt and to wear one of her long colorful skirts. When James pulled his Buick to a stop, she slid into the passenger seat in one fluid motion without a single twinge of pain in her injured leg. It was getting better by the day. She no longer had to take several awkward steps to get into the car: back up to the vehicle, stop, lower herself onto the seat, stop again, then slowly lift her feet from the pavement and plant them on the car's floorboards. This progress pleased her.

"You don't have to wait for me at the edge of the lot," he said. "I can walk up to your house to pick you up there."

She smiled. "You're very gallant, but it's too risky to leave a car like this unattended. By the time you got to my house and back, you'd lose your wheel covers and anything that wasn't hidden."

"Cars park here all week long without any problems."

"They have a guard here on weekdays."

"You're not speaking very well of your neighbors."

She laughed. "I love my neighbors, but some of them are desperate."

She had to tell him about Mrs. Bentley's objection to mixed-race couples. What were James' true feelings about all this? Unconsciously, she swatted the bench seat with her left hand.

They went to a movie that had recently opened in Tunis, *Annie Hall.* It started out funny, making them laugh as the younger, free-spirited woman became entangled with an older man from a very different background. Was this James and her? Feeling good, she leaned against his shoulder. Then the movie morphed into the breakup of the relationship that had been doomed from the start. Angie left the theater with a sense of foreboding.

James drove them to his apartment where he had prepared a dinner. It was a stew he had left in his refrigerator and only needed to warm up. She promised herself she would raise the topic of Mrs. Bentley as soon as dinner was finished.

She relished the old building where he lived, constructed during the French colonial period. At the end of the living room was a small balcony overlooking a quiet street with palm trees, elegant walkways, and a sidewalk café. The door to the deck was lined with blue Tunisian tiles. A colorful woven rug of red, white, and green stripes hung from one of the walls. And for Angie, these traces of both a French and Tunisian ambience created a romantic mood.

When they finished eating, she wandered to the balcony doorway and gazed down at the charming street where a young woman was pushing a baby in a stroller. As much as Angie needed to discuss her relationship with James, she dreaded the possible outcomes. What if James agreed with Mrs. Bentley? What if he just hoped Angie would be a casual sex partner while he looked elsewhere for some blond, Nordic type as a serious mate?

She pounded her fist on the wrought iron railing of the balcony. This was crazy. James had never given her any reason for thoughts like this. She went to the living room and sat down at the opposite end of the couch from where he was sitting.

"Mrs. Bentley treated me to lunch this week."

"That old biddy? What did she want?"

"Old biddy!" mimicked Angie. "That's no way to talk about your boss's wife."

He laughed. "It's not my fault she's an old biddy."

"She raised some questions about you and me."

"What!" He set his glass down so hard that wine sloshed over the rim onto the coffee table. He leaned toward Angie. "What did she say about me?"

"It wasn't so much about you as about me."

She folded her hands in her lap as she tried to frame what was on her mind. It had seemed so straightforward when she'd planned it that morning. However, her stomach churned as she tried to put into words the pain of Mrs. Bentley's insults.

"Are you going to tell me what she said?"

"She's worried that our relationship might progress to the point of marriage."

James' eyes widened at the word marriage. "And how is this any business of hers?"

"I asked myself the same question. However, I didn't say that to her, since she's married to your boss."

"What did she say?"

"You are putting your career at risk by involving yourself with a colored person. That was the word she used, *colored*."

James stared at her, unblinking. Angie swallowed hard.

"She didn't even give me the dignity of calling me Black or Cuban or Afro-Cuban or Hispanic. She pulled up this old, insulting word as though we had never left the 1940s."

She stared at James, whose eyebrows furrowed. This topic makes him uncomfortable, Angie thought. Good!

"She's absurd," he said. "You're no more colored than anybody here in Tunis. Or in Italy for that matter."

Her head jerked up. "What does that mean?"

"You could pass for white."

She jumped off the sofa.

"Pass for white!" she shouted. "I don't want to pass for white!"

James' jaw dropped in surprise at her outburst. "Calm down, Angie. I didn't mean to insult you."

She jabbed her finger at his face. "I speak three languages, play good chess, figure skate competitively, and was capable enough to get Doctors Without Borders to vaccinate the kids in Ettadhamen. I don't need some rich white guy to tell me what I can pass for."

"Some rich white guy! What the hell does that mean?"

"What the hell does 'passing for white' mean?" she retorted.

James paused before responding. She continued to stare at him.

Finally, he replied. "Angie, I did not mean to insult you. It just came out in reaction to Mrs. Bentley. I'm sorry I said it."

"You're sorry because it was wrong? Or you're just sorry for upsetting me?"

He looked down at the floor, then back up to her eyes. She crossed her arms over her chest.

"Tell me what you mean, James. You want me if you think I can pass for white? But you don't want me if I pass for something else? Tell me what you mean."

"Angie, please. Before we go over the edge."

She uncrossed her arms. "I have to go to the bathroom," she said as she marched away from him.

Let him fret, she thought as she entered the bathroom. Between the toilet and the sink was a French-style bidet. She sat down on the toilet lid and propped her feet on the bidet. Soon she began to twiddle her thumbs. Her only reason for coming to the bathroom was to let him panic while she took a moment to collect her thoughts. But she was the one fretting, stuck in the bathroom, while he had free run of the apartment. She flushed the toilet and ran the tap water to make it sound as though she'd used the facilities. Then she pushed open the door.

James rushed to her immediately. "Angie, I'm sorry. What I said was wrong. I try to live my life being respectful of everybody, and I would do anything to keep from hurting you."

He reached out to take her hands, but stopped before they touched. "I grew up in the same country you did, learned a lot of crap, and maybe I haven't completely purged all of it from my system."

She softened as she sensed anguish on his face. "Maybe I haven't, either," she said.

He pointed to the sofa. "Let's sit down. Have I ever said anything prejudicial about you or about anybody, for that matter?"

"Until now, no," she responded. She slipped onto the sofa, the opposite end from him.

"Angie, I love who you are and what you are. I love you! I don't care what anybody else thinks."

She blinked. "You love me?"

"Yes!"

"What about Mrs. Bentley's warning to us? If you keep associating with me, people will steer clear of us, locals as well as Americans. You'll be passed over for important posts, and you'll end up in the backwaters of the diplomatic world."

"That won't happen. Even if it does, I don't care, as long as I can keep seeing you."

She recalled the conversation they'd had while visiting Carthage, and how impressed she'd been at his passion for what he did in the Foreign Service. Was he really willing to chuck all of that just to be with her?

"How can you not care?"

"I'll admit that I love the Foreign Service. However, it wouldn't be catastrophic if I left to do something else."

"James, the Foreign Service needs you. We can't let our country be represented by the likes of Mrs. Bentley. And I don't want to be the person who forces you out."

James raised his hands to his cheeks in apparent exasperation. Then he relaxed and took one of her hands. "Forget what the Foreign Service wants and what Mrs. Bentley wants. Tell me what *you* want?"

She paused, then smiled. "I like being a catalyst."

"A catalyst?"

"Yes. The one who shows up and makes things change. Like I did with the vaccination project. And introducing the girls at Ettadhamen to roller skating. And getting a chess set that brought more boys into the Center."

"That's what you want to do for other people. What do you want for yourself?"

She sat erect on her end of the couch, folding her hands on her lap, feeling self-conscious about telling him the thought in her mind. She'd barely expressed this to herself, much less to anyone else.

"When I looked out from your balcony a moment ago, I saw a woman with a baby, which made me a little envious. It reminded me of how lonely it had been growing up as an only child with Charlie. It would be nice to have a home with a few children I could pamper. Not yet, but someday."

He bent forward, grabbed her shoulders, and kissed her.

"Marry me."

"What?"

"Marry me."

She reeled for an instant as a flood of different emotions hit her so fast she couldn't sort them out. Fear that Mrs. Bentley might be right. Apprehension that her life might change drastically. Excitement that somebody really wanted her. And she in turn really liked that somebody a great deal. But did she love him? How could she know?

"You can't propose marriage just because you're mad at Mrs. Bentley. Besides we've never talked about marriage."

"Isn't that what we've been talking about ever since we sat down?"

"James, we just had a very difficult conversation about a painful topic, and the fact that we could do it makes me feel better about us. However, we need more time before we can decide on something like marriage."

It wasn't just time that made her hesitate. Her limited experience with men had been disappointing. Especially the boy she'd paired with at the skating club. Given the shortage of boys in the competitions, the boys could practically pick the partner they wanted. She'd felt cheapened when she realized that a boy had partnered with her primarily to get her to sleep with him. This had disillusioned her on pairing, and she'd skated solo ever since. Would she be disappointed with James as well?

This comparison was off the wall. No matter what happened with James, he, at the very least, had approached her honestly without any ulterior motive, so far as she could see. Sometimes, you just have to gamble. With a twinge of anxiety, she edged toward him on the sofa. She draped her wrists over the nape of his neck to pull his face toward her. She liked the feel of their lips touching and his arms wrapping around her. She pulled back and motioned with her eyes toward his bedroom door.

When he turned on the light in the bedroom, she reached up to turn it off. "I don't want you to see my scar. It's ugly."

"You'll have to let me see it sometime."

"Maybe next time. Right now, you have to keep the lights turned off."

14

"That sounds like not attached."

December 1978

Tunis

Angie sat on the ground leaning against the outside wall of their house. She held *To Kill a Mockingbird*, and her eyes skimmed over the same paragraph three times. She wanted Sarah's opinion on James' marriage proposal, but she was afraid Sarah would feel deserted and betrayed if Angie suggested she might move on to a new life with someone else. Letting the book sit on her lap, she picked up a handful of stones and tossed them one by one back onto the ground.

Sarah came out with a cup of tea and sat near her to watch dusk descend over the neighborhood. "You look agitated," she said, as Angie continued tossing stones onto the ground.

Angie let her hand sink to her lap. "There's something going on that I haven't mentioned yet."

Sarah nodded for her to continue.

"James wants to marry me," said Angie. She bit her lip as she looked over to her friend.

"Well, bless his horny little body."

"You think that's all this is about?"

"No, but that's always where it starts."

Angie laughed, and Sarah continued. "So, he wants to get married. What do you want?"

"I could live with him very happily. He's fun and sensitive and shares a lot of my own values. He stood up for me when Mrs. Bentley tried to break us up."

Sarah shuddered. "I'm appalled at what she did. What did James do about it?"

"He complained to his boss, and a week later, I got a note of apology from Mrs. Bentley."

"He stands up for you. He's introduced you to a new ilk of interesting people. He's apparently not a turn-off in bed, and he even cooks. Obviously, you accepted."

"Not quite. We agreed that we need a little more time together before getting engaged. After all, marrying an FSO isn't like marrying the boy next door."

"How so?"

"They keep moving to new assignments every two or three years. That would be tough on friendships and any children we might have. At least that's what I hear from the wives of his Foreign Service buddies."

"I can see that," said Sarah. "And all this moving around from assignment to assignment would probably kill your skating career."

Angie grimaced. "It might already be killed. One of those tendons Stevie Parker sliced didn't heal properly, and I can't yet lift that leg as high as I should."

"When you do those exercises every morning, you lift your legs higher than anybody I know."

"I'm not competing against people you know; I'm competing with the most agile people in the country." She tossed another stone into the dusty street.

"I'm sorry, Angie."

"Don't be sorry yet. I'm still hopeful that the leg will come back enough to give me one more shot at the triple axel next November."

A panicked look spread onto Sarah's face. "Next November? But to do that, you'd have to start training immediately."

Angie nodded. She set her hand on Sarah's wrist. "I've got to start training as soon as I can get released from my Peace Corps contract. I feel terrible about deserting you."

Sarah swallowed and waited a moment before responding. "I do feel a little deserted. But the one you're really deserting is James. You'll be back home, and he'll still be here in Tunis."

"That's the other development. He's being sent to the U.S. next week to start language training in Farsi. I should probably go home as soon as I can in any case."

Sarah nodded. "Especially since you haven't given him a definitive yes to his proposal."

When she and Sarah finished talking, Angie went inside and composed a letter.

Dear Charlie,

Important things are happening here in Tunis. I've decided to leave the Peace Corps in February.

I've enclosed a photograph of me at the ruins in Carthage. The guy by me is James Whitcomb, a Foreign Service Officer from North Carolina. He was very helpful to me after my skating incident last summer, and we have been seeing quite a bit of each other. In February, he will start language study in Farsi at the Foreign Service Institute in D.C.

Also enclosed is a news clip about the vaccination project my partner Sarah and I organized last summer. This would never have been possible without your contribution to Doctors Without Borders. Most of your donations go to big organizations where your share gets merged with thousands of others. I thought you would like to see that this particular contribution had specific consequences.

Some people complain that it did no good to save kids in one poor neighborhood when other kids elsewhere do not get saved. But I disagree. Even if we can't save everybody, we should save whoever we can when we have the chance.

I'm proud that you paid for those shots. I haven't told anyone what you did, however, because I'm afraid it could harm my relations with everyone else here. I'm sure you'll understand.

Your loving daughter, Angelita

As she licked the envelope, she smiled. Charlie would flip out trying to determine who James Whitcomb was.

Arlington, Virginia, Foreign Service Institute

James was relocated immediately to Washington, where he started classes in Farsi. Groggy one morning after endless repetition of instructional dialogs, James was glad for the lunch break. The instructor, Delbar, was about James' age, with light blue eyes that seemed to gleam in the overbright fluorescent light of the cramped classroom. She was a stickler for pronunciation. At one point that morning she had kept James and the other two students repeating the same sentence for half an hour before she smiled in satisfaction and moved on to the next sentence in the dialog.

James grabbed a tuna salad sandwich from the buffet line and searched the cafeteria for an empty table. There were none, but he spotted Delbar sitting alone by the window, looking out on a covering of snow that had fallen the night before. She wore a bulky white, cowl-neck sweater. As she saw him approach her table, she slid her tray aside to give him room.

"Your pronunciation is getting much better, James," she said.

Thank you. If so, it's all due to you." He gave her a thumbs up to show his appreciation.

Her eyes widened and she raised her hand to her cheek. "Oh no. You never want to give that gesture to an Iranian," she said.

"Sorry," replied James, reddening. "What does it mean?"

She laughed. "You'll have to get someone else to tell you that."

James groped for something to say in return. Starting conversations with women had never been his strong point. He recalled his first conversation with Angie and how his gaffs had almost torpedoed their relationship. But he had to say something. Delbar was, after all, his Farsi instructor, and they were going to be stuck with each other for the next four or five months.

"You are the only Iranian I know who is blonde and blue-eyed," he said.

"It's common where I come from, by the Caspian Sea. Not so much so in the rest of Iran, however." She tilted her head down and looked up from the corner of her eye, smiling.

"If you prefer an instructor with dark hair, you can ask to be reassigned."

James laughed and touched his hand to her wrist. "No, no. I'm quite happy as things are.

They traded information about their backgrounds. How James had gotten into the foreign service, and how Delbar had managed to get from the Caspian Sea to the Foreign Service Institute across the Potomac River from Washington, D.C. How they were both single, living in small apartments. Just as he finished his sandwich and was about to leave, she set her hand on his wrist.

"Tell me, James. You're a charming, eligible, young diplomat living right now in a region with an overabundance of women compared to men. No one you're attached to?"

James startled at the question. Everything he had studied led him to expect Iranians to be evasive and indirect. But Delbar's question was as direct as one could be. "I don't know," he said.

She laughed. "How can you not know if you're attached?"

"I was very close to someone at my previous posting in Tunis. I even asked her to marry me, but she hasn't given me an answer." He shrugged. "So here I am in Washington, while she's back in Tunis for another month or so."

Delbar stood, getting ready to return her tray. She smoothed her skirt as she smiled warmly. "To me, that sounds like not attached."

New York City

Charlie studied the photo of Angie with the handsome young man. A man who had been very kind to her during her convalescence. This obviously was a message.

Although it would be good for her to have a man in her life, it was critical that she complete her college studies. This would be very difficult to do if she hooked up with a globe-trotting Foreign Service Officer.

Charlie was grateful she hadn't told anyone about his funding the vaccinations. If James Whitcomb knew that her family had enough money to fund such a thing, he might become a gold digger.

He dialed a number from the Rolodex on his desk. When the receptionist answered, Charlie asked to speak with an old friend, Delroy Brown.

"Who may I say is calling?"

"Charlie Parnell."

There was a pause before Delroy's voice boomed over the phone. "Charlie, my man. It's been ages."

"It has indeed. Life's been good for you?"

"Wonderful. I settled down with a great woman, and we've got a couple of boys."

"How are things at Protection Services Company?"

"I'm a division chief now and still grateful to you for helping me get my foot in the door. What can I do for you?"

"Do you have time to do a small job for me?"

"I can put someone on it."

"I don't want someone. The person I want is you."

"That'll take longer. I'm a little busy right now."

"I'm in no hurry. But I'd like to know everything you can find out about somebody."

15

"There must be some way."

February 1979

Greenwich Village

Angie's plane touched down at JFK during the afternoon rush hour. Having shipped the bulk of her possessions home, she had only a carry-on case that cleared customs in no time. She took a shuttle to the JFK Express subway line to Manhattan.

Coming out of the Washington Square subway, she faced a gray and dreary sky. She walked through the square, and the glow of old memories warmed her as she swiped her hand over one of the cold, empty concrete chess tables. As a teen, she'd sat at this table waiting for an unsuspecting tourist to stop and challenge her to a chess game. She stopped at a grocery store to pick up enough essentials to tide her over till morning. Then she walked down the street to her apartment building a block from Washington Square.

She owed her possession of the apartment to Charlie's new wife, Glenna, who persuaded him to move the family to a roomier co-op just south of Central Park. When he refused to sell the Washington Square unit, Glenna blew a gasket and accused him of wanting to keep it as a love nest for other women. Angie saw red when she heard about the accusation. But Charlie came up with an ingenious solution that satisfied all three of them. Angie would move in once she enrolled at the nearby New York University. This would give her a nice place to live, save Charlie the cost of her living on campus, and keep Angie away from Glenna. The two of them never got along.

After more than a dozen hours in airports, cabs, and subway trains, Angie relished her old apartment. She brewed a café con leche, sank into the living room sofa, and put her feet up on the coffee table. Cradling the warm cup in her hands, she looked up to the mantel which held a photo of her mother, Isabel, who had taught Angie how to mix the steamed evaporated milk with coffee and sugar to get the Cuban style café con leche.

Despite the cozy feel of being home, something felt oddly out of place. The apartment seemed too luxurious in contrast to her dingy house back in Tunis. A little empty without Sarah's quaint Kentucky idioms. And a little quiet without the Arabic voices of her neighbor, Rania, and the kids in the street out front.

She phoned Charlie. "It's me, Angie."

"Where are you?" She sensed the excitement in his voice.

"Home. I just got in. I want you to meet James."

"When?"

"How about lunch tomorrow? Just the three of us?"

He paused for an instant, and she thought she heard a sigh. He clearly wasn't comfortable with Angie's attempt to exclude Glenna. Angie resisted the idea of sharing her homecoming with Glenna, and in any case, it was much too early for James to meet her.

"It's your show," said Charlie, finally. "Where do you want to meet?"

"I'm taking him skating at Rockefeller Center in the morning. How about after that?"

"Perfect," said Charlie.

Rockefeller Center

Wearing a long overcoat, Charlie limped toward the skating rink that gleamed in the bright winter sun. He picked up a long stem rose from a vendor, bought a coffee from another, then sat at a table by the rink's edge. With no wind, the mid-thirties temperature felt comfortable. He looked forward to watching his daughter skate. Angie had barely been four when she'd first wobbled onto a rink. In no time, she'd gone from a little girl to a beautiful woman, a ballerina on ice. A ballerina who had come within an eyelash of making the Olympic figure skating team. And who now wanted to chuck all that so she could follow a globe-trotting diplomat around the world. He shook his head.

Angie walked up to the rink, her elite Don Jackson skates laced together and draped over her neck, just as she had carried her beginner skates as a child. She wore a white nylon jacket, tight leather gloves, and a long tartan tweed skirt.

She held the hand of a tall thin man in his twenties. Twenty-six, to be precise. Charlie had learned that from the background check he'd ordered. A registered voter with no legal problems, no troubles with the IRS, and no unexplained gaps in his biography, he appeared to be a model citizen. He didn't even seem to be the gold digger that Charlie feared. His father owned millions of dollars of stock in a North Carolina firm, Autumn Fresh Brands, where he was a vice president. The only red flag was that Autumn Fresh Brands produced cigarettes. Charlie had an aversion to cigarettes ever since a teenage incident with a pedophile who reeked of cigarette breath. The incident today was almost forgotten, but the aversion remained.

Charlie could hardly blame the son for the sins of his father. He shook hands with James, then handed Angie the long-stemmed rose. "Happy Valentine's Day. To both of you."

He put his hands on her shoulders to hold her at arms' length.

"My little Angelita has become a grown woman," he beamed.

She lifted the rose to eye level. "This is so sweet, Charlie. But Little Angelita is redundant. Let me take James for a spin around the ice. Then we can get a bite to eat and talk. He's never skated before. Can you believe that? I'm going to get him started, then run through some routines if the rink doesn't get too crowded. I'm so pleased that you came early to watch, Charlie. I haven't ice skated in two years, and I can't tell you how much I have missed it."

The words tumbled out of her mouth as she and James sat down to put on their skates. She pulled off the long tweed skirt and handed it to Charlie. Grinning, she stood in pink tights and a short skirt that came down to the top of her thighs.

"It's simple," she told James. "Push off from your right foot so your left foot glides forward, then do the same thing with the other foot. After that, it's natural."

Charlie smiled as he watched her take James' hands, skating backward and pulling him forward. When James gained momentum, she let go, but he teetered. She laughed as she steadied him, then glided backward again. Once James got the hang of it, Angie took off on a warm-up swing around the edge of the rink. She skated half speed to avoid colliding with anyone. She did a slow coast toward Charlie and tossed him her nylon jacket before she sped up again. With the statue of Prometheus behind her, she went into a haircutter spin, arching her back and raising her right leg behind her so she could reach back over her shoulder and grasp the skate blade in her hand as she spun.

Something was wrong. She wasn't raising her foot high enough to grasp it. Charlie frowned.

She completed the spin and glided over to James. They made a few circuits around the ice, then went back to Charlie's table to take off their skates. "Oh, God. I can't tell you how good that feels," she said, her face glowing in the crisp air.

———

Charlie led them to an elegant French restaurant halfway up the Rockefeller Center Tower. They sat at a window with a view of the skating rink.

"What's good?" asked Angie, as she scanned the menu.

"Try the Salade Rachel. I like the artichokes and asparagus," said Charlie.

He bought a bottle of Alsatian white wine. Half a glass was enough for him, but he wanted to find out how much James drank. He raised his glass to them.

"Sláinte," he said

"Salud," she replied.

They clinked glasses, and Charlie turned his gaze to James. "You're not worried about going to Iran in the current situation?" he asked. "There are so many things that could go wrong."

"Such as?"

"What if the shah tries to come back."

James shook his head. "The shah's gone for good. He's not coming back, thank God."

Charlie smiled. Another point for James. He wasn't hidebound to the policies that had kept the brutal shah in power. "Suppose the shah came to the U.S.?"

James looked wide eyed for an instant. "If he comes here, all hell will break loose in Teheran. President Carter will never risk that."

"Maybe not. But even if the shah doesn't come here, the situation in Iran could easily degenerate into a civil war while you're there, and such a thing would be tailor made for the Soviets to expand their influence."

James smiled. "All the more reason for us to be there. With the shah gone, we have an extraordinary opportunity to shift some of our military aid to economic aid. We can encourage a budding democracy."

Charlie forced himself not to roll his eyes. "It doesn't look like a budding democracy to me. It's an unpredictable revolution. Don't you worry for your safety?"

"Right now, Iran's the biggest game in foreign policy. If we play it right, we can bring prosperity and stability to the Mideast for the first time ever. If there's a big game like that coming up, who would want to sit on the sidelines?"

"Salud, again." Charlie raised his wineglass. "I admire your dedication. I just hope that, as your future father-in-law, I don't regret it."

Angie grinned. "So, you approve of our marriage?"

"Your happiness is my happiness," he said, smiling broadly and raising his glass to them.

James reached across the table and squeezed her hand. "Your strike against men went sideways." They both laughed, and she squeezed his hand in return.

Confused, Charlie smiled awkwardly. He had no idea what inside joke had triggered their laughter. "I request only one thing," he said. "That you hold the wedding at Our Lady of Pompeii."

She frowned. "We were thinking of doing it at City Hall. Who needs all that hoopla of a church?"

Charlie leaned forward in such a rush that the legs of his chair scraped on the floor. "Marriage isn't just a scrap of paper you purchase from the city for a legal convenience. It's a social contract you enter into publicly in the presence of the families you are bringing together."

Angie's frown deepened. "Whose wedding is this? Yours or mine?"

"Cut me some slack, mija. That church and its school have been a part of our life ever since we moved to New York. Just hold the wedding there so our family, James' family, and our friends can share in your happiness. I'll go along with anything else you want."

"James is Baptist. Our Lady of Pompeii isn't going to allow him to have a church wedding there, and I'm not going to submit him to the indignity of begging for it."

"Let me talk with the priest. If I can't talk him into it, then do it at James' church. Is that okay with you, James?"

James looked startled to think he had a voice in this matter. "I'm okay with having it at Angie's church, but it's really the bride's prerogative to have it where she wants."

"You can talk to the priest," said Angie. "But you're not going to get anywhere. And if you don't, you've got to go along with City Hall."

"Or James' church," Charlie added. Why hadn't she included that? Did she have some latent fear that her mixed-race background might raise eyebrows at James' church in North Carolina?

Before she could think up another objection, Charlie changed the subject. "When you were out on the ice, Angelita, you seemed to have trouble with your right leg."

She looked down at the remains of her salad. "I tried that haircutter spin to test how well my leg had recovered from my injuries last year. Unless I can do it properly, there's no point in entering any competitions."

Charlie set down his glass and gripped the table edge, stunned. "You told me you'd only had a minor injury from roller skating."

Angie dipped her head and brought her hands to her face. After a second, she reached down and set her hand on Charlie's wrist. "I'm sorry, Charlie. I was afraid that if I told you the full truth you would fly out to Tunis and drag me back to New York."

He stared her in the eye for a long moment before commenting. "What is the full truth?"

She told him about being slashed by Stevie Parker and the settlement she'd worked out with the State Department.

"I'm going to have my lawyer reopen that settlement. Whoever engineered it took advantage of you in a moment of anguish."

She took her hand from his wrist. "No, Charlie. I don't want to do that. I want to put this behind me."

"Angelita, listen. The first woman to do the triple axel will become the Babe Ruth of figure skating, a person remembered for decades. You did one in practice, which means you can eventually do one in competition. This Parker character robbed you of a shot at that."

"I already had my shot at it, and it's over now."

"He destroyed a promising career in figure skating, and he's liable for damages."

Angie shook her head. "He's got no money, Charlie. There's no point in suing him."

"Then we'll sue the State Department for hiring such a dangerous person to begin with."

She looked up to his eyes.

"Please. Let it be. The settlement I got meets my needs. And I'd sabotage James' career if I sued the State Department."

She leaned forward and set her free hand on top of James' hand. "I've got everything I want." She gazed at James with her lips turned up in a wistful smile, then turned back to Charlie. "Please. Let it be."

Charlie frowned as he leaned over the table. "Let it Be" had been the Beatles song playing in the background when she took that life changing fall at the Boston Garden. Then he raised his hands, palms up. "Okay," he said. "It's your life, and I support your right to live it anyway you want. I do have another suggestion, however."

"What?" she asked, squinting.

"You're planning your wedding for the fall after James finishes his Farsi classes. Is that right?"

"Yes."

"In the meantime, while you're taking classes at NYU and he's studying Farsi in D.C., the two of you will get together every other weekend?"

"What's wrong with that?" she said.

"Engaged people should see each other more often than twice a month. Why don't you experiment with every weekend instead of every other weekend? If transportation costs are a problem, I can help."

She squinted at Charlie's suggestion that she and James should double the number of times they slept together. Charlie suppressed a smile. The stress of traveling back and forth every week might give them second thoughts about rushing into the marriage.

"We'll talk about it," she said. She looked at her watch and stood up. "Thank you so very much for the lunch, Charlie, but we have to run. We agreed to see our Foreign Service friends Ken and Jenna this afternoon, and we barely have enough time to get to them."

Angie gave her father a kiss on the cheek, picked up the long-stemmed rose, and they headed out. Charlie leaned back in his chair and gazed through the window at the bustling ice rink.

She'd be much better off, he thought, if she delayed her marriage until after James returned from Iran and she finished her college degree. He couldn't fault the man she'd picked. He showed courage by his willingness to take on the risky assignment in Iran. He displayed an admirable amount of ambition in his desire to go where the action was. And he didn't seem at all to be the type who would make her miserable by drawing lines in the sand and demanding her compliance. He truly seemed to make her happy. What more could a father want from a son-in-law?

At some point, Charlie thought, the differences in their personalities would emerge. James' successes in life came from an easy-going nature that fit well in the reserved lifestyle of the diplomatic service. Angie's successes came from a single-minded dedication to whatever obsessed her. Mastering the triple axel and pulling off that vaccination project. He tapped his fork on the white tablecloth. She was bound to throw herself into some flashy project in the future. What would happen when her flashy project collided with James' best interests?

Monsignor O'Reilly's Office

Arranging a church wedding at Our Lady of Pompeii turned out to be just as complicated as Angie had predicted. The pastor, Father Dmitri Boromeo, could not allow the marriage of a non-Catholic in the sanctuary. The service could only be held in private in the parish rectory.

"Father Boromeo," Charlie argued, "My family has deep attachments to this parish. Angelita attended school here for eight years. We buried her mother at this church. And we have contributed generously to various capital campaigns. We very much want a nuptial mass in the sanctuary."

"I wish I could do that, Mr. Parnell, but I don't have the authority to permit it. Now if the young man converted to the Catholic church, there'd be no problem."

Charlie scowled. "I would be offended if somebody told me that my daughter had to become Baptist in order to marry her fiancé, and I refuse to offend Mr. and Mrs. Whitcomb by demanding that their son become Catholic."

"Only the bishop can grant dispensations. The person you need to talk with is Monsignor Kevin O'Reilly, one of the bishop's administrators at the chancery."

Oh, Jesus, thought Charlie. Probably an old, conservative Irishman who still said mass in Latin. There's no way he'd go along with this.

Monsignor O'Reilly turned out to be much more accommodating than Charlie had anticipated. He greeted Charlie at the door to his office.

"Ah, a fellow Irishman," the short and rotund monsignor boomed with a big grin. Monsignor O'Reilly pulled a pitcher from a small refrigerator behind his desk, filled two glasses, and pushed a slice of lime onto the lip of each glass. Handing one to Charlie, he raised his in a toast.

"Sláinte," he said as the glasses clinked.

"Sweet, but nice," said Charlie after sipping it. "What is it?"

The monsignor held up a bottle of Irish Mist liqueur. "This, pineapple juice, and syrup. It's called an Irish Fix."

After he set Charlie on a sofa in his ornate chancery office, the monsignor regaled Charlie with boring stories about the past. Midway through the tales, he topped off their glasses with more Irish Fix. By the time he got to the issue of the wedding, the Irish Fix was gone, and Charlie felt woozy. The prelate refilled the glasses with pure Irish Mist.

When Charlie suggested he might contribute to the archdiocese capital campaign, the monsignor held up his hand.

"We can't *sell* dispensations, my boy. That would have echoes of selling indulgences which provoked all that unpleasantness with Martin Luther. You remember the problems that led to."

The history of the Reformation had never been clear in Charlie's mind, and all the Irish Mist he'd consumed made it seem fuzzier. In any case, it seemed excessive that what happened five centuries ago should prevent Angelita from having a church wedding today.

"Monsignor," he pleaded, "My daughter is about two steps away from marching down to City Hall and getting married by a judge." He raised his glass to the prelate.

"There must be some way we can start off her marriage with the full blessings of the church."

"Ah, yes," said Monsignor O'Reilly. "Young people today sometimes have trouble seeing the wisdom of following in the steps of their religious traditions. We must do what we can to help them out."

When Charlie finally teetered out of the chancery he was pleased that he had gotten the dispensation. It didn't cost nearly as much as he had feared, and he felt an amused respect for the contorted logic the monsignor had used to get what he wanted. He couldn't accept payment for the dispensation, but he could get the dispensation granted if Charlie's investment firm, Zenith Capital Management, agreed to become the investment adviser for a million dollars of the archdiocese's finances. And waived its fee for the first three years. Monsignor O'Reilly wanted a five-year waiver, but Charlie bargained him down to three.

16

"Be good to each other."

July 1979

Washington, D.C.

At first, Angie and James followed Charlie's advice to get together each weekend. That pace soon became demanding. Almost eight hours were eaten up just travelling back and forth between Washington and New York. Eventually, they slipped to every other weekend. By the end of June, Angie was so busy with two summer school classes that three weeks passed before she could see him.

As she boarded the plane to visit him for their long Fourth of July weekend together, a little bubble of anticipation grew in her chest. Her arms tingled at the prospect of seeing him after all the time that had passed since their previous visit. It would be so much more comfortable if she just moved down to D.C. She didn't do that, though, because they'd both agreed on the importance of her staying at NYU to take classes toward her degree.

After three weeks without her, he must be climbing the walls, she thought, and grinned at the idea of it. Their separations seemed to make him appreciate her more. She relished how close they were becoming. Their bodies would touch as they sat and watched TV together, and they would hold hands as they walked down the street. And sometimes their conversations in the evening would run on to the point where she'd fall asleep in his arms. She'd never felt so good in the company of anyone else before.

This weekend they would have several days to make love as much as they wanted. She looked forward to a double date James had set up to attend the outdoor Fourth of July concert with their friends Ken and Jenna who had returned from Iran earlier that year.

Expecting the concert to be packed, they arrived early to stake out a spot on the National Mall by the Capitol. The lawn had been mowed that morning, and the aroma of freshly cut grass still lingered. It had drizzled that day, and they brought vinyl rain jackets in case the rain started up again. As Angie and Jenna spread a blanket on the grass, Ken commented to James, "Those Farsi instructors are like drill sergeants. How are you getting along with them?"

James' head jerked up in response, and Angie was startled at his reaction. She forgot about it an instant later when James and Ken went off to buy hotdogs from a vendor.

She sat down on the blanket and said to Jenna, "Now that we're alone, I want to ask you something,"

"What?"

"The closer we get to James' departure for Tehran, the more anxious I get. What would you think of me following him there?"

"You can't. The State Department no longer sends dependents to Iran."

"I know they won't send me, but they can't stop me from going on my own. James will need a lot of support, and there are probably many service projects I could do."

Jenna took off her glasses and stared at her friend for a moment. "Bad idea, Angie. It'd be sort of like you giving the finger to the State Department. What does James think of this?"

"He wants me to wait until he sees what it's like there first."

"The best thing you can do to support him is to finish off your degree. Every Foreign Service spouse I know has a college degree. If you want to fit in, you must get one."

"I'm signed up for the fall semester, but after that I'm going to look into seeing what I have to do to go there."

Jenna shook her head, but before she could reply, James and Ken returned with the hot dogs. Ken uncorked a bottle of Iranian Shiraz.

"Once upon a time, Iran produced the best wine in the world," he said as he filled their glasses. "But they're getting so much pressure from Islamic fundamentalists that they're closing the wineries."

"Poor James," said Jenna, teasing. "You might not get any of this delicious wine when you get there."

James laughed. "I can't say I care much whether the Iranians produce wine or not. What I do care about is that we do not poison our relations with them."

Angie said, "A lot of people are urging the president to allow the Shah of Iran into the U.S. so he can be treated for his cancer. It would be the humanitarian thing to do. But wouldn't that in itself poison our relations with Iran?"

Ken raised his wine glass toward her. "You hit that nail on the head. If Carter gives in on this one, there'll be demonstrations all over Teheran."

"Oh dear," said Angie, squinting at Ken. "Will James be safe?"

"No problem," said Ken, spreading his hands out and spilling some of the wine from his glass. "He'll be in the

Embassy. Embassies are sovereign territory. Nobody would dare break in."

"A mob broke into the Embassy there last February," Angie reminded him.

"And the government expelled them a few hours later."

Ken continued talking. "The big problem is that we and the Iranians don't see the world the same way."

"How so?" asked Angie, setting down her glass and leaning against James.

"We come out of the Enlightenment belief that we can make human conditions progressively better. They come from a tradition of traders trying to gain an advantage on their deals just as they've done for a thousand years."

Although Angie had heard about the Enlightenment in one of her classes, she couldn't remember much about it. But that wasn't something she would admit in front of James and their two friends. "Put that in practical terms," she challenged.

"When it comes to trading, we're no match for them. If you let them know you want something badly, they'll drive the price through the roof. At least that was my experience there."

"That's certainly the way it worked in the marketplace, when I'd go shopping," said Jenna.

"The president and his advisers must understand these nuances as well as we do," Angie replied.

"I'm not sure," said Ken. "I saw a photo of Carter and his advisers when they were allegedly discussing whether to let the shah into the United States. The president was surrounded by all these high-powered agency heads, but not a single scholar of Iranian studies or a Foreign Service Officer who could clue him in on how this might go over with the average Iranian."

Then, before anyone could respond, they all rose to their feet as the National Symphony Orchestra launched into the Star-Spangled Banner.

New York City Zenith Capital Management

Angie rapped her knuckles on the old oak door and peeked into Charlie's office. He lit up with a big grin. "Sit down. I'll get you a coffee. To what do I owe the pleasure of this visit from my favorite daughter?"

"I'm your only daughter."

"You're still my favorite." He limped out of the office for an instant and came back with two coffees in paper cups.

She took a drink of the coffee before mentioning what was on her mind. "Only getting to see James on the weekends leaves me with a lot of free time on my hands, and I've been thinking about applying for a position that's just opened up on the board of directors for the Skating Club of Manhattan. Do you think I'd have a shot at it?"

"You'd be a shoo-in."

"A shoo-in?"

"Just think of all the competitions you won for them when you were skating."

"Lots of girls have won competitions."

"But you've got something they don't. You're an ex-Peace Corps volunteer whose picture showed up all over the country because of that vaccination project you did in Tunis. You would be a public relations asset for the club."

"Do you think the board would see it that way? They're not very young, and they're almost all men."

"In that case they need another woman. Is Mrs. Vanderkellen still on the board?"

"Let me see. I've got the list right here." She pulled a sheet of paper from her purse. "Yes. She's on the fund-raising committee."

"Let me give her a call. She's been a client of ours for several years, and her investments have done well enough that she has a lot of reasons to be happy with the Parnell family."

A month later, James came up from Washington mid-week so he could attend Angie's installation as a board member of the Skating Club of Manhattan. Afterwards, Charlie and Glenna treated them to dinner along with Mrs. Vanderkellen.

Monsignor O'Reilly's Office

As a condition to having their wedding at Our Lady of Pompeii, Angie and James agreed to attend pre-marital instructions. Monsignor Kevin O'Reilly took a personal interest in their wedding and gave the guidance himself.

The idea of receiving marriage instructions from a presumably celibate man who'd never been married annoyed Angie. Her shoulders tightened as they entered his ornate office at the diocesan chancery. The dark, oak-paneled room was marked by plush velvet drapes covering deep-set windows. Designed to intimidate, she thought. The monsignor was so rotund he reminded her of a miniature sumo wrestler. What absurd conditions did he plan to impose on their marriage? James had already agreed that any children would be raised Catholic. What else might the monsignor prescribe? An end to their sleeping together before their wedding? A ban on birth control? Attendance at Sunday mass? A confession of their sins? A refusal to go along with the music she wanted?

Things started badly when she looked at the proposed wedding vows. "I will love and honor my husband," she read aloud, then looked up at the monsignor. "I refuse to say *obey*."

"You do understand that the word was put into the vow in medieval times to protect the bride?" said the smiling prelate.

Angie furrowed her eyebrows. "I don't see how that provides any protection."

"In exchange for pledging her obedience, she received the pledge of the groom that all of his possessions were hers."

"I don't need his possessions. I still object."

"In that case, my child, we will strike the word. Marriage is a partnership blessed by God, not a straitjacket."

Her antagonism ebbed as he used his pen to scratch out the word. It ebbed further when he suggested that James should invite his Baptist pastor from North Carolina to stand at the altar and assist in the exchange of vows.

By the conclusion of their first session of instructions, both Angie and James had warmed up to Monsignor O'Reilly. He turned to the small refrigerator behind his desk and pulled out a pitcher.

"I want to take a moment to applaud the courage of you both. You, James, for your accepting this dangerous assignment in Iran. And you, Angie, for your willingness to accept the anguish that is bound to come with your separation."

He filled three glasses from his pitcher, wedged a slice of lime over the lip of each glass, and handed one to each of them.

"There's nothing a poor prelate like me can say to alleviate your anxieties that will grow as James' departure approaches. I assure you that God will protect you if you are good to each other."

He raised his glass.

"To your betrothal," he said, raising his glass. "May the flower of your love never be nipped."

"I've never heard that saying before," said James, grinning, as he responded to the monsignor.

"It's an old Irish toast."

"And what is this delicious drink?" Angie asked, raising her glass

"That, my child, is an Irish Fix. What it's called is not important. What's important is that you preserve the sweetness of its taste in your lives together. Remember, if you are good to each other, God will protect you through your difficult times ahead."

Monsignor O'Reilly refilled their glasses, and by the time she left, Angie felt giddy. She stumbled into James as they came down the chancery steps, and they giggled as they linked arms on the walk to the subway station.

Monsignor O'Reilly was more accommodating than any priest she had ever met. She became suspicious of how Charlie had managed this.

The next time they talked, she teased him. "How much did all this cost you?"

"Love has no price, querida. In any case, it's an ecclesiastical secret."

17

"No other place I'd rather be."

October 1979

Our Lady of Pompeii Church

Charlie had been right to insist on a church wedding, she reflected, as she walked down the aisle with him so smashing in a tuxedo. A kaleidoscope of light streamed into the church from the stained-glass windows high on the side walls, and she glowed in a flood of pleasant memories from her time as a child at Our Lady of Pompeii.

Walking in front of her as flower girl was little Tamar, the daughter of her maid of honor, Evie. And trailing behind as ring bearer was her little half-brother, Michael. It felt wonderful that so many important people in her life took part in the wedding. She glowed when James' pastor handed the gold band to James and instructed him to place it on her finger.

They held the wedding reception at the Midtown Hilton. She and James stood side by side to greet a long line guests: relatives, old friends from the skating club and Angie's school days, and a multitude of Charlie's acquaintances whom she didn't know but who were important to him. A few pulled him aside for a private word, for what she had no idea. She found James' parents enchanting and regretted that she had so little chance to talk with them. And she beamed with pleasure as she danced a waltz with Charlie.

Everyone cheered when she and James cut the cake and fed each other a piece. She clapped her hands when Sarah caught the bridal bouquet Angie tossed over her shoulder. Finally, exhausted, she and James left hand in hand to ride the elevator up to their bridal suite.

The next morning, she woke to sunshine. James was still asleep, lying on his back, and her elaborate lingerie was now scattered on the floor. She kicked off the sheet and rolled to her side to get the sunshine out of her eyes. She threw her leg over him and lay there with her thigh resting on his genitals. Soon he would depart for Iran, and they needed as much closeness as they could squeeze in before that dreaded day.

JFK Airport

On a bleak Monday morning, Angie and James took a taxi to JFK, checked his bags, and sat at the gate waiting for his flight to board. She took his hand, but after a moment he withdrew it to check something in his carry-on bag. She pressed her shoulder against his, and they sat without speaking, but troubling thoughts plagued her mind. Other people had refused this assignment to Teheran. Why couldn't James?

The boarding call came, and they rose to their feet. Even in her heels, Angie was shorter, and as she threw her arms around his neck, her weight drew him forward. They held a kiss for a long time. She withdrew her lips, placed her fingers on his pale cheeks, and looked up with a strained smile.

"I'll come, James. I'll join you as soon as I can."

"Let me settle in first and get the lay of the land."

"I'll come. You can bank on it."

They stepped into the line of passengers and edged forward. At the counter, he set down his bag and grasped her hands. She didn't know what to say. Instead, she pushed against him and gave him another long kiss. The gate attendant cleared his throat, and other passengers stepped around them. Finally, James showed his ticket to the attendant and walked into the jetway, where he disappeared from her sight.

She trudged quasi-comatose toward the taxi stand. Conflicting thoughts struggled in her mind. Horror that he was going off to a place the State Department considered so unsafe they didn't allow dependents to accompany the diplomats. But also relief that the dreaded moment of departure had finally come and gone.

She gave her destination to the taxi driver, and he pulled out from his parking slot. He glanced at the open window between the front and back compartments. "Dropping off a friend, Miss?" he asked.

She nodded without speaking, but the driver missed the hint that she was too distraught to talk. She shot him a sharp look, then leaned back and her black hair splayed against the cushioning of the seat. He gave up on the attempt to converse and hauled the taxi onto the freeway. In the dark interior of the cab, the immensity of what had happened swept over her. She clenched her fists in horror at realizing she had been relieved that James' departure was over.

What kind of woman was she to feel relief at sending the man she loved to a dangerous country for two years? This awful question grew in her mind as the taxi sped up the freeway and the lights of the city drew closer. In the back of the cab, she pitched forward and wept.

Manhattan Skating Club

Angie slept till noon the next day. She made a Cuban café con leche, which she took to the living room. She slouched on the sofa and stared vacantly at the pictures on the weathered bureau across the room. Her husband James, her adoptive father Charlie, and her deceased Cuban mother Isabel. She brooded all day until she fell asleep at nine.

Nothing had changed when she woke up Wednesday morning. She felt disgusted with herself. What was wrong with her? When she had gotten depressed in Tunis, she had pulled out of it by jumping into the vaccination project. Even in figure skating, she'd always bounced back after taking a fall.

She had to find something to fill the empty hours. On Saturday, she tied the laces of her Don Jackson Figure Skates together, draped them over her neck, and set out for the skating club. Her friend Gilda, who'd been a bridesmaid in the wedding, would be giving lessons there.

When Angie arrived, Gilda was already on the ice with two preteen girls. Their breath condensed in the chilly air as Gilda guided them forward. Angie dropped her skirt to the floor, and in her pink tights, she glided onto the ice. She caught Gilda's eye and skated around the fringes of the class. On a whim, she tried an axel and was delighted to find that her jumping leg, the left one, was still strong enough to do it. Amazing that she could still jump that well after her long layoff. Maybe she could return to competition. She arched her back and lifted her right leg behind her to try her haircutter spin, but she still couldn't raise her right foot high enough to grasp it. Who was she kidding? No matter how high she could jump from her left leg, she needed two good legs if she wanted to skate competitively. And she only had one, thanks to that miserable Stevie.

But skating had been such a big part of her life, she couldn't give it up completely. Maybe she could learn to coach the sport. She coasted over to Gilda who was packing her things away. "Gilda," she said, "I'm on pins and needles since James left for Iran. How about hiring me as your assistant coach?"

"I'd love to Angie, but I can't afford it. I only have these two pupils right now, and their fees barely cover my costs for rink time." She waved her hand in the direction of the two skaters who were heading out with their parents.

"I'm going crazy," said Angie. "All I do is study for my classes and mope around at night for James."

Gilda grimaced. "I'm sorry to hear that, Angie, but I still can't afford to hire you."

"Pay me a dollar a week. If I dig up any new pupils for you, you can give me a bonus. Also, since I'm on the board of directors for the club, I'll check to see if we can get you a discount on your fees to use the rink."

"It's a deal."

Back at her apartment, Angie telephoned Evie, her close friend at Zenith Capital Management.

"Evie, how old is your little girl, Tamar?"

"Four. You should know that. She was your flower girl."

"Do you know what she needs?"

"You're going to tell me what my kids need?"

"Yes. Figure skating lessons."

"You're giving lessons now?"

"I'm helping out my friend Gilda. Bring Tamar to the Manhattan Skating Club on Saturday, and I'll put on a little demonstration to get her enthused."

"As long as I get back home for our Shabbat lunch."

"We meet at nine, and we'll be done by ten. I'll help you prepare the lunch."

"You know how to make a Shabbat lunch?"

"I can set the table and cut the vegetables for that salad you make."

Next, Angie called Charlie, and talked him into giving her four-year-old stepbrother Michael, a tryout.

The following Saturday, she grinned as she proudly introduced the two new students to Gilda. Somehow, Gilda meshed the preteens with the little kids and made it work.

NYU

Angie now had something to do on Saturday mornings, and she spent half an hour each day composing a letter to James. But the rest of the week dragged. Her first letter from James arrived in the mailbox as she was rushing off to classes at NYU. She resisted the temptation to rip it open immediately. Instead, she stuffed it into her purse and headed across Washington Square to the university. Tingling with anticipation, she sped to the classroom building and didn't look at the letter until she sat down in the back row of the two-hundred and fifty-seat lecture hall for Introduction to Sociology.

My Darling Angie,

I'm slowly adapting to Iran. At the embassy, I am one of only two people in the Political Section who speak Farsi well. We are very busy, and I have time for only a short note.

I miss your curly black hair and that Cuban café con leche you make for breakfast. But I haven't found an apartment yet, so we should hold off awhile on you coming here.

It's interesting that everybody here is young. Almost nobody over fifty. This means huge advancement opportunities, since this is where the action is. There's no other place I'd rather be right now.

Love, James

No place else he'd rather be? Wouldn't he rather be with her? What was happening to them? Was this separation going to disrupt the emotional intimacy they'd enjoyed since they'd met back in Tunis? Maybe he could take that R&R in Switzerland sooner than expected. They needed it.

Continuing to tune out the professor at the front of the lecture hall, she tapped a ballpoint pen on her lips as she thought up a response.

Dear James,

I miss you so much. I know you're doing important things, but the bed is so cold without you, and the apartment feels so empty.

My days drag, and I still want to go to Iran on my own, if I can just get you to agree to it. But while we're waiting, is there any way you could take your R&R in Switzerland a little earlier than you were scheduled?

In little more than a week, James' response came back, and Angie marveled at how quickly the State Department got mail into and out of Teheran. Once again, she pulled it from the old brass letter box in the lobby of the apartment building. Once again, she refrained from reading it until she got to the back row of her sociology class. And once again, James' letter was short on detail. But two items stood out.

My Darling Angie,

Please drop the idea of coming to Teheran. It is not safe for you. At least wait until after we no longer hear gunfire in the streets. As much as I love

Iranian culture, I would not stay here myself if I did not have diplomatic protection. Without the State Department's okay, you would not be allowed to use your diplomatic passport. You would have to come on your regular passport. It is not safe here for anybody who lacks diplomatic protection.

However, I love your other idea of taking an early R&R in Switzerland. I talked it over with my boss, and they're willing to give me the last two weeks of December.

Angie was so excited about the prospect of an early R&R that she threw a fist into the air. Then she withdrew it sheepishly when she saw the professor staring at her from the well of the large lecture hall.

18

"What is going to happen?"

November 1979

Washington Square

At 5:30 a.m. on Sunday the fourth, Angie's twenty-first birthday, the jangle of the kitchen phone jerked her awake. She swore as she stumbled toward it across the cold floor. It was Charlie.

"Why are you calling me at this hour?" she said. "Are you okay?"

"Turn on WCBS."

"Why?"

"Just turn it on."

"What number?"

"Eight-eighty on the AM dial."

When the sound came in, her eyes widened. A hyper announcer talked a mile a minute about a swarm of Iranian students invading the U.S. Embassy compound in Teheran. They had climbed over fences, thrown rocks through windows, and battered the door of the main building, however they had not yet gained entrance to it.

"Oh my God!" she shouted. "Is James in there?"

"In all likelihood," said Charlie.

"Oh my God!" she repeated. She sank down onto a kitchen chair and sucked in a long breath of air. Her hand shook as she clutched the handle of the phone.

What would happen to him? Would there be shooting, and would he get caught in a crossfire? Why hadn't she objected to his going when she'd had the chance? What could she have done differently?

"Angelita. Are you still there?" said Charlie.

"Yes," she said, scrambling to reach the small kitchen TV while still holding on to the phone. She twisted the tuning knob, but none of the channels had anything on the crisis. "Damn!"

"You shouldn't be alone right now," said Charlie, his voice cracking with anxiety. "As soon as it gets light, grab a cab and come up here until this blows over."

"Okay," she said, zombie-like.

Columbus Circle

At the first light of dawn, Angie staggered down the stairs to the street and found a cab circling Washington Square. She climbed into the taxi and said to the driver, "Fifty-Eighth Street and Sixth Avenue." When they reached Charlie's co-op on Fifty-Eighth Street, a few blocks from Columbus Circle, she realized she'd forgotten her wallet. She asked the cabbie to accompany her up to Charlie's unit to get cash for the fare.

"Give him a big tip," she said when Charlie answered the door. "I'll pay you back."

Charlie walked her across the parquet floor into a spacious living room. "Did you have any breakfast?"

"I'm too anxious to eat, Charlie, and I don't want to impose on you and Glenna. Could I just camp-out with the TV and radio in your den so I can follow the news?"

"I'll get you a coffee and some toast. You must eat something."

Visible on the wall as she entered the den was a Manuel Mendive painting of an Havana santeria. Until he married Glenna, Charlie kept the painting in the living room as a reminder that Angie's mother Isabel had once hidden her daughter with a santera until the two of them could escape Cuba. But his new wife, Glenna, did not want any reminders of Charlie's deceased first wife, and the painting got relegated to the den.

Angie slumped into the suede sofa while both a radio and a TV station played in the background. Every now and then, she would lean forward when the news gave an update on what was happening at the embassy. Everything was sketchy. After an hour she walked back to the living room. "The news people don't seem to know what's really going on, and I'm jittery sitting there. I have to go out and walk around a little bit, Charlie."

"I'll join you," he said.

They took little Michael with them and ambled along the sidewalk toward Central Park. Michael walked between them, and they each held one of his hands. The boy insisted on stopping by a horse and carriage that stood across from the Plaza Hotel, waiting for customers. Angie lifted Michael up so he could pat the horse's nose. Filled with anxiety about her husband, she treasured the warmth of the small boy in her arms. Charlie bought submarine sandwiches from a street vendor and brought them back to the apartment for lunch.

Angie had no appetite, but forced herself to eat half of her sub before she retired to the den to check out the TV once more. It wasn't until the evening news that an actual feed came in that showed rain falling on the embassy compound in Teheran. The front door of the embassy opened.

"Oh my God!" Angie shouted.

Charlie and Glenna ran to the den and glued their eyes to the television screen, where James emerged from one of the buildings. He stood in the doorway, speaking to the students.

A TV reporter said, "It looks like one of the diplomats is trying to persuade the mob of students to break up. He's speaking Arabic. And he seems to be having a calming effect."

"Farsi!" Angie screamed at the TV screen. "It's Farsi, not Arabic."

Charlie and Glenna exchanged glances at her outburst.

"Wait," said another reporter. "Something is happening."

Three students came up to James and pinned his arms to his side. A fourth threw a hood over his head to blindfold him. They led him off to the side and pushed him to a sitting position on the rainy ground.

The TV news switched from Iran to a local commercial.

"No! No!" shouted Angie.

Charlie sat down next to her and wrapped his arm around her shoulder. She leaned against him, trembling, staring transfixed at the TV screen that was now pitching a deodorant. "Oh, God, Charlie, what is going to happen?"

"The president will intervene," said Charlie.

"Are you sure?" she pleaded.

"I'm positive. Why don't you stay here tonight? You can use the guest bedroom, and we have some spare toothbrushes."

She considered it. The idea of riding the noisy subway back to the lonely apartment filled her with dread, and it would be a comfort to have Charlie and Michael around her right now. Over Charlie's shoulder, she spotted Glenna standing near the painting of the santeria. If Angie stayed much longer, she was bound to let slip out some resentment she had about Glenna's snubbing the painting that reminded Angie of her mother.

"No Charlie. I've bothered you guys enough. And the news isn't really telling what's happening anyway. Just call me a cab so I don't have to take the subway."

19

"Things will not go well for you."

November 1979

Teheran

James stepped out of the chancery building, the main administration building in the embassy compound. Speaking loudly and in Farsi, he urged the students to leave the embassy and was pleased when two of them stepped away from him. No sooner did they back away than two sets of strong hands grabbed his arms from behind and jerked him down to a sitting position on the wet stone. Someone wrapped a long piece of cloth around his head, blindfolding him. The last thing he saw was a team of student revolutionaries using a long pole as a battering ram to break through the chancery door. A dull thump echoed each time it struck. The picture he formed of what was happening came from the noise: the rain splattering on the pavement, the invaders yelling, and the battering ram as it thudded against the door. The thump of the battering ram stopped, and a cheer swept through the crowd. Someone bound James' wrists together, pulled him to his feet, and pushed him into the building, then up the stairs to the second story. He tripped twice. At the top, he was led to a room and knocked to the floor where he bumped against someone.

"Sorry," he muttered.

"That's okay. Don't give them any names or job titles or anything. Just bullshit them until the government comes and kicks them out," said the man. James didn't recognize the voice.

Someone pulled the blindfold from his head, and he watched one of the Iranian students pulling off blindfolds one after another. They were in the chancery's big conference hall, and the glare from the ceiling lights forced James to squint until his eyes adjusted. At least forty people were crowded onto the floor.

One student stepped in front of James and his neighbor. "What are your names and positions?" the student said in broken English.

"Mickey Mouse," said the neighbor. "Rodent Sniffer Outer."

"Donald Duck," said James, picking up on his neighbor's chutzpah. "Aquatic displays."

Looking puzzled, the student turned toward the only American who hadn't been pushed to the floor, an Army sergeant holding a yellow legal pad. "Thomas Smith, International Communications Agency, and James Whitcomb, Third Secretary Political Section," said the soldier. He wrote the names on his yellow pad.

James looked over to Smith, who shouted at the sergeant, "Peter Simon! What the hell are you doing?"

"Stop making this easy for them," shouted a second.

"Motherfucker!" screamed one of the embassy's Marine guards, who was sitting on the floor across the room, his wrists bound.

"Shut up!" shouted another one of the captors. "No speak!"

Despite the protests, Army Sergeant Peter Simon went around the room writing down the names of the people he knew. When he finished, he handed the legal pad to one of the militant students.

James seethed as he listened to the captors argue about what to do next. Most looked very young, some probably still in their teens. One looked to be in his early thirties, and he seemed to dominate. The others addressed him as Hossein. He pulled James and Thomas Smith to their feet.

"These two are troublemakers. Take them to that building next door."

A half dozen armed students marched James and Thomas Smith out of the chancery building to the ambassador's residence next door and pushed them into a musty room in the basement.

"You bastards are breaking international law," shouted James in Farsi.

A guard slammed him in the ribcage with the butt of his rifle.

"No speak!" he ordered.

Washington Square

Angie was grateful for having been able to spend Sunday with Charlie and Michael. But when she woke up Monday morning in the deafening silence of her empty apartment, a powerful sense of isolation dropped over her. She bit her nails for the first time since she was a little girl. She phoned the State Department for information but found out little that wasn't already on the news. Then she began phoning contacts among James' Foreign Service friends, but all they could do was trade rumors. If it wasn't for the task of going to her classes at NYU, she thought she'd go crazy.

Midweek, the phone rang and she snatched it out of its cradle. It was her friend Jenna.

"I'm having some people over on Friday night. How about joining us? You need to expand your support network."

The sun had set on that Friday when Angie showed up at Jenna's two bedroom on Thirty-Fourth Street, a convenient location for both Jenna and her husband, Ken. She was only a half hour subway ride to New York University, where she'd started a Master's program in Social Work. And for him, it was a short walk to the United Nations where he was starting a new assignment.

Most of the people at the party seemed obliged to reassure Angie that everything would work out okay for James and the other hostages. Others liked to show off their knowledge.

A balding FSO told her, "We know that the chargé d'affaires and two others are being held in the Ministry of Foreign Affairs. Then there are six more being hidden by the Canadians."

Angie noted the patches on the elbows of the man's herringbone jacket. Since none of this had been made public, this guy was abusing his access to classified information. Some people in the room did not have a security clearance, and at least one was not even an American citizen. If it got back to the Iranians that the Canadians are hiding the Americans, who knows what their reaction would be? They might attack the Canadian embassy as they had the American one.

"Your husband," the guy in the herringbone jacket went on, "is probably in the ambassador's residence where most of the hostages are being held. However, he could also be elsewhere in the compound, the consulate, the chancery, or even the warehouse."

"That place must be huge," said Angie.

"It is. I should show you the map," said Jenna.

"You have a map?"

"It's more like a schematic diagram showing where the buildings are located, plus floor plans of the main buildings."

"Can I see them?"

"I can't really dig them out now with all these guests here." She swept her hand toward the people in the room. "Let's have lunch on Monday, and I'll show them to you then? Can you think of a place near NYU where I'll be at class?"

"Lombardi's," said Angie.

Teheran

Each day, a guard with a rifle sat in the room with James and his roommate Smith who, James found out, went by Smitty. They sat on the floor, with each one's wrists bound in front of him. The bindings were removed only when they went to the bathroom. On day one, James had asked his roommate how he was holding up, and the guard shouted, "No speak!" A resounding quiet filled the room ever since. The only sounds came with the delivery of meals and the requests of James or Smitty to use the bathroom. There was no toilet in the basement, and a guard had to lead them up to a second-floor bathroom.

On the third morning, they were sitting in silence when the door burst open. Two guards yanked James to his feet, slipped a hood over his head, and led him out of the musty basement. They took him outside to a cold wind and pushed him along to a different building. From the number of steps to the door, he guessed it was the chancery building, the main office building of the compound. He was led along a hall, through a doorway, and shoved forward until his face bumped into a wall. Filled with rage, he pushed his wrists against the strips of cloth that bound them, to no avail. He cursed under his breath. The Iranian police should have shown up by now and kicked these bastards out.

"What is your job with the CIA?" someone asked him. He recognized the voice as that of Hossein. James did not respond.

A pointed object jabbed at his ribs. "I asked you a question," said Hossein. "What do you do for the CIA?"

"I don't do anything for the CIA. I'm a diplomat and I work for the State Department."

"I want the names of all the CIA agents here."

Oh my God, thought James. Unless the CIA personnel had shredded all their paperwork before the battering ram broke through the chancery door, the students would comb through their files for every Iranian contact they could find. They'd pick them up one-by-one, interrogate them, and most likely shoot them. James shuddered to think of the torture they would be subjected to before they were executed.

"Who are the CIA agents?" Hossein repeated.

"How would I know their names? I'm not CIA. I'm a diplomat in the Political Section."

Although James knew most of the CIA people, in truth he had very little contact with them. They pretty much stuck to themselves. He'd had a friendly chat in the cafeteria with William Daugherty one day. But Daugherty, like most CIA officers, had said nothing about his job responsibilities.

Nonetheless, James had no intention of divulging any more information than what he figured Hossein already knew. Let somebody else give out the names. James wasn't going to do it. Let somebody else tell them that much of the communications equipment on the top floor of the chancery had little to do with Iran. It collected data from the listening posts that tracked Russian aircraft and missiles, just across the Soviet-Iranian border. However, to clam up completely was to pass up an opportunity to dissemble and mislead his inquisitor.

"It would be easier to recall these things, Hossein, if you took off the blindfold and let me sit down."

A pair of hands yanked the hood from James' head and spun him around. Hossein sat behind the desk in the office of the *chargé d'affaires*. He directed James to a wooden chair in front of the desk. James' hands remained bound in his lap. Hossein tapped an eighteen-inch rubber hose against James' forehead. A wave of anxiety swept through James as he stared at the hose.

"How did you know my name?" asked Hossein.

"That's what somebody called you last Sunday when you sent Smitty and me to that basement room."

"You speak Farsi?" Hossein asked.

"Yes," said James. He gave Hossein what he thought was a disarming smile. "But not nearly as well as you speak English. You must have spent time in the U.S."

"I studied at Berkeley," said Hossein, with a smug smile. He slapped the rubber hose against the desktop. James jumped at the noise.

"You're refusing to answer my questions," Hossein shouted. "I want the names of all the CIA agents here."

"How am I supposed to know their names? I just got here a month ago. I barely know anybody."

"I'm going to read you some names, and I want you to tell me what you know about these people. Mr. Bruce Laingen. Is he CIA?"

"No, he's the chargé d'affaires. He's the one in charge of the Embassy."

"Which of the CIA people does he report to?"

"He doesn't report to any of them. He reports to the State Department."

"The CIA's in charge. We know that. Which one of them does Laingen report to?"

Oh, Jesus! Hossein seemed to believe that the CIA gave orders to everyone. "You studied at Berkeley," James replied. "You know that the U.S. is too big to be run by the CIA. Why do you pretend that it is?"

"We're not discussing the country. We're discussing this embassy." Hossein tapped the rubber hose on the desktop. "Which CIA person does the chargé report to?"

"He doesn't report to the CIA. He reports to the State Department. He runs the embassy. Or at least he did until you violated international law by your invasion."

Hossein got up from behind the desk and waved the rubber hose in front of James' face. "I have no more time for you right now," said Hossein.

The guards pulled James to his feet. Just before they dropped the hood over his eyes, Hossein tapped him on the cheek with the rubber hose. "I want you to think about what you are doing. If you persist in lying, things will not go well for you."

Lombardi's Pizza

Angie sat down at one of the square tables in the long narrow room at Lombardi's. She shook the rainwater off her wet umbrella, set it on the floor, and ordered a coffee to warm herself up while she waited. Jenna finally came in wearing a plastic raincoat that dripped water.

"I just had a bitch of a test," said Jenna, as she draped her raincoat over a nearby empty chair. "This master's degree in Social Work is turning out to be a lot more work than I anticipated."

"Why are you doing it?"

"The bigger embassies around the world all have a social worker position. With an MA, I can get one of them. You might want to think of something like that yourself. Sometimes you start feeling isolated overseas if you don't have enough to do."

Angie tapped her fingers on the checkered tabletop. "The maps, Jenna. That's why we're meeting here. Did you bring them?"

Jenna nodded. "Let's order before we look at them."

They flagged a waiter, and Jenna ordered two slices of pizza. Angie asked for an Italian salad.

"That's how you stay so trim, eating salads," said Jenna, smiling. "I wish I had your discipline."

"The maps, Jenna. I want to see the maps."

"They're not so much maps as schematic drawings," said Jenna. "We haven't looked at them since we got back from Iran, so it took a little digging to find them."

Angie looked on bug-eyed as Jenna fanned out four different schematics on their table. All were on letter-sized paper. The first showed the location of all the buildings in the compound. Even *The New York Times* hadn't printed this. A second showed the floor plans of both the chancery and the ambassador's residence which seemed to be the places where most of the hostages were held. Angie traced her index finger along the two floor plans as though that could help her figure out which room held James. Jenna continued talking. "I want to show you some snapshots of the compound. They'll give you a better idea than the maps of what the place looks like."

She spread out a dozen photos that showed the inside lobby of the chancery, several interior views of public rooms in the ambassador's residence, cottages next to the consulate building to the left of the chancery, and even an ugly warehouse building at the rear of the compound. She tapped the warehouse photo. "This one's got so much mold we called it "The Mushroom Inn."

Angie fingered each of the photos, moved the pictures of the buildings to their locations on the map of the compound, and stared intently at the photos of the ambassador's residence where she believed James was being held. She wiped away a tear that slid onto her cheek.

"May I keep these long enough to make copies of them?"

"Ken will be furious if I lose those schematic drawings of the compound."

"In that case, let's make a detour to Zenith Capital when we leave here. I can use the color copier to duplicate everything. It'll be on your way home, and that way, I can give the originals back to you immediately."

"Why are they so important to you?" Jenna asked.

She set her hand on Jenna's wrist. "Oh Jenna," she said. "Up till now, everything I know about where James is being held is so hazy. These photos and maps bring it to life for me." Angie gulped. "They help me feel closer to him."

20

What could she do?

November 1979

Teheran

In the basement of the ambassador's residence, James watched a young guard sitting in a straight-backed chair holding a rifle across his thighs. Every time James or his roommate Smitty attempted to get up to stretch their legs, the guard pushed them down to the floor. With their wrists bound, neither James nor Smitty could resist. They sat in silence in the damp room.

James worried about Angie and how she was holding up with the terrifying uncertainties of the situation. He hoped she was doing something to ease the tension. Maybe skating. He bit his lip in regret that he had been so unenthusiastic that day she'd wanted him to skate with her at Rockefeller Center. He recalled her in those pink tights speeding across the ice, going into that incredible spin, and then gliding toward him with that happy smile on her face. He'd never seen anything so graceful. And the vision of her in that short skirt and pink tights made him long to take her in his arms again.

Without warning, four guards burst into the room, shocking James out of his reverie. They blindfolded Smitty and led him away.

James had no way to know how long Smitty was gone, because his watch had been pulled off his wrist when the Embassy takeover began. Eventually, Smitty was pushed back into the room and knocked to the floor. James tensed, expecting that it was his turn to be marched off.

Instead, the guards left. For the first time since they'd been shoved into the basement room, James and Smitty found themselves unwatched.

"What the hell happened?" said James.

"Another half-assed interrogation. It's like these kids are doing this on their own without any supervision. All they care about is the CIA."

"That and haranguing us with their revolutionary philosophy."

Smitty laughed. "Yeah. Have you met Screaming Mary yet?"

James started to follow up, but the guards stormed into the room. "No speak," shouted one. The others wrapped a blindfold around James' head and led him out of the damp basement to another building. As he stumbled along, his pulse quickened. What now? Back to Hossein with his rubber hose?

He was pushed into a hard-backed chair, and the blindfold yanked off. James blinked at the sudden change of light and saw that, once again, he was back in the chancery building in the office of the chargé d'affaires. The official portrait of President Carter had been pulled off the wall and thrown on the floor, its frame broken. Piles of papers clustered in the room's corners.

Two armed guards took up positions on each side of the chargé's bare desk. James felt a sense of relief that Hossein was not standing there with his rubber hose. Instead, a short, plump woman stood by the desk chair. Looking to be in her late twenties, she wore the black chador, a head-to-toe robe that had become mandatory garb for women in public now that the revolution was in full swing.

"I am Nilufar Ebtekar," said the woman in English as she took a seat at the desk. "What is your job in the CIA?"

"I don't work for the CIA. I am a diplomat, and I work for the State Department."

"I want the names of all the CIA criminals."

"I don't know any CIA criminals," said James.

"You must answer the questions honestly," snarled Nilufar. "If you beat around the bush, things will not go well for you."

Beat around the bush, James noted. My God, her English is perfect. The idioms, the grammar, the accent. She must have grown up in America.

"Where did you learn such excellent English?"

"That is none of your business. Just answer the question. What do you do for the CIA?"

"I don't do anything for them. I work for the State Department. Why are you doing this?"

"Doing what?"

"Helping oppress women in Iran today. Forcing them to wear that black robe." He raised his hands that were bound at the wrists, and he pointed toward the chador she wore. James felt a small twinge of elation when her eyebrows narrowed in annoyance. This must be Screaming Mary, although she hadn't actually screamed. With any luck, he could sidetrack the interrogation into a political discussion.

She waved her hands. "It is Western women who are oppressed. They suffer from satanic commercialism and the exploitation of their sex. I wear my chador freely and proudly as a protest against the Western enslavement of women."

She stood up and spread her arms to emphasize her point about the chador. She launched into a monologue. "America is the Great Satan. Only a Great Satan would have dropped the atomic bomb on Japan."

How the hell did we go from the rights of women to the atomic bomb? His arms tensed in anger, and he responded off the top of his head. "We wouldn't have done that if they hadn't bombed Pearl Harbor first." Even in his own mind, he knew that this argument was a non-starter. He was stunned with her response.

"What is Pearl Harbor?"

"You lived in America, and you don't know what Pearl Harbor is?"

Frowning, she turned her back on him and returned to the swivel chair behind the desk. She spun around until she faced him. "You're getting off the issue. The issue is America's oppression of the world. The revolution will bring freedom to the world. To all the peoples of the world. Even to the Black people and the women and oppressed peoples of your own country."

"If African Americans and women agreed with your revolution, they would be speaking out in support of you taking us as prisoners. But they're not." Of course, James was only guessing at that. He had not heard a word of outside news since the takeover.

She jabbed her finger in his direction, and the volume of her voice began to rise. "Your government censors the truth. You've refused to let your women and Black community learn about the transcendent wisdom of our revolution."

"You are breaking international law by occupying this Embassy and holding us as prisoners."

"You are not prisoners."

"Nonsense," he said loudly.

She paused for a moment and stared him in the eye. "You are guests of the Ayatollah."

James rolled his eyes, but she didn't seem to notice. "What you are doing is an affront to human values," he said.

"You must raise your consciousness, Mr. Whitcomb." She took a breath and seemed to calm down as she spoke in a softer voice. "Human values have to be seen in the context of the broader issues facing the world. You put the shah in power by overthrowing Prime Minister Mossadegh. You supported the terror, torture, and killings that the shah imposed on the Iranian people. You have suffered no treatments like that. Keeping you here enlightens the whole world about the treachery of the Great Satan."

"Nilufar, I was two years old when the shah took power. You can't blame that on me."

"You share the collective guilt of all Americans for what the shah did."

"Rubbish!"

"You must learn to cooperate, Mr. Whitcomb. If you persist in your obstruction, I will not be able to protect you."

Protect him? Did she think she was protecting him by haranguing him while he sat bound in a chair? He blurted out, "That's bullshit!"

She stepped around the desk, slapped him in the face, and marched out of the room. The teenage guards led James back to his musty basement cell. Exhausted after the tense confrontation with Nilufar, he felt relief to be back in the silence of his room. Almost as though it were a refuge.

His conversation with her left him very disturbed. Better than anyone he had talked to, she articulated the purpose of the takeover. It was a cathartic justification of the Iranian Revolution itself. Taken to its extreme, the revolution justified anything its leaders wanted to do.

How was he going to survive this? How would he even make it through the night?

Washington, D.C.

Angie stepped tentatively through the State Department's main entrance. The building had never felt as intimidating as it did at that moment. The marble lobby and the display of flags along the wall seemed cold and threatening. She felt dwarfed as she entered the massive auditorium, with its sloped seating and big stage.

Each hostage family had been given a round trip ticket to attend a briefing on the crisis. Angie took a seat a third of the way back from the front. On her seat she found an introductory letter written by Mrs. Penne Laingen, wife of the chargé d'affaires, Bruce Laingen, who was now held hostage in the Iranian Ministry of Foreign Affairs.

> Many of us are angry. . . Mistakes have been made.
> But dwelling on the mistakes will not be helpful.
> We should set our anger aside and stand behind
> our President.

A young woman to Angie's left sat drawing black lines through the letter. Once the room was full, the program was about to begin. The woman stood up and held the letter high above her head. She waited for all eyes to focus on her, then tore the letter to shreds.

Angie said to the woman, "It's my husband who's stuck there. Yours as well?"

The woman looked down at the letter in Angie's hand. She made a face, annoyed that Angie hadn't followed suit and also ripped up her letter.

"It's my father," she snapped, then stared up at the stage. She sat rigid and taut, looking as though she were about to explode.

This seemed over the top, Angie thought, as she set her letter on her lap. Even though we're angry, we should see what the president has in mind before we make hostile gestures. We should appreciate his willingness to consult with us.

Her commitment to patience dwindled as Secretary of State Cyrus Vance failed to satisfy the angry people who shot accusation after accusation at him. President Carter should have anticipated that violence would result if he admitted the Shah of Iran to the U.S. He should have shut down the embassy beforehand. At the very least, embassy staffers should have been given the opportunity to come home before the shah was admitted. He should have gotten them freed by now. There was no end to the complaints.

When the secretary of state iterated the administration's position that the embassy takeover had been a violation of international law, several people stood up to speak. "If it violates international law," said one, "then we should send in the Marines and put an end to this."

This provoked a counter-response from several others. A tall, attractive woman with long black hair said, "We can't do that. It's impossible to use force without some hostages getting killed. I don't want my children to become orphans."

Secretary of State Vance tried to retake control of the meeting. He admitted that mistakes had been made, but he pleaded with people to unite behind the president's leadership. The best thing they could do at the moment was keep writing letters to their family members who were being held hostage.

Angie furrowed her eyebrows when a young presidential adviser announced that the president was doing everything possible to show the Iranians how important the hostages were to him, and how committed he was to negotiating a successful outcome.

According to James and Ken at their discussion on the Fourth of July, this was the wrong way to deal with the Iranians. Ken was a veteran of Iran, and James had become a diligent student of the country's culture. She trusted their opinions more than those of the young aide who had just spoken.

Angie fidgeted in her seat waiting for the meeting to end so she could present this thought to the big shots on the stage. She made her way forward, edged aside the tall, black-haired woman, and planted herself in front of the Secretary of State. Her hands were shaking.

"Sir," she said, her voice quivered, "you must tell the president that he misunderstands how to deal with the Iranians."

Secretary Vance raised an eyebrow.

Angie continued before he could say anything. "Iranians come from a long tradition of commerce and trading. If you let them know something is vitally important to you, they'll react like most merchants and raise their price. If we look like we're begging them to release the hostages, they'll up their demands. Once they release the hostages, that will be the time to be conciliatory and address their grievances about the shah."

The Secretary frowned. "And did you get these insights from a Ph.D. program in Iranian studies or from extended living in the country."

"No, but I've lived in the Muslim world, as has my husband. Please, sir. Just raise this issue with President Carter and his other advisers."

"I must leave now," said Vance. "Please give your name to my assistant here so we can get back to you." He pointed toward a young woman, then walked off stage.

Angie sped out of the auditorium. Her shoulders tensed as she rode the high-speed Metroliner back to New York. She was convinced from what she'd heard that the administration lacked a coherent plan for the crisis. All she had tried to do was communicate the ideas of James and Ken to the Secretary of State. And she had failed.

She was furious, and even the lulling sway of the train failed to settle her. By nature, she was not a passive, sit-back-and-wait type of person. But what could she do? What could any of them do? There had to be something she could do.

Teheran

A guard escorted James to the second floor of the ambassador's residence and gave him a moment of privacy in the restroom. Once elegant and smelling of air fresheners, the room now smelled of urine. The mirror over the sink was cracked, and Iranian newspapers were spread on the floor to sop up the water.

James spotted a bar of soap on the sink and scratched "res cellar" and the initials JBW and TS into the bar. He was desperate to communicate with other hostages. If his captors didn't confiscate the soap, maybe someone else would add another message on the back side of it.

Sitting on the toilet, his eye drifted down to one of the Teheran newspapers that had spread out on the floor. A shocking headline in Farsi caught his attention. He read as much of the story as possible before the guard pounded on the door for him to hurry up.

The next morning, just as James and Smitty were waking up, four guards burst into their room and dropped a hood over James' head. He clenched his fists to keep his hands from trembling as he was led, blindfolded, into the unknown. Again, he was taken outside, and counting the steps toward the next building they entered, he calculated that he was back at the chancery. This was confirmed when a guard pushed him into a chair and yanked the blindfold from his head. He was back in the office of the chargé d'affaires, and sitting behind the desk was Hossein, with his rubber hose. He sat leaning back in the desk chair, a lit cigarette suspended between his thumb and index finger.

One of the guards untied the cords that bound James' wrists together. James rubbed the wrists and looked up. "Thank you," he said to Hossein.

"I have given you time to reflect on your situation, Mr. Whitcomb. Now I want to find out who are the CIA people here, and we'll start with William Daugherty. Is he CIA?"

This gave James a chance to dissemble. Daugherty's role as a CIA agent had already been exposed, as James had discovered from the newspaper he had seen in the toilet the day before. An American newspaper had published a U.S. Government cable identifying Daugherty as a CIA undercover man in Teheran, and the story got reprinted in the Iranian newspaper.

Clever, James thought, that Hossein asked a question to which *he* knew the answer. If James denied that Daugherty was CIA, Hossein could conclude that James was lying. With Daugherty's cover already blown, there was nothing James could say about the man that the Iranians didn't already know. However, there was no point in making Hossein's job easy, so James feigned ignorance.

"He might be CIA."

Hossein smiled at the admission. "Is he your boss."

"No. I'm a diplomat. My boss is the chargé, whom we haven't seen since your illegal takeover. What have you done with him?"

Hossein refused to take the bait for an argument, although he scowled in annoyance. He snuffed out the cigarette in the desktop and handed his rubber hose to a young guard. "Put your hands on the desk," he barked at James. "Palms up."

Adrenalin rushed through James as he leaned forward to do as he was told. His eyes fixated on the rubber hose.

"Give me the names of the other CIA agents."

"They are secret. Nobody knows who they are."

Hossein nodded to a young guard, who lifted the rubber hose. He waved it in front of James' face, then slapped it hard against the palm of James right hand. A jolt of pain shot through the hand. When the guard raised his arm to strike the left hand, James flinched and pulled his hand back. Two other guards grabbed the arm and forced his hand back on the table. Pain radiated through the hand as the hose struck his palm again.

"This will happen every time you lie," said Hossein calmly. He ordered the guards to tie James' wrists to the desktop. They looped a rope around each wrist, fed them over the desk and then under it to the front of the desk where two guards sat on the floor tugging the ropes tight. This pulled James to the edge of his chair and left him leaning forward with his hands exposed on the desktop. The remaining guard twisted James' wrist so that the palm was up.

"Who is your CIA boss?" asked Hossein.

"I don't have a CIA boss."

Swish. Another jolt of pain. James tensed, waiting for the second blow. The guard grinned and waited before delivering it. James made a fist of the other hand to protect his palm, and the hose slammed down on his knuckles. The pain was even worse than on the palm.

"No more bullshit," said Hossein. "I want the names of the CIA agents."

"Why do you care?" James pleaded. "They're already locked up here along with the rest of us."

"It's none of your business why I care. Just give me the names of these criminals."

He nodded at the guard who raised the hose. James trembled waiting for the blow. Desperately, he shouted, "How am I supposed to know them? I told you before that I'm new here. I've met very few people." He shouted in Farsi rather than English, hoping this might appease Hossein.

Hossein gave another nod to the young guard, and James flinched. Swish. The rubber hose struck an already bruised spot and blood began to ooze. James stared in dismay at the wound.

"Tell me the names."

"I don't know. Nobody knows," he lied. "They're all secret."

He tensed, expecting that the lie would bring another blow from the rubber hose. How much longer could he keep this up before spilling out everything he knew? He looked fearfully up to the guard with the hose, but the guard did not hit him.

"You speak Farsi very well," said Hossein. "Is that so you could do a better job of spying for the CIA?"

"No."

This time two sharp slaps came. James screamed and laid his head on the desk in agony. There was no consistent reaction to whatever James said. The truth brought a blow, but a lie did not. Sometimes it was the reverse. Not knowing how to avoid the blows left him trembling.

"What other CIA people here speak Farsi so they can spy on us?"

"I don't know. You'll have to ask them."

The questions were making less and less sense. Hossein didn't ask about things James did know. And some things he did ask about were inconsequential. Hossein was one of the best educated of the guards James had met, but all he seemed to care about was the names of the CIA people. Maybe he hoped that compiling a list of CIA agents would boost his stock with the Revolutionary Guard, a powerful paramilitary arm of the Revolution.

Eventually, Hossein seemed to run out of patience.

"Get him out of here."

Two guards untied the ropes and pulled James from the chair. As he stumbled, blindfolded, back to his room, he tried flexing his hands to relieve the pain, but he couldn't spread the fingers apart.

21

"Hostage wife blasts president."

November 1979

Teheran

James flexed his fingers as he leaned back against the musty basement cell he shared with Smitty. Range of motion was coming back to his fingers, and the sores on his palms had become bearable. He was proud that he had given Hossein no useful information, and he vowed to stay defiant. Nonetheless, he trembled when the door to the room opened, and a tall thin man with a mustache entered.

"Call me Akbar," the man said in English. "I've come to move you to new quarters."

James' pulse quickened. Anything would be better than this moldy basement, but he was wary. "Why?"

"You speak Farsi quite well, and we need another interpreter upstairs."

"So you're going to move me. What about my buddy?" James nodded toward Tom Smith.

"Buddy?"

"My pal. Smitty's my friend."

Akbar tugged at his mustache. "Buddy. I must remember that." He asked Smitty a question in Farsi, and Smitty looked bewildered.

"He can't speak the language," said Akbar in Farsi to James. "We don't need him."

"If he can't go, I don't go."

"Mr. Whitcomb, we'll drag you up there."

James paused before replying. "If you do that, I won't translate."

Akbar shook his head, resignedly. "Grab your things, both of you."

James smiled as he stood up and motioned for Smitty to get up as well. This was the only successful thing he'd done since the takeover.

James and Smitty were led to a bedroom on the second floor that already held two other hostages whom James recognized. Jerry Miele was a communications technician and Gordon Taylor an army lieutenant. The room was bare of furniture except for half a dozen mattresses on the floor. James plopped down on the one nearest the window. Compared to the damp floor in the basement, this room felt like luxury.

"We will call you when we need you," said Akbar. "In the meantime, is there anything I can do for you?"

James should have shown some gratitude, since this was the first time anyone had offered to do something for him. But he resented the beating he'd endured and the fact that he'd lost control over his life. As a diplomat pledged to work within a system of international laws, he was infuriated that the sanctity of foreign legations could be violated by the ragtag group of students who were now in charge of the embassy. In Farsi, he said, "Yes, there is something you can do. You can get the fuck out of this embassy and take your thugs with you."

He probably hadn't translated "get the fuck" correctly, but it didn't matter. Akbar tugged at his mustache as though he understood.

"Things would go more smoothly, Mr. Whitcomb, if you and your friends were less hostile."

James lifted his manacled wrists. "We might be less hostile if you untied our hands."

"That is not possible. Some of you have been very abusive to the guards, and they fear what you might do if your hands were freed. Mr. Metrinko, for example, does everything he can to disrupt our order."

"You want me to tell Mike Metrinko how to behave?" James shuddered at the reaction his outspoken colleague would have if James demanded that he tone down his behavior.

"Mr. Metrinko and several others. If they would stop trying to escape, stop taunting the guards, stop throwing things, everything could be much easier. Perhaps we could dispense with the handcuffs and provide more amenities."

James felt a sense of glee. "Metrinko escaped?"

"No, but he is what you Americans would call a pain in the ass."

James' lips curled up with an involuntary grin. The acerbic Metrinko would be pleased to know that the guards considered him a pain in the ass.

"Mr. Akbar, if you want us to be more cooperative, all you have to do, as I said before, is to get out of the embassy."

"And, as I told you, that is not possible. We only planned to hold this protest for a few days until the government ordered us out."

"The few days are up, and you've made your point. You can leave now."

"When Ayatollah Khomeini praised what we did, all of Teheran cheered for us. Now everybody thinks we've

171

pledged to hold you until your President Carter releases the shah to us."

Carter had made a big mistake in letting the shah into the States, James believed. But he wasn't going to admit that to Akbar.

"The shah is dying of cancer. Providing medical treatment for him was the humane thing to do. The Koran, after all, preaches mercy. It calls Allah the Beneficent, the Merciful."

Akbar smiled. "I applaud your knowledge of the Koran, Mr. Whitcomb. It also calls for repentance. I see no sign that the shah has repented. Until he is returned to Iran, we can't release you."

"There is no way that President Carter will turn him over to you."

"Then, unfortunately, we have a difficult situation. You Americans have a phrase for it." He paused, then said in English, "We're at log ends, or something like that."

"Loggerheads," James said, chuckling. "We're at loggerheads."

"Loggerheads," repeated Akbar as he turned to leave.

Despite James' anger, he appreciated Akbar's attempts to pick up English idioms. He was also the only guard James had met who seemed to enjoy give-and-take conversations. He might be a worthwhile person to cultivate. Lord knows that the hostages could benefit from having a friend among their captors.

The conversation had also confirmed something James had suspected. Neither the Americans in the embassy nor their Iranian captors had any control over when or if the hostages would be released. That was now in the hands of President Carter and Ayatollah Khomeini, the Iranian national leader.

As Akbar left the room, James called after him. "Your English could use a little work, Akbar. If you want to practice it, stop by any time."

Columbus Circle

Angie spent Thanksgiving at Charlie's co-op near Columbus Circle. An inch of snow covered the ground, and Charlie's son Michael talked her into taking him sledding in Central Park. They laughed when he hit her in the head with a snowball and she fired one back at him. By the time they returned to the co-op, she was grateful to the boy for diverting her away from the awful situation of James' captivity in Teheran. She maintained a civil peace with Glenna throughout the day, even managing to stifle a curse when Glenna criticized her for using the wrong fork to eat the pumpkin pie.

James kept coming back into her mind. She recalled how relaxed it had been sitting around on Sunday mornings drinking coffee and working through the mammoth weekend edition of *The New York Times*. She recalled how her anxiety had escalated as his departure date grew close and how a surge of relief flowed through when he'd finally walked into the jetway at the airport. Now she felt guilt at having had that sense of relief.

As dusk fell, she told Charlie, "I think I'll head out now."

"How are you getting home?" he asked.

"I'll take the subway."

He grimaced. "On Thanksgiving? The only people on that train will be drunks and deviants. Let me call you a cab."

The taxi sped through the empty holiday streets and pulled to a stop at her apartment building just north of Washington Square Park. As she stepped out of the cab, she was approached by a man in a Mets jacket who introduced himself as a newspaper reporter. A camera flashbulb popped.

"Mrs. Whitcomb, could you tell our readers how you feel about the embassy takeover in Teheran?"

"How do you know who I am?"

"I came across a human interest story our paper ran about your wedding and your husband being assigned to Iran." He held up a newspaper photo of Angie and James next to their three-tiered wedding cake.

"Could you say something for our readers?"

"There is nothing I can say. I don't know any more than you know."

"What do you think of President Carter's statement on the hostages?"

She didn't know which statement the reporter meant, so she said, "The president got us into this, and I hope he will get us out."

She was stunned the next morning to see her twisted, anguished face on page one along with a bold headline, "Hostage Wife Blasts President."

She gripped the paper so tightly it ripped. The reporter had manipulated her into criticizing the president. This was a no-no for a foreign service wife, and she was angry at having let herself be used this way. However, another part of her was pleased. The president deserved to be blasted. She should have blasted him at the State Department meeting when she had the chance. Then she shuddered. Blasting the president, as some of the hostage relatives had done, wouldn't make James safer, and it might make him less safe.

22

"He threw it in the toilet."

December 1979

Teheran

One of the guards, Habib, kept telling James that something special was coming up for Christmas. Habib was an emaciated twenty-something university student who wore a faded Army jacket. James called him Habib the Liar because of the frequent times he had deceived the hostages. Having been tricked before by Habib, James was skeptical. Then, on Christmas morning, guards untied the hostages' wrists and led them to the back of the compound to a warehouse so damp and musty the hostages called it The Mushroom Inn.

"Amazing," said James to the man nearest him. "They do their best to isolate us, then they bunch us together for Christmas."

"No speak," warned Habib the Liar, as he led James to one of the tables.

At one end of the room stood a Christmas tree and at the other end a banner of, "America, the Great Satan." Tables were spaced around the room, and at three of the tables stood American clergymen. As Habib led James to one of the tables, an Iranian student tracked them with a video camera.

A tall American clergyman with a receding hairline and gray hair curling about his ears placed himself between James and Habib. With a welcoming smile, he said, "I am the reverend William Sloane Coffin from Yale University and the Riverside Church. As a sign of solidarity, we are going to join hands and sing Silent Night."

"Solidarity with whom?" James demanded.

Coffin gave him a kindly, pastoral look. "Solidarity between ourselves, the American people, and the Iranian people," he said, still smiling.

"Bullshit." said James.

Coffin called for everyone to clasp hands, and he extended his left hand toward Habib. The pastor apparently did not know that you never offer your left hand to a Middle-Easterner. Habib had a strange look and grabbed Coffin's wrist instead of his hand.

"Sigh-a-lent night!" sang the reverend in a powerful, resonant voice. James stood without singing, his eyes seeking out familiar faces in the room. Several men had grown beards, and their faces looked just as haggard as James' had looked in the bathroom mirror that morning. Some of them joined in the singing, but most didn't. Coffin looked dismayed at the hostages remaining silent.

Four hostages walked up to the table beneath the banner "Death to America." Three of them read statements critical of U.S. policy toward Iran, leaving James and several other hostages glaring. The fourth stepped forward holding a microphone and a sheet of paper.

"I am Sergeant Peter Simon," he said into the microphone. James noticed the colorful sweater that Simon wore, a gift from the Iranian guards in exchange, James assumed, for Simon's frequent collaboration with them. In his travels around Iran, Simon said, he had seen more and more of the evils done by the shah. He lifted the piece of paper, saying it was a Christmas card the hostages had prepared for the Ayatollah Khomeini. He read from his paper, wishing the Ayatollah a Merry Christmas filled with loving memories.

James snarled as he stared, stupefied, at the scene. He waited until the TV camera panned across his table, then raised his right fist and flipped the bird to Peter Simon and the other three. Reverend Coffin reached over to rest his hand on James' wrist. He whispered, "Please don't do anything to hinder the harmony we are establishing to ease your burden."

With the cameras rolling and the American clergy present, the guards could not maintain complete silence among the hostages. James asked the man to his right, "Where's Metrinko? Why isn't he here? I'd like to see his reaction to this."

"He's in solitary confinement," said James' colleague.

"Well, if all of us can't be here, none of us should be here. We should all refuse to eat."

He pushed his chair away from the table. A tall thin Iranian took James' arm and nudged him to his feet. It was Akbar.

"Mr. Whitcomb, I ask you again to cooperate. We offered to let your friend Metrinko come to this party, but he refused. So, it is his own fault that he's not here."

"You could have at least offered him the Christmas dinner." James pointed to the plates of turkey and mashed potatoes that were being set on the tables.

"I personally had a guard take the meal to him. Do you know what he did?"

James refused to respond. Akbar had the look of disappointed resignation a grade schoolteacher might have in dealing with a misbehaving pupil.

"He threw it in the toilet."

James' beamed with a big grin. "Good for him!"

Akbar frowned. "I implore you, Mr. Whitcomb, do not spoil this for your friends. If you don't want to eat this dinner, you don't have to. But don't spoil it for everyone else."

James sat back down at the table. His empty stomach growled as he looked at the food on his plate. Due to weight loss, he had taken in his belt by two notches since the takeover, and he salivated at the aroma of the turkey, potatoes, and stuffing. It was the best food he'd seen in almost two months. After his display of defiance, he refused to touch the meal.

With the festivities complete, the guards led the hostages out of the room. James' guard pushed him against a wall.

"How dare you refuse the Ayatollah's merciful generosity. Raise your arms!"

James raised his arms above his head. The guard jabbed him in the ribs with his baton. "Out. Arms straight out."

James lowered his arms so they were parallel to the floor, like a cross. He could only hold them that way for a few minutes, however. When they sagged, the guard rapped him on the shoulder.

"Out! Arms out!"

"Enough! Enough!" shouted someone. James turned and saw Akbar pull the guard away. "Christmas is their holy day. We must respect their holy day."

Lombardi's

Jenna invited Angie to another lunch at Lombardi's Pizza. Angie found her friend in the long narrow side room with the brick wall and its montage of photographs ranging from football players and astronauts to family members. Angie shook the snowflakes off her coat before draping it over the back of her chair.

Jenna smiled warmly. "I thought you could use a chance to relax."

"That I can," said Angie.

They decided to split a small pizza and gave their order to the waiter. Jenna put her hand on Angie's arm. "I haven't seen you for a while, and I've been wondering how you're doing. Are you still active in that skating club?"

"Everything's falling between the cracks, Jenna. I haven't been to a board meeting since the embassy takeover. Maybe I'll go in February, but right now I can't focus." She struck her fist on the tabletop. "I'm livid, Jenna. Livid! Livid! Livid!"

Jenna recoiled. "The briefing at the State Department was that bad?"

"It was useless, but what's really got me upset is that propaganda stunt the Iranians pulled for Christmas. According to the *Times*, some of the hostages were coerced or tricked into reading those horrible statements. Accepting blame for everything the shah did."

"We were just children when the shah came to power in the fifties," said Jenna, shaking her head.

Angie clenched her stomach muscles and made a fist. "What pissed me off the most was that pious attitude of those ministers who were brought in for the Christmas event."

Jenna turned her nose up. "Did you hear those things Sloane Coffin said? The hostages should guard against self-pity. And then he wanted them to join hands with him and sing Christmas carols."

"He'd sing a different tune if his spouse was the one penned up over there," said Angie.

"The shah was terrible. I get that," said Jenna. "But Ken and I didn't mistreat anybody when we were there. And James didn't even get there till after the shah had fled. Why do those ministers make us out to be the bad guys?"

Angie stopped speaking. She set her hand on Jenna's arm and stared her in the eye. "The question," she said, "is what are we going to do about it?"

Jenna furrowed her eyebrows. "What can we do? We're half the world away from there."

"Coffin is back from Iran, and he preaches regularly at the Riverside Church here in Manhattan. Suppose we gather a few other Foreign Service dependents, draw up some posters, and interrupt the next sermon."

Jenna's head snapped back. "You're out of your mind."

"Why?"

"That's one of the most prominent churches in the country."

"My dad always used to tell me that audacity wins the day."

"Win the day? The only thing we'll win if we do this is the prize for looking stupid and petty."

"A woman protesting for her loved one never looks stupid or petty."

"Angie, the Iranians will retaliate against James, and it will be a black mark against him in the State Department."

"The State Department!" Angie shouted.

She jumped up, pushed her chair back, and it screeched along the floor. Other customers looked over at the two of them.

"They're doing nothing to rescue the hostages. Nothing. Neither is anyone else."

"You'll ruin James' career."

Angie snarled. "James' career! What kind of career can he have there after this? What kind of career can any of them have? You said they were betrayed by those ministers. Well, I say they're betrayed by our government if it fails to rescue them."

With a pained look of sympathy, Jenna motioned for her friend to sit back down. "Oh, Angie, I feel so bad for you. You and the other families are in a horrible situation. But how would the government ever pull off a rescue plan? There are almost sixty of them, which would make a rescue mission practically impossible. It's not like that trick Ross Perot pulled off last year."

Angie sat back down. "Who's Ross Perot?"

"You never heard of him? He's a rich Texan. Built his fortune on some computer software company. When the Iranians arrested two of his employees last year, he organized a rescue mission that plucked them out and brought them home."

Angie slapped the tabletop. The slap was so loud that customers looked over from other tables again. Angie froze. If Jenna was afraid to picket the minister's church, there was no way she'd encourage the thought that had just popped into Angie's mind.

23

"Maybe the Israelis could pull it off."

January 1980

Teheran

James ambled with a guard to a makeshift library room that had been put together in the chancery building. The guard prodded him to move faster, but James treasured the few moments outside the room where he was held captive and he moved slowly. The library room had been put together from books brought to the embassy from the American school when it closed. The few English-speaking guards took turns sitting at a desk to handle the check-in and check-out of the books.

In charge of the desk today was Habib the Liar. James watched Habib's bony fingers trace through the pages of the book James was returning to ensure no secret messages had been written in it. At home, such a meaningless display of control would have infuriated James. Here he was grateful. With nothing to do all day, time dragged. Each minute spent at the library was a minute less to be spent mute sitting on the floor in a locked room.

A spark of anger flashed in his mind when he noticed the Omega watch on Habib's wrist. It was the one Angie had given him for a wedding present. He would wait until he got his new book before he complained.

While he waited, he scanned the row of available books on the shelves behind Habib. The corners of his mouth turned up as he spotted the one he coveted. When Habib let him pass through to the shelves, James grabbed his prize. He continued browsing. Anything to fill up the empty time.

"Hurry up," said Habib. "You're only allowed one book, and you already have it in your hand."

James placed his selection on Habib's desk to be checked out.

"*War and Peace*," said Habib. "This is the most popular book I've got. Why are you Americans so eager to read about Russians?"

"It's a classic," said James. And it's big, he thought. With no activities to fill the long days, the hostages prized the longest books. A lengthy book like this could occupy him for days. He had seen one hostage borrow a dictionary and go through it word by word just to kill the time.

With the book tucked under his arm, James pointed at Habib's wrist.

"That is my watch you are wearing."

"Do not lie. This is my watch."

"Look at the back, you'll see the inscription from my wife."

"You do not have a wife. She sleeps with other men now. I heard she also sleeps with women."

"You're in trouble," said James.

"What kind of trouble can you cause me?" sneered Habib. "You're a worm."

"You're in trouble with Allah. You took somebody else's property without their permission, and that is forbidden by the Koran. None of your fasting or your prayers will help you."

Having just mentioned both Allah and the Koran, James tensed, expecting the guard at the door to slam a rifle butt into his back. The guard failed to react, however. Maybe he disliked Habib as much as James did.

Habib's face grew red. "How dare you mention Allah! Get out of here!"

James let a smile creep onto his lips. In the sea of misery where the hostages struggled to stay afloat, every little jab he could make at his captors helped him keep his head above water.

Plano Texas

Angie got the company's name and phone number from the public library at Bryant Park. When she phoned the company, the person she reached was polite, but not helpful.

"We can't make appointments over the phone. Please send us a letter detailing who you are and why you want the appointment."

Angie typed the letter immediately and put it in the mail for overnight delivery. She feared, however, that it would end up in a slush pile unread. Maybe she should fly to Dallas to press her case in person. She could pay for the airline tickets from James' allotment check that came into their joint account each month. She felt awkward tapping into that. Instead, she withdrew the money from the financial settlement she had negotiated with the State Department after Stevie Parker's assault.

She flew into Dallas, rented a car, and drove to EDS Inc in suburban Plano. The guard at the gate gave her directions to the administration building. When she got there, however, the security guard at the entrance desk refused to let her pass through to the elevators.

"I sent a letter to Mr. Perot and called his office. They're expecting me."

The guard looked again at the names on his clipboard. "Your name is not on the list of people they gave me. I'm sorry, Miss, but I can't let you in."

She searched her brain for a way to make a connection that might bend the guard's adherence to policy. He was young and handsome and looked to be Hispanic. She flattened her lips into a look of distress. "I'm desperate, amigo. My husband is one of the hostages in Iran. I've come all the way from New York to ask the advice of Mr. Perot, who is sympathetic to the hostages. Wouldn't you seek all the help you could if your chica was held captive?"

With a sigh, he swept his arm to the side. "Take that elevator. If I get any flack, I'll say you snuck past me when I got distracted."

When Angie reached Perot's office, she ran into more resistance. The receptionist furrowed her eyebrows and looked annoyed.

"We received your letter, but you didn't wait for us to get back to you with a specific appointment time. We can't just let people pop in unannounced. He'd never get any work done."

Angie pursed her lips, looking forlorn. "Please ask if he will see me. He'll want to know what I can tell him about the Iranian hostage situation."

"He is tied up in meetings all afternoon."

"I don't mind waiting. Please stress that I have important information for him."

While she waited, Angie browsed a huge collection of Perot memorabilia, looking for anything she might use to break the ice with him. Hanging on the walls were accolades he had received from various units of the armed services. The most touching, she thought, was a flag emblem worn by a GI who had been killed in Vietnam. Accompanying it was a letter the GI's buddy had sent to Perot along with the flag emblem. That fit with what she had learned about Perot when she'd researched him at the library. A Navy vet himself, he liked military people.

Her anxieties built as she sat, much in the way they had in the past when she waited for her time to get onto the ice in competitions. And she used the anxiety now as she had then by visualizing her plan of action. If she got a chance, she would take advantage of his warm spot for service members by pointing out that her stepdad, Charlie, was a veteran. Adrenalin pumped into her veins three hours later as the receptionist ushered her into Perot's seventeenth floor office.

He was much shorter than she'd anticipated, standing no taller than she was when she was barefoot. He kept his hair in the same type of crew cut he'd worn as a cadet at the Naval Academy many years earlier. That, his trim figure, his straight posture, and his confident smile gave him a commanding presence.

"Welcome, Mrs. Whitcomb. I regret the sad circumstance you are in, but I am honored to meet you."

Surprised by his nasal twang, she extended her hand. He clasped it warmly with both hands before gesturing for her to sit at one end of a couch. Off to her side, a huge window looked out over the suburban sprawl of Plano. And on the wall, she spotted a famous Norman Rockwell painting, *The G.I. Homecoming*, from World War II. Before joining her on the couch, he pulled her letter from his desktop and set it on his lap.

"I wouldn't bother you, Mr. Perot, but I don't know where else to turn."

"Although I don't normally see people on the spur of the moment, I was touched by your letter." He lifted it off his lap. "And I am outraged by this situation. These are our people over there, and I want them back. The least I could do was talk with one of the relatives."

Angie's pulse quickened. At last! Someone who might act. Before she could respond, the secretary came in with a silver tray and a matching coffee set. Perot poured coffee into two fine china cups and handed one to her.

"Before we get to the hostages," he said, "it would help me to find out a little bit about you."

"How much do you want to know?"

"Everything, if you're thinking of what I suspect. Start with where you were born."

"Havana."

He raised an eyebrow. "Havana?"

"My father died before I was born. When I was three, my mother fell in love with an American soldier who had some kind of assignment in Cuba."

She led him through her story of migrating with her mother to New York, being brought up by her hedge fund manager stepfather, and then taking a break from college to join the Peace Corps where she met her future husband, James.

Perot grimaced. "Then right after you get married, he goes to Iran and is taken hostage?"

"Almost immediately," she replied.

"Right after my wedding, I was put on a long cruise for the Navy, so I understand what the separation was like. But we never had a hostage situation on top of it." He shook his head. "What a terrible thing, especially for two newlyweds."

"It's so frustrating, Mr. Perot. The president should have closed the embassy down a year ago, before those revolutionaries had a chance to take it over. Now that this has happened, all he does is try to negotiate with the Iranians. And they keep refusing to budge. Carter is doing nothing to rescue them."

"I offered to consult with him if he was planning a rescue mission."

She brightened. "What happened?"

"He never responded."

Angie winced as Perot went on talking. "We don't know why he didn't reply. Maybe they already have something in the works that they need to keep secret. If so, their lack of response is a good sign."

Nonsense, she thought. Why was he sugar coating this?

"Mr. Perot, you're the only person I know of who has rescued anybody from Iran. Will you help us?"

"True, we rescued two of my employees." He paused and a wide grin broke out on his face. "Oh, that was a grand moment. What a joy it was to get those two people home."

His words energized her so much she reacted with a grin of her own. She leaned toward him in anticipation.

"But you must understand something," he said.

It took her a moment to realize he was not taking the idea where she wanted it to go.

"I had a responsibility to rescue them. I was the one who sent them there in the first place."

"President Carter sent James there. He's also responsible. But he's not doing anything."

"The situation today is very different. We only had to rescue two people, and they were both in the same prison. Today, there are at least sixty, and we don't know precisely where they are."

"Three are in the Ministry of Foreign Affairs and another fifty are in the Embassy compound." She paused. Should she tell him about the ones hidden with the Canadian ambassador? Probably not. This was classified information she wasn't supposed to have. Better to wait until she got a commitment out of him.

From her briefcase, she pulled the schematic of the embassy compound. Perot did a double take.

"You're full of surprises. How'd you get that?"

She smiled. "My husband works there. Why wouldn't he have a drawing of the premises? Here's where he is." She pointed to the ambassador's residence. "That's where most of them are. A few are here in the chancery." She tapped her finger on the big, rectangular office building facing the entrance to the compound. "A few more are in these cottages by the consular building. There might even be some in this warehouse building at the back."

She pointed at the buildings as she mentioned them. He followed her finger as it moved across the page. She pulled another sheet from her briefcase.

"This is the floor plan of the ambassador's residence. It tells us what rooms we have to look into to find the hostages. James, for example, was down here in a miserable cellar room with another guy."

"You said was, not is."

"The letter that told me this is a month old. So by now he might be in a different room."

"You get to exchange mail?"

"I write almost every day, but I've only received two letters from him since the takeover, which tells us they are intercepting a lot of stuff. The point is, Mr. Perot, that we know what buildings they're in. Once we got a team of rescuers on the ground, they would know exactly where to look for the hostages."

Perot frowned. "It helps to know where they are, but there's another problem."

She didn't want to hear about other problems. Her big smile disappeared.

"The Iranians allowed me to visit our two employees in the prison. This enabled me to give them instructions. Then we were able to incite revolutionaries to storm the prison and create confusion. In the confusion, my workers followed my instructions and fled to a rendezvous point I had specified. From there we put them in a van and drove them to Turkey."

Perot grinned at the memory and slapped his hand on his thigh. She nodded.

"However, none of that is possible in this case," he said.

"There must be a way."

Perot softened his voice and took on a paternal tone.

"Think of the logistics, Mrs. Whitcomb. We'll have to land half a dozen helicopters in the embassy yard which will be surrounded by hundreds of screaming, enraged student revolutionaries in the street. There also will be armed guards in the compound. We'll have to fight them off while we search several buildings. Once we get everybody loaded into the helicopters, we have to fly hundreds of miles to a friendly border and hope that the Iranian Air Force doesn't see us. And worst of all, for you personally, how will you feel if we can only locate fifty of them before we have to leave? And suppose James is one of those left behind?"

Her hopes sank at the discouragement in his voice. He lifted his hands in sympathy.

"I'm sorry for sounding so negative, Mrs. Whitcomb. You've put a lot of thought into this, and I hate to disappoint you. I don't see any way that I could succeed at something like this."

"You're saying it's impossible."

"Impossible for anybody I know. Maybe the Israelis could pull it off. They rescued a hundred people at Entebbe a few years ago. But the costs would be out of sight."

"Even for you?"

Perot grinned. "I admire your spunk, so I hate to discourage you. But I won't mislead you. Your best hope lies in supporting the president and whatever he's doing."

She slumped forward, as though a load of bricks had been dropped on her back. She gathered her schematics to slip back in her briefcase.

"I'm terribly sorry Mrs. Whitcomb. If I thought there were a decent possibility of succeeding at this, I would jump at the chance. I'm not your man for this one."

24

"Four, Three, Two, One."

January 1980

Teheran

It had been dark for hours, but James was awake, sitting on the mattress and leaning back against the wall. Although the outside cold seeped into the building, at least he and Smitty were out of the damp basement. He was composing a memoir in his mind. He could not put it on paper for fear that his captors would confiscate it. Each day he picked a scene and reviewed it word by word, hoping to etch it so sharply in his brain that it would pour out when he eventually returned to civilization and got to a typewriter. Tonight, he was trying to recall the details of his bitter Christmas party exchange with the Reverend William Sloane Coffin.

His attention kept wandering, his head would droop, and he would nod off. Then his head would snap up as he'd come alert. A picture of Angie soon floated into his mind. They'd sleep in late on Saturday mornings, and he treasured her look as she lay naked on her side running her fingertips over his chest. But he wasn't getting the hard-on he'd usually get from that image. What was happening to him? His head dropped forward again, the image faded, and he nodded off once more.

Suddenly, the lights flicked on as four armed men burst into the room and yanked him to his feet. He screamed just before they wrapped a blindfold around his head. He could tell from shouts that the same thing was happening to his roommates. Pushed from behind, he moved into the hallway where he and others were herded through a doorway and into a room. The ambassador's bedroom, James guessed, based on the turns and the number of steps it took to get there from his room. The guards yanked the blindfolds off their heads.

"Against the wall," one of them shouted.

James moved toward the wall and tried to identify the guards. None of them looked familiar.

"Raise your hands. Put them on the wall," shouted the guard.

Six sets of hands went up against the wall.

"Spread your legs!" The guard nearest James kicked at his ankles to get him to spread his legs, then jammed the muzzle of a gun into his ribs. When James tried to edge away, the guard jabbed the muzzle even harder against his ribs.

His heart thumped out of control. An image of his mother flashed through his mind. Then other images: the Farsi instructor at the Foreign Service Institute; Angie in a baggy sweatshirt reading the Sunday newspaper. He struggled to break his hands free, but the strips of cloth on his wrists failed to loosen. To stop him from moving, the guard kicked him in the ankle again. The man next to him, Richard Queen, lacked the strength to keep his hands raised. Even with a guard jabbing a rifle muzzle at his back, he could keep his hands no higher than his forehead.

Behind the spread-eagled hostages stood the guards. They slid back the bolts of their rifles, and James trembled in fear at the snap-clack sound of the rifle bolts sliding into place. He felt a powerful urge to urinate, and he clenched his pelvic muscles as tightly as he could. Whatever happened, he'd be damned if he'd let them see him wet his pants.

Then the chief guard began a backward count down.

"Five."

"Four."

"No!" a voice shouted, followed by a blow of some sort and a grunt.

"Three."

James clenched his muscles tighter, but it no longer worked. He filled with shame as the warm urine poured into his pants.

"Two."

"One."

The guard paused several seconds.

"Zero," he shouted.

Firing pins of several guns clicked against empty chambers. The guards spun the hostages around to leer at the terrified looks on their faces. One of the guards pointed at James' wet pants and roared with laughter.

They marched the hostages back to their rooms, pushed them inside, and slammed the doors. James lay on the floor trembling in the dark.

Columbus Circle

Angie sat on the parquet floor of Charlie's living room helping Michael build a house with the Lego Duplo she had brought for his fourth birthday party. Charlie's co-op was two blocks from Columbus Circle. The unit was high enough that in the distance a small patch of Central Park could be spotted through the window. A far cry from her Greenwich

Village apartment whose windows looked out on other buildings. She pushed the birthday wrapping off to the side, then smiled with delight as she guided Michael's hands to snap a particularly obstinate block into place.

Her mind wandered back to her conversation with Ross Perot. Although he had the resources, he was incapable of mounting a rescue operation. But the Israelis had pulled off an even bigger rescue mission at Entebbe in Uganda. Somewhere there must be somebody who had the resources and the expertise to do it.

As Angie pondered this, Glenna huffed and bent over to snatch the gift-wrap off the floor. Glenna's fastidiousness had always been an irritant to Angie. She decided to head back to her apartment off Washington Square as soon as Michael got his birthday cake.

She looked up to see Charlie watching them, a satisfied smile on his face. She knew he had always wanted to have a child with her mother so Angie could grow up with a biological sibling. Sadly, that had never worked out, but she felt as close to her stepbrother Michael as she would to any biological brother or sister. Charlie looked so pleased at the two of them sitting together on the floor that this might be a good time to ask him something that was on her mind.

"Just out of curiosity, Charlie, who is our wealthiest client?"

"Probably Jim Bob Jones who runs an oil services firm in Dallas. Why?"

"My Sociology prof gave us an assignment on wealth concentration."

Charlie's warm smile changed to a stern frown. "You stay away from Jim Bob Jones. I don't want you or your professor conducting any projects with our clients. And in any case, he isn't the kind of guy anyone wants to fuck around with."

Angie did a double take, because Charlie seldom swore. Jim Bob Jones must be a very interesting person.

Tehran

At mid-morning, three days after the mock executions, James banged on the locked door of his room. Habib the Liar opened it. "What's wrong?"

"I have to use the bathroom."

Halfway to the bathroom, they crossed paths with Press Attaché Barry Rosen, and James said, "Good morning, Barry."

He was surprised when Habib failed to object.

"You forgot to tell me, No speak," challenged James.

"Through the mercy of Ayatollah Khomeini, we now give you times when you can speak. And you will get thirty minutes a week to walk outside."

Was this an attempt to apologize for the mock executions? They certainly ought to.

The very next day, James was pleasantly surprised when Habib escorted him through the front entrance of the ambassador's residence to the crisp winter air. Habib sat on the steps and gestured for James to wander the yard. Armed guards stood at the front gates to prevent any escape attempts. Fat chance of that, thought James. If he ran through the gate, where would he go?

James spotted one other American pacing the yard, Kathryn Koob, the director of the Iran America Society. She had lost considerable weight, he noted, and her dress now hung on her body. James fell in step beside her, expecting Habib to pop up at his side and separate them. But Habib left them alone.

"Ms. Koob," said James, "I haven't seen you since the takeover."

"I was at the Christmas party."

"If you're like me, you probably wished you were someplace else."

"If I had kept my wits about me, I almost certainly would have been someplace else," she said.

"What do you mean?"

"When the student revolutionaries showed up at the Iran America Society on the day of the takeover, I escaped to the German Goethe Institute not far away. They offered me safe haven."

James looked wide-eyed at her. "And you didn't take it?"

She shook her head. "When we got word that the students vacated my offices at the Society, I figured my duty was to go back and phone Washington with a report on what was happening. Eventually the students returned and took me captive."

Noble, James thought in admiration, but a horrible miscalculation. If she had just stayed with the Germans, she wouldn't now be penned up inside these walls pacing back and forth on a brown lawn whose grass was dying in the winter cold. And no one would have faulted her for it.

"Do you know anything about Ann Swift? She's my boss."

Kathryn made a wry smile. "She also made a big mistake."

"What?"

"When our student captors asked for our names and titles, she gave her title as First Secretary, and she got annoyed when the young guard wrote that down as typist. She insisted on correcting him."

James laughed. First Secretary was one of the most important positions in the embassy. "Why was that a mistake?"

"A couple weeks after the takeover, the Iranians released the Black and female hostages. They thought this would inspire women and African American citizens to rise up in rebellion in the U.S."

"I remember that's exactly what Screaming Mary told me."

"Nilufar?"

"Yes."

"It's not nice to call her Screaming Mary."

"But what's this got to do with Ann not being sent home?"

"If she had just kept quiet and not let them know how important she was, she would have been sent home with the other women."

"So, she was too important to be released?"

"Exactly."

"And I'm guessing that you also were too important to be let go, since you ran the Iran American Society."

"Screaming Mary, as you call her, believes the Society was a front for the CIA in its attempt to destroy Iranian culture."

"So, you share the collective guilt we all share for the Shah's oppressions?" James gave a bitter half laugh.

"Don't laugh. She wants me to be prosecuted by the Iranian Revolutionary Council for Justice."

They walked quietly for a few paces before James asked, "How do you keep your sanity?"

"Because we were forced to sit still all day, I began to experiment with exercises I could do without leaving my chair. Muscle contractions and stretching exercises and things like that."

James grinned. "I did the same thing. And now that the guards let us move around, I do a whole regime of calisthenics every day."

"The big thing for me," said Kathryn, "was realizing that the guards' no speak rule could be seen as a monastic silence. I do meditations and devotions."

"Prayers?"

"It's more than prayers. I developed a schedule to keep at it. I have one devotion for morning, then afternoon, then evening, each with a different goal. One day I devote them to world crises, then another day to my family, and I dedicate prayers to each of my family members. In time, all this began helping me maintain an inner peace."

They reached the other end of the yard and turned around. Smiling, she looked up at him.

"How do you cope, James?"

"I'm not sure I do. After that mock execution, my hands shake every time a guard comes into the room. And my heart starts pounding so hard it feels like it's going to break through my chest."

"Mock execution?" she asked.

"I guess there's no way you could have known, given how we're kept isolated from each other." He described the event, and her mouth gaped open.

"That's horrible."

"You asked how I cope. Once they unshackled us and I was able to do calisthenics, that helped. I also try to get in a dig at the guards every chance I get." He pointed at Habib who was still sitting on the chancery steps. "Habib over there takes himself so seriously it's easy to yank his chain."

"Hostility won't bring you inner peace."

If she had gone through a mock execution, she'd be a little hostile, too, but he refused to criticize her. Each person coped in their own way.

"Inside!" shouted Habib. "Inside! Time is up!"

Habib was still sitting on the steps when James walked past him. He pointed at the wristwatch on Habib's wrist.

"When are you going to give me back my watch?"

"Stop lying about this watch," said Habib. "It is my watch."

New York, Public Library

As she walked up the steps of the public library at Bryant Park, Angie patted the big stone lion on the paw. She stepped through the massive double doors at the entrance and asked for help finding information on a specific business leader from Texas. The reference librarian loaded her arms with three volumes and she brought them to one of the polished oak tables in the library's ornate reading room.

Jim Bob Jones was indeed just as interesting as she'd suspected. He ran an oil services firm, JBJ Enterprises, whose value had skyrocketed to the billions in the 1970s, along with the inflating price of petroleum. With a personal net worth of several hundred million, he certainly had the resources to fund a hostage rescue attempt. Could she talk him into doing it?

Angie found nothing, however, to suggest that Jim Bob Jones was as dangerous as Charlie had made him out to be. She returned to her Greenwich Village apartment, phoned the number she'd located at the library, and requested an interview. At the end of the day, the man's administrative aide phoned back and invited her to Dallas.

Dallas

Jim Bob Jones seemed too informal a name for a man who ran a billion-dollar oil services company, Angie thought as she swept her eyes across the lobby of his office. It seemed drab compared to the museum-like appearance of Ross Perot's offices. Instead of memorabilia and Norman Rockwell art, Jim Bob's walls held photos of oil platforms, helicopters, derricks, and sweaty men muscling pipes into place.

She sat in a chair reviewing her pitch when a huge man in his fifties walked up to the receptionist. His face had the creases and dried skin of someone who'd spent too much time in the sun. He was dressed like a cowboy, complete with heeled boots and a blue denim shirt. He reminded Angie of a cuddly grandpa who couldn't possibly be as dangerous as Charlie had told her. He handed a sheet of paper to the receptionist before turning toward Angie.

"Mrs. Whitcomb?"

"Yes, sir," she said, standing up.

"I am happy to make your acquaintance. Please come into my office." He swept his hand in an arc for her to pass through a doorway.

Angie smiled. Things were starting well. Then she frowned when Jones added, "You look just like your father described you."

"I didn't ask my father to call you."

"He didn't call me; I called him."

Oh God, thought Angie. Charlie's going to throw a monkey wrench into this.

Jim Bob guided Angie into his office and sat them in two upholstered chairs half-facing each other. Between them sat a glass-topped end table. The chairs were upholstered in pastel desert colors as were the walls in the room. His desk had a spotless glass surface with only two objects on it: a big Stetson hat on one side and a copy of the Frederic Remington bucking bronco statue on the other. Off in the distance, the Dallas skyline shined through the window.

"This situation with the hostages is an outrage," said Jones. "Three families in and around Dallas have members who are hostages, and from what I understand, they feel like they're living with a sword over their head. So, the moment you said you were a hostage wife, I had to give you an appointment."

A gray-haired woman entered the office, and Jones said, "This is my administrative aide. She is the person who talked with you on the phone."

Angie smiled at the woman who smiled back. She set the tray on the coffee table and closed the door as she left. Before they went any further, Angie needed to find out what Charlie had told Mr. Jones.

"Out of curiosity, if you were committed to seeing me, why did you call my father? And how did you even know he was my father?"

"You identified yourself as Angela Parnell-Whitcomb, and my administrative aide said you had a New York accent.

Maybe it's a mere coincidence that I now know two Yankees named Parnell. Or maybe not. So, I phoned him to ask if the two of you were related. He seemed surprised that you had called me."

She lowered her head and grimaced. "Oh, he's going to be mad at me."

"He certainly didn't sound pleased, and I hope you understand that I want to maintain a friendly relationship with him."

If she wanted any help from Jones, she needed to be frank with him. "May I explain what I did and why I didn't tell my father?"

"Please do."

"I needed to find someone with substantial resources who also had a background as a patriotic American."

Jones folded his muscular arms across his chest, skeptically.

"When I asked him if we had any clients who fit that description, he mentioned you."

"You said, 'if *we* had any clients,' almost as though the fund was yours, not his."

"I've worked for the fund off-and-on ever since I was a teen, so I guess I do feel like I'm part of it. I'm also a shareholder, although my shares are held in a trust, and I can't access them for many years."

"So, he gave you my name and told you to call me?"

"No, sir. He emphatically told me not to call you. Please don't blame him for my contacting you."

"I don't blame him for anything," said Jones. "But why did you want to see me?"

Angie paused. She took a nibble from a pastry sitting on the coffee tray. Her eye fell on the bucking bronco statue on his desk. It looked strange among all the pictures of oil services equipment dotting the walls. Jones motioned for her to reply.

She swept her hand toward the pictures on the wall. "Your company has access to boats, machinery, helicopters, and trucks."

"And?"

Angie inhaled deeply.

"My husband and the other hostages are being left to rot in Teheran. The president is well meaning, but every offer he makes to Iran is met with a snub. A humiliating snub. He has no hope of negotiating an end to their captivity any time soon. And he refuses to mount a rescue effort."

"We don't know that. Such a thing would never become public until it was over. And in any case, what has this to do with me?"

"Will you help mount a rescue operation?"

Jones shook his head, stood up, and paced. He looked out his window at the Dallas skyline.

"The obstacles to such a thing are formidable."

Angie brightened. "But not unsurmountable."

"For me, they are," said Jones, and Angie's shoulders sank. He sat down opposite her again and leaned forward. "My men are very good at what they do, but they're not commandos. There are more than fifty hostages to get out, which would pose enormous logistical problems. And Teheran must be at least four hundred miles from any possible launching site in the Persian Gulf."

"At Entebbe, the Israelis rescued over one hundred people, and they were two thousand miles from home."

Jones came back to his chair. "I'm impressed that you know that. The hostages in Entebbe were all concentrated at an airport, where a transport plane could land to pick them up. Ours are in the middle of a crowded city. In at least two separate locations."

"I realize that the two situations pose different problems. But if we apply the same kind of creativity to Teheran that the Israelis applied to Entebbe, a rescue would be possible."

"Mrs. Whitcomb, even if it is possible, my men have no experience in this sort of thing. As I told you, they are not commandos."

"If we can find the commandos and someone to direct the operation, would you help?"

Jim Bob froze. "You mean pay for it?"

She reddened with embarrassment. "Yes, sir."

"Do you have any idea how much that would cost? We'd have to use those big Chinook helicopters they used in Vietnam. If one of them crashed, that's ten to fifteen million dollars right there."

"If we find an experienced person to plan and run the operation, nothing will crash."

"Why don't you ask your father to fund this?"

"He would never do something like this. His money is all tied up in that fund you're in. If he pulled out any significant amount, it would have a negative impact on his clients. For him the clients always come first."

Jim Bob grinned. "As one of his clients, I'm glad to hear that."

"You're my last hope, Mr. Jones," said Angie. "The last hope for those families you've told me about in Dallas who also go to bed every night biting their nails."

Immediately, she curled her fingers into fists so she wouldn't show her own bitten nails. She raised her eyes to his and saw the look of a man trying to avoid being scammed by a flimflam artist.

"Here's what I will do," he said. "For your sake and the sake of the other hostage families, I'll consider it. Only if you can find experienced people who can produce a plan with an excellent chance of success."

Angie jumped to her feet, beaming. She extended her hand for him to shake. "Can you do one other thing for me?" she asked.

"What?"

"Do you have somebody who can find out who led the raid on Entebbe and get me an appointment with him?"

"The only person I've got is a geologist, Jacob, who works in Israel. Let me see what he can do."

––––––––––

Jim Bob picked up the Stetson from his desk and placed it on his head. Then he escorted her out, ducking his head to get through the door. Once she was gone, he spoke to his administrative aide.

"Contact Jacob in Israel so I can talk with him. Then make arrangements to fly Mrs. Whitcomb to Tel Aviv."

"Why Tel Aviv?"

"She has a crazy idea that the Israelis can get her husband and the other hostages out of Iran."

"If it's crazy, why are we getting involved?"

"She's extremely anguished, and I do business with her father. So, I don't want to be the one to burst her bubble. Let the Israelis do it."

"Flights to Tel Aviv aren't cheap."

"Call it an investment. Who knows what it might lead to?"

25

"You deserve the chance to try."

January 1980

Teheran

Each night after the mock executions, James became plagued with nightmares, sweating, and shortness of breath. Even in daytime, the details popped into his mind. The whimpering of his fellow captives. A rifle pressed into his back. The countdown. The click of the rifle's firing pin on an empty chamber. The shame of wetting his pants. The taunting laughter of the guards. He tried to divert himself by focusing on the memoir he'd been composing in his mind. Inevitably his mind would wander after a few moments.

Maybe he should try Kathryn Koob's approach of inner peace through meditation. He leaned against the wall as he sat on the floor and tried to empty his concerns from his mind, but nothing like her inner peace came to him. Maybe he needed a mantra. "Ooohm," he whispered. Even whispering it aloud made him feel self conscious, because he shared the room with other people. He tried to do the mantra under his breath so he wouldn't be overheard by his roommates. "Ooohm, Ooohm," he chanted. His heart palpitations continued.

The lock turned in the door, and he jumped. What now? Then he relaxed when Akbar came into the room.

"What brings you here?" James asked.

"I had a free hour and remembered your invitation to come and practice my English."

James edged to the side so Akbar could join him on the floor.

"You don't look good," said Akbar.

"I think I've been having heart attacks."

"Why do you think that?"

"My chest tightens up. Sometimes I can barely breathe and my heart just thumps. Right now it feels like it's going to explode."

Akbar got to his feet. "Let me see if I can find a doctor or somebody to talk with you."

Half an hour later, he returned with a medical student. The student felt James' pulse, tapped his back, and put an inverted cup on James' chest to hear the heartbeat.

"There's nothing wrong with you," the medical student proclaimed. "You must try to relax."

"Relax?" James shouted. "How do you relax when every noise at night makes you expect another monstrous trick like the last one?"

"You're too weak, mentally. You should toughen up. The soldiers and marines you've got here don't complain like this."

James rolled his eyes. He held out his hand, which was shaking. "So, you're telling me I should just pretend all of this is a dream?"

"I'll see if I can find you some valium," said the medical student.

Washington Square

On Friday afternoon, Angie attended a meeting of the Skating Club board of directors, the first one she'd attended since the embassy takeover. However, her mind kept dwelling on the horror of James languishing in captivity, and she quickly grew tired of the bickering over agenda items. She had to stifle a desire to roll her eyes. Fortunately, no one at the meeting had the chutzpah to give her any assignments.

When she returned home, she called her answering service. She'd subscribed to the service after James had left for Iraq so she wouldn't miss any important calls. Just one message had come in, and adrenaline hit her when she learned it was from Jim Bob Jones. She returned his call immediately.

"Can you fly to Dallas on Wednesday?"

Her winter term classes started that day, and she considered putting off Jim Bob until Saturday. But that might lead him to think she wasn't serious about the rescue plan.

"I'll crawl across the Sahara if that's what it takes to meet the guy who organized the Entebbe raid."

Jim Bob chuckled. "Flying to Dallas will be enough. We booked you a seat leaving LaGuardia at 9:30 Tuesday morning. Pack enough clothes for five or six days and bring your passport. My driver will pick you up at the baggage carrousel when you arrive. To make it easy for him to spot you, wear a blue scarf."

A chill ran though her as she put down the phone. An Israeli who had helped rescue a hundred of his people two thousand miles from home, could certainly rescue fifty hostages a mere four hundred miles from the Persian Gulf. All Angie had to do was talk him into it.

Teheran

In mid-afternoon, James, Smitty, and their two roommates sat on the floor reading. James had trouble concentrating, because his heart had started thumping again. Three months now he'd been in Teheran, and two of them in this miserable captivity. Suddenly, he got pulled out of his introspections by the sound of Smitty slapping his ankle.

"Shit!"

The other roommates looked over at him.

"Bug bite," said Smith. He wiped the dead insect from his hand, then rolled down his sock to examine the growing red spot just above his ankle bone. He raised his hand to his throat and began to gasp.

"Smitty, what's wrong?" asked Lieutenant Gordon Taylor.

Smith pointed to his throat, continuing to gasp.

"Get the doc!" shouted the lieutenant.

James banged on the door and shouted in Farsi to the guards.

"Get the Army medic. We've got a man choking to death."

The guard unlocked the door and gaped at Smith, who was on the floor leaning forward, wheezing audibly.

"Get the Doc," James shouted again.

"There is no doctor here," said the guard.

"Sergeant Hohnan, the medic, two doors down the hall," said James, pushing the guard out the door. He calculated that the guard didn't know that medics were the Army's first responders and typically called "Doc."

The guard returned barely a minute later, followed by a soldier with sergeant first class chevrons on his sleeves and a combat medic badge sewn onto the breast of his shirt. He had been posted to the embassy, James knew from previous conversations, only because the State Department hadn't been able to find an embassy nurse willing to accept an assignment to Teheran. Hohnan touched the round red spot on Smith's ankle and looked into his mouth.

"Allergic reaction. He needs a shot of epinephrine. Mr. Whitcomb, tell the guard to take me over to the dispensary in the chancery so I can get my supplies."

While James explained that to the guard, the medic said to the lieutenant, "Sir, while we're gone, try to keep Mr. Smith as relaxed as you can."

The guard led the Doc out of the room, but Hohnan stopped, grabbed James' sleeve, and pulled him forward. "Follow us. If anybody stops us on the way over, I'm going to need you to translate."

Doc ran into the hallway but was stopped by two Iranians. James shouted at them in Farsi, "Let the Doc get his medicine from the chancery, or a man's going to die on your watch!"

Once they grasped the situation, they led James and the Doc out of the building. However, they didn't run fast enough for the medic, and he pushed them forward. James trailed along shouting at the guards behind to speed up.

Doc grabbed a medical kit from the chancery and sped back to the ambassador's residence. By the time they had raced up the steps to the second floor, James himself was gasping for breath. He hadn't sprinted like that since he'd been a teenager.

Smith's situation had worsened, and he struggled desperately to get air through his swollen throat. Red blotches broke out on his face as his lungs heaved. Doc unhitched Smith's pants and plunged the syringe into his thigh.

James knelt on the floor and watched as the man's breathing slowly grew easier. Smitty grabbed Hohnan's hand, squeezed it, and with a sound that was barely audible, he mouthed "Thank you, Doc."

The guard nudged Doc to his feet. "Good job," he said in broken English. "Back to you room, now."

"It's going to take a while for him to get back to normal," Hohnan said to James. "If we were back in the States, I'd run him into an emergency room, but here I'm afraid to let him out of our sight. So keep a close eye on him, and if he regresses, call me back."

He turned to the guard. "And if they call me back, you're going to have to get him to a hospital. Immediately. This is life threatening."

James translated, and the guard nodded that he understood. Then he said, "Now back to you room."

James walked Doc and the guard to the door. Lieutenant Taylor scowled at them. "Back to you room," he mimicked. "Back to you room. You room. You room."

"Jesus Christ, Lieutenant, that guard just helped save Smitty's life. What more do you want from him?"

"Why doesn't he learn to speak English?"

"It's his country. Why don't you learn to speak Farsi?"

"It's our embassy, and these guys are killing us. Stop being so goddamned nice to them."

"Fuck you!" said James.

He picked up the book he had set down at the start of the emergency, but he couldn't concentrate. He should be modeling civil behavior among the hostages, not confrontation. The stress was getting to him. It was getting to most of them. Petty grievances sometimes led to shouting matches or shoving incidents. Even strong friendships felt the strain.

He looked across at Smith sitting on the floor, leaning against the wall, staring down at his feet. His breathing continued to improve, and the color of his face was returning to normal.

James shifted his view to the angry lieutenant who was pacing the floor.

"Sorry, Gordon. I agree with you that most of these guards are fanatic jerks who have no right to be in this embassy. And I enjoy getting digs in at them as much as anybody else does. Every now and then, for whatever reason, one of them does something decent. If being nice to that guy sows some little seed of mistrust between him and the rest of them, then that's what I think we should do."

Lieutenant Taylor grumbled, but he didn't reply. James noted that his own heart had stopped its palpitating, and his breathing was back to normal.

He walked over to Smitty to place his hand on his shoulder. Smitty looked up and said, "When the hell is Carter going to show some guts and send in the Marines to get us out of here?"

Dallas

Jim Bob's driver identified Angie by her bright sapphire blue scarf and carted her luggage to a Cadillac Seville in the short-term parking area. The moment she slid into the passenger seat, she pulled off the scarf.

She arrived at Jim Bob's office just before noon, and he led her to a private dining room where a small buffet was laid out. "I didn't know what to offer for your lunch, so I ordered the fixings for a salad or a sandwich." He pointed to the buffet bar. "You can choose whatever you like. Or, if you want a real treat, you can have a burger of good old Texas beef, like I'm going to have."

"Thank you, Mr. Jones. That was very thoughtful."

She put together a small salad of lettuce, cherry tomatoes, avocados, hearts of palm, and slices of cheese for protein. A waiter filled two cups of coffee and set Jim Bob's burger before him.

Who the hell would have an appetite with all this going on? But Jim Bob had no trouble taking a big bite from his burger.

"Setting up this meeting for you was not a piece of cake," he said. "It was done by my seismologist, Jacob, who is helping us look for oil in Israel."

"I didn't know Israel had any oil."

"They're searching for it, and we're happy to help them."

"So was Jacob able to get me in to see the leader of the Entebbe raid?"

"No."

No? Why the hell did Jim Bob fly her halfway across the country if he couldn't get her in to see the leader?

"The original leader, a guy named Yonatan Netanyahu, was killed in the mission. To honor him, the Israelis named an anti-terrorist institute after him.

"How does that relate to your seismologist?"

"Before we get to that, you have to understand how critical it is that we keep your mission secret. I don't want to be identified in any way with you asking the Israelis to organize a rescue mission."

"You don't have to worry about me keeping it secret. I haven't talked to anybody about it, and I won't.

"I believe you, but I had to figure out a cover for you, so that I could keep Jacob in the dark."

How could Jacob set up a meeting with whoever took over after Yonatan Netanyahu and be kept in the dark about it? Mystified, Angie folded her hands on the table and waited for Jim Bob to explain.

"All Jacob knows is that I'm disappointed we haven't found any oil yet, and I'm sending you to Israel to find out if there is anything wrong with his seismic vibrator."

Seismic vibrator? I'm not even going to touch that one, she thought as she stifled a chuckle.

Jim Bob must have been used to this reaction, because he smiled in return. "Jacob will explain it to you when you get there. He'll give you a demonstration and hand you a written report to bring back to me."

"So, he thinks I'm an employee of yours?"

"You will be on assignment to us. That's part of your cover. I plan to ask your father to invest some money in our Israel exploration project. Who better to evaluate the exploration than his own daughter who understands how his fund operates because she worked there off and on."

Angie squinted. "True, I know quite a bit about the fund, but I know absolutely nothing about oil exploration."

"Jacob won't know that. All you need to do is pretend you understand what he's saying, ask him a few questions from a sheet I'll give you, and make sure he gives you his written report."

"How is all of this going to get me in touch with whoever took over the Entebbe raid?"

"Jacob knows that your husband is a hostage in Teheran, and he will think it is the most natural thing in the world for you to contact Israelis who have dealt with hostages. He has a close friend at the Yonatan Netanyahu Anti-terrorism Institute who got you an appointment with an important officer who took part in the Entebbe raid."

"And who is this officer?"

"Jacob will give you all the details. I've already hired a security firm to assess whether he is competent and trustworthy, so you don't have to worry about that."

She stared him in the eye "What is it that I do have to worry about?"

"Talking him into it."

"If he checks out and I talk him into it, you'll fund it?"

"If." Jim Bob paused. "And this is a big if. If he comes up with a viable plan and he convinces me he can keep it secret. Just in case anything backfires, I don't want the FBI breathing down our necks. And neither do you."

She had to force herself to keep a stoic look. If the cost of setting James free was to have the FBI breathing down her neck, she'd gladly run that risk. She couldn't let Jim Bob know that. She simply asked, "What do I do next?"

"You fly from here to Tel Aviv tomorrow afternoon, and Jacob will meet you at the Renaissance Tel Aviv Hotel on Thursday evening to brief you on the details. For him, the real issue is convincing you that his seismic vibrator works properly. Putting you in contact with the guy from the

Entebbe raid is just enabling you to pursue a private interest of your own.”

“And you’re certain he won’t be suspicious of my intent?”

“He’s always suspicious. It’s a natural consequence of the Holocaust and being surrounded by neighbors who want to destroy his country.”

He slid a white number ten envelope across the table to her.

“What’s this?

“Five-hundred dollars in shekels. You’ll have some expenses, and I want you to pay them in cash. I don’t want you leaving a trail of credit card receipts.” He tapped the envelope with his finger.

“I can’t imagine that I’ll spend that much money in such a short trip.”

“If anything’s left over, you can return it to me when you get back.”

He looked at his watch and pushed his chair back from the table. “I’m sorry to desert you, Angie, but I have an important meeting with my auditors coming up. And you have several things to do before you take off for Tel Aviv. Check with my administrative aide for your flight information. Then my driver will take you to a hotel where my wife will pick you up at three.”

“Your wife?”

“She’ll take you to Neiman Marcus to get some appropriate clothing.”

Angie looked down at the chic satin blouse she was wearing. “Appropriate clothing?”

Jim Bob smiled. “Well, if you were meeting a Hollywood casting director, that mini skirt you’re wearing now would be perfect. However, the guy you’re trying to impress is an Israeli commando. My wife has an Israeli friend who suggested how you should dress.”

Angie looked startled. “Does she know why I need these clothes?

"Only that you're going to accompany Jacob out to the desert to evaluate some equipment."

Angie stood up and extended her hand. She smiled. "Thank you for everything, Mr. Jones. You've been most gracious. I'll try not to disappoint you."

Jim Bob cocked his head to the side and looked down at her.

"It's a gamble. And I'm not sure you understand what the consequences might be."

She gulped. "Then why are you helping me?"

"You deserve the chance to try. And I deserve the chance to see what we can make of it."

He grinned. "I got my first break in oil as a wildcatter, Angie. Risk taking is in my blood."

26

"That won't do it."

January 1980

Teheran

James lay on the floor watching the light in the window turn from a dim gray to the glow of sunshine. When the last trace of nighttime disappeared, he stood up to start his exercises.

He stretched his arms toward the ceiling, and lowered them to the shape of a cross, twisting left, then right to stretch his back and sides. He did this ten times as slowly as possible. With nothing to do throughout the waking hours, it was important to drag exercises out for as long as possible. He bent over, with knees locked, to reach down to the floor. When he'd started this routine, he could barely touch his toes. Now he could place his palms on the floor and hold them there to a count of twenty.

He followed this by running in place, then doing push-ups, crunches, arm curls, and pullups. As a bar for the pullups, he curled his fingers over the molding above the door mantel. The strain on his fingers was so great, he could do no more than two or three repetitions.

His appetite grew as he exercised, and he heard guards in the corridor bringing breakfast. A guard James didn't recognize unlocked the door and set the trays for the hostages on the floor. James lifted his tray and looked at its meager contents, two slices of unbuttered bread and a serving of Wheaties that had been taken from the Embassy commissary. "We need more food than this," he said.

The guard spat onto one of the bread slices. James' head snapped forward in rage, and he spat twice at the guard's chest. Looking dumbstruck at the spittle sliding down his shirt, the guard jerked his fists up into the tray James was holding. The tray flew into the air, then spilled its contents on the floor when it landed. He ground his shoe into the bread, slammed the door shut, and locked it.

The lieutenant, who a few days earlier had complained about James being too nice to the guards, put his hands on James' shoulder. "I'm glad you did that, Mr. Whitcomb. Served the bastard right. Here, have a piece of my bread." He picked his tray of food off the floor and handed one of the bread slices to James.

James took the bread and sank down to a sitting position on the floor, leaning against the wall. His pulse raced, and he waited for it to calm down before biting into the bread. What the hell was wrong with him? He should behave with the dignity of the diplomat he was, not get into a spitting contest with a teenage guard. What would the guard's revenge be? His pulse refused to slow down, and James cursed the medical student guard who had never returned with the anxiety pills he had promised. James began his deep breathing exercises in hopes he could keep his palpitations from coming back.

Tel Aviv. Ben Gurion International Airport

Angie's plane bounced once as it touched down and steadied itself to taxi smoothly to the terminal. Her passage through customs and immigration control also went without a hitch. Not surprising, she thought. At the Dallas airport she had been peppered with questions before getting on the flight, and her baggage had been thoroughly searched. What did surprise her was the absence of armed guards inside the Tel Aviv airport, given how vulnerable Israel was to terrorist attacks.

She no sooner reached the baggage claim than a man in a tan colored short sleeve shirt came up to her. "Mrs. Whitcomb?"

"Jacob," she asked.

He nodded.

"I was wondering," she said, "if we could stop for a bite before we drive into the city. I got nauseous on the plane and wasn't able to eat."

"Certainly, but your hotel has an excellent restaurant that serves some wonderful Mediterranean dishes."

"I don't need anything that elaborate just now. Maybe a slice of pizza."

In fact, she hadn't been nauseous, but she wanted to pick Jacob's brain and was afraid she would lose the chance to do that if he just dropped her off at the hotel and drove away. He led them to a café in the airport where they ordered a small pizza to split.

"Let me say how sorry I am to hear about your husband," said Jacob, as they waited for the food to arrive.

"Thank you," said Angie. She touched the back of his hand, then withdrew. She wasn't sure how to start, but things would go more smoothly if she reassured him that she was not there to investigate how well he was doing his job.

"The real reason I accepted this assignment is the chance it would give me to meet with someone from the Entebbe raid."

"So, you don't want the report I prepared for you?"

"Mr. Jones does indeed want me to get your report and observe the seismic vibrator in operation. That's what he's paying me to do. But, as long as I'm here, I want to use my free time to meet the person you found from the Entebbe operation."

"I'll hand you my report when we get to the car, so you have time to look at it if you wish before we go out to the desert on Sunday to inspect the vibrator at work."

"Sunday?"

"Yes, Saturday's the sabbath. And tomorrow I've scheduled you to meet with the person from the Entebbe raid. I'm quite confused about why you want to see him."

She twirled one of the strands of her curly hair. "Every day, I'm on pins and needles worrying about my husband, James, in Iran. I'm terrified that President Carter will try some reckless commando raid. And I just need some kind of reassurance from someone who's already been through a raid that James will be safe."

"All you want is reassurance?"

She frowned. "If your spouse were held captive wouldn't you want some reassurances?"

Jacob raised his hands, palms out. "I'm sorry. I shouldn't have said that. What do I tell people if I'm asked why you are here?"

"Just tell them the truth. I'm here on business for Mr. Jones. If anyone presses you on my interest in Entebbe, tell them you set up the meeting as a personal favor to me. With all the attacks that Israel has suffered, you yourself must have had moments of terror about somebody's safety. And you empathized with my situation."

There was a long pause until Jacob suggested, "Maybe I should tell you a little about this person you're meeting tomorrow. His name is Daniel Laveen, and he was second in command to the guy who took over after Yonatan Netanyahu was shot. He was a captain in the IDF."

"IDF?"

"Israeli Defense Forces. He's an ideal person to answer any questions you have about hostages in general."

"What's he been doing since Entebbe?"

"He left IDF to form a private security firm that has become very successful."

"Do I meet him at his office? Or what?"

"I made a reservation for you to have dinner with him tomorrow on the patio at your hotel. The patio restaurant is laid out in a way that will give you the privacy and informality you need. Mr. Jones stressed that both of those are essential."

Another question nagged at the back of her mind, and Jacob had just given her a way to segue into it. She was grateful to Jim Bob for the help he was giving her. She wondered, though, how much she could trust him.

Before she could pursue that, the waiter set their pizza on the table. Angie slid a piece onto a plate for herself and another on a plate for Jacob.

"Suggesting that you keep my meeting with Mr. Laveen informal was very thoughtful of Mr. Jones." She tapped her fork nervously on the white tablecloth as she stared at Jacob's impassive face, wondering if he'd be receptive to questions about Jim Bob. "What is it like to work for him," she asked.

Jacob swallowed a bit of the pizza before responding. "Just don't get in his way."

She looked at the Israeli, startled. "Meaning?"

"When I started with the company, some workers in Texas tried to unionize. One night, a group of thugs cracked the heads of several union leaders. The unionizing effort collapsed, and there have been no attempts at it since then."

Angie's stomach churned.

"I'm not saying it was Mr. Jones who did this, and nobody knows who gave the order. The net result is that the company remains non-union."

"Won't he get mad at you for telling me that story?"

Jacob shrugged. "Why would he? The more people who hear about it, the more he gets treated with kid gloves."

Renaissance Tel Aviv Hotel

At 7:00 p.m. the next day, Angie took the elevator down to the lobby of the hotel. Although she felt underdressed in the navy blue slacks and tan cotton shirt she wore, that was what the Israeli friend of Jim Bob's wife had prescribed for her. No sooner did she step from the elevator, than a man of medium height approached her.

"Mrs. Whitcomb?"

"Yes. But how did you know it was me?"

He grinned. "You're the only woman in the lobby."

"And you must be Daniel Laveen."

"In person," he said. "Let's go out to the terrace where we can talk in private."

Like most men she had seen so far in Israel, Daniel Laveen wore a plain-colored short sleeve shirt instead of a suitcoat. Broad shoulders that filled out the shirt and muscular arms descending from the short sleeves gave him the appearance of being a physically powerful person. That would be an asset in any rescue attempt.

He led her to a table so close to the beach she could smell the salt water. A wind blew across the water, and the waves formed white crests just before they crashed onto the shore with a roar that drowned out nearby conversations. "It will be easier to hear each other if we move away from the surf," she said.

Daniel smiled. "The noise will shield us from eavesdroppers."

"You think we have eavesdroppers?"

"No. It's just that old habits are hard to break."

Then he changed the subject. "Could we get acquainted over a glass of wine before we do anything else? How about a Cabernet Sauvignon from Galilee?"

She nodded, trying to look sophisticated. There was no point in tipping off Daniel that she couldn't tell a Galilee Cabernet from a Mogen David. He placed the order with a waiter and pulled out the bio sheet he had received from Jacob.

"I'm curious how you came to speak three languages," he said. "That's extraordinary for an American."

She laughed. "I had no choice. The Peace Corps sent me to Tunis where I had to learn Arabic if I wanted to talk with anyone. English, of course, I grew up with. And Spanish I learned from my Cuban mother who refused to talk with me in English because she didn't want me to lose our native language. That was annoying at times, but the Spanish was ingrained in me by the time I turned nine."

"What happened when you turned nine?"

"My mother was piloting a small airplane that crashed."

Daniel winced. "What happened?"

"She was flying some Cuban freedom fighters someplace, but nobody knows why the plane crashed."

"Your mother was a political activist. And your father, Mr. Parnell? Is he an activist as well?"

She chuckled. "Charlie? Heavens no. He did some work for Bobby Kennedy once. But all his energies are consumed by a small hedge fund he operates."

"The other thing I'm curious about," said Daniel, tapping the edge of the bio-sheet on the tabletop, "is why your husband didn't ask for a hardship deferment on the assignment to Teheran. After all, you had just started your honeymoon."

"James refused to ask for it. 'I want to go where the action is,' he told me. He didn't want to sit on the sidelines if he could be part of helping to stabilize the Middle East."

"That speaks well of him," said Daniel. "And of you for going along with it."

Their conversation lagged for a moment, and Angie picked anxiously at her fingernails. She hadn't had a chance to broach the question of a rescue mission, and so far, he had learned a lot more about her than she had about him.

"That's my background." She smiled coyly. "Tell me a little about Daniel Laveen."

"I worked for several years in Sayeret Matkal."

"What is that?"

"It's the branch of military intelligence that carried off things like the Entebbe raid you apparently are curious about."

"But you're not with them anymore?"

"As time passed, I grew impatient with the military bureaucracy. I quit to form a private security firm. We got a big boost when we snatched two Kuwaitis from the hands of Iranian police, and our business has been pretty steady since then."

He raised the glass to his lips, took a drink, and set it down. His smile faded. "Somehow, I think there's more to you wanting to see me than what your friend Jacob told me. If I'm wrong, tell me. But there's only one reason why the spouse of a hostage would travel halfway around the world to consult with somebody like me who has a record of rescuing hostages."

"You're on the mark so far."

"You want me to find a way to con your husband's guards at the embassy in Teheran into moving him someplace, intercept the move, pluck him from their clutches, and transport him to safety."

Angie's stomach sunk. "That won't do it."

"Then, what do you want from me?"

"I want you to rescue all of them."

Daniel's eyes widened. "All of them?"

She twirled her wine glass on the tabletop. "The State Department wants all of them released or none of them, and the hostage families agree with that. To negotiate for the release of anything less than all the hostages will increase the bargaining clout of the Iranians."

"But you're not asking me to negotiate a release. You're asking for a rescue."

"The same logic prevails. If only one is rescued, the well-being of the others becomes more precarious."

Without pause, Daniel replied. "Do you understand the complexity of rescuing that many people?"

"At Entebbe, you rescued a hundred people two thousand miles from home. In Teheran you've got fewer people, and you're a much shorter distance to friendly territory, the Persian Gulf, or even Israel itself. How could this be more complex than Entebbe?" She looked him in the eye, without further comment.

"We succeeded at Entebbe in part because our leader, Muki Betser, had lived in Uganda and had detailed knowledge about the airport where the hostages were held. We flew in at night because we knew that the Ugandan Air Force didn't fly after dark. We also knew they tended to line up their fighter planes in formation on the ground which made it easier for us to blow them up and prevent them from chasing us on the way out. The situation in Teheran is much more difficult. In Entebbe, as I said, the hostages were all concentrated right next to an airport runway where we could land a transport plane. In Teheran, the embassy compound is surrounded by mobs of angry students, some of whom are armed and disruptive."

She slouched back in her chair, dispirited.

"Are you saying it's impossible?"

"Not at all. With careful planning, adequate resources, a clear chain of command, and absolute secrecy, we could do it. I'd love to do it. But I want you to weigh the risks."

She nodded.

"At Entebbe, nobody doubted that the terrorists would carry out their threat to kill all the Jewish people on board. Even if our mission fell far short of our goal and some of them got killed, most of them would have been saved. In your case, the Iranians probably wouldn't dare kill the hostages. So you have to weigh the risk that some of them might get killed in a rescue attempt versus the probability that all of them will be set free someday."

"That day might be ten years from now. Iran threatens to put them on trial as spies."

"They can't."

"Why not?"

"That would give the American Air Force the excuse it wants to wipe Teheran off the map."

"But what if this rosy scenario of yours doesn't work out, Daniel? I can't just sit back twiddling my thumbs."

"Suppose we do undertake this mission. We'll need adequate resources: personnel, equipment, several helicopters, and a way to get them in and out of Iran. Have you considered how expensive something like this will be?"

"We've got funding for it if we can find a competent person to run it." This was an exaggeration. Jim Bob had said only that he would consider funding it. And only if he had confidence in Daniel.

It was Daniel's turn to lean back in his chair. He steepled his fingertips under his chin and sat that way for a few minutes without replying.

"When do you leave Tel Aviv?"

"Sunday night."

"Just before you leave, I'll hand you a brief outline of a plan. You can show this to no one but your financial backer, whoever he is. And as soon as he sees it, I want you to shred it. It will give him a very good idea of how much this will cost him, and he can check me out to see if he's satisfied with my abilities. If he wants to proceed, I will make a formal proposal wherever and whenever you two want to meet me."

Angie's jaw gaped open. This guy had not only been a leader at Entebbe, he'd mounted his own rescue operations. And he was sensitive to secrecy.

"Thank God!" A huge grin broke out on her face.

She flagged a white coated waiter who was standing by the terrace entrance with a towel draped over his forearm.

"Bring us a menu and give my friend whatever he wants. I'll take an Irish Mist, if you have it."

27

"Doonesbury Cares."

February 1980

Teheran

James stepped into the yard of the embassy compound for his weekly half-hour outdoors. He kicked at the dying brown lawn and shook his head as he glanced up at the empty flagpole. Press Attaché Barry Rosen was already walking in the yard, and James quickened his pace to catch up with him.

"One of the things I miss," he said, "is sitting around on Sunday morning with Angie working our way through *The New York Times*. But here we've been blacked out on everything outside this compound." He swept his hand from the ambassador's residence to the chancery. "For all I know, we've disappeared from the front page, and everybody at home is going on with their normal lives. Do you think anybody other than our families really cares about us anymore?"

"They care," said Barry.

"How do you know?"

"Look at this."

Barry pulled a tattered comic strip from his pocket. It was in color, from a Sunday newspaper.

"Where'd you get that? They toss out all the newspapers so we can't see them."

"They let the comic strips slip by, figuring they won't disclose anything important. Some guy in Boston mails them to us."

"What do they tell us?"

"Take a look."

He folded the paper over to a *Doonesbury* strip satirizing an American minister sympathetic to the Iranian Revolution. Iranians had invited the minister to visit the hostages, but he kept putting off the visit until a mob could be organized to demonstrate against the Americans. James laughed and handed the paper back to Barry.

"*Doonesbury* cares," he said.

Seeing James laugh at the cartoon strip, Habib the Liar ran over to them and grabbed the newspaper page from Barry. He unfolded it, turned it back and forth, and inspected it for any hidden messages. Not recognizing the strip as a parody, he handed it back.

"Time's up!" he barked. "Get back inside."

James continued smiling as they walked back to the residence. *Doonesbury* cares, he thought. Somebody's thinking of us.

Dallas

Angie stepped confidently into Jim Bob's office at nine o'clock in the morning. She finally had a commando capable of organizing a rescue and a Texan rich enough to fund it.

She couldn't wait to give Jim Bob the good news about Daniel, but his opening words brought her up short.

"It is always a pleasure to see your smiling face, Angie. To tell the truth, I never thought you'd be back."

"Then why did you send me to Israel in the first place?"

"Not to be crude, but I didn't want to be the one to convince you your plan was hopeless. I thought this Israeli would do that for me."

"Nope." She handed him the two-page outline Daniel had given her. "After you read it, Daniel wants me to shred it. He's ready to develop a complete proposal and give us a presentation whenever and wherever you want."

She sat on the chair in front of Jim Bob's desk while he read the outline. He slowly went through it twice. As he handed it back to Angie, he said, "Knowing the uphill battle this thing faces, you nonetheless found someone who held out the illusion of success so he could make a buck?"

He pointed at Daniel's bottom line estimate of what the project would cost. Her excitement shifted to anger, and she furrowed her eyebrows at him.

"His motive's not money. He already runs a security business that provides him a generous living."

"If not money, then what's he after?"

"As long as he's willing to run this for us, what difference does it make?"

"That's the same thing I thought when I was young and looking for partners to get me started. As time goes on, you'll learn that the motive of the other guy always makes a difference."

She pointed at Remington's *Bronco Buster* sculpture on his desk. "Does it make any difference why that cowboy got on top of that horse? Isn't it enough that he did it? Or for that matter, does it make any difference why the artist made the sculpture? He captured the way humans strive to do something difficult."

Jim Bob shook his head as he glanced at the sculpture. "Considering that bronco busters are plagued with broken bones, something reckless would be more like it."

She tapped her fingers on her knees. "Jim Bob, I don't know why the cowboy got on the horse, and I honestly don't know why Daniel Laveen wants to do this. Maybe he sees some glory in it. Maybe this project will catapult his company into the biggest security firm in the world. Maybe he truly believes in justice."

Jim Bob rolled his eyes, and she spread her hands out, palms up.

"We can drive ourselves nuts trying to guess his motives," she said. "What we know for certain is that he has done rescue operations before. He played a key role at Entebbe, and he rescued two Kuwaitis from Iran last year. He wants to show you his ideas for this one. Aren't you at least curious?"

"Skeptical would be more like it."

She flashed a broad grin. "Aha! You're as curious as I am. When will you see him?"

He looked at the calendar on his desk and leaned back in his chair, reflective. Angie restrained herself from interrupting him.

He tapped a pencil on his desk before returning his stare to her eyes. "You realize, don't you, that doing something like this is illegal. You could be prosecuted."

"Ross Perot wasn't prosecuted when he plucked two of his employees from Iran, and we won't be prosecuted either. When those hostages arrive in the U.S., public support will be so huge, nobody will dare prosecute the people who rescued them."

"Ross Perot was lucky. You might not be as lucky. The FBI might hear about the plot before it even gets off the ground. Or some of the hostages could get killed in the process."

She shuddered. "I've had nightmares over that possibility. But if we don't act, some of them might die in captivity anyway. Others will be put on trial and sent to prison for ten years or more."

"You could be the one ending up in prison."

She looked down at her hands in her lap and then up to Jim Bob's eyes before saying in a soft voice. "If I can get James free, all of them free, I'll gladly go to prison. I'll go to hell if that's what it takes."

Jim Bob's head snapped up in reaction. He paused, then said, "I'll talk with your friend Daniel, but his plan better be foolproof, because I'm not as blasé about going to prison as you are. I want absolute secrecy. This meeting has to be set up in a way that never links you and me to your friend Daniel."

"But we're already linked," she said. "I've been here twice, I've met your wife, and you sent me to Tel Aviv to meet with both Daniel and Jacob."

"No," said Jim Bob, shaking his head. "Don't tell the story that way. Tell it like this. I sent you to Israel to conduct some business for my company JBJ Enterprises. My wife helped you pick out clothes for the desert. If you somehow met Daniel Laveen while you were there, that's your business, not mine. I don't have to worry that you will blab about that, because you don't want to be prosecuted. I don't have to worry about my wife saying she met you, because people can't be forced to testify against their spouses. And my background check on Daniel Laveen tells me that I don't have to worry about him blabbing. As long the mission succeeds, we're all scot free."

Angie was astounded at the self-centered calculating mind Jim Bob was showing. "So how do I get the two of you together?" she said.

"First, until I set up a secure communications method, get yourself a bag of quarters so you can call him from public telephones. Tell him to fly to Monterrey as soon as he can. We'll reimburse him."

"Monterrey? In Mexico?"

"I already told you we want secrecy. Weren't you listening? We've got to meet him without him ever entering the U.S. or us going abroad."

Puzzled Angie squinted and furrowed her eyebrows.

"Just let me know when he'll be in Monterrey, and I'll tell you what to do next."

Near South Padre Island

Angie clung in terror to the gunwales of the speedboat as it bounced over the choppy waters of the Gulf of Mexico. Why did it have to be so windy on the day she had to do this? The Mexican-American captain of the boat shared none of her anxiety and didn't even flinch when they slammed into a giant wave. Following Jim Bob's instructions, he kept the boat far enough at sea to stay out of sight from the shore. He finally turned West, and in a few moments, she spied land in the distance.

"Playa Bagdad?" She shouted to be heard over the sounds of the engine and the waves.

The captain nodded. As he got nearer to land, he veered left, slowed down, and began cruising parallel to the beach. The waves now hit the boat from the side, causing it to roll, which was almost as frightening to Angie as it had been hitting waves head-on. Thank God she'd taken Dramamine. They cruised southwardly for twenty minutes before a solitary man came into view.

"Allí. Ese hombre," she shouted and pointed.

They headed toward the figure, who began waving at them, and the captain moved the boat slowly toward the beach. Angie kicked off her shoes and jumped into the water to hold the bow of the boat steady against the sand as the man threw a briefcase into the boat, then climbed aboard. She pushed the bow off the sand and scrambled back into the boat, her jeans were now drenched with sea water, but she barely noticed. She gave the man a big grin.

"Welcome, Daniel."

They sped back out to sea and cruised for half an hour until they reached an offshore oil rig. A tower of steel rose above them several stories into the sky. There was no walkway from the boat's mooring dock to the rig itself. As the boat idled next to the mooring dock, Angie grabbed a rope to swing over the open water to the rig, exhilarated when she reached the other side. Daniel sent his briefcase across first, then swung onto the rig himself.

Jim Bob met them and led them along a series of stairs and catwalks into the rig. My God, she thought, as they progressed. This is a miniature city. They passed by a cafeteria, a gym, a game room, and what looked to be a movie theater. The constant clanking of machinery assaulted her ears.

Jim Bob led them into a conference room and shut the door, finally blotting out the thunderous noise. The room was complete with a whiteboard and a pull-down projection screen. The smell of fresh coffee came from a sideboard. They each took a cup and sat around the end of the conference table nearest to the projection screen. Angie's clothes were still damp from her drenching, and scales of salt clung to her blouse and jeans.

"The floor is yours, Mr. Laveen," said Jim Bob. "I'm curious to find out what you've brought us."

Daniel projected his first slide onto the screen, an image of the look-down, schematic drawing of the Embassy compound that Angie had gotten from her friend Jenna.

"We'll do this on a night with no moon. To gain the element of surprise, our helicopters will sweep in under the radar and land in this big open area in front of the chancery building."

"What kind of helicopters?" said Jim Bob, interrupting him. "No chopper I know of has the range to get that deep into Iran."

"I'll get to that Mr. Jones." He used a long wood pointer to indicate the compound's courtyard on the screen.

"When do you plan to carry this out?" demanded Jim Bob.

"There's a new moon in mid-April. We can go then if we have everything ready. But mid-May is more likely."

Jim Bob drummed his fingertips impatiently on the tabletop. "Even if you come in under the radar, you'll get shot down by the guards in the compound."

Daniel smiled. "It turns out that Iran has a fleet of its own Sea Stallions, which is the helicopter we plan to use, so no one will be surprised to see them flying over Teheran. By the time the students at the embassy realize we're not Iranian, we'll be close enough to saturate the compound with tear gas. That will immobilize the guards long enough for our men to get on the ground and tie them up. There are typically a dozen of them in this area at night, most of them asleep on the ground."

"How do you know that?"

Daniel paused. "I'm not free to give out my source for that information. Even if there are half again that many and they are awake, they will be overwhelmed in minutes by the tear gas and our men."

For the rest of the day, they delved into questions. Sandwiches were brought in at noon, and they ate while they continued their discussion. Angie was amazed at the rapidity with which Jim Bob grasped the plan and raised serious issues. By mid-afternoon, his comments began to suggest that he was buying into the idea.

"Where will you do your training and your dry runs?"

"If my government is willing to keep its nose out of my business, we'll do it in the Negev Desert."

"And if they don't cooperate?"

"We don't need them to cooperate. We just need them to look the other way, as you Americans say."

"And why would they do that?"

"If they look the other way, they get plausible deniability even as the operation goes forward. And if the operation succeeds, their big adversary, Iran, gets a black eye."

"They might look the other way," said Jim Bob. "But what if they don't?"

"If they ask too many questions, you'll need to find a secret training site here in the U.S."

"Impossible," said Jim Bob. "Angie was supposed to tell you that this entire operation has to be handled outside of the U.S." He cast a frown in her direction. "And the trouble I took to meet you here on this offshore rig, outside of both Mexico and the U.S., should tell you how important this is to me."

"I'll figure out something," said Daniel. He replaced the slide of the compound with one showing a huge helicopter.

"This is the Sea Stallion I mentioned. It carries thirty-seven people and has the range to fly round trip from Kuwait to Teheran, if we augment its fuel capacity with drop tanks. So we need three of these to assault the compound, one more to pick up the three hostages at the Ministry of Foreign Affairs, and two more for backup if anything goes wrong."

Angie smiled. The term *pickup* made it sound as easy as a bus pulling up to a street corner to take on passengers.

"You're going to launch from Kuwait?" asked Jim Bob, frowning. "How the hell are you going to get the Kuwaiti government to go along with that?"

"I'm not. I have one highly placed person in Kuwait who's grateful to me for saving his sons' lives and who hates the Iranians for arresting them in the first place. All he has to do is file the paperwork for an oil tanker to dock at Kuwait City. We'll weld steel landing pads onto the deck of the tanker, and we'll be well outside of Kuwaiti territory when our helicopters launch."

Daniel sorted through his overhead slides and put up a map of the Arabian Peninsula. "When I'm satisfied with our preparations and our dry run, we'll move everything to the tanker that we'll dock at the port of Eilat." He used his wooden pointer to trace a route from the desert to the Port City of Eilat, through the Red Sea, around Saudi Arabia, and into the Persian Gulf.

"And how much is this tanker going to cost me?"

"Forty-five hundred dollars per day if I have to lease a modern super tanker. Less if I can find a smaller, older version."

Angie expected Jim Bob to object to the price, but he merely nodded for Daniel to continue.

"When our helicopters return from Teheran, they land at the Kuwait airport. This gives the emir of Kuwait the pleasure of calling President Carter to come and pick up his hostages."

"What's the downside for the emir?"

"None. If the mission succeeds, he gets enormous leverage over the American government for several years to come."

Angie fidgeted. She didn't like the word if.

Jim Bob asked, "What if it doesn't succeed?"

"The emir still has no downside. As I said, our helicopters will be launched from the tanker in international waters."

"It's no-lose for Kuwait?"

"Correct," said Daniel, "but one of the most important things for me is control over the operation. If you provide adequate funding, I will get you the best equipment and the best people we can find. In turn you give complete operational control to me." He pointed at his chest and paused. "If not, I won't do it."

"Adequate funding, you say," said Jim Bob. "Let's start with the copters. How much do they cost?"

"Brand new, thirteen million dollars each."

Jim Bob bolted forward. "Times six! That's seventy-eight million dollars just to get us there."

Why is Jim Bob haggling over this detail? Angie wondered. He's already gotten Daniel's ballpark estimate of the costs.

Daniel smiled again. "That's if we have to buy them brand new. Used they'll be cheaper. And you'll be able to recoup most of the cost by reselling them afterwards."

The questions went on through the afternoon. Finally, at 4:30, Daniel returned to the issue of money. "On my end, I've already set up a corporation in Switzerland to buy the supplies, recruit the personnel, and handle the logistics. We can start as soon as we have the financing."

Jim Bob responded. "Each time you submit an itemized list we'll transfer the requested money to a bank in Switzerland from a subsidiary we'll set up in Grand Cayman. Before the money reaches your account, we'll transfer it through enough other banks that it will be almost impossible to trace. Only one other person will know about these transfers from our subsidiary."

"What will this subsidiary be called?"

"Emergency Services Program, or ESP, for short."

"And who is this person that will run it?"

Jim Bob pointed at Angie. "You're looking at her.".

Angie did a double take. "Me? I don't know how to make payments from a secret bank in the Cayman Islands to another secret bank in Switzerland."

"I need somebody I trust and somebody I can train. You worked in the accounting department of your father's hedge fund which moved money around all the time. What you didn't learn there, I can teach you. To do that, however, I'll need you here in Dallas. Can you move down here for the duration?"

Angie wrinkled her nose. "It's so early in the semester at NYU I could drop my courses with no penalty. But what would be my reason for doing that? My father will want to know why, and so will a lot of other people."

"Do you have any friends here you could say you needed to visit for some reason?"

Angie grinned. "My Peace Corps partner, Sarah. She just started law school in Fort Worth. I'll tell Charlie I want to spend some time catching up with her. Give her some support while she adjusts to this new phase of her life."

"While you're here," said Jim Bob, register for a course at Southern Methodist University that will teach you how to use a spreadsheet. You'll need that for what I have in mind."

"What's a spreadsheet."

It was Jim Bob's turn to grin. "One of the most useful things you'll ever learn."

Oil Rig Restroom

By five, the smell of coffee from the sideboard had grown stale, and they ran out of issues. The only thing left was putting Daniel back on the speedboat, while Angie and Jim Bob headed to the helipad where a copter was waiting to whisk them back to Dallas.

On the way out of the conference room, Jim Bob said, "We should all make a pit stop before we head out." He went into a men's room in the corridor.

Daniel followed him in and said, "You had a strange look, Mr. Jones, when I mentioned there was a market for reselling those Sea Stallions."

Jim Bob put his hand on the younger man's shoulder. "You come out of a military background, Daniel, where there's no incentive to keep prices down. Here in the real world, price is everything. Get me the best prices you can on the purchase and resale of those Stallions, and I'll give you ten percent of the profit. And you can earn another bonus if you get your Kuwaiti friend to arrange for me to load my tanker with oil and transport it someplace. I might as well make a little money off that ship while it's in the neighborhood."

"That's very generous, Mr. Jones."

"Generosity has nothing to do with it. I'm giving you an incentive to keep costs down. Instead of paying seventy-eight million dollars for those six helicopters and reselling them for sixty-eight, let's say you do the reverse. That will give me an unexpected $10 million profit. I'm more than happy to give you one-tenth of it."

28

"I believe in moral patriotism."

April 1980

Teheran

At Easter, the Iranians accepted a request from left-leaning American religious leaders to offer religious services for the hostages and to meet with them in small groups. James, an Army major, and four others met with a Catholic Priest, Father Darrell Rupiper. Among the group was Marine guard Kevin Hermening, the youngest of the hostages. Hermening offered to do the Bible reading at the service. Afterwards, he carried the Bible as the group was led to a table in a different room where they were permitted to converse informally.

Hermening squeezed in front of James. He whispered that he needed to get next to the priest so he could give him a message to take home about the shitty way the hostages were treated.

"Jesus Christ, Kevin, the guards will haul you off to join Metrinko in the Mushroom Inn when they hear you tell that to the priest."

"I wrote it on a gum wrapper, so they won't hear anything. Then I stuck the gum wrapper inside this Bible."

James watched Kevin bend forward and whisper something as he handed the book to Father Rupiper. The priest gave a quick glance down at the Bible placed in his hands. He combed through the pages, and the book opened at the gum wrapper. He quickly closed it and glanced up to see if he were being watched by the two guards at the door.

Regaining his composure, Father Rupiper introduced himself. He served with the missionaries of Mary Immaculate in Omaha. Thin, with long brown hair and piercing eyes, he projected an intensity that, in James' mind, gave him a captivating presence.

"I believe in moral patriotism," he said after everyone settled into their chairs at the table.

The Army major scowled at the term moral patriotism, and James stiffened.

"What does that mean?" said James. "Moral patriotism?"

"Our country has abandoned universal moral standards. It is our duty as moral patriots to hold our nation accountable for its actions."

James frowned. "And how does that relate to us here?"

"I have spoken out against your captivity. It is wrong. But our support of the Shah was immoral, and the Iranians have legitimate grievances."

This was the kind of thing James himself had said before he became a hostage. But five months of harsh captivity had ended his sympathy for the revolution.

"With all respect, Father," said James, "it is easy for you to say things like that when you have the freedom to fly out of here tomorrow. It's much different if you're in our shoes."

"You are right," said the priest. "I've decided to follow the example of Jesus and put myself in your position."

"You're going to do what?" challenged the Army major from across the table.

"I'm going to offer to take the place of one of you."

James blinked. That was insane. Or, if not insane, maybe a meaningless pandering to the hostages. He looked at the other men around the table. One drew his hands over his eyes, another smoothed his hair, both looking dumbfounded. Hermening, sitting next to James, looked aghast. His mouth fell wide open. It was critical to him that Rupiper leave, taking the Bible and the message Kevin had inserted.

"You don't have to do that," James said to Rupiper. "There's no help you can give us here. Go home to your family and your congregation so you can do some good for them."

"I must do this," said Rupiper. "Who should it be? Whose place should I take?"

"Miele," said a quiet voice from across the table.

"Jerry Miele," echoed James. "If you're going to do it, take his place. He's in bad shape."

"Bad shape?" asked the priest.

James paused, wondering how much he should tell. He looked toward the door to see if the guards were following the conversation, but they seemed to be paying no attention.

If Rupiper was doing nothing more than pandering to them with an empty gesture he never intended to carry out, maybe he should get a dose of reality. Would he make this offer if he really understood the kind of treatment he'd be letting himself in for?

"When the guards discovered that Jerry worked for the CIA," explained James, "they took particular delight in tormenting him. It would be an act of mercy to get him out of here."

"What did he do for the CIA?"

"Why should that matter?" barked the Army major who had earlier questioned what Rupiper had meant by saying he would put himself in the position of the hostages. James held his hand up for the major to wait, then he addressed Rupiper.

"He was a communications technician. He didn't run agents or anything like that. One day the guards bound him to a chair, stripped the insulation from an extension cord, and wrapped the bare wires around him. One guard carried the plug over to the wall outlet, threatening to plug it in and electrocute him. Jerry was sweating like a pig and was screaming, *No!* The guard stepped away from the outlet. But when Jerry slumped forward in relief, the guard brought the plug near the outlet again. He did this four times, like a cat toying with a mouse. As Jerry broke into tears, Smitty and Lieutenant Taylor started screaming at the guards. When it looked like we might riot, the guards finally put an end to it."

The priest's head drooped forward.

"Ever since then, Jerry's lived in terror that they might actually carry out an electrocution," said James. His heart palpitations starting to return and his voice starting to crack. He paused to stare at the priest. "One day he tried suicide because he was so anguished. Another day I found him curled on the floor in a fetal position, trembling and shaking."

Father Rupiper paused, his hands clutching the table.

"If you're going to do this," said James, wanting to find out if the man was really going to follow through on his offer, "you should do it now while you've got the chance."

The priest still didn't move.

James shrugged and added, "But as I said, "you don't have to do this. No one at home will think less of you if you just walk away." He stressed the term *at home* as though the hostages in Teheran might not think as generously of him as the people in his congregation at home.

"I will think less of myself," said the priest. He pushed himself away from the table and headed toward the ambassador's office where the student leaders were headquartered.

James felt stunned, deflated. The priest hadn't been posturing after all. Instead of exposing the man as a fake, James had goaded him into carrying out the insane idea. If Rupiper ended up in their midst, James would be responsible. He sucked in a gulp of air to catch his breath. But it didn't stop the thumping of his heart in his chest.

"Nice going, wise guy," snarled the major from across the table. "You just made it impossible for him to back out and keep his dignity."

"I'm sorry," said James. "I really thought he was just sucking up to us."

"You're sorry?" said the major, his voice rising. "I hope you've figured out how you're going to protect him when he starts pushing that moral patriotism crap down our throats. Better hope that Metrinko doesn't get out of solitary and cross paths with him."

"If he stays, at least Jerry can get out."

"Stop bullshitting yourself. They're not going to let Jerry out, and you know it."

The hostages sat in exhausted silence for the next half hour. James closed his eyes and concentrated on slow, deep breathing to ease his anxiety attack. They all looked up when footsteps sounded in the hall. Father Rupiper came back into the room. His tall, thin form was bent forward and his eyes cast toward the floor.

"They turned me down," he said. "They feared that their message to the world would be diluted if a man of faith joined you. It would be harder to portray you as international criminals doing the evil work of the CIA."

James stiffened. Had Rupier actually made the offer or was he still posturing? But it no longer mattered. Kevin's message would get out, and the major would be freed from talk about moral partriotism.

"Tell Miele I'm sorry," Rupiper said to James. "I tried."

He shook hands with the men, and the guards took them back to their rooms. James was sitting on the floor, with his heart rate back to normal when one of the guards burst in. He waved a gum wrapper in the air.

"Who did this?" he shouted, bending over and pushing his jaw toward James' face. "Who wrote this? It came from somebody at your table. You will be sorry if you fail to tell me who did this."

Had Father Rupiper handed over Hermening's note? More likely, the guard had inspected the Bible and found the note on his own. But James wasn't going to expose who it was that had tried to smuggle out a message. He'd done enough shitty stuff for one day. Hermening had shown guts in writing the message, and he didn't deserve to be ratted out. The guard left, and James' heart began to thump. Some, or all, of them would pay a price for this episode.

Israel, Negev Desert

At 2:00 a.m., the Sea Stallion flew through the dark, moonless desert toward its target. Five others followed. Angie sat near the front in the lead copter, leaning against the bulkhead, the black camouflage paint itching her cheeks. Daniel sat at the rear where he could guide his troops out the exit ramp. From the copters' rocket tubes, a barrage of canisters shot out. As each one hit the field in front of the chancery building, it unleashed a plume of tear gas. Within seconds, the grounds were saturated with the disabling gas. The copter landed, and Daniel stood at the exit door, rushing out his teams of commandos. All wore gas masks.

Angie stood in line for her turn to jump out, with adrenalin coursing through her system. Being in the middle of the action felt more dicey than it had seemed when she'd first asked Daniel to let her participate in the dry run. Maybe she should have listened to him when he'd rejected the idea. She'd still be safe and comfortable in Dallas.

"Never!" he had said. "We're using live ammo, and it's too risky to have a non-combatant with us."

"Daniel, I was the catalyst for this whole operation. If it weren't for me, none of us would be doing this."

"Never," he repeated.

"It's my husband who's at stake here. You can't deny me the chance to observe how his rescue will be carried out."

"Never," he shouted. "You'll get in the way. Everybody's got a role to play, and you'll interfere with that."

"I'll just be an observer. You must have had observers on some of those missions you did for the IDF. Just let me come and watch so I can see how this is going to work out for my husband."

Daniel finally relented. "You can be an observer. Nothing more. You sit against the bulkhead of the helicopter, and after it lands you can't wander more than ten meters from it. No. Five meters. I don't want you getting shot or breaking your leg from a fall. We'll paint observer on your uniform so no one will try to involve you in what they're doing. Put some padding around your waist so you look like a man. I don't want any of my men distracted by you. Pin your hair up tight so it will all fit in your helmet and make yourself look as much like a man as possible."

She beamed. "You've got it, Daniel. I'll keep so much out of the way, you won't even know I'm there."

"You're going to cause me logistical problems. I don't want any record of you entering Israel. So arrange your flights into and out of Amman, Jordan. I'll send a jeep to pick you up and sneak you across the border."

As she jumped to the ground, Daniel's men shot out the overhead lights, and the compound went dark. She pulled down the night vision scope fixed to her helmet. The first team of commandos were wrapping duct tape around the ankles, wrists, and mouths of lifelike dummies in the field, while other commandos trained their weapons on the scene. When one of the dummies sprang up from the ground, simulating a defender, it was immediately shredded by a *pop pop pop* of bullets. The rifle's suppressor muffled the noise, so the silence of night was broken only by the helicopter rotors and the muted bursts from the AK-47s. Angie gasped as pieces of the dummy flew through the air, realizing what those bullets would do to a person.

One team went to search for hostages in the cottages to the left of the chancery, and another headed up the chancery steps. Off to the right, a second copter had landed in front of the Ambassador's residence, and commandos were already storming the big house. Three backup copters landed and waited in readiness on the open field behind the chancery. The sixth headed off to the Ministry of Foreign Affairs to rescue the three hostages being held there.

She was struck by how real the mock-up embassy compound appeared. It looked just like the schematics and photos she had obtained of the real embassy grounds, except that everything here was constructed from plywood and two by fours she had paid for from the secret bank account in Grand Cayman.

The lead commando on the chancery steps found the door locked. He blew the lock off with successive bursts from his AK-47. Daniel lobbed in a stun grenade that went off in a super-bright flash of light and an ear splitting bang.

Ignoring Daniel's order to stay within five meters of the helicopter, Angie followed him into the building. The lobby was saturated with tear gas, and the commandos duct-taped the lifelike interior dummy guards just as they had the ones outside. A lone dummy came tumbling down the stairs of the chancery, mimicking a defender, and one of the commandos ripped it open with his silenced automatic rifle.

The commandos went in pairs to search each room and pull out the dummies serving as hostages. They herded the dummy hostages into the lobby, then searched the second floor and finally the basement.

Before Daniel could see her and discover that she'd disobeyed his order to stay near the helicopter, she began running back to the aircraft. Its rotor blades kicked up such a sandstorm from the desert floor that it was hard to see, and she moved in a zigzag pattern toward the ship. Her eyes stung from the traces of tear gas that had leaked into her gas mask.

She watched the commandos carry dummy hostages toward the helicopter and load them on board. One commando was carrying two dummy hostages, and one of them fell out of his grasp. She ran to retrieve it and drag it to the helicopter.

Dragging the dummy slowed her down, and she was the last person to reach the copter. Terrified that it would take off without her, she scrambled toward it as best she could and dumped the hostage dummy on the floor. One of the men grabbed her hand to pull her aboard, and the door thudded shut behind her the instant she got inside. Daniel shot her an angry look and pushed her down to a sitting position by the exit door.

She leaned back in relief. Looking forward through the bulkhead door, she could see one of the commandos positioned to fire the copter's Sidewinder heat seeking missile in case they should be pursued by any fighter planes.

Israel, Command Post

The helicopters circled over the desert, then landed at a makeshift command post only a few miles from the target. The commandos carried the hostage dummies into a big tent, where a pair of combat medics simulated a check-up of each hostage.

Angie and the others followed Daniel into a second big tent. Despite the cold desert night, she was drenched in sweat. She grabbed a coffee, and it was only then that she noticed her hands shaking. She squeezed the cup with both hands to hold it steady, but even so, coffee sloshed over the rim of the cup. As she sank onto a metal card table chair, she pulled a reporter's notebook from her pocket to take notes on the debriefing for her report back to Jim Bob in Dallas. The sweat on her back began to dry, sending a chill along her skin. And the acrid smell of the tear gas on their clothes hung in the air. No longer needing to disguise herself as a man, she pulled off her helmet and shook her head to let the hair fall free.

Daniel conducted the debriefing with the same thoroughness with which he had organized the dry run. He spoke in Hebrew and assigned one of his men to translate for Angie.

Standing at the front of the room with a clipboard, he asked for reports from the team leaders and the pilots. Each one found a detail that hadn't gone as planned, which left Angie flabbergasted. Except for the one hostage dummy she had to drag to the helicopter, it had looked to her like a flawless operation.

By 6:00 a.m., people were stifling yawns. Daniel looked at his watch. "Any last comments before we call it a night?"

One of the commandos spoke. "We need a faster way to handle the guards. It takes too many of us and too much time to tie them all up. Once we get them unarmed, why don't we just herd them into one of those cottages and barricade the door?"

"Meet with me later today and we'll brainstorm it," said Daniel. "Any other final comments?"

When no one replied, Daniel announced, "Let's wrap it up, then. I'll meet with each of the team leaders and make whatever modifications we need to the plan. We'll do another dry run based on that. Then we'll do the real thing, give you guys the rest of your pay, and let you go back to your lives."

He refilled his cup at the coffee urn and walked over to Angie, his eyes blazing with anger. "I told you to stay by the helicopter. You interfered with the operation when you picked up that dummy."

"I felt I had to. You had stressed with us that no one should be left behind."

"The one who almost got left behind was you," he shouted. "Somebody else had the job of going back to pick up that dummy. If somehow it gets into the back of his head that you'll be there to backstop him, he might get careless."

She felt chagrined, but she refused to take her eyes from his.

He paused for an instant and seemed to cool off. "Angie, this is one of the reasons I didn't want you there in the first place. I didn't want any civilians. But as long as you're here, what are your observations?"

"As I was out there by the helicopter, all that gunfire was so realistic I almost expected the Iranians to break into the embassy compound with a counterattack. And the longer we stood out there in the open, the more nervous I got. It seemed like a long time."

He looked at a stopwatch on his wrist. "Forty-three minutes. We'll brainstorm ways to speed things up."

One of the commandos overheard the exchange as he walked past them on the way out of the tent. He said, "We could save a lot of time if we'd just shoot the guards when we get off the helicopter instead of tying them up."

Daniel scowled at him. "We're soldiers, not murderers. Nobody gets shot unless they're a threat."

He turned back to Angie. "As we try to speed up the operation, we must be careful not to rush so much that we make mistakes. As it is, we only recovered fifty-two of the fifty-three dummy hostages. We don't want to make mistakes like that when we do this under fire."

Angie swallowed. If they miss a hostage in the actual mission, it might be James. "Which one was it?" she said.

"The one in that warehouse at the rear of the compound, the one you said they call the Mushroom Inn. We should land one of the helicopters closer to it. That would reduce the time it takes to get the hostages into the helicopters. We could cut off a couple minutes if we did that."

"When do we carry this out?" asked Angie.

"Ideally, when there's no moon."

"But that's not till May. I looked it up."

"I know, and that's too far away. Everyone is psyched up for this, but we can't stay that way if we wait much longer."

She nodded and recalled from her skating competitions that her performance suffered if she overtrained or psyched herself up too soon. That was too trivial a comparison to mention to Daniel, but the factor of psychological readiness would be similar.

"What do you do now?"

"I'll have a driver smuggle you back to Jordan where you can get your flight back to the U.S. While you're doing that, our construction people will tear down this place. We leased an oil tanker that's currently docked in the Port of Eilat. We've welded the steel landing pads onto the deck, so we're ready to load the helicopters, cover them with tarp, and set sail for the Persian Gulf. From the air we'll look just like any other oil tanker sailing for Kuwait. As soon as we get positioned in the Gulf, we'll launch. We'll take off from the oil tanker and land in Kuwait on our return. Just like we planned."

29

Protections for Jim Bob, not her.

April 1980

En route to Dallas.

Angie had slept and eaten very little since she'd arrived for the dry run almost two days earlier. On the plane back to Dallas, she forced herself to stay awake long enough to get the airline meal, and then she fell into a fitful sleep.

She dreamed the real assault was taking place and James was the hostage left behind in the Mushroom Inn warehouse at the back of the compound. Once again, the rescuers missed him. Just as the helicopters were set to take off, an Iranian military truck with a squad of soldiers broke through the compound gate and the soldiers began shooting at the helicopters. A ferocious firefight erupted, and all the Iranian soldiers were killed. Suddenly, she was in one of the helicopters with the hostages, and the floor was covered with blood. Then her dream put her back in the warehouse, huddling with James as they waited for the Iranian guards to come and take whatever vengeance they could for the mayhem. She and James clung to each other, the cloying smell of their sweat and dirt and teargas stinging her nostrils.

She jerked awake, and the passenger next to her recoiled. Angie ran her trembling fingers through her hair as she grappled with the meaning of the dream. That nightmare was not going to happen, she told herself. Daniel was so good at rescue missions that none of the hostages would die. They all would be freed. She had to believe that.

Teheran

James lay on the floor mattress trying to control his heart palpitations with the meditation exercises Kathryn Koob had urged on him. Just as he began to relax, a key turned in the door, and his pulse jumped. Relief flooded through him when he saw that it was Akbar.

"You look better than the last time I saw you," said Akbar.

"No thanks to your medical student who never brought me the Valium he promised." James sat up and made room for the Iranian to sit next to him on the mattress.

"You seem to be doing okay on your own, so no harm done," said Akbar.

James rolled his eyes. "What's up?" he said.

Akbar looked puzzled. James laughed. "Just another piece of English slang. What's up? What's happening? What have you been doing?"

"'What's up?' I'll try to remember," said Akbar. "I found something for you. A book on the history of Persia."

Akbar handed the book to him, and James did not know what to say. Amid the daily cruelty the hostages faced, every now and then someone would make a kind gesture. More often than not, it was Akbar.

"I've enjoyed the discussions you and I have had," said Akbar. "As a man with a philosophical bent, you might find this a help in understanding our traditions."

James turned the book over and back. He patted the Iranian on the shoulder.

"Thank you, Akbar. I, too, have enjoyed our talks. I will start reading it this afternoon."

When Akbar left, Lieutenant Taylor snorted from the other side of the room. "Why do you keep being so goddamned nice to these fuckers?"

James reflected for a second before pointing his hand at the other man. "I keep telling you, Gordon, if you want to survive in this world, you have to learn to draw distinctions between the fuckers, the naïve ideologues, and the decent people, like Akbar."

Dallas

With the dry runs completed, everything now depended on Daniel fine tuning his plan, bringing his commandos to their peak psychological readiness, and launching the operation. Angie found herself with a backlog of work that had piled up at Emergency Services Program while she'd been in the Israeli desert.

She drove on Thursday morning to the ESP office she had rented in an old warehouse building on the edge of downtown. She had picked the location because it was semi-deserted. Nowhere on the building was there a sign with the name of the office or even the initials, ESP. However, the empty liquor bottles and trash strewn on the pavement by the entrance always made her wary of who might be lurking, and she closed her hand around the mace container in her purse.

Once in the building, she turned on the teletype machine connected to Daniel's headquarters through a secure communications service called Telex. It flashed new bills to be paid. She arranged transfers from the Grand Cayman account through banks in St. Kitts, Bahamas, and Liechtenstein, to Daniel's numbered account in Zurich.

It took most of the morning to make the telephone calls and draft the telegrams to accomplish these tasks. As she sat back to relax afterwards, she noticed the dust that had built up in the office while she'd been out in the Israeli desert. Still filled with nervous energy, she grabbed a cloth to wipe off all the surfaces. Anything to keep her mind off Daniel's upcoming operation and the dangers it posed to James and the other hostages.

She appreciated the responsibilities Jim Bob had given her. Added to the experience she'd picked up working summers in the back office of Charlie's hedge fund, she was learning a great deal about managing finances. Especially useful had been a course at Southern Methodist University in the VisiCalc spreadsheet that Jim Bob had insisted she take. Without it she'd never have been able to keep track of the millions of dollars passing through ESP.

"You can't let any of this leak out, Angie," Jim Bob had stressed at the start. "With all these circuitous transfers of funds you will make, we've built a security firewall. But, if any snoopy reporters get an inkling of what we're doing, they'll bust their balls trying to breach that firewall. So will the FBI. They would make your life a living hell. And if the White House decided we were interfering with their foreign policy, who knows how much prison time we'd be risking?"

In her mind, it would be worth the risk of jail time if she could free James and the other hostages. Why Jim Bob ran that risk, she wasn't certain.

Nonetheless, she shared his obsession with security. In event they were raided, she wanted to leave no incriminating evidence in the office overnight. So mid-afternoon that Thursday, just as she did every afternoon, she saved the spreadsheet to floppy disks and erased all data from the Apple II 8-bit computer. To use the spreadsheet the next day, she would need to reinsert data from the previous day's floppies. She stuffed every critical paper document into a folder and shredded the rest.

It took two trips down to her car to carry her personal belongings, the floppies, the documents, and the bag of shredded paper. She tossed the bag into a dumpster and brought the other materials to a safe deposit box for Jim Bob. The ESP office, itself, was stripped of any information that could link Jim Bob to what Daniel was doing in Teheran. Even the teletype machine had been turned off, and turning it back on the next day, required a password that only Angie knew.

All these precautions, she realized, were protections for Jim Bob, not her. If for whatever reason, she might someday need to dig out anything from the record, she wouldn't have access to it. Accordingly, she made duplicate copies of everything for herself. After she dropped Jim Bob's copies in his safe deposit box, she drove to her own bank to deposit her copies of the records in a safe deposit box of her own. Jim Bob, she reasoned, would be happier if she didn't tell him about this second safe deposit box.

Picking up a gyro sandwich and a can of Coke from a nearby Greek deli, she went home with hopes of relaxing by the TV. She fell asleep in the middle of the show *Taxi*, woke up at midnight, and went to bed.

30

"A guest of the Revolution."

April 1980

Dallas

The phone jarred Angie awake at three a.m.. She was lying on her side with her arm curled around a pillow, as if it were James. My God, she thought, glancing at the alarm clock, something must have happened to Charlie. Completely awake now, she jumped out of bed and ran to the phone hanging on the wall in the kitchen.

It was Jim Bob. "Take a look at the TV! Then get to your office, and I'll meet you there."

She clicked on the TV, wondering if Daniel had carried out his mission already. With any luck she would see his helicopters on the ground in Kuwait, with 53 smiling hostages now returned to freedom.

She sucked in her breath as the stunning picture came into view. The blackened hulk of a helicopter and the carcass of a four-engine plane lay immobilized next to each other in a treeless desert. In the background, someone in a strident voice read a White House announcement about the failure of a daring raid. "The president has ordered the cancellation of an operation in Iran which was underway to prepare for a rescue of our hostages."

Without bothering to brush her hair, she stepped into a pair of jeans and pulled on a baggy SMU sweatshirt with red spaghetti sauce stains on the front. She stopped at an all-night diner to pick up coffees. If the deserted location of ESP was dicey during the daytime, it was downright scary at three in the morning. She parked on the sidewalk next to the entrance, gripped her mace container, hurried through the outer door, locked it behind her, and sped up the steps to the ESP office on the second floor.

While she waited for Jim Bob to arrive, she switched on the office TV. The photo of the burned-out planes had been replaced by an angry looking U.S. Army colonel wearing the distinctive green beret of the Special Forces. A cigarette dangled from his lips.

Colonel Charles Beckwith had led several helicopters, planes, and more than a hundred Special Forces commandos to a staging area in the Iranian desert in a rescue mission called Operation Eagle Claw. From their staging area, they intended to assault the U.S. Embassy compound in Teheran, but equipment failures forced Beckwith to abort his mission. On the way out, a helicopter collided with a tanker, sparking massive explosions of fuel and ammunition that destroyed both planes and killed eight men. Beckwith flew his remaining men and planes out to safety. Angie shuddered as she watched the screen.

She handed Jim Bob one of the coffees when he showed up. Then she sank into the swivel desk chair in front of the computer. He sat in a hardbacked chair off to the side and pulled the lid off his coffee cup. Muting the TV, she repeated the latest announcement to him.

"What now?" she asked.

"It's off."

"I don't mean them," she said, using the coffee cup in her hand to point at the TV. Some of the coffee spilled on her sweatshirt to mingle with the spaghetti stains. "I meant us. Our mission. What do we do now?"

"It's off," he repeated.

Teheran

James hooked his toes under the radiator to begin his twenty sit-ups. Habib and four guards burst into his room. They screamed at the hostages to stop what they were doing. While one guard pointed his rifle at them, Habib the Liar and the other guards shackled their wrists and pulled blindfold hoods over their heads. They pushed the men out of the building and into the back of an empty van.

Every pothole they hit sent shockwaves up James' spine. Fortunately, the ride was short. When Habib pulled the blindfold off their heads, James looked up, dismayed at the sign on the building. Evin House of Detention.

"So, you're putting us in a prison now, Habib. You finally admit that we are prisoners you are holding illegally under international law."

"You are not a prisoner, Mr. Whitcomb. You are a guest of the revolution. In his great mercy, the Ayatollah wishes you to be in a place where you will be safer than you were before."

The prison guards pushed James into a cell along with a man he knew to be a CIA officer. This meant, James reasoned, that the guards still believed he was CIA. Had the revolutionaries finally decided to execute the CIA officers and brought them to the prison for that purpose? None of it made sense. After six months being held in the embassy, what happened to dictate this sudden move? James' heart palpitations, which had abated in the morning, returned. He sat on the floor, closed his eyes and tried to meditate away the anxiety.

By next morning, the heart beats had returned to normal. James and his cellmate were sitting on the floor, leaning against a wall, trying to ignore the smell from the slop bucket of urine and feces in a corner of the cell. Suddenly, they both jumped at the unmistakable sound of a whip's crack. Just like the sound made by a lion tamer's whip.

After the whip crack came the victim's voice pleading in Farsi, "Mercy, please."

The whip cracked again, followed by more begging. James turned to his roommate and saw the same look of terror in his eyes that James felt.

Then, the sound of the whipping was blotted out by the loud crescendo of the finale to Tchaikovsky's *1812 Overture*, with drums beating and cannons firing. The rest of the piece was not played. Just the thunderous finale over and over. Some guard, with access to a tape recorder, must have made a loop of the finale to cover up the sounds of the Iranian being whipped.

But there was a small gap between the end of the tape and its start-up again, and the crack of the whip sneaked into that gap. James clasped his hands over his ears and focused on his breathing. But the music, the crack of the whip, and the screams of the victim were fixed in his brain. This was a piece of music he never wanted to hear again.

Emergency Services Program

"Off?" Angie repeated what Jim Bob had just said, her eyebrows furrowed in a befuddled look. "But we've come so close. There must be some way Daniel can pick up the hostages while the Iranians are distracted by that mess in the desert." She pointed again at the image of the blackened aircraft on the TV screen.

Jim Bob leaned forward and set his coffee cup on the computer desk. He spoke softly. "Unless he's already launched, he has to abort. He's lost the critical element of surprise. You know that, and so does he. At this point, the Iranians will shoot down any planes that violate their air space. And they'll scatter the hostages around the country to make another rescue impossible."

She sank back into her desk swivel chair, deflated. All that work for nothing. James and the other hostages might be worse off now than they were before. Her lip quivered at the thought of what might happen to him.

"What do we do now?" Her voice was hoarse, almost whispery.

"I need you to close down this office. Transfer the balance of our Grand Cayman account into Daniel's account in Switzerland so he has enough cash to pay off his people and his contractors. Then close the Grand Cayman account."

"What if that's not enough money for him? Or too much?"

"I have a secure phone number where he can call me. We'll sort things out that way."

"What else do you want me to do?"

"Before you close out the bank account, give yourself a five-thousand-dollar bonus, so you can relocate somewhere. I want you out of Dallas as soon as we close this office. We want to wipe out any trace of it. Shut down your telephone lines, your mail delivery, your newspaper subscriptions, anything that connects this office with the outside world. I'll send my driver over this morning to help you remove every single thing from here."

She began to swivel listlessly in the computer chair. "We did all this work and came so close, and it all falls apart at the last minute."

"We're lucky it was the president's operation that collapsed. If it had been ours, the dead people would be our responsibility, not the president's. We'd have the FBI on our backs and dozens of TV reporters shouting questions at us."

She glanced down at the paper cup in her hand, the once fresh aroma of the coffee now gone flat. "You and Daniel have thrown heart and soul into this mission. I'm sorry now I got you into it," said Angie.

"Don't be sorry about that. Daniel can use a lot of the equipment for his security business. He'll find some people to buy the helicopters at a markup, for which he'll get ten percent. And his Kuwaiti contact will arrange for us to load oil into the tanker. This will get us into the oil shipping business. That's where the money is."

Angie stopped swiveling. Her jaw dropped "Oil shipping? Ten percent? Where the money is? You've been doing all this just to make a quick buck? I thought you were doing it to save them."

"We did our best, but there were huge costs involved in this project. Any businessman would do what he could to cover them. There isn't any necessary conflict between patriotism and turning a small profit."

"People could have been killed on this operation. You were risking peoples' lives just to make more money? Don't you already have enough?" Her voice grew louder, and Jim Bob rose to his feet, taking on a more commanding position.

"I was the one risking their lives? What makes you so high and mighty? You knew people might get killed when you first talked to me. You saw how dangerous it was when you went on that dry run. And you plowed ahead anyway."

"I trembled at the idea that one of the hostages might get killed, but I didn't take that risk to make money. I did it so we could save them. You don't really care about them."

"Of course, I care. But you can't blame me for hedging my bets. Christ, your father runs a hedge fund. Didn't you ever pay any attention to what that means?"

Angie stood up. She'd focused so much on the mission itself, she'd paid too little attention to Jim Bob's motives. She'd been naïve. A fool. A wave of anger grew inside her.

She jutted her jaw at Jim Bob, who towered over her. She was so angry it was hard not to scream at him. Forcing herself to speak slowly in a controlled soft voice, she said, "I'm out! You can keep that five-thousand-dollar bonus. You can close this place down by yourself. And if the FBI comes around asking about all the things we've been doing, don't expect me to be the fall guy who goes to prison while you try to cover your ass."

She stepped out of the room and sped down the hall to the stairs. Jim Bob rushed after her, but she was already down the stairs and at the door by the time he got to the top of the steps.

"Stop right there," he shouted. "Nobody runs out on me."

She pushed the door open to step through, and he screamed as she slammed the door behind her. "You'll regret this!"

Dallas, On the Run

Fuming, Angie roared away from the parking lot. She clenched the steering wheel and let up on the gas pedal. This was no time to get stopped for a traffic violation.

She took her right hand off the steering wheel and pounded the dashboard. She'd always suspected Jim Bob was untrustworthy. That was why she'd kept all those backup copies. Just in case Jim Bob tried to double-cross her. She should have been ready for something like this. She slapped the dashboard once more.

Jim Bob's last statement echoed through her mind. What did he mean when he said she'd regret deserting him? Charlie had warned her early on that Jim Bob was dangerous. And Jacob the seismologist had accused him of violence to keep his workers in line. Why had she so stupidly threatened to rat on him if she got trapped by the FBI? Would he send thugs after her as Jacob said he had sent after the union organizers in his company?

Even more urgent in her mind was James. Up until now, at least she had known that he was being held at the embassy compound. If the hostages got scattered around the country as Jim Bob predicted, she'd have no idea where James was. Would the Iranians retaliate for Carter's rescue attempt by torturing the hostages? Shooting them? A shiver ran up her spine as the possibilities stampeded through her mind.

Her mind also ran wild with all of the things Jim Bob might do to take revenge on her. Instead of fretting about the threat he posed, she needed to calm down and move out of her apartment into a secure hotel where she could safely stay until she made arrangements to head back to New York.

She found a Hilton Inn on Mockingbird Lane, within walking distance of SMU. It was much pricier than she wanted, but it would only be until she decided what to do, and she had plenty of money left from the State Department settlement to pay for it. Still wearing the baggy SMU sweatshirt with coffee stains, and surrounded by people wearing suits and dresses, she felt ill at ease standing by the check-in desk asking for a room.

With her housing secured, she went to clean out her apartment. She drove around the block once to make sure no one was sitting in the parking lot waiting for her. Flustered, her rear wheel bounced over the curb, and she almost hit a woman who was walking her dog. Angie rolled down her window to apologize, but the woman flipped her the bird.

As quickly as possible, she cleared everything out of the apartment and cancelled her newspaper subscription so unread papers would not collect at her doorstep.

Thoughts raced breakneck through her mind as she drove her belongings to her new quarters. She should give Charlie her new phone number at the hotel. But she hadn't figured out yet what to tell him when he inevitably hit her with a barrage of questions about why she'd moved into a hotel.

It wasn't until two-thirty that she called Evie at Zenith Capital. "Would you give Charlie my new phone number?"

"Where are you? Your phone's been disconnected."

"Oh dear," said Angie. "Maybe you should transfer me to him."

"Okay. But make sure you're sitting down." The phone went silent for a moment until Charlie's voice came on.

"What the hell have you been doing?" he screamed.

"I've been busy."

"You're so busy you had to disconnect your phone?"

"It's complicated."

"You're goddamned right it's complicated. Jim Bob's threatening to pull his money out of my fund."

"I'm sorry, Charlie."

"You're sorry? He's got five million dollars he might pull out. Do you have any idea how many peoples' salaries that represents?"

"I'm sorry," she repeated. She twirled the phone cord between her fingers.

"He called you a spoiled brat. I told you to stay away from him. What the hell did you do?"

"I need your advice, Charlie, but it's too complicated to explain over the phone. Can I fly up to New York and talk to you in the morning?"

"No! Tell me now."

"It's not something we can talk about over the phone. I'll get a flight out of here this evening. Can you stop by my apartment in Greenwich Village on your way to the office in the morning?"

"Since you're the one causing problems for me, rather than vice versa, I want you to show up at my office when it opens."

She shook her fists in exasperation, but realized he couldn't see her. "Charlie, I'm telling you. We can't let anybody overhear us when we talk. I mean *anybody*. Please stop by the apartment."

Washington Square

When she heard Charlie's steps on the stairs, Angie set a pot of coffee and a plate of bagels on the coffee table in front of the sofa. She opened the door for him and said, "I would've made you breakfast, but I got in late, and the only thing I could find were these bagels and cream cheese."

He simply draped his coat over the back of the sofa and sat down before he said a word.

"I didn't come here for breakfast, Angelita, I came here to find out what the hell's been going on with you and Jim Bob Jones."

Nonetheless, he spread cream cheese on the bagel and took a bite. "You owe me an explanation."

"I'll tell you everything," she replied. "But you have to understand that I will be in deep legal trouble if you let any of this slip out to the public."

"Legal trouble?" He squinted.

"Yes."

"Then you'd better be very careful in what you say. A father is not protected from testifying against his child like he is from testifying against his spouse. I could be forced to repeat everything you tell me."

"If it stays secret, it will never come to a trial. But if it does, your testimony won't hurt me. The only honorable thing I can do is admit what I did. Jim Bob and I organized a mission to rescue James and the other hostages."

The bagel fell from Charlie's fingers onto the plate. "You did what?"

"Let me start at the beginning."

The more she told him, the more agitated he became. He spilled coffee when he lifted his cup off the tray. He paced the length of the floor. He looked out the window. He sank down into the seat and stared at her.

"What were you thinking? If the FBI finds out about this, you could go to prison."

"Only if they find out."

At that point, the kitchen phone rang, and Glenna's voice came through the receiver when Angie picked it up. She handed the phone to Charlie and returned to the living room sofa where she toyed with the ivory chess pieces on the coffee table. She never played chess these days, but she kept the set on display because it brought back warm memories of the boys in Tunis who had given it to her. Angie heard Charlie tell Glenna he would have to miss their luncheon date. He'd explain when he got home.

Angie looked up alarmed when he returned to the couch. "Charlie, you can't tell Glenna anything about Jim Bob and the rescue attempt. She'd never be able to keep it a secret."

"Stop worrying that I might tell anyone. Your big worry is Jim Bob's fear that *you* will let the story slip out."

"You think he might send out his goons to shut me up?"

"He's done it before with others."

"That'll backfire. I kept copies of all the spreadsheets, correspondence, and invoices in my safe deposit box. I have account numbers, receipts, notes on his instructions to me. Just let him know that you'll send it all to the FBI if anything happens to me."

"Move all that stuff to your safe deposit box in Switzerland."

"Why?"

"The FBI can force its way into your safe deposit box here, but it can't for the one in Switzerland."

She curled her hands and glanced at the bitten fingernails. "If only Daniel had launched his mission two days earlier, James and the other hostages would be out of there now."

Charlie straightened up in his seat. "And some of them would be dead."

She gritted her teeth.

"Angelita, what makes you think Daniel Laveen could have succeeded when the president failed, despite all the resources he had? The Navy, the Air Force, the Army, the

Special Forces, the CIA, and the White House. If they couldn't run an operation without getting eight men killed, you would also have had people killed."

"Charlie, you should have seen the dry run. It was a lightning strike with tear gas, night vision capability, and overwhelming fire power that grabbed control of the compound the moment we touched down. We were in and out in forty minutes."

Charlie shook his head. "Everything depended on achieving complete surprise, so that nobody could shoot back at you. In real life, that's unlikely. And once the shooting starts, everything changes. I know that from my own experience."

"You might be right." She tugged at a strand of loose thread on one of the couch pillows. "What really grates on me is that I let myself be duped by Jim Bob. I should have paid more attention to his motives for helping me out. All he wanted was to use me for a money-making operation."

"So what if he wanted to make a little money? He went along with the rescue plan. Hell, he funded it. Doesn't that count for something?"

"I guess," she said. "Maybe it was a mistake to desert him at a critical moment. But I can't undo what's already been done."

"What are your plans now?" he asked.

"I'm too depressed to make plans. Even before all this happened, I'd sit around biting my nails while I worried about James." She curled her fingers again to glance at the nibbled ends of the nails.

31

"There have to be consequences for what you did."

May 1980

Teheran

A week passed for James with no more sounds of flogging, but the incident had etched itself in his mind. He paced back and forth in the small cell, tensing his shoulders involuntarily each time he heard footsteps outside the cell door. Was he the next person to be dragged out and whipped? Or his cellmate? Suddenly, the sound of guards chattering came through the eye-level slit in the steel door. James stopped pacing and put his ear to the opening.

"What'd they say?" whispered his cellmate, moving next to James.

James motioned for his friend to stay away from the window. If the guards saw two people at the slot, they might slide the window shut. After a moment, James turned slack-jawed to his companion.

"Carter tried a rescue attempt."

"Jesus. And they missed us?"

"It sounds like they missed everybody." James jerked his thumbs to the guards in the corridor. "The only thing those guys seem to know is that two of our planes crashed in the desert, and we're being scattered around the country."

"Any casualties in that attempt?"

James shrugged. His friend let his head bump against the cold metal door. "Oh, God. We might rot here forever."

James slid down to a sitting position, a piece of peeling paint falling into his lap. He rested his elbows on his knees and placed his head in his hands. The Iranians were bound to retaliate somehow. He shuddered as he recalled the cries of the prisoner being whipped the week before. Would he ever get out of this alive and return to Angie? He lifted his head and forced himself to rework a segment of the memoir he was mentally composing. Try as he might to ignore it, he couldn't stop a churning in his stomach.

Two days later, guards pulled James and his friend out of their cell. They did not put blindfolds on the heads of the two hostages, and this change in routine convinced James that they were being led to the torture cell to be whipped. He dug in his heels, but the guards dragged him out anyway. When he saw they were being led outdoors to the prison yard rather than to a torture cell, his terror spiked. This must mean that they were going to be tied to an execution stake and shot. He forced himself to stand erect and march forward. Damned if he was going to cringe.

Instead of being tied to stakes, they were pushed into the back of a van. With wrists bound in front of him, he leaned against the side panel of the van and closed his eyes. He was bathed in sweat, despite the chilly Spring morning.

An elbow nudged him in the ribs, and he opened his eyes to see Smitty. James smiled at his friend. "Hey, old buddy. Good to see you in one piece."

"No speak," shouted one of the guards, jabbing his rifle into James' ribs for emphasis.

Where were they headed? And for what purpose? He bounced on the floor each time the van hit a pothole or bump. They stopped at another prison, where the three of them were placed in a big cell already holding another of the Embassy's CIA officers. Why were the guards always putting him in with CIA officers? They must still think he was CIA.

Their new prison was less terrifying than Evin Prison had been. There was no whipping of prisoners, but it was still a prison. He was locked in a cell that, like the old one, smelled of urine, and he faced a constant battle to keep the cockroaches at bay.

Zenith Capital Management

Charlie motioned for Angie to sit in the chair facing his desk. He was still pissed, she saw. He usually offered her a coffee and sat with her on the couch. Charlie leaned his elbows on the desktop as he started to speak.

"I talked with Jim Bob Jones."

Her shoulders tensed. Although the threat of Jim Bob had never disappeared, she'd been able to push it into the recesses of her mind.

"I convinced him not to harm you in any way whatsoever."

Angie leaned forward as the tension went out of her shoulders. "Oh, Charlie, I'm so relieved. And grateful. How did you do that?"

"Last month, you mentioned a lot of incriminating materials about that crazy rescue scheme you and he concocted."

She bristled at the word crazy, but the stern look on Charlie's face deterred her from objecting.

"Did you take your materials to Switzerland, as I advised, and stick them in your safe deposit box there?"

She nodded.

"Good, because that's what I told him, and he doesn't want to go to prison for money laundering or any of the other crimes you and he committed. I promised him that all of those materials will stay under lock and key as long as you stay healthy and unmolested. He in turn agreed to leave you alone as long as those materials never see the light of day."

She grinned and tossed her head at Charlie's chutzpah, her long curly hair fluffing with the motion.

"However, all of this comes at a cost." He slid a sheet of paper across his desk toward her. It listed half a dozen names.

"What's this."

"Jim Bob is pulling his assets out of our fund. At our two percent management fee, this will cause enough loss of revenue that two of the people listed on this page will have to be let go."

Grimacing, she looked down at the list and recognized every name.

"Why are you showing me this?"

"If you'd stayed away from Jim Bob like I told you to, they wouldn't be facing dismissal. Why shouldn't you know who's paying the price for your actions?"

Shocked at his bluntness, she looked into his unblinking eyes. "Isn't there some way to absorb the costs?"

"That simply pushes the costs onto the shareholders of the company. Glenna's a shareholder. How do you think she'll react to sharing the costs? And Michael's shares are reserved to pay for his college, just as yours were. Why should he have to pay the price?"

Angie bent forward and stared at the names. "Oh God, I never intended for anything like this to happen. There has to be some way to get around firing these people."

She looked up at him. He had leaned back in his chair and steepled his fingertips.

"I've got it," she said. "Couldn't we handle it by attrition? Continue their salaries until two people resign and move on to something else?"

"The economy is in a recession right now. Nobody's going to quit their job during a recession."

"Eventually people will move on, and eventually you'll get enough new clients to make up for the loss of Jim Bob."

"And how do I pay these salaries in the meantime?"

She slouched back on the chair and closed her eyes to avoid Charlie's gaze. When she opened them, he was still staring at her.

"I never meant for this to happen, Charlie, but I concede that I'm to blame. I'll do whatever you want to make up for it."

"I want you to contribute your monthly trust fund allowance to help cover these salaries."

"What'll I live on?"

"Like everyone else in the world, you'll have to figure that out. You still have funds from your settlement with the State Department. You get an allotment check from James' salary each month. Or, I suppose, you could get a job."

"How long do we do this?"

"Until two people on this list voluntarily move on to other jobs or until new investors come in to make up for the revenue that you cost us."

She nodded. "That's fair."

"There have to be consequences for what you did," said Charlie, "and this is the only thing I have control over. Even though the money's substantial, that's not the big issue."

He stood up and walked to the front of the desk where he towered over her. "Somehow, you sucked two people into a scheme that was unbelievably reckless and dangerous. You're lucky that you aren't in prison or that you didn't get somebody killed. I don't know any other way to impress on you the gravity of what you did. And given your ability to persuade others to join something like this, I fear for what you might do in the future."

She was speechless as she sat staring at him. For as long as she could remember she had shared a bond of trust with Charlie. As much as she hated to admit it, he was right. She had been reckless. She stared down at her feet, wanting the meeting to be over, but not knowing how to end it. Fortunately, his secretary popped her head through the door to announce that his next appointment had arrived.

32

"That's a bad idea."

July 1980

Teheran

Two guards pulled James out of his cell, and he quivered as they rushed him down a corridor. What now? Every change in routine made him fear the worst. Maybe it was his turn to be flogged while the finale of "The 1812 Overture" played in the background.

His fears eased as the guards stopped in front of an office. They pushed him into the room, and he broke into a broad grin as he saw Akbar sitting at a table. If this ordeal ever ended and the hostages were set free, Akbar would be the only Iranian he would miss. James hadn't seen him since the day Akbar had given him the book on Persian history. James sat down across from him and said, "I started reading the book you gave me, but it got lost when we were moved to Evin Prison, so I couldn't finish it."

"No need to apologize. I have news about one of your colleges," he said.

"Colleges?"

"Yes. One of your friends here."

James laughed. "Colleague, not college. You mean one of my colleagues."

Akbar tugged at his mustache. "I must remember. Colleague. One of them is being sent home."

James snapped to attention. If one person was being released, others would undoubtedly follow.

"Which one?"

"Richard Queen. His health is deteriorating," said Akbar.

James grimaced. "You should have listened to us back in November when we told you that. He was already complaining about numbness and dizziness. And his hands were always shaking. He was right next to me when you guys put us through that mock execution, and he could barely hold his arms up."

"We're not the ones who did that," protested Akbar. "We were just student guards at the Embassy. The ones who did that were soldiers in the Revolutionary Guard who snuck into the building that night."

James started to object, then stopped. There was a clear distinction between the student guards at the embassy and the Revolutionary Guard organization that was aligned with the Ayathollah to preserve the revolution. Akbar was the closest thing he had to a friend among the guards and accusing him of being part of the mock execution might jeopardize their friendship. Especially if there was any chance of James being released.

"Well, if you're sending people home for health reasons, take a look at Jerry Miele, wherever you've put him. He's in bad shape."

"Queen's health got so bad, we took him to a neurologist, and he seems to have developed multiple sclerosis. Sending him home was the humane thing to do."

Humaneness had nothing to do with it, James thought bitterly. They simply didn't want the bad publicity that would result if word got out that they imprisoned someone diagnosed with MS.

"Send the rest of us home. That would also be humane."

"That's out of my hands, and you know it."

James was pleased at Queen's release, but the visit from Akbar worsened his depression. Nothing in Akbar's words or tone suggested that any more hostage releases would take place. When he got back to his cell, he banged his fists on the wall in frustration.

Brooklyn

After the frantic winter organizing Daniel's rescue mission, spring and summer dragged for Angie. She resumed her attendance at the board of directors' meetings for the Manhattan Skating Club. To fill her time, she volunteered for every task that came up. By August, she was the most active member of the board. She upped her skating sessions to four times per week to cope with her anxieties, and she skated so strenuously that her clothes were soaked with sweat by the end of each session.

Her mind, however, could not ignore the fact that she hadn't received a single letter from James since January. She continued writing weekly letters to him and sending them to the State Department to be forwarded. It was unlikely he got any of them, and when she put them in the mail box, she felt as if she were dropping them into a black hole. Even if there was only one chance in a hundred a letter went through, she had to keep writing them.

Desperately needing something to fill in the long gaps of time on her hands, she phoned Barbara Rosen, wife of the press officer in Teheran. "I'm calling about the Family Liaison Action Group you helped start. I'm going nuts with anxiety, and the media seems to have put us on the back burner. Is there anything I can do to help you guys out?"

"Could you come over to Brooklyn for lunch?"

"No problem."

"Meet me at my house and I'll find a place where we can go."

When she reached Barbara's address, Angie pushed a bell at a gate in front of the house. A lone photographer snapped her photo as she was admitted. He was still there a moment later when the two women came out. Angie tried to avoid him, but Barbara made a joke with him before pulling open the door on a nearby car.

"They camp out in front of your house?" Angie asked.

"Not so much anymore. At the moment there's only that one photographer. They never camped out in front of your house?"

"Only once," she said, then laughed.

"What's so funny," asked Barbara as she started the car.

"You've probably saved me."

Barbara smiled. "How so?"

"I've seen you on TV. You're so poised and telegenic, that once they found you, they were apparently too lazy to go looking for anyone else."

"I'll admit that intellectual diligence doesn't seem to be an important quality for television. But the newspaper reporters are a lot sharper."

Barbara drove to a Jewish deli, where they compared notes on their lives. Angie felt an immediate connection to the tall, thirtyish woman. They both came from culturally mixed backgrounds. And both married men outside the Catholic religion they grew up in.

"I envy you," said Angie, toying with a napkin on the table.

"You envy me?"

"I live alone in an apartment off Washington Square Park. You've got this big family for comfort. Your children and your parents all living together."

"When this is all over, you can start your own family. And you've got some enviable traits yourself."

Angie smiled. "Thank you."

Barbara continued. "The first time I saw you was at that big meeting the State Department set up for us last Fall. You pushed me out of the way in your rush to get to Secretary of State Vance."

Angie blanched, but Barbara laughed. "But I loved it when you said the president was misunderstanding how to deal with the Iranians. Those were my thoughts exactly."

"Why didn't you say that?"

"I'd been at an earlier meeting with the president, a smaller meeting with only a few of the hostage families. I expressed my views then."

Angie shot up straight in her chair. "What an honor!"

"He was very sympathetic. I asked him not to take any military action that would put the hostages' lives at risk, and I showed him pictures of my children so he could see what was at stake."

Angie froze. As bad as her own situation was, what must it be like to tell small children that their father was locked up and might never return? She didn't know how to express her empathy without making it sound like pity, so she moved the conversation away from children.

"I admire the work you've done with the Family Liaison Action Group. It was brilliant the way you guys got the Europeans and the pope lined up behind us."

"We were grateful that the pope met with us, but his message would have had a bigger impact if he'd given us an exclusive audience."

"What about the European leaders?"

"I thought the German chancellor, Helmut Schmidt, was the most helpful. He said we should resist the feeding frenzy of the media over the hostages."

"What feeding frenzy?" Angie objected. "The media has forgotten about the hostages."

"According to him, that's exactly what we want."

"I don't see why."

"The more we criticized President Carter, the more popular the student revolutionaries became in Iran. If they hadn't gotten that publicity, their public support might have dropped and made it easier for the Iranian government to release the hostages."

Angie shook her head. "Maybe, but I'm skeptical."

"Then consider this. When Vance met with us in November, do you remember him saying he would avoid military action?"

"Yes," said Angie.

"But day after day the president was bludgeoned by the media to do something. So he mounted a rescue mission that ended up killing eight soldiers. It could just as easily have been Barry who was killed. Or James." Barbara's eyes hardened as she said this.

"I understand what you're saying," said Angie. "But it's hard for me to sit back and do nothing."

"You could come out to our next Family Liaison Group meeting. Can you afford to fly to San Francisco?"

Even though her monthly trust fund allowance had been eliminated so she could pay back what she owed to Zenith Capital Management, she still had the State Department settlement to help with her travels and activities. Barbara and most of the other active spouses squeezed the costs of their activities out of their own middle-class incomes. "I can manage," she said.

"Good. One of the items on our agenda will be whether we should try to send a delegation of clergy to console the hostages next Christmas."

Angie's eyes widened. "Oh, Barbara, that's a bad idea."

Barbara's face lit up in a big smile. "Yes, it is. Personally, I'm grateful to Reverend Coffin for some courtesies he extended to Barry and me last year. But let's face it, the Iranians turned that Christmas pageant into a propaganda stunt. We don't need another one. I'd like to have you at the meeting to help me argue against it."

33

Imagine.

December 1980

Teheran

James's conditions improved as summer gave way to autumn. The harsh treatment he and the other hostages received immediately after the takeover diminished. His hands remained unbound unless he was being transported somewhere. He conversed often with other hostages and he was given times each week when he could walk outside.

Often, he found himself dwelling on pleasant moments in his life. He'd recall the day he and Angie had ice skated at Rockefeller Center. How she'd steadied him until he got the hang of it. How alluring she had looked in her pink tights and skimpy skirt. And the grace with which she did leaps and spins and glided on one foot with the other one pointing out behind her. He cringed at the lack of enthusiasm he had shown at skating with her. It was an activity that meant so much to her he should have been more supportive. He vowed that he'd make it up to her if he ever got out of Iran. He would skate with her at least once a week.

One night he lay awake and the picture of Angie in his mind faded into that of his Farsi instructor back at the Foreign Service Institute. He clenched his fists to force the image from his mind. He never should have had that affair with her. It had happened when he didn't know where he stood with Angie. She had not yet accepted his marriage proposal, and he wasn't sure she was going to accept it. She had remained in Tunis while he went off to D.C. to start the Farsi classes. And the friendly, blue-eyed Iranian Farsi instructor had been so available. James broke off the affair the moment Angie accepted his proposal. But the image was fixed in his mind of the first time the Farsi instructor pulled off her sweater, revealing her bare breasts. He forced himself to think of Angie on the ice rink in her pink tights and sexy little skirt.

Once, in September, a Russian MIG warplane flew in low over the city. Iran didn't use Russian planes, he knew, but Iraq did. Less than a minute later came the thump, thump, of distant explosions. Two guards came out to push James toward the building. Before being shoved inside, he looked over his shoulder and saw other warplanes in the sky. Iran was obviously at war with Iraq. How long had this been going on? He strode rapidly back to his cell, eager to share the news with his cellmate Smitty. War with Iraq would pressure the Iranians to release the hostages. A country can handle only so many crises at one time.

Early in December, the guards put blindfolds on the hostages, bound their wrists, and once again loaded them into vans. James rubbed his head against the wall of the van to loosen his blindfold. By tilting his head back, he could peer through an opening below the blindfold and see where they were heading. Hopefully to the airport. But, no, instead of going in that direction they were driving north toward the city's affluent neighborhoods. Near the edge of the city, they passed through the gates of what appeared to be a large estate.

"Where are we?" James asked the driver of the van.

"You're at a guesthouse the government maintains," answered the driver as he pulled to a stop.

Despite its peeling paint and cracked floor tiles, the mansion looked luxurious compared to the prisons where James had spent the previous half year. He, Smitty, and two other men were given beds in a room that had a view of the outdoors. Adjacent to their room was a bathroom with a shower. When James turned the faucet to see if it worked, he was astounded to discover hot water flowing out of the shower head. He quickly undressed and ducked into the stream of water.

He lingered for several minutes to luxuriate in the pleasure of the hot water flowing over his body, and eventually Smitty shouted, "Give someone else a chance at that shower, James, before you use up all the hot water."

Outside their window was a school, and they awoke the next morning to the sound of children chanting, "Death to Carter! Death to Saddam Hussein!" Maybe the chants were aimed at the school's new American neighbors. Or maybe they were just part of the curriculum. James shook his head in dismay that children would be taught to chant death, whatever the target.

The next day, other hostages poured into the guest house. They were herded into small groups and shunted to separate rooms. Along with them came Habib the Liar, whom James hadn't seen since they had been rushed out of the embassy compound. Habib smiled, lit a cigarette, and slapped James on the back as though they were old friends rather than adversaries. He lit a cigarette.

"Your people threw out that devil, Carter. Reagan beat him."

"Reagan won the election?" the four hostages said, almost in unison. Smiles broke out on all their faces.

"Your people now support us and our revolution," said Habib.

"Nonsense," said James. "Reagan called you barbarians and uncivilized."

"You lie!" shouted Habib.

"You yourself told me that several months ago," retorted James.

Like most other Foreign Service Officers, James kept his political partisanship private, but he felt certain that Reagan's victory increased their chances for release. If the Iranians wanted a negotiated settlement, they had a lot of incentive to conclude it before the hardliner Reagan became president on January 20. The four Americans gave each other high fives and speculated on how soon they would be released. Habib looked on puzzled at why the hostages thought they would be freed so quickly.

Christmas came and went, but the hostages remained stranded in the guest house mansion. Although it was the best accommodation they'd had since April, it was nonetheless still a prison. A prison from which their hope of a quick release was dwindling.

New York

For one of the few times in her life, Angie found herself with too little to do. Fearing that her anxiety over James would make it difficult to concentrate on her schoolwork at NYU, she had dropped down to the one course which captivated her, Introduction to Kinesiology. She harbored dreams of opening a skating academy for underprivileged kids, and kinesiology would be useful. She remained on the board of directors for the Manhattan Skating Club, but board meetings were infrequent. On top of that, her hopes to become more involved with FLAG didn't materialize. The main activity she looked forward to each week was a Friday lunch with her friend Jenna.

Late in the evening On December eighth, Angie had radio music playing in the background as she crammed for a test the next afternoon. Suddenly, the music stopped, and the disk jockey announced that the famed musician and ex-Beatle, John Lennon, had just been shot and killed outside his Manhattan apartment.

Angie had been a Beatle fan since she'd been a small child, and this was just one piece too much of dreary news. She recalled times when one or another Beatle song spoke to some difficult moment in her life. She turned off the radio and put the first Beatles album she found onto the stereo. It opened with John Lennon himself singing "Imagine." But with James now a hostage, and one of her favorite singers now dead, she found it impossible to imagine a world without nations and wars and conflict, as the song urged. If only we could imagine that, she thought.

The next morning, she dragged herself to the subway station and headed uptown to Lennon's apartment building off Central Park. Hundreds of people crowded around the building. Maybe thousands. Many were in tears. Several carried placards expressing their concerns.

LOVE!
JOHN!
WHY?

Why indeed? she thought as she elbowed her way through the crowd to set a rose amid the dozens of others that had already been placed there. She stood mingling with the somber crowd but found no one in the mood to talk. Wiping a tear from her eye, she ambled back to the subway and rode down to NYU to take her kinesiology test.

34

"We just passed out of Iranian airspace."

January 1981

Teheran

On January nineteenth, a doctor came to the guest house to give each hostage a cursory exam. "This has to be it," exclaimed Smitty, giving James a high five. "Why bother giving us a physical, if they weren't shipping us out."

But nighttime came with nothing else happening. James' anxiety began to rise again.

"What time will it be here when it's noon tomorrow in Washington," he asked Smitty.

"Eight-thirty at night. Why?"

"That's when Reagan's inauguration takes place. If the Iranians can't strike a deal with Carter to get us out, they'll never be able to strike one with a hardliner like Reagan."

In the morning, Habib ordered the hostages to pack their things into plastic bags and take them to a large reception room. Noontime came without a meal being served. One by one, the hostages were taken from the room and not returned. Was James being left behind while the others headed to the airport?

Habib tapped him on the shoulder in mid-afternoon and led him to the dining room where Nilufar, in her long black chador, sat at an old mahogany table. A guard stood to the side with a video camera.

Oh God, James said to himself. Not Screaming Mary! Not now!

Nilufar waited for the camera to point in her direction before she spoke. "Through the generous mercy of the Ayatollah, we want to give you the opportunity to express your appreciation for the care you received after your president abandoned you."

"He didn't abandon us. You invaded the U.S. Embassy and took us prisoner."

"That was no embassy. It was a den of spies that we returned to the rightful possession of the Iranian people. We will convert it into the Museum of the Revolution."

James refused to respond. He had no desire to argue philosophy at this point.

"Were you fed well?" she asked.

He didn't want to antagonize her, but he also didn't want to humiliate himself by making a televised statement that could be used for propaganda.

"We were fed."

She scowled. "And did you receive good medical care?"

"I had overwhelming headaches and persistent heart palpitations, and all you gave me was aspirin."

"We brought in a doctor to see you."

"It was a fucking medical student, and he said it was all in my head. He didn't even get me the Valium he promised."

She jumped up. "Ingrate!" Then she screamed at a guard, "Get that devil out of here."

Habib and a guard pulled him into the kitchen and bound him by the wrists to an old cast-iron stove.

"Why are you so hostile?" Habib shouted at him. "Don't you want to go home?"

James' heart pounded faster. He was becoming as recalcitrant as Metrinko. He recalled his acerbic colleague railing about Nilufar when the hostages had been first brought to the guest house. "If she were on fire on the street, I wouldn't piss on her to put it out."

The guards' afternoon call to prayers came, and James sat alone bound to the stove. The afternoon teatime passed with no food being served. The light streaming through the window began to fade as the sun went down, and guards in the hall began to murmur their early evening prayers. Somebody should start moving fast if they were going to get the hostages out of Iran by the critical moment of eight-thirty.

Still, no one came to get James.

Washington Square

On the morning of the twentieth, the State Department phoned Angie as she washed her breakfast dishes. An agreement had been signed to release the hostages, but they had not yet left Iran. She should watch the news for updates.

Elated, she threw the dishrag in the sink and turned on a twenty-four-hour news channel. Too excited to sit still, she paced the room. Then, she made café con leche, dusted the furniture, and paced the floor again. She sat down and buffed her nails, staring at the nubs left from her biting them. She turned the television to full volume so she could take a shower without fear of missing anything.

Dripping water on the floor she went back to the TV to turn it down. The television toggled back and forth between the endless parade of inauguration details and a jetliner parked on an airport tarmac in Tehran. Three hours to go. It was only nine in the morning.

She called her friend, Jenna. "James might get released today, and my anxiety is through the roof. Could you stop by to spend a little time before you go to class this afternoon?"

"I'd be honored to spend that moment with you. Give me an hour to get there."

She should serve Jenna something when she arrived. Somehow, coffee seemed too tame for the occasion. She poured half of a bottle of Irish Mist into a pitcher and added a small amount of pineapple juice. She set the pitcher on the living room coffee table, along with glasses and a bowl of ice cubes.

The phone rang while Angie waited for Jenna. A reporter from the *Daily News* wanted to know how she felt about President Carter's statement earlier that morning.

"I can't talk," she said. "The State Department might call, and I need to keep the line open." She set the phone back in its cradle.

Ten minutes later, the phone rang again. A reporter from *The New York Times* asked her to update him on the situation. She gave him the same message she'd given the other reporter and hung up.

Half an hour later, the *Daily News* reporter phoned back. "Did you get your call from the State Department yet?" he asked. She hung up without responding.

She didn't want to leave the phone off the hook, just in case she did get a call from anyone important to her. On the other hand, the State Department and all her friends had the number of her answering service and would leave a message.

She threw a blanket over the phone to muffle it, while she resolved to check her messages every half hour.

Teheran

With his wrist tethered to the iron stove and nothing to do, James fretted. Had he just wiped out his only chance to get out of Iran? If this anticipated release fell through, he might go mad. With his recurrent heart palpitations, periodic shortness of breath, and persistent depression, he feared that he was already halfway there.

He forced himself to think of something pleasant. And immediately coming into his mind was the image of his blonde, blue-eyed Farsi instructor unbuttoning her blouse. No! He must put that behind him. He recalled waking up in the mornings with Angie. She would always be the first one up, and she'd start the elaborate stretching exercises she said she needed to do to re-enter competitive skating. He found it erotic to watch her. She'd bend over on each side to an impossible degree. She'd balance on one leg at the foot of the bed and lift the other leg up until her toes pointed at the ceiling. When she felt playful, which was often, she'd bend over and hold her palms on the floor while she wiggled her butt before him. He would get up and pull her back to the bed. There must indeed be a God in heaven to have brought such a woman into his life. He yanked at the bindings that fastened his wrists to the cast iron stove. But the only thing he accomplished was to dig the bindings into his wrist.

———

The sun had already set when Habib returned, placed a blindfold over James' head, and led him outside. He guided James up the steps of what was obviously a bus and pushed him down the aisle to the rear. Half a dozen steps into the aisle, he stumbled over someone.

"Sorry," he said. "I can't see where I'm going."

"Don't worry about it," said the other. "Let's just hope we're getting out of here."

"No speak!" shouted a guard. Then came the sound of the door closing. The bus started to move.

They bumped along the roads in the dark, and James gritted his teeth in fear that this was just going to end up in another disappointment. He tried to see out from under the bottom of the blindfold, but it was too tight.

The bus finally stopped, and a guard pulled the hostages to the front. When James reached the door, someone ripped off his blindfold, and in the dim light, he could barely make out the words Mehrabad International Airport in both English and Farsi. A roar of shouting reached his ears. Between the bus and an Algerian airliner on the tarmac, a mass of Iranian young people stood screaming and shaking their fists. A path opened up, and the hostages were pushed one-by-one toward the plane. As each hostage passed through the gauntlet, the demonstrators jeered and shouted, "Death to America!"

James grinned in admiration as his fellow hostages held their heads high while being pushed through the corridor of abuse. Ahead of him was Kathryn Koob, whom he had come to admire for her composure. She paused and looked shaken as the demonstrators screamed, but she squared her shoulders and marched proudly between them.

As James stepped forward, one student struck him on the shoulder with a placard and shouted, "Death to Carter." James raised his two fists and extended his middle fingers. "Death to Khomeini!" he shouted in Farsi.

"Get those fingers down Whitcomb," yelled the man behind him. "Don't screw things up at this point."

As James stepped into the Boeing 727, a pretty stewardess said, "Welcome."

"Thank you," he replied in Arabic, drawing a smile from her. He turned toward the cabin of the plane and was astounded to realize how few people he recognized. Having been separated into small groups and kept isolated from each other for fourteen months, they seemed more like strangers than colleagues who had shared a common ordeal.

Finally, the plane began edging toward the runway.

James looked at his wrist to check the time, but he had no wristwatch. Habib had never given the stolen watch back to him. "What time is it?" James asked the man next to him.

"Eight-thirty-two," he said. "Two minutes into the inauguration."

After takeoff, James stared through the window, but saw nothing below, due to the wartime blackout. With an enormous sense of relief, he slumped back into his seat. But his fingers still clenched the armrests. Were they really being released? Or was this one more instance of the on-again-off-again life the hostages had lived over the previous months? It seemed like more than an hour of flight before the voice of the pilot came over the plane's intercom, "We just passed out of Iranian airspace."

The cabin exploded with cheers and shouts. James clapped his neighbor on the shoulder, and the two of them embraced. Bottles of champagne appeared. The hostesses moved up and down the aisle passing a glass to each person.

He toasted his neighbor and drank the champagne. Then the two of them stepped into the aisle to join the sea of people hugging each other and raising their glasses in jubilation.

Greenwich Village

"Why'd you put a blanket over the phone?" asked Jenna when she arrived.

"To mute the ringing. It's been going non-stop, and it's driving me nuts."

"What if an important call comes in?"

"They'll do what you do when you can't reach me. They'll leave a message at my answering service."

She sat Jenna on the couch, put ice cubes in two glasses and filled them from a pitcher that was sitting on the coffee table. "Voila!" she chirped as she handed the glass to Jenna.

"A little sweet, but tasty," said Jenna. "What is it?"

"An Irish Fix."

"You're not Irish."

"It's in honor of James."

"He's not Irish, either."

"When we had our pre-marriage instructions, they were conducted by this cute, old Monsignor O'Reilly. Halfway through each session, he served us each an Irish Fix."

She lifted her glass. "Salud!"

They leaned back on the couch and watched the inaugural proceedings. President Reagan made no mention of the hostages in his inaugural address. But an hour later, CNN filmed him addressing a post-inaugural reception in the Capitol rotunda. When he announced that the hostages had left Iranian air space, the crowd erupted with applause.

Jenna and Angie joined the celebration, standing up, hugging each other, and dancing in a circle. Grinning, Angie refilled their glasses, and they collapsed on the sofa.

"Ironic," said Angie.

"What's ironic?"

"Carter spends a year negotiating for a release, and Reagan gets the credit."

"Why shouldn't he get some of the credit?" said Jenna. "With the specter of a hawk like him coming in to call the shots, the Iranians had to cut a deal with Carter while they could."

Angie leaned forward, squinting, suspicious. "What kind of deal?"

"Ken hasn't told me all the details. But we agreed to release all the Iranian financial assets that we've kept frozen since the crisis started. Billions of dollars."

"That sucks. We should keep them frozen so there'd be something there for the hostages to get when we sue Iran for illegal imprisonment."

"Apparently, we can't do that."

Angie's mouth gaped open. "Why not. Most of those hostages come from middle class families. Suppose it was Ken, and supposed you'd spent the last year with FLAG travelling around the country trying to help them. You'd have spent a fortune that you didn't have."

"It doesn't matter. As a condition for releasing the hostages, Iran demanded immunity from any suits like that."

Angie shook her head in dismay.

"Are you all right?" asked Jenna.

"This has gone on for so long. So much has happened. So many ups and downs. I'm elated, but I'm also exhausted."

Jenna stood up. "Will you be alright if I leave to go to my class?"

Angie laughed. "Yes, but after all that Irish Mist, I hope you don't have to take a test right now."

"Nope. Just a lecture on dealing with PTSD."

Angie had never heard of PTSD, and she didn't bother to ask. She ushered Jenna to the door, then leaned back on the couch and eyed the TV to find out what would happen next. The hostage plane was headed to Algiers. From there it would go to the Rhine-Main Air Force base in Germany. After physical examinations and debriefings, the hostages would fly to the Military Academy at West Point, New York, where their families would join them.

A shiver of excitement cascaded through her chest as she thought of seeing James again.

She teetered to the kitchen to make herself another batch of Irish Fixes.

35

A taste of her baklava.

January 1981

Wiesbaden Air Force Hospital Germany

Doctor Anderson, an Army captain, took one last listen to James' heart and lungs. He moved from the examining table to a desk and motioned James to the side chair while he looked through a folder of lab test results.

"Other than being severely underweight, you're in excellent condition. Your EKG and blood test results all look good. Extraordinary for what you've been through. I'm not even seeing muscular atrophy."

"The only way I could cope with all the empty time we had was to do a daily routine of stretching and calisthenics."

"Well, the results are palpable, and all that exercise undoubtedly helped you keep your sanity."

James frowned. "I'm not sure I did keep my sanity. I've been plagued for a year with headaches and shortness of breath and heart palpitations. Even this morning, when I woke up and had that moment of not knowing where I was, my heart started pounding."

"It's your body's reaction to the enormous stress you've been under. This should go away as your life gets back to normal."

"You think I'll live?"

"Spectacularly long, I hope," laughed the doctor, as he stood up and shook James' hand. "Before you go, however, stick around for a few minutes so Lieutenant Larson can make one last check of your blood pressure."

He started out the door, stopped, and turned around. "Yes, it might be a good idea for you to get a decent meal tonight. Maybe some of that great German sauerbraten."

Dr. Anderson no sooner left the exam room than Lieutenant Larson stepped in and wrapped a blood pressure cuff around James' arm. She was the nurse who had checked him in for Dr. Anderson's visit. As she began pumping the pressure cuff, James noticed her long blond hair, bright blue eyes, and a strong scent of perfume.

"You remind me of my Iranian Farsi instructor," he said, inadvertently shifting in his chair as he said it.

"Hold still, so I can get a good reading," she replied.

After a moment, she unwrapped the cuff, smiled, and said, "Perfectly normal. A blond Iranian?"

"What?"

"Your Iranian Farsi instructor? She was blond like me?"

"They exist. Mostly around the Caspian Sea area where she was from. She used to bring delicious halvah bars to our classes. These were a delicacy in the region."

Ms. Larson smiled. "After all you've been through, I'm impressed that you have a fondness for these Iranian halvah bars or anything at all Iranian for that matter."

James shrugged. She looked down at the floor and blushed before raising her eyes to him. "I heard Dr. Anderson say you needed a good German meal. If you wanted, I could take you to a gasthaus I like, then drop you off back here at the hospital afterward."

James' chin lifted in surprised. Women seldom came on to him. But Lieutenant Larson wasn't really coming on. She was just offering to share some good German sauerbraten and then return him to the hospital.

"What time's your last appointment?" she asked.

"We're going shopping for some clothes to tide us over until we get home. Then I meet the shrinks at three. I'm sure we'll be finished by five."

"Wait at the main gate," she said with a coy grin. "I'll pick you up at five-thirty when I get off. Look for a green Volkswagen."

Washington Square

On the morning after the hostage release, Angie woke with her head pounding. She knocked a water glass off her nightstand, and the shattering pieces echoed through her brain with the fury of billiard balls clanking into each other. The room spun dizzily as she headed to the bathroom, but she puked on the floor before she could reach the toilet bowl.

"I swear to God, I will never touch another drop of alcohol," she pledged as she fell back on her bed.

By Sunday, she was back to normal, except for a sky-high anxiety. She started to bite her nails, then pulled her hand down. She had to break that habit. What would James think if he saw her doing that?

The ETA of the hostages was 3:00 p.m. at Stewart Air National Guard base near West Point. Angie planned to take the two-hour bus ride up to the airport and join the other hostage families as they waited for the plane to land.

Despite fourteen months anticipating this moment, the reality of it filled her with apprehension. She looked forward to being wrapped in James' arms, but so many things had happened since the last time they'd embraced, she feared that things might not be the same.

How would he react when she told him about the hostage rescue mission she'd almost pulled off? She had to tell him, because a marriage couldn't work if the partners kept secrets from each other. But he didn't have to hear about it immediately. She would wait for an appropriate moment a week or so after they got settled in. The same thing was true about the realization she had come to that she wanted to get pregnant and raise a family.

She folded his charcoal gray suit and put it into a suitcase along with enough underwear and accessories for the three days the hostages would spend at West Point. That would carry him over until they had a chance to shop for what he needed. She put on a maxi-length, body hugging tartan wool skirt and mid-calf leather boots. For that evening, she gently folded the lingerie ensemble and black nylons she had worn on their wedding night. After fourteen months of celibacy, James wouldn't need any extra stimulation, but she loved the look on his face when he saw her in something sexy.

En Route to the U.S.

Except for the hum of the engines, the plane was quiet as it soared across the Atlantic. The White House had dispatched one of its Boeing 707s for the voyage and temporarily redubbed it Freedom One. The hostages were scattered through the spacious plane.

James morosely stared down and fingered an empty china coffee cup with the presidential seal. His seatmate, Smitty, nudged him in the ribs.

"Why so glum, James. In five hours, you'll be home with your gorgeous wife."

James raised his coffee cup toward a stewardess who was coming up the aisle offering refills from a carafe. "I did something I shouldn't have done."

"So? Everyone in the world occasionally does something they shouldn't do."

"Remember when Carter flew to Wiesbaden to talk with you guys in the hospital."

"Yeah. You weren't there. I figured you were boycotting him."

James drank from the coffee refill. "I spent the night with one of the nurses."

Smitty beamed. "Way to go, James. Which one?"

"That's none of your business. We went to a gasthaus for some sauerbraten, and I was telling her about that delicious halvah we used to get in Iran before the embassy takeover. She said it sounded like the baklava she had back in her apartment. It was the only Middle Eastern food she knew, and she loved the nuts, the sweet honey taste, and the pastry flakes. She wanted me to taste her baklava to make a comparison with the halvah. Before I knew it, we were in bed."

"Taste her baklava?" Smitty roared with laughter. The stewardess, still walking with her coffee carafe, looked at them.

"It's no joke, Smitty. What am I going to tell Angie?"

"Angie?"

"My wife! The one you called gorgeous."

"James, every man on this plane would have done what you did if he'd had the chance. Every single one. Christ, we've been celibate for fourteen months."

"What do I tell Angie? She deserves to know."

Smitty banged his coffee cup down on the tray hanging down from the seat in front of him. He stared at James a moment before saying anything. "Deserves to know? You're telling me she deserves to have her guts ripped out just because you've got a guilty conscience?"

James didn't reply.

"If that highly developed brain of yours is still working, James, you won't tell her anything. You'll just take up your role as a loving husband and forget about Lieutenant Larson who gave you a taste of her baklava."

"I didn't say it was Lieutenant Larson."

Smitty laughed again.

Stewart Air National Guard Base

The airport was packed when Angie arrived. Yellow ribbons and welcome home signs bloomed throughout the area. Other hostage families gathered silently in small groups in the terminal. She started to go over to Barbara Rosen, who had her hands on the shoulders of two small children. But it was such an intimate scene that Angie feared she would be an intruder. She envied Barbara. What a comfort it must be to have her children with her at a moment like this. Would Angie ever have something like that?

A loudspeaker announced that the hostages were arriving, and the crowd poured out of the building onto the tarmac. Angie's chest tingled as the plane taxied toward them, the words UNITED STATES OF AMERICA painted in bright blue on the white fuselage. In a strange way she didn't understand, she felt bonded to James, the other hostage families, the plane with its big blue lettering, the historic moment, and the Star Spangled Banner being played by a military band waiting on the Tarmac for the plane's arrival. Her own experiences as a Peace Corps volunteer and a hostage wife somehow brought her into union with all this. Although not given to overt patriotic displays, she felt a powerful pride in all of it.

A ground worker waved batons to guide the big plane to a stop only yards from where the crowd stood. The Marine guards from the embassy were the first ones to emerge onto the stairway that had been rolled up to the plane, and a loud roar erupted behind Angie. She turned to see hundreds of townspeople, reporters, and safety officers cheering wildly. When a bearded man stepped down the stairway, one of Barbara Rosen's children broke from her and ran to the man, wrapping his arms around his legs.

Angie turned her eyes back to the plane to watch for James. Being tall, he stood out the moment he appeared, and Angie was stunned at how skinny he looked. She pushed through the crowd, and the moment he reached the ground, she wrapped her arms around his neck, pulling him forward so they could exchange a long kiss.

He pulled his head back. "Oh, Angie, I thought of you all the time. I couldn't wait for this moment."

"James, James, James. I'm so grateful you're safe. I was petrified I was never going to see you again."

She pulled him forward again into a long, silent embrace, tears streaming down her cheeks. Slowly, they backed off and joined hands. It felt as though they were the only people there as they stood holding hands, waiting to be led to the buses for the drive to West Point. The crowds were so thick along the route it took an hour to make the fifteen-mile trip. She leaned against James throughout the ride, waving through the window at the well-wishers. He draped an arm over her shoulder. She grinned up at him when a loudspeaker blared the song *Tie a Yellow Ribbon Round the Ole Oak Tree*. But James grimaced.

"What's wrong?" she asked.

"All this noise and these colors after all those months of being cooped up in drab silence. I think I've got sensory overload."

The buses pulled up to West Point's historic Thayer Hotel, a huge red brick, fortress-looking building with three wings and a gothic stone portico at the main entrance. To shield the hostage families from the hundreds of journalists and television cameramen, military police and their dogs had been trucked in from Fort Dix in New Jersey. They established a perimeter that kept gawkers at a distance.

"If we'd been guarded this well at the embassy in Teheran," James joked to Angie. "We'd have never been captured."

It was six o'clock by the time they entered their room. Though not huge, it was elegant. A queen-size bed had pillowcases emblazoned with the hotel's logo. The paned window looked out over the Hudson River, with its black water flowing between white snowy shores. A comfortable chair sat next to a writing table. On top of the table, a vase of yellow roses and a basket of fruit had been set. Next to the vase was an envelope with a note written by one of the cadets at the Academy. Angie's eyes moistened as she read it aloud to James. "Welcome home. And God bless you."

She wanted to be alone with him in their room, separate from the crowd of people in the hotel. "James," she said, "instead of eating in the dining room, why don't we just order room service."

"I've been pent up in small rooms for a long time. I'd rather go downstairs," he said.

"Of course." Why hadn't she thought of that? "Let me freshen up in the bathroom first."

She dug into her luggage for her toiletries and spotted her diaphragm case. She hadn't used it in fourteen months. She picked it up, and the image of Barbara Rosen's beautiful children popped into her mind. If she didn't use the birth control device now, maybe she could have a child too. She stood looking at the case in her hand, trying to decide what to do. Then she set it back in the suitcase. She could decide later when they came back from dinner.

36

"Stop that music."

January 1981

West Point, New York

Angie clutched James' hand as they walked through a polished oak archway into a carpeted dining room with chandeliers hanging from the ceiling and support beams covered with gilded decoration. On a wall by the entrance was a portrait of the room's namesake, General Douglas MacArthur.

"Welcome home, sir," said the maître d'. He led them to a window table with a majestic view of the Hudson.

Angie broke her pledge from the previous Wednesday never again to touch a drop of alcohol. She ordered an Irish Mist with Coke, while James ordered a Scotch and Soda.

"What were your days like?" she asked, trying to get a conversation started. But she bit her tongue the instant the words came out. What a stupid question to pose.

"Mostly boring. And yours?"

She felt perplexed at this curt answer. "I tried to keep busy. I got to know Barbara Rosen, who was very effective at keeping public attention on the situation."

When he had no response, she smiled and tried another tack.

"I'll bet you guys cheered like crazy once that plane took off from Teheran."

"Really not until it exited Iran's air space."

But he didn't elaborate. After failing to get a conversation started, she felt grateful when a waiter came up to them. She ordered a trout filet and James a sirloin cut with a baked potato and a second scotch. They ate in silence, and for dessert, Angie chose a baklava. James' fork stopped in mid-air, and he squinted questioningly at her.

"Why that strange look, James?" she said, jokingly. "You used to love baklava back in Tunis."

"My steak was a little heavy. I'll just have a scoop of ice cream."

When the dishes were cleared from the table, she slipped James a credit card so he could pay, but the waiter refused it.

"It's on the house, Sir. It's the least we can do for you."

As they sat for a moment before leaving, James nodded to a fellow hostage who entered the restaurant alone. "That's Smitty," he said. "We were roommates for awhile right after the takeover. He actually wanted Carter to do his rescue operation. Can you believe that?"

"If it had worked, you'd have been home a long time ago."

"Some of us would have gotten killed. What if I'd have come home and someone else hadn't, how would I be able to look that person's widow in the eye?"

"I don't know," she admitted. In light of what he'd just said, she also didn't know how she was ever going to tell him about her own attempt at a rescue. She had to at some point, she realized, but not tonight. Maybe in a few weeks, after they'd gotten comfortable with each other again.

They left the restaurant, and he pointed to a small tavern down the corridor from the dining room. "Let's stop in here to relax for a moment before we go upstairs."

She didn't really want another drink. What she wanted was to wrap her arms around him. To relieve the overpowering physical ache she'd felt since the moment they'd embraced on the airport tarmac. To lounge in bed recapturing the sexual and emotional intimacy they'd always had. And he must surely want the same thing.

Nonetheless, she nodded and followed him into the bar. As with the restaurant, the walls were adorned with portraits of the tavern's namesake, General George Patton.

They sat at a corner table sipping their drinks when she spotted Barbara Rosen in the corridor with her husband.

"James, you should see the two beautiful little children she's got."

He didn't respond, and they fell into an awkward silence. She edged her chair as close to him as possible, leaned her shoulder against his, and rested her hand on his thigh. He sat like that for a moment before gulping down the last of his drink. He stood up, took her hand, and led her out of the bar.

Up in their room, they took turns using the bathroom. Her diaphragm was still sitting at the top of her suitcase. She really wanted to leave it where it was and hope she'd get pregnant. But doing that without discussing it first wasn't fair to him.

She took the diaphragm as she went into the bathroom after James came out. She brushed her teeth, touched up her hair, and let her outer clothes drop to the floor. Standing in her heels, she looked into the full-length bathroom mirror to admire the white garter belt and black nylons. Her wearing something sexy had always put James in the mood, and she relished what his reaction would be to this.

She glided to the bed and struck a ta-da pose next to where he sat propped up by a pillow against the headboard. She slipped under the sheet, nuzzled next to his shoulder, and slid her hand down to his penis. He was still flaccid as he lay on his back staring at the ceiling, looking embarrassed.

"Angie, I don't know what's wrong. I used to day dream about you all the time, but things feel strange now, like we're in some new territory."

"It feels strange for me, too, James."

"Maybe we could just lie here for a while."

She took her hand off his penis.

"But you don't have to let go."

She lay huddled next to him under the sheets, until he slowly got aroused enough to make love. He fell asleep, and Angie lay staring at the ceiling. Their readjustment to each other was starting out to be more difficult than she'd expected. At least they'd been able to make love. She'd be good to him, as Monsignor O'Reilly had advised, and eventually the old talkative James would come back. Their emotional intimacy would return.

In the middle of the night she awoke to find James thrashing next to her and calling out, "No! No!"

She shook his shoulder to wake him. "You had a nightmare," she said. He popped up, stared at her vacantly, then lay down and fell back to sleep.

When she asked him the next morning about the nightmare, he couldn't remember.

"You kept saying, 'stop that music'. What music? What did you dream about?"

"I told you, I can't remember."

West Point Conference Room

Later that morning, she and James streamed with the hostages and their families into the hotel's biggest meeting room. James paused when he saw a bank of television cameras and a phalanx of journalists eager to grill the hostages. "It was too much to hope that we'd get a few days of peace before we were put on stage," he complained.

Angie squinted in dismay, but didn't reply. The country wanted to see the hostages. Why would he not want to be seen? She didn't understand his reticence, but was determined to accept it.

The reporters were sympathetic as they questioned the hostages about their treatment. Family members gasped as the hostages replied. Angie cringed as James recounted the terror of the mock execution. But she didn't understand why he took the microphone to make that statement after having said earlier that he didn't want to be on stage. Why did he talk about the horrible event in public before mentioning it to her in private.

The reporters cheered as the hostages described tricks they used to annoy their guards and insult the Ayatollah Khomeini. The room erupted with laughter when one of the Marine guards related that he phrased his requests to use the toilet by saying, "I need to take a Khomeini."

That evening, they dined at the Military Academy. The cadets lined up in their elaborate blue-gray uniforms with brass buttons and white sashes across their chests. They gave the hostages a ten-minute cheer when they entered the dining hall.

Several hostages seemed to enjoy the attention, but James muttered, "Why are they cheering us? We didn't do anything heroic."

"You survived, James," said Angie, "and we are all proud of you for it."

The White House

The next few days flew by in a blur. They went by bus to Washington, where two hundred thousand people lined Pennsylvania Avenue to cheer them along their route to the

White House. President Reagan praised them, shook hands with each hostage, and gave each one a small silk flag in a personalized rosewood box. The State Department gave its hostages the department's Award for Valor, and the Pentagon presented its Meritorious Service Award to all the military hostages except Peter Simon.

James remained stoic through it all and didn't complain, even though he didn't seem to enjoy it as much as other hostages. He gasped when they were ushered into a room at the White House to meet family members of the eight servicemen who had been killed trying to rescue the hostages the previous April. He whispered to Angie, "What can we possibly say to these people whose husbands and fathers died trying to save us?"

Angie found herself equally tongue-tied. If her own rescue plan hadn't been aborted, she herself would be responsible for some deaths. With tears streaming down her cheeks, she stood by James' side as he said to the family members, "I am so sorry. I don't know what to say. I'm grateful we are all back, but I'm so sorry for the price you paid."

One of the dead servicemen's wives replied. "We are just glad everyone is back."

Angie grabbed James' hand and held it as they were led out of the White House and back to the bus.

New York, Ticker Tape

The following Friday they were back in New York where a ticker tape parade was planned. James balked.

"Angie, this week has been one PR event after another. Why can't they understand that we need some alone time, not an endless succession of promotional activities for somebody else's benefit?"

"A lot of people put enormous effort into setting up this parade. You'll be sticking your thumb in their eye if you skip it."

"Half the hostages have already gone home. So why should we attend? There will only be a few of us."

"We have to go, James. The whole country's looking at this, and if nobody shows up it will be a national embarrassment."

"Let the extroverts go. They love this kind of crap."

She put on her coat and handed him his jacket. "James, you didn't want to go to the White House either, but it's a memory we'll carry forever. If you don't do this ticker tape parade, you're going to regret it for the rest of your life."

His lips tightened. "What you mean is that you are the one who will regret it."

The comment stung, because James wasn't completely off the mark. She indeed did look forward to the parade and knew that it would be fun. But she was convinced that he, too, would enjoy the event once it started. In future years, they would proudly show photos of the parade to their children.

A Rolls Royce convertible carried them through New York's canyon of skyscrapers. Yellow ribbons were decked out all along the route, and an estimated two million people cheered them.

Angie sat in the back seat of the Rolls waving at the crowd as tons of ticker tape, computer paper, phone book pages, and newspaper strips rained down on them. Bits of the paper clung to her hair and clothes. There was so much of it that the floor of the car was ankle deep in paper. She laughed as it spilled out to the street when she pushed the door open.

When they got back to their apartment, James slammed the door shut. He spotted the State Department Award for Valor which Angie had set prominently on the mantel in the living room, its ten-carat gold medal suspended from a blue and gold ribbon. He threw it on the floor, then sank into the couch and buried his head in his hands.

"No more parades, Angie!"

Startled, she didn't know what to say.

"This was not a national victory. And I'm not a hero. They've got to stop calling me a hero."

Had she called him a hero? She couldn't remember.

"I didn't do anything heroic. I tried to do the right thing. But Angie, I did things I'm ashamed of. We all did."

"That doesn't matter, James. What matters is that you stuck it out and did your duty under horrible conditions. Somewhere in this country is a little boy or a little girl who's heard about you guys and gotten determination to stick it out in the face of whatever problems they face. You inspire people. All of you do."

James looked up, with an enigmatic smile and a shake of the head. She sank down next to him on the couch, and they fell into each other's arms. They stayed that way, clinging to each other without talking. After several minutes, he stood up, took her hand, and led her to the bedroom. This was the first time he'd taken the initiative since he'd returned home.

37

With all my love.

February 1981

Washington Square

Angie continued helping her friend Gilda teach figure skating. Just before Valentine's Day, Gilda asked Angie to help transport five of their students to Poughkeepsie for a competition. One of them was Angie's five-year-old stepbrother, Michael, who'd been taking lessons for more than a year. She took great pride in the progress he'd made as a result of her coaching and saw it as an encouraging sign that she might indeed be able to run a skating academy someday far off in the future.

Angie hesitated. "Things are so fragile with James right now, I'm afraid to leave."

"It's only a weekend, Angie. I realize he's horny after all those months of celibacy, but he can do without you for two nights."

Horniness was no longer the problem, now that their sex life had returned to normal. A pleasant normal to be sure. The problem was that she was hoping to tell him this weekend about the rescue plan she'd organized. She was worried about his reaction. If he got upset about her going off to Poughkeepsie for the weekend, it might not be possible to discuss the hostage rescue.

"We were separated for so long by that hostage crisis, we really treasure our time together."

"Bring him with you."

That could solve her problem, Angie thought. A mini vacation might relax him and facilitate the discussion she felt compelled to have about her attempt at a rescue mission. And if that discussion went okay, she could tell him she wanted to get pregnant.

When he returned to the apartment late that afternoon for dinner, Angie greeted him at the door with a kiss. He smiled.

"Angelita, my little angel."

"That's redundant."

He laughed. "How am I supposed to know what's redundant in Spanish? I don't speak it."

He was in a good mood, so she thought there would be no better time to suggest a mini-vacation to Poughkeepsie. "Sit down while I get you a glass of wine. I have an idea for us." She disappeared into the kitchen and returned with two glasses of pinot noir. She pushed her hip against his as she sat on the sofa.

"James, how would you like to take a small trip to Poughkeepsie for the weekend? We could have our Valentine's dinner there Saturday night."

"Poughkeepsie?" he asked, wrinkling his nose.

"Gilda needs me as a driver for a skating competition she's taking the kids to. You'll get to see what a great job I've done with Michael. He can glide on one skate now."

"I love your little brother, Angie, but figure skating's not my thing."

Hurt, Angie resisted the urge to pout. Not only did she want to show off Michael, this would be their first Valentine's day together since getting married. Who needed her more? Gilda or James?

"I don't want to leave Gilda in the lurch, James, and I really want to see how Michael does. If you don't want to come, we'll have to have our Valentine dinner on Sunday when I get back.

"That's okay, because I've got a lot of paperwork for the State Department that will keep me busy."

She squinted. "Are you sure."

He smiled. "Go ahead and have a good time. I'll get us a dinner reservation for Sunday when you get back."

Poughkeepsie

On Saturday morning, Michael woke up with a fever. "I hate to desert you, Gilda," Angie said after phoning back to Charlie and Glenna. "But his mother wants me to bring him home immediately."

Angie lay Michael in the back seat of her car for the two-hour drive back to Manhattan.

"Pobrecito," she said, furrowing her eyebrows into a sympathetic look. "You'll miss out on the Valentine's party Gilda planned. But I brought your present with us."

She set a heart shaped box of candies next to the boy.

"Thank you," said Michael.

At noon, Angie dropped Michael off at home, near Columbus Circle. Then she brightened at the realization that she and James could have Valentine's dinner that night after all. By this time, it would be impossible to get a table at a fancy restaurant, so she called Lombardi's Pizza. James had never liked Lombardi's much, but he would accept it, knowing how many fond remembrances she had of it from her childhood with Charlie. With dinner nailed down, she had time to buy him a Valentine gift.

Washington Square

In mid-afternoon, she skipped up the steps to their apartment. An overnight bag hung by a strap from her shoulder, and in her hand was a box containing a watch she'd just bought to replace the one that had been stolen in Teheran. She had the jeweler engrave the back.

James, with all my love,
Angie

She pushed open the apartment door, but the living room was empty, as were the kitchen and the bedrooms. She set the box with his Valentine's gift on the mantel in the living room and spotted a note he had left there.

Angie,

I didn't want to spend the weekend alone. I took the Metroliner to D.C. so I can turn in my paperwork Monday morning. I'll be back Monday or Tuesday night.

James

What kind of passive-aggressive bullshit was this? He didn't want to stay in their apartment alone, but he didn't mind being alone in D.C.? And even though he knew she'd be back on Sunday, he planned to stay away two extra days. She picked his Valentine's gift off the mantel and felt tempted to throw it on the floor. Instead, she brought it to the bedroom where she tucked it into the top drawer of her dresser. She returned to the kitchen to pour a glass of Irish Mist.

James returned on Tuesday afternoon, and Angie bristled when he sat down on the sofa with no explanation for his absence.

"What's going on, James? I don't hear from you for three days, and then you just show up with nothing to say for yourself."

"Jesus Christ, Angie, cut me some slack. I've got a lot going on." He jumped up and stormed into the kitchen where he poured a glass of scotch. She sank into the couch, pulled a copy of his *Foreign Service Journal* off the coffee table and leafed through the pages without reading them.

For fifteen minutes, the apartment remained so silent that the slightest noise echoed. His glass striking the table when he set it down. The soles of her shoes rubbing on the carpet when she moved her feet. She went to the kitchen and sat across from him at the old wooden table.

"I'm sorry for snapping at you. Please tell me what's wrong."

He raised his palms. "I'm lobbying to get that Mideast desk job at State, but they're nowhere near a decision. Until they make one, I'm in limbo with nothing to do all day. I'll try to be more considerate."

He reached across the table and took her hand.

38

"Maybe you two should try counseling."

Spring 1981

Manhattan

Angie felt that part of James' problem stemmed from him having so much free time. Maybe they needed more to do.

"James," she said one morning, waving her hand toward the street below their window, "While we've got the chance, we should take advantage of this great big city."

"This wondrous toy," he quipped, a twinkle coming to his eye for the first time in days.

"Just made for a girl and boy," she followed up and laughed.

"An isle of joy," he added, hugging her and picking her off her feet. She loved it and thought about the Valentine's Day gift for him that was still hidden in her dresser drawer. Maybe she could give it to him for Easter.

"James, you're not a native New Yorker, and there's so much you don't know about the city. We should go exploring."

They climbed the Statue of Liberty, walked the Brooklyn Bridge, saw the Rockettes, and visited the Cloisters. James seemed to get in the spirit of things. He took her hand and suggested ice skating together at Rockefeller Center.

She grinned. Maybe James was coming out of his malaise.

"When I was locked up in Teheran, I felt bad that I'd been so unenthusiastic about skating that day you introduced me to your dad at Rockefeller Center. I vowed I would make it up to you."

She smiled. "We can't go there, since they closed for the season in April. But we could go to the Manhattan Skating Club, where I'm on the board of directors. Nobody would complain if we used the rink for an hour."

They visited the club, and she wore the same pink tights and skimpy skirt she'd worn the previous time. She refrained from doing any fancy maneuvers for fear of embarrassing him, and she showed him how they could hold hands and skate side by side. After circling the rink a few times, she became antsy at having to skate so tamely, and James grew bored. The pink tights did their job though, since James rushed her home and to bed.

They spent a sunny Saturday strolling Manhattan from their Washington Square apartment to Central Park where they ate a leisurely lunch at Tavern on Green. They sat in the Crystal Room, drinking Irish Mist and gawking through the glass walls at people in the park. But James didn't talk much, and it was hard for her to keep a conversation going.

When they arrived home both exhilarated and tired from the long walk, they found a letter from the State Department in the mailbox. Angie held her breath as James tore it open. He scanned it without comment, then handed it to her.

"James, this is wonderful," she said. "They're giving you a temporary assignment to the United Nations here in New York until the Mideast Desks opens up in D.C."

"You know what that means. Temporary assignments have a tendency to become permanent. By the time the desk job opens up in Washington, they won't want to move me out of the United Nations."

Why was he so negative? At least it would give him something structured to keep himself busy, she thought. That would take some of the stress out of their lives, and she would be able to approach him about her dream of starting a family.

Jenna's Midtown Apartment

Angie rode the subway up to Midtown for lunch with Jenna in her apartment. They sat across from each other at the dining room table, and Angie frowned as she mentioned the letter James had received from the State Department.

"It was almost like we had each read a different letter, Jenna. He's depressed, because he thinks the U.N. assignment is a tactic to prevent him from getting the Mideast Desk he really wants. I'm excited, because it lets us stay here in New York a little longer, and it gives him something to keep him busy. His moping around with nothing concrete to do has been driving me nuts."

"Moping around doesn't sound like James. I picture him as a 'take-charge' type of guy."

"It's like he's become a different person."

Jenna frowned, sympathetically. "The psychologists have come up with a new term, PTSD, for people's difficulty in recovering from a terrifying ordeal."

"PTSD?"

"Post Traumatic Stress Disorder. He can't recover overnight from what happened in Teheran, and neither can you. It's going to take time."

"I understand that in my head, Jenna. But it's so hard to deal with. At Valentine's Day, he deserted me for three nights. It was the first Valentine's Day we've had together since we got married, and he just deserted me."

"Angie, you deserted him first. You left him alone so you could go to that figure skating meet."

"I know. I know. I know," said Angie, pounding her fist on her thigh. "I shouldn't have done that. But he's changed, Jenna. He's different."

"So are you."

Angie looked up, startled. "So am I what?"

"Different. When I first met you, you were like a girl barely out of high school. James took care of you in Tunis after that horrible slashing attack. Now you're more of an in-charge person, and you're the one taking care of him."

"Taking care of him?" She exploded. "I'm walking on eggshells trying not to trigger some outburst. I don't want another fight like the one we had after Valentine's Day. That was so bad I was afraid for a while that we were done for."

Jenna leaned forward. "You're not thinking of leaving."

"No. What I really want is a family. I wish we had some children."

"What does James think of this?"

"We haven't discussed it yet."

Jenna shook her head, then sat still for several minutes before responding.

"Maybe you two should try counseling."

Washington Square

Bit by bit, Angie and James began to share more of their experiences. He mentioned how much he had admired the quiet calm of Katherine Koob during the hostage crisis. Angie mentioned that she had met Ross Perot who had rescued two of his employees who had been imprisoned in Teheran. If James responded well, maybe she could tell him about her own rescue plan attempt.

James shook his head. "Thank God he wasn't in a position to try that on us. Some of us would be dead now."

James' new assignment to the U.N. in New York required him to take occasional overnight trips to Washington to consult with the State Department. The small separations unexpectedly helped ease the tensions between them.

Maybe there was some hope for them after all. Angie looked forward to a cozy evening with James on Memorial Day watching a holiday concert on TV. James prepared a big bowl of popcorn, and she made a pitcher of the Irish Fix drinks.

"To Monsignor O'Reilly," she toasted, raising her glass. James clinked his glass against hers.

They sat languidly on the couch watching the program. Angie fantasized about having a little boy there to enjoy it with them. Absentmindedly, she fingered the hair on the nape of James' neck.

Near the end of the concert, James got up to go to the bathroom. Just as he returned, the orchestra had reached its finale, Tchaikovsky's *1812 Overture*. The music reached its crescendo, with bells ringing, cannons exploding, and the volume rising.

"Shut that goddamn thing off!" James threw his glass at the TV screen, and amber liquid trailed on the floor as the glass sailed through the air, shattering against the wall, and just missing the TV set by inches. The cannons continued to explode, and James twisted the on-off dial so hard it broke loose and fell to the floor.

"Don't ever play that fucking song again."

"James, I didn't play it. It was just part of the concert."

But James didn't hear. He stormed out the door and slammed it behind himself.

She cleaned up the mess James had made, put the TV knob back into place, and refreshed her Irish Mist. She sat on the couch and stared blankly at the wall as she waited for him to return. When he showed up two hours later, he smelled of scotch. She was holding a glass of Irish Mist, her second since he'd left.

"I'm sorry, Angie. I shouldn't have done what I did."

She sipped from the Irish Mist. "Why did you do it?" she asked. "What did I do to you?"

"You did nothing." He sank onto the sofa and put his head in his hands, looking more like a boy than the six-footer of the man he was. He told her of the flogging incident at Evin prison in Teheran. How he'd cringed in fear and horror at hearing the prisoner beg for mercy, then the crack of the whip, the screams, and the tape at full volume playing the finale of the *1812 Overture* to drown out the crack of the whip and the screams.

"So, when I came into the room and heard that music, I went berserk."

She lay her head against his chest, grabbed his hands, and sobbed.

39

"I can't live with I think so."

July 1981

Washington Square

They both needed a getaway, Angie decided, and the Fourth of July provided the perfect occasion. The board of directors of the Skating Club of Manhattan had organized a retreat for that weekend.

She suggested the idea to James on a Sunday morning as they lounged around the Washington Square apartment, drinking coffee and leafing through *The New York Times*. They were leaning back on the sofa with their feet propped up on the coffee table.

"James, you'll love it," she told him. "You're a history buff, and this retreat's at one of the most historic spots in the country."

"Where?"

"Lexington-Concord in Massachusetts."

He pursed his lips. "It's tempting, but I'd feel like a fifth wheel among all those skating insiders."

"I feel like a fifth wheel at some of your State Department functions. But I go to them, anyway."

He squinted. "Fifth wheel? You and the other Peace Corps volunteers in Tunis did more to help out real people with real problems than all the rest of us in the embassy together."

She lay her hand on his arm and smiled. "Thank you for saying that. I doubt that your Foreign Service buddies feel the same way. There's a pecking order among them. Being the wife of a rising star in diplomatic circles doesn't put me at the bottom of the pecking order. But being a former Peace Corps volunteer doesn't add much in the way of status."

She paused, then said. "Besides, you won't be a fifth wheel. These are sophisticated people interested in world affairs, and they'll eat up everything you tell them."

"Give me a pass on this one, Angie. I've got a ton of stuff to catch up on at the U.N. Having that weekend free to work on it would be very helpful."

She smoothed her hands over the fabric of the cushion on the couch in resignation. "Okay. If that's what you want."

Lexington, Massachusetts

She drove alone to the retreat on the evening of July second and had dinner with Mrs. Vanderkeller. During the next day's noon hour break, she strolled along the town's well-tended Battle Green where the Lexington Minutemen had started the Revolutionary War. In a gift shop, she found the perfect present for James, a print of the scene, entitled *The Shot Heard Round the World*. She still hadn't given him the watch she'd bought for Valentine's Day. Now, she could give them both at the same time.

She got the gallery owner to engrave a small brass plate that he embedded at the bottom of the picture frame.

James, with all my love,
July 4, 1981
Angie

As she waited for the engraving, she began feeling guilty about leaving James alone with his boring U.N. paperwork. And her chest tingled as she anticipated his reaction to the two gifts. Maybe this would be the time she could open up to him about her aborted rescue mission escapade. As soon as she got back to the conference hall, she told the board president that something had come up requiring her to leave the retreat early.

Greenwich Village

Traffic on the Interstate was light, and she reached New York late in the afternoon on the third. When she got to Greenwich Village, she stopped at a flower shop to buy a new plant for the coffee table.

She left her bags in the trunk of the car to pick up later. Then she hopped gleefully up the steps to their apartment, carrying only the potted plant and the gift for James. She relished the look she'd see on his face that she'd come home early to be with him.

She pushed open the apartment door, but the room was empty. He must still be at his office. Strange, she thought, a small red and white sweater was draped over the couch. She set the plant and the gift she'd bought on the coffee table next to the ivory chess set she'd brought back from Tunis. Then she went to get the Valentine's gift from her dresser so she could give him both gifts at the same time.

Her mouth gaped open as she stepped into the bedroom. James lay naked in the bed with a blonde, their heads buried in each other's thighs. The two jerked up and scrambled to cover themselves.

"Out!" Angie screamed. "Out of my bed!"

They grabbed for their clothes, while she marched back to the living room. In a moment, both came out and stood next to the coffee table. With their shirts and pants misaligned from having dressed so hurriedly, they cast their eyes down to their feet on the floor.

"I'm sorry, Angie," James mumbled.

"Save it!" She picked the sweater off the back of the couch and threw it on the floor at their feet. "Just get out."

They stood watching her, immobilized. She picked up the plant she had just brought in and threw it down at their feet. Potting soil spilled over the chic sweater. Startled, they took a step back.

"Out!" Angie screamed. "Out of my house!"

The woman grabbed her red and white sweater from the floor, and the two of them rushed out the door to the stairway.

Enraged, Angie strode to the bedroom and threw open the window to let out the faint, lingering scent of the woman's perfume. She ripped the sheets from the bed and took them to the washing machine, then stopped. No. She didn't want to clean the sheets. She wanted to trash them. She stuffed them into a pillowcase. The rest of the bedding also had to go. She stuffed that into two white thirty-gallon garbage bags.

Struggling, she dragged her stuff down the stairs and outside to a row of garbage cans for the building. She managed to cram the pillowcases into the can for her unit, but the garbage bags of bedding wouldn't fit. She set one bag on top of the can and left the other on the ground in front of it. The management company for the building would complain about this, but she was too upset to care. Maybe some needy person would grab the bedding before the management company saw it.

When she got back up to the apartment, she poured herself a glass of Irish Mist and sat on the couch sipping it. How could James do this to her? What had she done wrong? And what the hell was going to happen to her? Absentmindedly, she grabbed one of the chess pieces from the set on the table. It was cold and hard and lifeless, just like the knot that was forming in her gut. She refilled her glass.

The next morning, her head throbbed from too much of the alcohol. She brought a café con leche to the sofa, propped up her feet on the coffee table, next to the Tunisian chess set, and took two small sips before setting the cup down.

Until now, James had always been a good man. He had been supportive after Stevie's slashing attack and the harassment by Mrs. Bentley. He never cracked racial jokes. But now, here he was in bed with a blonde woman. Angie looked at her own light-brown wrists. How could he do this to her? In her own bed?

He'd never really been the same after his hostage experience. She recalled how he'd screamed at her on Memorial Day. She'd been tiptoeing around him ever since.

She would make sure they discussed this when he finally came back to talk. Which he would. As humiliated as he must feel, he would be driven to return and talk with her.

She gave him a week.

Washington Square

In fact, he stayed out only three days. Late Tuesday afternoon, she heard a tap on the door. When she peeked through the eyehole, James was standing there, sweating from the heat wave that smothered the city. Her anger flared as she opened the door. But she contained herself and dropped onto the couch, leaving him to sit on a straight-backed chair opposite her. He pulled at his shirt collar.

"God, it's stifling out there. Can I get a glass of water?"

"No."

They stared at each other in awkward silence for a long moment, before she said, "What do you have to say for yourself?"

He raised his hands, palms up, and his face was so contorted he looked as though he wanted to weep.

"Angie, I am sorry. I am so sorry."

"You're sorry for what you did? Are you sorry that you did it in our bed? Or are you just sorry that I found out?"

He set his hands in his lap and looked down at them.

"Who is she?"

He looked up. "My Farsi instructor."

"But it's been almost two years since you studied Farsi."

Then the implication of what she'd just said dawned on her. This affair had started in the earliest days of their engagement. It picked up again when he got back from Teheran. Tears streamed from her eyes, and she bent forward, covering her face with her hands.

"A blue-eyed, blonde Iranian?" she asked when she finally looked up.

"She's from the Caspian region. It's common there."

"If what you wanted was a white woman, why didn't you marry her instead of me?" But she knew the answer to that one even as she asked it. A light-brown Cuban-American as a spouse would not hinder his career in the State Department, no matter what Mrs. Bentley had said. But an Iranian spouse might, especially amid all the hostility and mistrust that surrounded U.S.-Iranian relations.

"Please, Angie. That's not it at all."

She jutted out her chin. "Then what is it?"

"I started seeing her during that short period of time before you came back from Tunis when it wasn't clear where you and I stood."

"So it's my fault you did this?"

"As soon as you returned from Tunis and accepted my proposal, I cut it off with her. I was able to get different Farsi instructors so we wouldn't have to have contact with each other. Once I got assigned overseas, I figured it was all over."

She snarled. "Obviously you were wrong."

"The truth is I never saw her again until one day after I got back from Iran and ran into her at the State Department."

Angie slapped the coffee table. "That's bullshit, James. You couldn't have just run into her. The State Department's in D.C. She worked at the Foreign Service Institute which is across the Potomac in Arlington. You had to go out of your way to find her."

She continued glaring at him. "For the past several months, when you took those trips to Washington, they had nothing to do with the State Department. They were just an excuse to see the Farsi instructor."

He looked down at the floor.

"And when I went on the retreat in Massachusetts, that gave you the chance to bring her up here."

Her anger was growing difficult to control. She almost said 'up here to my bed.'

"I'm sorry, Angie, I should have broken it off."

"Broken it off?" she screamed. "You shouldn't have started it in the first place."

He looked down at the floor again. She leaned forward and bit her lip to keep from lashing out at him. "There's something I should tell you, James. I took an enormous risk for you while you were stranded in Iran."

"What risk?"

She had fully intended to tell him about the rescue mission she had organized. It would be gratifying to watch him squirm when she contrasted his betrayal of her with the extraordinary measures she had taken in her effort to get him freed. Measures that could easily have sent her to prison.

And it was that realization that stopped her. She no longer knew if she could trust that her marriage to James was secure. Before she could even think of trusting him with her secret, she had to know where she stood with him. Should she take him back? Did he even want to come back? And if she did take him back, how long would it take before she could touch him without that image of his Farsi instructor popping into her mind. She stood up and went to the window to look at people walking by on the street.

"What risk?" he repeated.

"It can wait," she said. "What do we do now?"

"I don't know. Doing what I did to you was horrible, and I'd do anything in my power to make it up to you."

"If we start over, can you be faithful?"

"I think so."

Stunned, her lips tightened. "James, I can't live with I think so."

40

Spring had already begun

September 1981

Zenith Capital Management

Despite James' inability to promise he would never see the Farsi instructor again, Angie agreed that he could stay in the second bedroom of the apartment until he found a place of his own. Maybe that would make it easier for him to come to his senses. And for the next week she bounced back and forth between hoping he would say he wanted her back and then feeling incensed when the words never came. She couldn't wipe from her mind the image of him in bed with the Farsi instructor.

She had to share her distress with someone, and at the end of the week she took the subway down to Evie's office. She sank into the chair facing Evie's desk, her eyes resting on the brass-plated sign, Zenith Capital Management, behind Evie's shoulder. Angie gritted her teeth and blurted out, "James and I are getting divorced."

Evie's mouth sagged open. "Why?"

Angie blinked back tears as she told Evie about finding James with his blonde, blue-eyed Farsi instructor.

"A blonde Iranian? I didn't know there were any blonde Iranians."

"What difference does it make if there are blonde Iranians? James was cheating on me. That's what matters."

Evie nodded. "You must be livid."

"I'm so angry I go into my shower and scream. My mind is so bent out of shape it's excruciating." Her face twisted into an anguished contortion as she gulped back the start of a sob.

Evie came around to the front of her desk, put her arm around Angie's shoulders, and led her to a couch. "Has he moved out?" she asked.

"Not yet. He's sleeping in the second bedroom until he finds a place."

"As long as you're both still under the same roof, you'll be forced to talk now and then. Maybe you can sort things out."

"That's what I'd hoped when I agreed to let him stay. But it's not working out that way. I can't get rid of that image in my mind of him in bed with her."

"A onetime event isn't necessarily the end of a marriage," said Evie.

"It wasn't just an event." She pounded her fists on the cushion for emphasis. "Even before I got back from Tunis, he was doing it with her. He said he broke it off when we got engaged. Then, sometime after he returned from Iran, he started it up again."

Evie squinted. "If he dumped her once, why would she take up with him again?"

"Marrying him would be her best shot at not having to go back to Iran someday. And let's face it. He comes from a rich family."

"Okay. I can see that a marriage to him would benefit her. But it would have a huge downside for him. An Iranian wife in the current environment would undermine his career at the State Department. He'll come crawling back to you long before he marries her."

"Even if he does, he'll still be fantasizing about her instead of me."

"Every man has fantasies. What does it matter where he gets his appetite as long as he comes home to eat?"

Angie shook her head. "Your husband might have fantasies, but in the last analysis, you're the one he wants. I'm not the one James wants. I'm determined to get divorced."

Angie began twirling one of her curls with a finger. Evie leaned back against the couch. She folded her hands and stared at Angie.

"It's your life, so you get to do it anyway you want. But I have one important piece of advice for you."

"What?"

Evie leaned forward. "Wait at least six months to start the divorce."

"Things will only get worse if we do that," said Angie. She let go of the hair she was twirling and leaned toward Evie. "The other day when he couldn't make the trip to D.C. to see her, he moped around like he wanted to do it with me. Soon I'll give in. We'll be like those couples I've heard of who break up, then get back together, then break up again, and carry this on for years. I've got to cut this off before I fall into that trap."

"Live separately for a few months. Tell people he just needs some space to decompress, or whatever the psychobabble is these days. After a decent time, you can start the divorce."

"That doesn't change anything. I want to do this now."

"There's a problem with that."

"What?"

"New York doesn't have a no-fault divorce law, so you need to give a reason in order to get a divorce. The easiest reason is a permanent separation, which requires living apart for at least six months."

"I can't wait that long."

"In that case, you have to give some other credible reason. And you only have one. James doesn't smoke. He barely drinks. He doesn't beat you or steal from you. In fact, he's an upstanding citizen in a distinguished profession who got you invited to the White House and to a ticker tape parade. He's practically a national hero. I repeat. The only reason you've got for divorce is that he cheats on you."

"Don't rub it in, Evie."

"I'm not rubbing it in. I'm saying that you can't get an immediate divorce unless you tell a judge, in open court, that James has been cheating on you."

"So what?"

"It becomes part of the public record that anyone will be able to look up. Anybody. Do you really want to wash that dirty linen in public?"

Angie's head snapped forward.

"What?" said Evie.

"Nothing. Something just occurred to me." It was bad enough having to charge James with adultery, but what if somehow her own behavior came under scrutiny? What if James found out about her hostage rescue attempt? If she publicly charged him with adultery, he could retaliate by reporting her illegal hostage rescue attempt to the Justice Department. In terms of legality, what she'd done was much worse than what he'd done. And the potential consequences much more severe. She shuddered.

"What occurred to you?" Evie asked.

"You're right. It's not a good idea to wash our dirty linen in public." She leaned back onto the couch, rested her head on the cushion, and stared at the ceiling. She blinked back tears.

Neither woman spoke.

Finally, Evie asked. "So, what are you going to do?"

"James can find a room in midtown where his U.N. office is, and he can commute back and forth to that blonde pig in D.C. I'll have my lawyer file for divorce now and pick a court date far enough out to show that we've been permanently separated for six months."

Evie nodded, and Angie snarled, "And when things fall apart between them, that will be James' problem, not mine.

Columbus Circle

Angie waited until Labor Day weekend, after James had moved out, before she rode up to Columbus Circle to tell Charlie about her impending divorce. Glenna had taken Michael out to buy school supplies, and Charlie was alone.

He welcomed her with a big hug, and her heels clicked on the parquet floor as he led her to the living room. He brought a tray with a silver serving set to the coffee table in front of the couch. The rich aroma of French pressed coffee wafted into the air.

Angie was unsure how to broach the topic of her upcoming divorce. She wandered around the living room and stopped in front of the window, looking out at people strolling on the street below.

"I love this place," she said.

"Glenna wants to move north a few blocks so we can look out on Central Park."

Sitting down next to him on the couch, Angie scrunched her nose at the mention of Charlie's wife. It was just like Glenna not to be satisfied with what she had.

"Central Park would be a stretch, wouldn't it?"

He laughed. "Unless the market triples in the next six months."

"How likely is that?"

"It's never happened before." He poured coffee into her cup. "Sugar?"

"I'll pass," she said, patting her stomach.

"You said you came over to tell me about a decision."

"Two decisions, actually. On one of them, I'm going to follow your advice."

"Well, that's the first in a long time."

She squinted and pursed her lips. "Don't be mean, Charlie. But let me tell you about the other decision first. James and I are getting divorced."

Charlie banged his cup down on the serving tray so hard that coffee sloshed over the rim. She explained how tense their marriage had become and how she had found him in bed with the Farsi instructor.

"I feel so bad for you, mija. Is there no way you can patch this up? If he stayed faithful?"

She shook her head. "If I thought he was truly remorseful, and if he convinced me that I'm still the woman of his dreams, of course I'd patch things up. But he can't. He's already moved out."

Charlie leaned back against the couch and steepled his fingers, as if he were debating something he wanted to say.

"What?" she said.

"Are you also going to ask the church for an annulment?"

"Never!"

"It would simplify your life if you ever wanted to marry again."

"It's dishonest. An annulment says I was never married to begin with."

"At heart, maybe you weren't. James concealed his desire for another woman, so he married you in bad faith. Wouldn't that be grounds for annulment?"

Angie tugged at the hem of her skirt while she pondered the question. "I know it's important for you to be in the good graces of the church, Charlie, but I don't feel the same way. When I think about it, the idea of an annulment makes me furious."

She paused for him to respond. But he just sat silently next to her waiting for her to continue.

"How can I agree to something that says we were never married to begin with? We lived together as husband and wife, and while he was captive, I wrote to him all the time. I tried desperately to get him freed. And when he came home, I did the best I could to deal with the PTSD we both had. To say that doesn't count as a marriage is demeaning and insulting."

She reached over and patted her father's wrist. "I know this isn't what you wanted to hear. But James and I have both agreed to this, so I hope you'll accept it."

He nodded, and she smiled. "Let me tell you about my other decision."

"I hope I like this one better."

"I decided to go back to school full time this fall to finish off college."

Charlie wrapped his arms around her shoulders. "That's fantastic. If I'd known that was the decision, I would have served you champagne instead of coffee."

"I can probably cover it from what I've got left of that settlement with the State Department. But if I run short, can you help me?"

"Of course. And just stay in the apartment. That will save you a bundle in housing costs."

"I'm transferring to SMU."

Charlie took his arm from her shoulder and sat up rigidly.

"Southern Methodist! But that's in Texas. Halfway across the country."

She looked down, abashed. "That's the point."

"The point is to get half a continent away from your father?"

She set her hand on his shoulder. "No, Charlie. It's not you I want to get away from."

"Then what is it?

"My demons are here."

He didn't respond. He just kept his stoic look. She removed his hand from her shoulder and tapped the backs of her hands on her thighs.

"Think about it," she said, her voice starting to crack. "It was here that I heard about Mama's plane crash. That I had a wedding I should have avoided. That I spent so much time biting my fingernails with worry about James in Teheran. That I started looking for someone to help me mount that insane rescue plan." She paused. "And it was here that I found him cheating on me."

She swallowed, trying to keep the lid on a flood of bitter emotions. Charlie seemed to have no idea how to comfort her. He set his hand on her shoulder, then pulled it back.

"I know he went through a horrible trauma in Iran. But my life here wasn't just a piece of cake. It's like a big wall has grown up between us, and we're each wandering around on our separate sides of it."

She stood up and smoothed out her skirt to give her hands something to do. To keep them from shaking with the anger that was welling up within her. "Then I come home one day and find him with a woman. In *my* bed!" She clenched her fists. "And when I say we can start over if he'll stop, he can't promise that he will."

"I get it," Charlie said. He stood and wrapped his arms around her shoulders. After a moment he backed off, held her at arm's length, then motioned for them to sit.

"But you have to understand that your demons will follow you wherever you go. The only way you can get rid of them is to confront them."

She furrowed her eyebrows. "What are you saying?"

"You've been through one shocker after another through the past few years. And then finding James the way you did. That would give anybody demons."

"That's why I've got to get out of here."

"If that's all you do, it's just the geographic solution. And that rarely works."

"The what solution?"

Charlie rubbed his chin. "I once had a friend Louis who lived in a cheap apartment in Boston, but he had a very unhappy marriage, which he figured was because of their cheap apartment. When he could afford it, they moved to a better apartment, but the marriage was still unhappy. Then they figured their problem was the cold weather of Boston, so they moved to Florida. But their marriage was still unhappy. Geography didn't solve anything for them."

"But I'm not moving to Texas to improve the marriage. I'm ending the marriage."

"True, but whatever nightmares you have from James' captivity won't stop just because you move to Dallas. Nor will whatever nightmares you have about the slashing attack. Or the ones about the failed rescue mission. Or even the ones about that skating accident."

"I never said I had nightmares about those things."

"Well, if they'd happened to me, I'd have nightmares about them."

She nodded. "The ones I have about the rescue mission are the worst. I keep dreaming there's blood all over the helicopter we're in."

"I almost killed a man once. I had him in my crosshairs and I was on the verge of pulling the trigger before I raised the rifle to shoot over his head."

Angie recoiled. She'd never heard this before, and she didn't want to hear about Charlie setting out to kill someone. But he continued talking.

"No matter where I moved, the nightmares never went away until I finally accepted the truth about myself, that I'd once been willing to kill another person. And the only thing I could do about it was to try and live the rest of my life in a better way."

He paused for a long moment, and she was afraid to interrupt. "All I'm saying is that there was no geographic solution to my demons, and there won't be to yours either."

She covered her face with her hands. "Oh, Charlie you must think I'm the world's biggest loser."

"No!" he almost shouted. "You're not a loser. You're a talented person. And judging from the things you've done, a powerfully persuasive person. If you can accept yourself, both the good and the bad, it doesn't matter where you live. But if you can't accept yourself, your demons will follow you wherever you go."

"I need a rebirth, Charlie, like the earth gets a rebirth in spring."

"But it's not spring. It's almost Autumn."

She smiled. "For an ice-skater, that's when the new season starts."

He paused before lifting up his hands. "Then SMU it is."

The Skating Club of Manhattan

Angie's heels clicked on the sidewalk as she left Charlie's building. She took the subway to the Skating Club of Manhattan to pull her gear from a locker. Sitting in her pink tights on a bench lacing up her skates, she watched a trio of children follow instructions from a teacher on the ice. A small boy teetered as he tried to skate backwards, and the sight brought warm memories of herself when she had mastered that movement.

She glided onto the ice, and the four youngsters stared as she did a graceful figure eight. The seasoned skater giving an example of what the novice skaters could become. To the outside world, spring wouldn't arrive for several months. But for Angie, on the ice with the children, it was already here.

The End

HISTORICAL NOTE

Having been a member of the U.S. Foreign Service and having served abroad in an American embassy, I had a powerful gut reaction in 1979 when militant students overran the embassy in Teheran. They captured five dozen American workers, and held most of them hostage for the next fourteen months. *Goodbye Demons* is a work of fiction set around that crisis.

It seeks to relate historical events accurately, but in a purely fictitious manner stemming from my opinions and understandings. Everything that happens to James in Teheran happened to someone. They just didn't all happen to the same person or exactly as they do in this fictionalized account. All actions, thoughts, and speech attributed to historical figures are based on writings by participants or reputable researchers. The only direct quote is that of Mike Metrinko in chapter 34, which can be found in Mark Bowden, *Guests of the Ayatollah* (NY: Atlantic Monthly Press, 2006). The fictional characters and Angie's attempt at a rescue mission are products of my imagination. Any resemblance of these characters to any persons living or dead is purely coincidental.

ACKNOWLEDGEMENTS

Goodbye Demons has relied heavily on the help of many people. Several hostages wrote memoirs and articles giving detailed accounts of their experiences. Among the surviving hostages, Kathryn Koob, Kevin Hermening, and Barry Rosen offered me insightful comments. Historians and journalists have built a substantial body of research that was helpful. And numerous people critiqued the manuscript in whole or in part. To all of them I am grateful. Tyrone Babione, Tricia Carlsberg, Chansy Charles, Don Deline, Jane Farrel, Eleanor Fritsch, Avron Gordon, Lynn Hanson, Kristin Harley, A.P. Harper, Mark Hollock, Kathleen Huffman, Molly Kelash, Brian Keller, Miranda Kopp-Filek, Tim Mahoney, Cesar Mantufar, Rebekah Moir, Matthew Morrison, Leah Omar, Leah Otto, Timya Owen, Eleanor Pearson, John Rhodes, John Rogers, Jody Schmiesing, Susan Stradiotto, Val Solar, Dale Vee, Doug Williams. Thanks also to my beta reader, Deb Rhodes. I'm especially thankful to my wife Sandy who has patiently supported this project.

ABOUT THE AUTHOR

 JJ Harrigan writes historical thrillers that stem from his experiences as a soldier stationed in Germany during the Cold War, a U.S. foreign service officer in Latin America, and a professor of Political Science. He graduated from Loyola University, got an M.A. in International Relations from the University of Chicago, and a PhD from Georgetown University. Today he scribbles his tales of intrigue on the banks of the St. Croix River in Minnesota where he lives happily with his wife Sandy.

www.jjharrigan.com

If you enjoyed Goodbye Demons, consider JJ's other works of historical fiction. All are available as print, audio, or e-books. To learn more or to purchase, go to the author's website at www.jjharrigan.com

Cuban Missile Crisis of 1962.

Silver award by Reviewers Choice, 2024

Lt. Charlie Parnell is coerced into a black ops mission in Havana. He falls for single-mom Isabel Fernandez, who is ordered to spy on him for Fidel Castro's security services. The Cuban Missile Crisis erupts, Havana gears up for an invasion, and Charlie ends up running for his life along with Isabel and her three-year-old daughter, Angelita.

https://amzn.to/47bicOJ

Bobby Kennedy, Sr. and a quest to end the Vietnam War. 1968

Eric Hoffer Award Finalist 2025

Now a widowed businessman raising Angelita, Charlie Parnell accepts a dangerous mission related to Robert F. Kennedy's Sr.'s presidential campaign and his intent to end the War in Vietnam. This puts not only Charlie at risk, but Robert Kennedy's presidential campaign, and nine-year-old Angelita as well.

https://amzn.to/4qkp70I

The Home front during the Korean War. 1953

Frustrated over racial and class divisions in their 1950s industrial town, Charlie Parnell and his friends form a dance band and organize an integrated sock hop they hope will bring black and white teenagers together. What could possibly go wrong? This is the backstory for Charlie who appears in all of the Goodbye Books.

https://amzn.to/3NdHRQH